Marie [...]
RITA® Award-winn[...]
[...]an 200 books fo[...]
[...]me Marie Nicole. Her romances are beloved by fans
[...]rldwide. Visit her website at www.marieferrarella.
[...]m

Jennifer Taylor has been writing Mills & Boon novels
[...]r some time but discovered Medical Romance books
[...]latively recently. Having worked in scientific research,
[...]e was so captivated by these heart-warming stories
[...]at she immediately set out to write them herself.
Jennifer's hobbies include reading and travelling. She
[...]ves in northwest England. Visit Jennifer's blog at
[...]nnifertaylorauthor.wordpress.com

[...]hree-times Golden Heart® finalist **Tina Beckett**
[...]arned to pack her suitcases almost before she learned
[...] read. Born to a military family, she has lived in the
[...]nited States, Puerto Rico, Portugal and Brazil. In
a[...]dition to travelling, Tina loves to cuddle with her
p[...]g, Alex, spend time with her family, and hit the trails
[...] her horse. Learn more about Tina from her website,
[...] 'friend' her on Facebook.

Pl[...]
Dy[...]

Summer of Love

Summer of Love: Second Chance at Sunset

MARIE FERRARELLA

JENNIFER TAYLOR

TINA BECKETT

MILLS & BOON

First Published in Great Britain 2021
By Mills & Boon, an imprint of HarperCollins*Publishers* Ltd
1 London Bridge Street, London, SE1 9GF

www.harpercollins.co.uk

HarperCollins*Publishers*
1st Floor, Watermarque Building,
Ringsend Road, Dublin 4, Ireland

SUMMER OF LOVE: SECOND CHANCE AT SUNSET
© 2021 Harlequin Books S.A.

The Fortune Most Likely To... © 2018 Harlequin Books S.A.
Small Town Marriage Miracle © 2011 Jennifer Taylor
The Soldier She Could Never Forget © 2015 Tina Beckett

Special thanks and acknowledgement to Marie Ferrarella for her contribution to the *Fortunes of Texas: The Rulebreakers* continuity.

ISBN: 978-0-263-29940-3

MIX
Paper from
responsible sources
FSC® C007454

THE FORTUNE
MOST LIKELY TO...

MARIE FERRARELLA

To
Susan Litman,
with thanks
for her
patience

Prologue

It was time that he finally faced up to it. He had never gotten over her.

Sitting on the sofa in his living room, Dr. Everett Fortunado frowned as he looked into the glass of expensive whiskey he was sipping. The single glass, two fingers, was his way of winding down. Not from a hectic day spent at his successful, thriving medical practice, but from the stress of terminating yet another less-than-stellar, stillborn relationship.

How many failed relationships did that make now? Ten? Twelve? He wasn't sure.

He'd honestly lost count a number of years ago.

Admittedly, the women in those incredibly short-lived relationships had all become interchangeable. Now that he thought about it, none of them had ever stood out in his mind. And, if he was being honest about it, Everett couldn't remember half their names.

As for their faces, well, if pressed, he could give a general description, but there again, nothing about any of them had left a lasting impression on his mind. Strictly speaking, he could probably pass one or more of them on the street and not recognize them at all.

A mirthless laugh passed his lips. At thirty-three he was way too young to be on the threshold of dementia. No, that wasn't the reason behind this so-called memory loss problem. If he were being entirely honest with himself, he thought, taking another long, bracing sip of whiskey, this cavalcade of women who had been parading through his life for the last thirteen years were only poor substitutes for the one woman who had ever really mattered to him.

The only woman he had ever been in love with.

The woman he had lost.

Lila Clark, the girl he'd known since forever and had barely been aware of until he suddenly *saw* her for the first time that day in Senior English class. Though a straight A student, Everett had found himself faltering when it came to English. Lila sat next to him in class and he'd turned to her for help. She was the one responsible for getting him through Senior English.

And somewhere along the line during all that tutoring, Lila had managed to make off with his heart. He was crazy about her and really excited when he found out that she felt the same way about him. Not long after that, they began making plans for their future together.

And then it had all blown up on him.

When he'd lost her, his parents had told him that it

was all for the best. They had pointed out that he was too young to think about settling down. They wanted their brightest child to focus on his future and not squander his vast potential by marrying a girl from a working-class family just because he'd gotten her pregnant. To them it had been the oldest ploy in the world: a poor girl trapping a rich boy because of his sense of obligation.

But Lila really wasn't like that. And she hadn't trapped him. She'd walked out on him.

Everett sat on the sofa now, watching the light from the lone lamp in his living room play across the amber liquid in the chunky glass in his hand. He would've given anything if he could go back those thirteen years.

If he could have, he wouldn't have talked Lila into giving up their baby for adoption.

Because that one thing had been the beginning of the end for them.

He'd been at Lila's side in the delivery room and, even then, he kept telling her that they were doing the right thing. That they were too young to get married and raise this baby. That they could always have more kids "later."

Lila changed that night. Changed from the happy, bright-eyed, full-of-life young woman he'd fallen in love with to someone he no longer even knew.

And that was the look in her eyes when she raised them to his. Like she was looking at someone she didn't recognize.

Right after she left the hospital, Lila had told him

she never wanted to see him again. He'd tried to reason with her, but she just wouldn't listen.

Lila had disappeared out of his life right after that.

Crushed, he'd gone back to college, focusing every bit of energy entirely on his studies. He'd always wanted to be a doctor, ever since he was a little boy, and that became his lifeline after Lila left. He clung to it to the exclusion of everything else.

And it had paid off, he thought now, raising his almost-empty glass in a silent toast to his thriving career. He was a doctor. A highly successful, respected doctor. His career was booming.

Conversely, his personal life was in the dumpster.

Everett sighed. If he had just said, "Let's keep the baby," everything would have been different. And his life wouldn't have felt so empty every time he walked into his house.

He wouldn't have felt so empty.

Blowing out a breath, Everett rose from the sofa and walked over to the liquor cabinet. Normally, he restricted himself to just one drink, but tonight was different. It was the anniversary of the day Lila had ended their relationship. He could be forgiven a second drink.

At least, he told himself, he could fill his empty glass, if not his life.

Chapter One

"**Y**our problem, brother dear," Schuyler said after having listened to him tell her that maybe he'd made a mistake talking Lila into giving up their baby all those years ago, "is that you think too much. You're always overthinking things and making yourself crazy in the process."

"Says the woman who always led with her heart," Everett commented.

"And that seems to be working out for me, doesn't it?" Schuyler asked.

He could hear the broad smile in her voice. It all but throbbed through the phone. Everett had no response for that. All he could do at the moment was sigh. Sigh and feel just a little bit jealous because his little sister had found something that he was beginning to think he never would find again: love.

"By thinking so much back then about how everything would affect your future," Schuyler went on, "I think you blew it with Lila. You were so focused on your future, on becoming a doctor, that you just couldn't see how badly she felt about giving up her baby—*your* baby," she emphasized. "And because you didn't notice, didn't seem to feel just as badly as she did about the adoption, you broke Lila's heart. If it were me, I would have never forgiven someone for breaking my heart that way," Schuyler told him.

"Thanks for being so supportive," Everett said sarcastically.

This was *not* why he'd called his sister, why he'd lowered his guard and allowed himself to be so vulnerable. Maybe he should have known better, he thought, about to terminate the call.

"I *am* being supportive," Schuyler insisted. "I'm just calling it the way I see it. I love you, Ev, and you know I'm always on your side. But I know you. I don't want you to get your hopes up that if you just approach her, she'll fly back into your arms and everything'll be just the way it was back then. Not after thirteen years and *not* after what went down between the two of you back then. Trust me, Lila is not going to get back together with you that easily."

"I know that and I don't want to get back together with Lila," he insisted defensively. "I just want to talk to her." Everett paused because this next thing was hard for him to say, even to Schuyler, someone he had always trusted implicitly. Lowering his voice, he told his sister, "Maybe even apologize to her for the way things ended between us back then."

He could tell from Schuyler's voice that she felt for him. But she was far from optimistic about the outcome of all this. "Look, Everett, I know that your heart's in the right place, but I really don't want to see it stomped on."

"No worries," Everett assured her. "My heart is not as vulnerable as you think."

What he'd just said might have been a lie, but if it was, it was a lie he was telling himself as well as his sister.

He had a feeling that Schuyler saw it that way too because he could hear the skepticism in her voice as she said, just before she ended their call, "Well, I wish you luck with that. Maybe Lila'll listen to reason."

Maybe.

The single word seemed to throb in his head as Everett decided to find out as much as he could about Lila and what she was doing these days.

It had all started two months ago when he'd taken the day off, gotten another doctor to cover for him and had driven the 165 miles from Houston to Austin to pick up his sister, Schuyler. At the time, he was supposed to be bringing Schuyler back home.

Given to acting on impulse, his younger sister had initially gone to Austin because she had gotten it into her head to track down Nathan Fortune. The somewhat reclusive man was supposedly her cousin and the ever-inquisitive Schuyler was looking for answers about their family tree. The current thinking was that she and the rest of their brothers and sisters were all possibly related to the renowned Fortune family.

It was while Schuyler was looking for those answers that she decided to get closer to the Mendoza family whose history was intertwined with the Fortunes. She managed to get so close to one of them—Carlo Mendoza—that she wound up completely losing her heart to him.

Confused, unsure of herself for very possibly the first time in her life, Schuyler had turned to the one person she was closest to.

She'd called Everett.

Listening to his sister pouring out her heart—and citing her all uncertainties, not just about her genealogy investigation but about the direction her heart had gone in—he had decided he needed to see Schuyler and maybe convince her to come home.

But Schuyler had reconciled with her man and decided to stay in Austin after all. Everett returned home without her. But he hadn't come away completely empty-handed. What Everett had come home with was a renewed sense of having made a terrible mistake thirteen years ago. And that had come about because while he'd been in Austin, he had run into Lila.

Sort of.

He saw Lila entering a sandwich shop and it had been a jarring experience for him. It had instantly propelled him back through time and just like that, all the old feelings had come rushing back to him, saturating him like a huge tidal wave. At least they had in his case.

However, he'd been struck by the aura of sadness he detected about her. A sadness that had *not* been there when they were in high school together.

He'd thought—hoped really—that when he got back to Houston, back to his practice, he'd be able to drive thoughts of Lila back into the past where they belonged. Instead, they began to haunt him, vividly pushing their way into his dreams at night, sneaking up on him during the day whenever he had an unguarded moment.

He began wondering in earnest about what had happened to her in all those years since they'd been together. And that sadness he'd detected—was *he* responsible for that? Or was there some other reason for its existence?

He felt compelled to find out.

Like everyone else of his generation, Everett turned to social media in his quest for information about Lila Clark.

He found her on Facebook.

When he saw that Lila had listed herself as "single" and that there were only a few photographs posted on her page, mainly from vacation spots she had visited, he felt somewhat heartened.

Maybe, a little voice in his head whispered, it wasn't too late to make amends after all.

Damn it, Everett, get hold of yourself. This is exactly what Schuyler warned you about. Don't get your hopes up, at least not until you talk to Lila again and exchange more than six words with her.

Who knows, she might have changed and you won't even like Lila 2.0.

Everett struggled to talk himself out of letting his imagination take flight. He tried to get himself to go slow—or maybe not go at all.

But the latter was just not an option.

He knew he felt too strongly about this, too highly invested in righting a wrong he'd committed in the past. Now that he'd made up his mind about the matter, he needed to make Lila understand that he regretted the way things had gone thirteen years ago.

Regretted not being more emotionally supportive of her.

Regretted not being able to see the daughter they had *both* lost.

Still, he continued to try to talk himself out of it for two days after he found Lila on Facebook. Tried to make himself just walk away from the whole idea: from getting in contact with her, from apologizing and making amends. All of it.

But he couldn't.

So finally, on the evening of the third day, Everett sat down in front of his computer, powered up his internet connection and pulled up Facebook. Specifically, he pulled up Lila's profile.

He'd stared at it for a full ten minutes before he finally began to type a message to her.

Hi, Lila. It's been a long time. I'm planning on being in Austin soon. Let's have lunch together and do some catching up. I'd really welcome the chance to see and talk with you.

Those four simple sentences took him close to half an hour to settle on. He must have written and deleted thirty sentences before he finally decided on those. Then it took him another ten minutes before he sent those four sweated-over sentences off into cyberspace.

For the next two hours he checked on that page close to a dozen and a half times, all without any luck. He was about to power down his computer for the night when he pulled up Lila's Facebook page one last time.

"She answered," he announced out loud even though there was no one around to hear him.

Sitting down in his chair, he read Lila's response, unconsciously savoring each word as if it was a precious jewel.

If you're going to be here Friday, I can meet you for lunch at 11:30. I just need to warn you that I only get forty-five minutes for lunch, so our meeting will be short. We're usually really swamped where I work.

Everett could hardly believe that she'd actually agreed to meet with him. He'd been half prepared to read her rejection. Whistling, he immediately posted a response.

11:30 on Friday sounds great. Since I'm unfamiliar with Austin, you pick the place and let me know.

After sleeping fitfully, he decided to get up early. He had a full slate of appointments that day. Best to get a jump on it. But the minute he passed the computer, he knew what he had to do first.

And there, buried amid approximately forty other missives—all of which were nothing short of junk mail—was Lila's response. All she'd written was the name of a popular chain of restaurants, followed by its address. But his heart soared.

Their meeting was set.

If he'd been agile enough to pull it off, Everett would have leaped up and clicked his heels together.

As it was, he got ready for work very quickly and left the house within the half hour—singing.

The second Lila hit the send button on Facebook, she immediately regretted it.

What am I thinking? she upbraided herself. Was she crazy? Did she actually *want* to meet with someone who had so carelessly broken her heart? Who was responsible for the single most heart-wrenching event to have happened in her life?

"What's wrong with you? Are you hell-bent on being miserable?" she asked herself as she walked away from her computer. It was after eleven o'clock at night and she was alone.

The way she was on most nights.

Maybe that was the problem, Lila told herself. She was tired of being alone and when she'd seen that message from Everett on her Facebook page, it had suddenly stirred up a lot of old memories.

"Memories you're better off forgetting, remember?" she demanded.

But they weren't all bad, she reminded herself. As a matter of fact, if she thought back, a lot of those memories had been good.

Very good.

For a large chunk of her Senior year and a portion of her first year at community college, Everett had been the love of her life. He'd made her happier than she could ever remember being.

But it was what had happened at the end that outweighed everything, that threw all those good recollections into the shadows, leaving her to remember that awful, awful ache in her heart as Emma was taken out of her arms and she watched her baby being carried away.

Away from her.

She'd wanted Everett to hold her then. To tell her that he was aching as much as she was. That he felt as if something had been torn away from his heart, too, the way she felt it had for her.

But all he had said was: "It's for the best." As if there was something that could be described as "best" about never being able to see your baby again. A baby that had been conceived in love and embodied the two of them in one tiny little form.

Lila felt tears welling up in her eyes even after all this time, felt them spilling out even though she'd tried hard to squeeze them back.

She wished she hadn't agreed to see Everett.

But if she'd said no to lunch, Everett would have probably put two and two together and realized that she hadn't the courage to see him again. If she'd turned him down, he would've understood just how much he still mattered to her.

No, Lila told herself, she had no way out. She *had* to see him again. Had to sit there across from him at a table, making inane conversation and proving to him that he meant nothing to her.

That would be her ultimate revenge for his having so wantonly, so carelessly, ripped out her heart without so much as a moment's pause or a word of actual genuine comfort.

"We'll have lunch, Everett," she said, addressing his response that was posted on her Facebook page. "We'll have lunch, and then you'll realize just what you lost all those years ago. Lost forever. Because I was the very best thing that could have ever happened to you," she added with finality.

Her words rang hollow to her ear.

It didn't matter, she told herself. She had a couple of days before she had to meet with him. A couple of days to practice making herself sound as if she believed every syllable she uttered.

She'd have it letter-perfect by the time they met, she promised herself.

She *had* to.

Chapter Two

Half the contents of Lila's closet was now spread out all over her bed. She spent an extra hour going through each item slowly before finally making up her mind.

Lila dressed with great care, selecting a two-piece gray-blue outfit that flattered her curves as well as sharply bringing out the color of her eyes.

Ordinarily, putting on makeup entailed a dash of lipstick for Lila, if that. This morning she highlighted her eyes, using both mascara and a little eye shadow. She topped it off with a swish of blush to accent her high cheekbones, smoothed her long auburn hair, then sprayed just the slightest bit of perfume.

Finished, she slowly inspected herself from all angles in her wardrobe mirror before she decided that she was ready to confront a past she'd thought she'd buried—and in so doing, make Dr. Everett Fortunado eat his heart out.

Maybe, Lila thought as she left her house, if she took this much trouble getting ready for the occasional dates she went out on, she might not still be single at the age of thirty-three.

Lila sighed. She knew better. It wasn't her clothes or her makeup that were responsible for her single status.

It was her.

After breaking up with Everett, she had picked herself up and dusted herself off. In an all-out attempt to totally reinvent herself, Lila had left Houston and moved to Austin where no one knew her or anything about the past she was determined to forget and put totally behind her.

She'd gone to work at the Fortune Foundation, a nonprofit organization dedicated to providing assistance to the needy. Through hard work, she'd swiftly risen and was now manager of her department.

And because of her work, Lila's life went from intolerable to good. At least her professional life did.

Her personal life, however, was another story.

Sure, she'd dated. She'd tried blind dates as well as online dating. She'd joined clubs and had gone to local sporting events to cheer on the home team. She'd gone out with rich men as well as poor ones and those in-between.

It wasn't that Lila couldn't meet a man, she just couldn't meet *the* man.

And probably even if she could, she thought, that still

wouldn't have done the trick. Because no matter who she went out with, she couldn't trust him.

Everett had destroyed her ability to trust any man she might become involved with.

Try as she might, she couldn't lower her guard. She just couldn't bear to have a repeat performance of what had happened to her with Everett.

Rather than risk that, she kept her heart firmly under lock and key. And that guaranteed a life of loneliness.

At this point in her life, Lila had decided to give up looking for Mr. Right. Instead, she forced herself to embrace being Stubbornly Single.

As she took one last look in the mirror and walked out the door, she told herself that was what she really wanted.

One day she might convince herself that was true.

Her upgraded appearance did not go unnoticed when she walked into the office at the Fortune Foundation that morning.

"Well, someone looks extra nice today," Lucie Fortune Chesterfield Parker noted the moment that Lila crossed the threshold. "Do you have a hot date tonight?" she asked as she made her way over toward Lila.

"No, I don't," Lila answered, hoping that would be the end of it.

Belatedly, she thought that maybe she should have brought this outfit with her and changed in the ladies' room before going to lunch instead of coming in dressed like this.

Lucie and she were friends and had been almost from

the very first time they met at the Foundation, but Lila really didn't want to talk about the man she was having lunch with.

Initially from England, Lucie was married to Chase Parker, a Texas oil heir who had been her teenage sweetheart. Because of that, Lucie considered herself to be an expert on romance and she felt she had great radar when it came to the subject.

Her radar was apparently on red alert now as she swiftly looked Lila over.

Studying her, Lucie repeated, "Not tonight?"

"No," Lila said firmly. She never broke stride, determined to get to her office and close the door on this subject—literally as well as figuratively.

"Lunch, then?" Lucie pressed. "You certainly didn't get all dolled up like that for us."

Lila looked at her sharply over her shoulder, but her coworker didn't back off. The expression on her face indicated that she thought she was onto something.

When Lila made no response, Lucie pressed harder. "Well, *are* you going to lunch with someone?"

Lila wanted to say no and be done with it. She was, after all, a private person and no one here knew about her past. She'd never shared any of it. No about the child she'd given up for adoption or the man who had broken her heart. However, it wasn't in her to lie and even if it were, Lucie was as close to a real friend as she had in Austin. She didn't want to risk alienating her if the truth ever happened to come out—which it might, likely at the most inopportune time.

So after a moment of soul-searching, she finally answered Lucie's question.

"Yes."

Lucie looked at her more closely, obviously intrigued. "Anyone I know?" she asked.

"No," Lila answered automatically.

Not anyone I know, either. Not really, Lila silently added. After all, it had been thirteen years since she'd last been with Everett. And besides, how well had she known him back then anyway? He certainly hadn't behaved the way she'd expected him to. It made her think that maybe she had never really known Everett Fortunado at all.

"Where did you meet him?" Lucie wanted to know, apparently hungry for details about her friend's lunch date.

"Why all the questions?" Lila reached her office, but unfortunately it was situated right next to Lucie's. Both offices were enclosed in glass, allowing them to easily see one another over the course of the day.

"Because you're my friend and I'm curious," Lucie answered breezily. "You've practically become a workaholic these last couple of months, hardly coming up for air. That doesn't leave you much time for socializing."

Pausing by her doorway, Lila blew out a breath. "It's someone I knew back in high school," she answered. She stuck close to the truth. There was less chance for error that way. "He's in town on business for a couple of days. He looked me up on Facebook and he suggested having lunch to catch up, so I said yes."

Lila walked over to her desk, really hoping that

would be the end of it. But apparently it wasn't because Lucie didn't retreat to her own office. Her friend remained standing in Lila's doorway, looking at her as if she was attempting to carefully dissect every word out of her mouth.

"How well did you know this guy—back in high school, I mean?" Lucie asked, tacking on the few words after a small beat.

Lila stood there feeling as if she was under a microscope.

Did it show, she wondered. Did Lucie suspect that there had been more than just high school between her and Everett?

"Why?" she asked suspiciously, wondering what Lucie was getting at. It wasn't that she didn't trust Lucie, it was just that inherently she had trouble lowering her guard around *anyone*.

"Well, if someone who I knew back in high school suddenly turned up in my life," Lucie said easily, "I don't think I'd dress up in something that would make me look like a runway model just to go out to lunch with him."

Lila shrugged, avoiding Lucie's eyes. "I'm just showing off the trappings of a successful career, I guess."

"Are you sure that's all it is?" Lucie asked, observing her closely.

Lila raised her chin, striking almost a defiant pose. "I'm sure," she answered.

Lucie inclined her head, accepting her friend's story. "Well, if I were you, I'd remember to take a handkerchief with me."

Lila stared at the other woman. What Lucie had just said made absolutely no sense to her.

"Why?"

Lucie's smile was a wide one, tinged in amusement. "Because you'll need a handkerchief to wipe up your friend's drool once he gets a load of you looking like that."

Lila looked down at herself. Granted, she'd taken a lot of time choosing what to wear, but it was still just a two-piece outfit. "I don't look any different than I usually do," Lila protested.

Lucie's smile widened a little more as she turned to leave. "Okay, if you say so," she answered agreeably, going along with Lila's version. "But between you and me, you look like a real knockout."

Good, Lila thought. That was the look she was going for.

There were mornings at work when the minutes would just seem to drag by, behaving as if lunchtime would never come. Lila would have given anything for that sort of a morning this time around because today, the minutes just seemed to race by, until suddenly, before she knew it, the clock on the wall opposite her office said it was eleven fifteen.

She'd told Everett that she would meet him at the restaurant she'd selected at eleven thirty.

That meant it was time for her to get going.

Lila took a deep breath, pushed her chair away from her desk and got up.

When she stood up, her hands braced against her

desk, her legs felt as if they had suddenly lost the power of mobility.

For a moment, it was as if she was rooted in place.

This was ridiculous, Lila told herself, getting her purse from her drawer.

She closed the drawer a little too hard. The sound reverberated through the glass walls and next door Lucie immediately looked in her direction. Grinning, Lucie gave her a thumbs-up sign.

Lila forced herself to smile in response then, concentrating as hard as she could, she managed to get her frozen legs moving. She wanted to be able to leave the office before Lucie thought to stick her head in to say something.

Or ask something.

This was all going to be over with soon, Lila promised herself.

Once out of the building, she made her way to her car. An hour and she'd be back, safe and sound in the office and this so-called "lunch date" would be behind her, Lila thought, trying to think positive thoughts.

It would be behind her and she'd never have to see Everett again.

But first, she pointedly reminded herself, she *was* going to have to get through this ordeal. She was going to have to sit at a table, face Everett and pretend that everything was just fine.

She was going to have to pretend that the past was just that: the past, and that it had nothing to do with the present. Pretend that those events from thirteen years ago didn't affect her any longer and definitely didn't get in the way of her eating and enjoying her lunch. Pretend that the memory of those events didn't impede her swallowing, or threaten to make her too sick to keep her food down.

Reaching her car, Lila got in and then just sat there, willing herself to start it. Willing herself to drive over to the restaurant and get this lunch over with.

Not a good plan, Lila. This is not a good plan. You should have never agreed to have lunch with Everett. When he wrote to you on your Facebook page, asking to meet with you, you should have told him to go to hell and stay there.

You've got no one to blame but yourself for this.

Lila let out a shaky breath and then glanced up into the rearview mirror.

Lucie was right. She looked fantastic.

Go and make him eat his heart out, Lila silently ordered herself. *And then, after you've finished eating and he asks if he could see you again, you tell him No!*

You tell him no, she silently repeated.

Taking another deep breath, she turned the key in the ignition.

The car rumbled to life. After another moment and a few more words of encouragement to herself, Lila pulled out of her parking space and drove out of the parking structure and off the lot.

The restaurant she'd selected was normally barely a five-minute drive away from the Foundation. Even with the sluggish midday traffic, it only took her ten minutes to get there. Before she knew it, she was pulling into a space in the restaurant's parking lot.

Sitting there, thinking of what was ahead of her, Lila found that she had to psych herself up in order to leave the shelter of her vehicle and walk into the restaurant.

To face her past.

"No," she contradicted herself through gritted teeth. "Not to face the past. To finally shut the door on it once and for all and start your future."

Yes, she had a life and a career, a career she was quite proud of. But she also needed to cut all ties to the woman she had once been. That starry-eyed young woman who thought that love lasted forever and that she had found her true love. That woman had to, quite simply, be put to rest once and for all.

And she intended to do that by having lunch with Everett, the man who had taken her heart and made mincemeat out of it. And once lunch was done, she was going to tell him goodbye one last time. Tell him good-bye and make him realize that she meant it.

Lila slowly got out of her car and then locked it.

Squaring her shoulders, she headed for the restaurant. It was time to beard the lion in his den and finally be set free.

Chapter Three

This was absurd, Everett thought. He was a well-respected, sought-after physician who had graduated from medical school at the top of his class. Skilled and exceedingly capable. Yet here he was, sitting in a restaurant, feeling as nervous as a teenager waiting for his first date to walk in.

This was Lila for God's sake, he lectured himself. Lila, someone he'd once believed was his soul mate. Lila, whom he'd once been closer to than anyone else in the world and had loved with his whole heart and soul. There was absolutely no reason for him to be tapping the table with his long fingers and fidgeting like some inexperienced kid.

Yet here he was, half an hour ahead of time, watching the door when he wasn't watching the clock, waiting for Lila to walk in.

Wondering if she wouldn't.

Wondering if, for some reason, she would wind up changing her mind at the last minute and call him to cancel their lunch. Or worse, not call at all.

Why am I doing this to myself? Everett silently demanded. Why was he making himself crazy like this? So what if she didn't show? It wouldn't be the end of the world. At least, no more than it was all those years ago when Lila had told him she didn't ever want to see him again.

The words had stung back then and he hadn't known what to do with himself, how to think, what to say. In time, he'd calmed down, started to think rationally again. He had decided to stay away from her for a while, thinking that Lila would eventually come to her senses and change her mind.

Except that, when he finally went to see her, he found out that she was gone. Lila had taken off for parts unknown and no one knew where. Or, if they did know, no one was telling him no matter how much he asked.

That was when his parents had sat him down and told him that it was all for the best. They reminded him that he had a destiny to fulfill and now he was free to pursue that destiny.

Not having anything else to cling to, he threw himself into his studies and did exactly what was expected of him—and more.

He did all that only to end up here, sitting in an Austin restaurant, watching the door and praying each time it opened that it was Lila coming in and walking back into his life.

But each time, it wasn't Lila who walked in.

Until it was.

Everett felt his pulse leap up with a jolt the second he saw her. All these years and she had only gotten more beautiful.

He immediately rose in his seat, waving to catch her attention. He had to stop himself from calling out her name, instinctively knowing that would embarrass her. They weren't teenagers anymore.

Lila had almost turned around at the door just before she opened it. It was only the fact that she would have been severely disappointed in herself for acting like such a coward that forced her to come inside.

The second she did, she immediately saw Everett and then it was too late to run for cover. Too late to change her mind.

The game was moving forward.

She forced a smile to her lips despite the fact that her stomach was tied in a knot so tight she could hardly breathe. It was the sort of smile that strangers gave one another in an attempt to break the ice. Except that there was no breaking the ice that she felt in her soul as she looked at Everett.

All the old heartache came rushing back to her in spades.

"I'm sorry," she murmured to Everett when she finally reached the table. "Am I late?"

"No," he quickly assured her. "I'm early. I didn't

know if there was going to be a lot of traffic, or if I'd have trouble finding this place, so I left the hotel early." A sheepish smile curved his lips. "As it turned out, there was no traffic and the restaurant was easy enough to find."

"That's good," she responded, already feeling at a loss as to what to say next.

She was about to sit down and Everett quickly came around the table to hold out her chair for her.

"Thank you," she murmured, feeling even more awkward as she took her seat.

Having pushed her chair in for her, Everett circled back to his own and sat down opposite her. He could feel his heart swelling just to look at her.

"You look really great," Everett told her with enthusiasm.

Again she forced a quick smile to her lips. "Thank you," she murmured.

At least all that time she'd spent this morning fussing with her makeup and searching for the right thing to wear had paid off, she thought. Looking good, she had once heard, was the best revenge. She wanted Everett to be aware of what he'd given up. She wanted him to feel at least a little pang over having so carelessly lost her.

The years had been kind to him, as well, she reluctantly admitted. His six-foot frame had filled in well, though he was still taut and lean, and his dark hair framed a handsome, manly face and highlighted his dark-blue eyes. Eyes that seemed to be studying her.

"But you do seem a little...different somehow," Everett said quietly a moment later.

She wasn't sure what he meant by that and it marred her triumph just a little. Was that a veiled criticism, she wondered.

"Well, it has been thirteen years," she reminded Everett stiffly. "We knew each other a long time ago. That is," she qualified, "if we ever really knew each other at all."

He looked at her, wondering if that was a dig or if he was just being extremely touchy.

It seemed there were four of them at the table. The people they were now and the ghosts of the people they had been thirteen years ago.

The moment stretched out, becoming more uncomfortable. "What's that supposed to mean?" Everett asked her.

"Just an observation," Lila answered casually. "Who really knows who they are at that young an age?" she asked philosophically. "I know that I didn't."

He sincerely doubted that. "Oh, I think you did," Everett told her.

Seeing the server approaching, she held her reply. When the server asked if he could start them out with a drink, Lila ordered a glass of sparkling water rather than anything alcoholic. Everett followed her example and asked for the same.

"And if you don't mind, I'd like to order now," Lila told the young server. "I have to be getting back to the office soon," she explained.

"Of course."

After he took their orders and left, Everett picked up the thread of their conversation. "I think you knew just what you wanted years ago," he told her. "I'm the one who got it all wrong."

Was he saying that out of pity for her, she wondered, feeling her temper beginning to rise as her stomach churned.

"On the contrary," Lila responded. "You were the only kid who was serious when he said he wanted to play 'doctor.' If you ask me, 'Dr. Fortunado' achieved everything he ever dreamed about as a kid."

Everett's eyes met hers. Longing and sadness for all the lost years filled him. For the time being, he disregarded the note of bitterness he thought he detected in her voice.

"Not everything," he told her.

This was an act. She wasn't going to fall for it, Lila thought, grateful that the server picked that moment to return with their drinks and their orders. Everett wasn't fooling her. He was just saying that so that she would forget about the past. Forget her pain.

As if that were remotely possible.

Silence stretched out between them. Everett shifted uncomfortably.

"So, tell me about you," he finally urged. "What are you doing these days?"

Lila pushed around the lettuce in her salad as if the fate of the world depended on just the right placement. She kept her eyes on her plate as she spoke, deliberately avoiding making any further eye contact with him. She had always loved Everett's dark blue eyes. When they'd been together, she felt she could easily get lost in those eyes of his and happily drown.

Now she couldn't bear to look into them.

"I'm a manager of one of the departments at the Fortune Foundation. My work involves health outreach programs for the poorer families living in the Austin area."

That sounded just like her, Everett thought. Lila was always trying to help others.

But something else she'd said caught his attention. "Did you say the Fortune Foundation?"

"Yes," she answered. Suspicion entered her voice as she eyed him closely and asked, "Why?"

"Well, it just seems funny that you should mention the Fortunes. My family just recently found out that our last name might very well be 'Fortune' rather than 'Fortunado.'" He pulled his face into a grin. "Crazy coincidence, isn't it?"

Coincidence. Lila had another word for it. Her eyes narrowed as she pinned him with a look. "Is that why you wanted to get together for lunch?" she wanted to know. "To ask me questions about the Fortunes and see how much information you could get?"

He stared at her, practically dumbstruck. What was she talking about?

"The fact that you work for the Fortune Foundation has absolutely nothing to do with my wanting to get together with you," Everett insisted. Thinking over her accusation, he shook his head. "I'm not even sure if the family *is* connected to the Fortunes. It could all just be a silly rumor or a hoax.

"And even if it *does* turn out to actually be true, my family's not positive if we want to reveal the connection. It sounds like there are a lot of skeletons in the

Fortune closet. Actually," he confessed, backtracking, "maybe I spoke out of turn, talking about the possible connection. I'd appreciate it if you didn't say anything to anyone at the Foundation."

Did he think she was going to go running back after lunch and act like a human recording device, spilling every word that had been said between them? Just what sort of an image did he have of her?

Lila found herself struggling to tamp down her temper before she said anything.

"Well, obviously not everyone at the Foundation is a Fortune," she pointed out icily. "And anyway, the Fortunes are a huge family. I don't think anyone would be surprised to find out that there's another branch or two out there. There've been so many that have been uncovered already."

Everett nodded. "Makes sense," he agreed, even though he still felt a little leery about having the story spread around that the Fortunados believed that they were really Fortunes. Trying to steer the conversation in a different direction, he asked, "I'm curious—what do you think of the Fortunes?"

Lila's smile was reserved. She remembered hearing a great many unnerving rumors concerning the Fortune family before she began working at the Foundation. But most of what she'd been told turned out not to be true. For the most part, the stories were just run-of-the-mill gossip spread by people who were jealous of the family's success as well as their money.

"In my experience," she qualified in case he wanted to challenge her words, "they're a great family. A lot of people hold the fact that they're rich against them, but the family does a lot of good with that money. The Fortunes I've met aren't power hungry or self-centered. A great many of them have devoted their lives to the Foundation, to doing as much good as they can," she emphasized.

"Power-hungry and self-centered," Everett repeated the words that she had used. "Is that the way you think of most rich people?" he asked. Then, before Lila could answer, he went on to ask her another question—the question he *really* wanted the answer to. "Is that how you think of me?"

Her eyes narrowed again as she looked at Everett intently. Rather than answering his question, she turned it around and asked Everett a question of her own. "Did I say that?" she asked pointedly.

"No," he was forced to admit. She hadn't said it in so many words, but he felt that Lila had implied it by the way she'd structured her sentence.

"Then let's leave it at that, shall we?" Lila told him.

It was obvious to Everett that he was going to have one hell of a rough road ahead of him if he ever hoped to win her over. And despite what he had told his sister to the contrary, he really did want to win Lila back.

He admitted to himself that Lila was the missing ingredient in his life, the reason that every triumph he had had felt so hollow, so empty. It felt that way because Lila wasn't there to share it with him.

For now, he changed the subject to something lighter. "You know," he said as he watched Lila make short work of her Caesar salad, "as a doctor I should tell you that eating your food that fast is really not good for your digestion."

"And being late getting back from lunch isn't good for my job approval," Lila countered tersely. Finished, she retired her fork.

Was she really serious about needing to get back so quickly? Initially, he'd thought it was just an excuse, a way to terminate their meeting if she felt it wasn't going well. Now she seemed to be waving it in front of her like a flag at the end of a marathon.

"I thought you said that you were the manager of your department."

"I am. And as manager, it's up to me to set a good example," she told him.

If she really wanted to leave, Everett thought, he couldn't very well stop her. "Can't argue with that, I guess."

"No, you can't," she informed him, a stubborn look in her eyes as they met his.

He gave it one last try. "I suppose this means that you don't want to order dessert. I remember that you used to love desserts of all kinds," he recalled.

"I did," she acknowledged. "But then I grew up," she told him crisply. "And right now, I'm afraid I have no time for dessert."

He nodded. "Maybe next time, then."

Lila was about to murmur the obligatory, "It was good seeing you again," but his words stopped her cold. "Next time?" she echoed, surprised and stunned.

She sounded far from happy about the prospect. Everett did his best to ignore the coolness in her voice. Instead, he explained his comment. "I might be spending more time in Austin over the next few months."

"Oh?" She could feel the walls going up around her. Walls meant to protect her. She could feel herself struggling with the strong desire to run for the hills. She forced herself not to move a muscle. "Why?"

"Well, with Schuyler engaged to Carlo Mendoza and living here, I thought I'd be the good brother and visit her from time to time to make her transition here a little easier for her." This was harder than he thought it would be and it took him a few moments before he finally said, "I was wondering if it's all right with you if I call you the next time I'm in Austin."

His question was met with silence.

Chapter Four

Despite the fact that the restaurant was enjoying a healthy amount of business with most of the tables taken, the silence at their table seemed to wrap tightly around Everett and Lila.

Lila realized that Everett was waiting for her to answer him. And unfortunately, the floor hadn't opened up and swallowed her, so she was forced to say *something*. At a loss and wanting to stall until something came to her, Lila played dumb.

Clearing her throat she asked, "Excuse me? What did you say?"

Everett had a sinking feeling in the pit of his stomach as he repeated, "I asked if it would be all right with you if I called you the next time I was in Austin. You know, so we could get together again," he added and then watched her, waiting for an answer.

Again? Lila thought, astonished. *I'm barely surviving this time.*

She debated just shrugging her shoulders and saying, "Sure," with the hopes that if and when Everett called, she would have been able to come up with some sort of a viable excuse why she couldn't see him again.

But if she didn't put him off now, there was the very real possibility that she'd be doomed to go through another uncomfortable meeting in the near future.

Gathering her courage, Lila told him, "Um, I'm not sure if that's such a good idea."

If he were being honest with himself, Everett had half expected her to react this way. Still, actually *hearing* Lila say the words was very difficult for him.

Nodding grimly at her rebuff, he told her, "I understand."

But he really didn't understand because he didn't think it was a bad idea. He thought it was a perfectly *good* idea, one that would allow him another chance to convince her that they should try making their relationship work again after all these years.

Because they *belonged* together.

"Well, I really need to get going," she told Everett, rising to her feet. When he began to do the same, she quickly said, "Oh, don't leave on my account. Stay," she urged. "Have that dessert," she added. And then she concluded coldly, "I wish you luck with the rest of your life."

Then, turning on her heel, she quickly left the restaurant without so much as a backward glance.

Lila didn't exhale until the restaurant doors closed behind her.

Her heart was hammering hard and the brisk walk to her car had nothing to do with it. Lila didn't come anywhere close to relaxing until she reached her vehicle and got in.

Then she released her breath slowly.

She'd done it, she thought. She'd survived seeing him again.

She really hoped that Everett hadn't realized just how affected she was by his presence. With that in mind, there was just no way she could see him again, Lila thought. She was certain that she wouldn't be able to endure being face-to-face with Everett a second time, even if it was only for a couple of minutes.

But she'd done it. Lila silently congratulated herself as she started up her car. She'd sat across from Everett Fortunado and she hadn't bolted. She'd held her ground until she announced that she had to be getting back.

And now, having made it through that and gotten it out of the way, she could go on with the rest of her life.

Everett left the restaurant a couple of minutes after Lila did. There seemed to be no point in staying. He'd only mentioned having dessert because he remembered how fond of sweets she had always been. The thought of dessert had no allure for him, especially now that Lila had left. So he paid the tab and walked out.

He had barely managed to get into his car and buckle

up before his cell phone rang. His first thought when he heard the phone was that it was Lila, calling to say she had changed her mind about having him call her the next time he was in Austin.

But when he answered the phone, it wasn't Lila. It was Schuyler.

"So how was it?" his sister asked in lieu of a hello.

Trying hard not to sound irritated, he asked her, "Why are you calling? I could have still been at the restaurant with Lila."

"I took a chance," she told him. "If you were still with Lila, I figured you wouldn't have answered your cell. But you did," she concluded with a resigned sigh. "So I take it that she really did have a short lunch break."

He didn't have it in him to lie or make something up, so he just said vaguely, "Something like that."

He should have known Schuyler wanted to know more. "What was it like *exactly*?" she asked him.

Everett sighed. There was no point in playing games or pretending that everything was fine. He'd been pretending that for the last thirteen years and it had just brought him to this painful moment of truth. And he knew that Schuyler would just keep after him until he told about lunch.

"I think Lila might hate me," he said to his sister. He'd said "might" because stating it flatly just hurt too much.

"Hate you?" Schuyler questioned in surprise. "Why? What happened at lunch?" Then she chuckled. "Did she try to set you on fire?"

Everett laughed dryly. "No, she stopped short of that.

But when I asked if I could call her again the next time I was in Austin, she told me she didn't think that was such a good idea."

"Wait, back up," Schuyler told her brother. "You *asked* her if you could call?"

"Yes." Schuyler was making it sound like he'd done something bad, but he had just been trying to be thoughtful of Lila's feelings. He didn't want Lila thinking he just presumed things. He was proud of the fact that he was first and foremost a gentleman.

He heard his sister sigh in disbelief. "Everett, you are a brilliant, brilliant doctor and probably the smartest man I know, but what you know about women could be stuffed into a walnut shell with room for a wad of chewing gum. You don't *ask* a woman if you can call her. You just call her."

He didn't operate like that. "What if she doesn't want me to call?"

"Then you'll find that out *after* the fact," Schuyler told him. "Believe me, if she doesn't want you to call, she'll let you know when she answers the phone. But if you hold off calling because she said she doesn't want you to, then you might wind up missing out on an opportunity."

This was making his head hurt. "Nothing is straightforward with you women, is it?"

"That's where the aura of mystery comes in," Schuyler told him with a laugh. And then her voice sobered. "*Are* you planning on seeing Lila again?"

Lila had as good as told him not to—but he couldn't bring himself to go along with that. Not yet. Not while he felt that there might be the slimmest chance to change her mind.

"I'm going to try," he confessed.

"When?" Schuyler questioned. "Now?"

"No." He was still smarting from Lila's rejection. "I think I'm going to give her a little time to mull things over. I'll probably talk with her the next time I'm in Austin."

"Talk with her about what?" Schuyler wanted to know.

"I want to make things right," Everett explained simply. "Maybe even tell her—"

Schuyler cut him off before he could say anything further. "Ev, not even *you* can bring back the past, you know that, right?"

"Yes, I know that," he said impatiently, "but I just want Lila to know that I wish I'd handled things differently back them. Schuyler, you have your happy ending in the works," he pointed out, "but I wound up driving away the best thing that ever happened to me and I'll do anything to get her back."

"Oh Everett," Schuyler said, emotion in her tone, "that is deeply, deeply romantic—and deeply, deeply flawed. You're going to wind up failing and having your heart broken into a thousand little pieces, and then ground up into dust after that."

"I don't want to hear about it, Schuyler," he told his sister with finality. "I don't need you to tell me how I can fail. I need you to tell me that I'll get her back. I *need* to get her back," he emphasized.

He heard Schuyler sigh, as if she was surrendering.

"Okay. Just please, *please* don't do anything stupid," his sister warned.

"I already did," Everett told her. "I let Lila go in the first place."

"Everett—"

"I'll be in touch, Schuy," he told her before he terminated the call.

Everett gave it to the count of ten, then opened his phone again. He had a call to make and then he had to get back on the road if he wanted to reach Houston before nightfall.

Lila didn't need to get back to the office that quickly. She'd just told Everett that she did so she had a way to end their lunch. She'd estimated that half an hour in his company was about all she could take.

She had a feeling that if she came back early, the people she worked with, the ones who seemed to take such an inordinate interest in her life, would be all over her with questions.

Especially Lucie.

But if she timed it just right, she could slip into the office just as they were coming back from their own lunches. That way she stood a better chance of avoiding any questions.

She thought it was a good plan and it might have actually worked—if it hadn't been for the flowers. Two dozen long stemmed red roses in a glass vase to be precise. They were right there, in the middle of her desk, waiting for her when she walked into the office an hour after she'd left.

And there, right next to the vase, was Lucie. With a broad smile on her face.

"You just missed the delivery guy," she told Lila. "I signed for them for you."

"Um, thank you," Lila murmured, although what she was really thinking was that Lucie shouldn't have bothered doing that.

"No problem," Lucie answered cheerfully. Her eyes were practically sparkling as she looked from the flowers to her friend. It was obvious that she had barely been able to curtail her curiosity and keep from reading the card that had come with the roses. "Who are they from?"

"I have no idea," Lila murmured, eyeing the roses uneasily, as if she expected them to come to life and start taunting her.

"You know a really good way to find out?" Lucie asked her innocently. When Lila glanced in her direction, Lucie told her with great clarity: "Read the card."

Lila nearly bit off that she *knew* that. Instead, resigned, she said, "I guess I'll have to."

"Boy, if someone sent me roses, I'd sound a lot happier than that," Lucie commented.

"Want them?" Lila offered, ready to pick up the vase and hand it over to her friend.

"I'd love them," Lucie said with feeling. "But I can't take them. They're yours. Now who sent them?" Her eyes narrowed as she looked directly into Lila's.

Steeling herself, Lila reached over and plucked the small envelope stuck inside the roses. Slowly opening it, she took out the off-white rectangular card.

Till next time. Everett.

Her hand closed around the card. She was tempted to crush the small missive, but something held her back.

Damn it, why couldn't the man take a hint? Why was he determined to haunt her life this way? Why couldn't he just stay away the way he had done for the last thirteen years?

"Well?" Lucie asked, waiting. She tried to look over her friend's shoulder to read the card. "Who sent the flowers?"

"Nobody," Lila answered evasively.

"Well 'nobody' must have some pretty deep pockets," Lucie commented, eyeing the roses. "Do you know what roses are going for these days?"

"I don't know and I don't care," Lila answered defiantly. She was debating throwing the card into the trash.

"Well, 'nobody' certainly does. Care, I mean," Lucie clarified. "By any chance, are these flowers from the guy you went out to lunch with?"

Lila closed her eyes. She really did wish she could convincingly carry off a lie, but she couldn't. Absolutely no answer came to her, so she found herself having to admit the truth.

"Maybe."

Lucie gave a low whistle as she regarded the roses. "All I can say is that you must have made one hell of an impression at lunch."

"No, I didn't," Lila replied. "He asked if he could call me again and I told him I didn't think that was such a good idea."

Taking in the information, Lucie nodded. "Playing

hard to get. That really turns some guys on," she confided. "They see it as a challenge."

"I'm not playing hard to get," Lila stressed between gritted teeth. "I'm playing impossible to get."

"Same thing for some guys," Lucie responded knowingly. "What you did was just upped the ante without realizing it. Play out the line a little bit, then tell him that you've had a change of heart because he's so persistent. Then reel him in."

She felt like her back was up against the wall and Lucie was giving her fishing analogies. She looked at the other woman in disbelief. "You're telling me I should go out with him?"

"What I'm telling you is that you should give him another chance," Lucie told her.

Another chance. She knew that was what Everett wanted as well, even though he'd started out by acting as if he didn't, Lila thought. But there was no other reason why he would want to call her the next time he was in Austin *unless* he wanted another chance. It certainly wasn't because they'd had such a spectacular time today at lunch and he wanted to continue that.

They hadn't been spectacular together in a long, long time, Lila thought.

She tried to close her mind off from the memories, but they insisted on pushing their way through, punching through the fabric of the years.

Echoes from the past both softened her and squeezed her heart, reminding her of the pain she'd gone through at the end.

How could she willingly open herself up to that again? She'd barely recovered the last time.

Lila blinked. Lucie was standing in front of her, waving her hand in front of her eyes.

"Hey, Earth to Lila. Earth to Lila," Lucie called out.

"What?" Lila responded, stopping short of biting off an angry cry.

"I was talking to you and you seemed like you were a million miles away. Where were you just now?"

Lila blew out a quick breath and pulled herself together.

"You called it," she told the other woman. "I was a million miles away. And now it's time to come back and get to work," she announced. "I've got a stack of reports to review so I can make the rounds tomorrow."

Lucie inclined her head. "I can take a hint."

"I certainly hope so," Lila murmured under her breath.

Hearing her, Lucie added, "For now," as she left the room.

Lila suppressed a groan. Glaring at the roses, she moved the vase to the windowsill.

It didn't help.

Chapter Five

"Have you given 'Mr. Roses' any more thought?" Lucie asked her a few days later completely out of the blue.

They were each preparing their input to submit for their departments' monthly budget and, taking a break, Lucie had peered into her office to ask about Everett.

Surprised by the unexpected salvo—she'd thought she was out of the woods since Lucie hadn't brought the subject up for several days—Lila answered, "None whatsoever." She deliberately avoided Lucie's eyes as she said it.

"You're lying," Lucie said.

This time Lila did look up. She shot her a look that was just short of a glare, but Lucie wasn't intimidated.

"You know how I know?" Lucie asked her.

Lila braced herself inwardly. Her outward countenance didn't change. "Please, enlighten me," she requested coolly.

"You're blushing," Lila pointed out triumphantly. "Every time you say something that you're not entirely comfortable about—like a little white lie—you start to blush."

Lila drew herself up. "I do not," she protested. But even as she said it, she could feel her cheeks getting warmer.

"Got a mirror?" Lucie asked. She appeared to be serious. "I'll show you."

Lila sighed, dropping her head back. "Okay, so I've thought about him, but the answer to your next question is still 'no.' I'm not going to be seeing him again anytime soon—*or ever.*"

Lucie shook her head. It was obvious by her expression that she thought Lila was turning her back on a golden opportunity.

"I think you're making a mistake," Lucie told her in no uncertain terms.

"My mistake to make," Lila informed her cheerfully. And then, because she knew that Lucie was only looking out for her, she relented. "No offense, Lucie. I know you're a romantic at heart. I'm aware of your story," she went on. "You and Chase were teenage sweethearts who, despite a few bumps on the road—"

"Big bumps," Lucie emphasized, interjecting her own narrative.

"—were meant to be together," Lila continued, pushing on. "But not everyone is like you. Most teenage sweethearts usually outgrow each other and are meant to be apart."

"Aha," Lucie exclaimed. "So you two were teenage sweethearts."

Lila stared at her. That had been a slip. "I didn't say that," she protested.

"Not in so many words," Lucie countered. "But you definitely implied it. Lila," she said, lowering her voice as she put her hand over her friend's. "The heart wants what the heart wants and it doesn't always make perfect sense. But old loves imprint themselves on your heart and on your brain. Take it from me. They *always* stay with you."

"That might have been your experience," Lila granted. "And I know that you and Chase are extremely happy—"

"We are," Lucie assured her.

Lila forged on. "—but not everyone is like you," she concluded. "As a matter of fact, I'm pretty sure that very few people are like you."

Apparently her remark didn't satisfy Lucie, who went on. "Why don't you give this guy another chance and see if you belong to the 'very few?'" she suggested.

Lila went back to looking over her notes and figures for the budget. "Not going to happen."

Lila might have wanted to drop the subject, but Lucie obviously didn't. The subject of reunited lovers was something that was near and dear to her heart.

"Why?" Lucie asked her. "What are you so afraid of, Lila?"

Lila's eyes met her friend's. "I'm afraid of not getting my budget done in time," she said in a crisp voice.

"Seriously," Lucie coaxed.

"Seriously," Lila insisted, refusing to be distracted from the subject any further.

Just then, she saw a movement out of the corner of her eye. She looked toward the doorway. For a split second, she was afraid that Everett had found his way up to the office, but then she realized, as the man drew closer, that it was a deliveryman—and he was carrying another vase filled with flowers.

Not again!

"Oh, look, more roses," Lucie announced gleefully. "Just in time to replace the ones that are beginning to wilt," she added, grinning at Lila.

"How do you know they're for me?" Lila asked almost defensively. "There are plenty of other people who work here."

"Oh, I just have a feeling," Lucie told her, her eyes sparkling as she looked at her.

Her grin grew wider as the deliveryman came over to Lila's office where they were working.

"Ms. Clark?" the deliveryman asked, looking from one young woman to the other.

"That would be her," Lucie said, pointing toward Lila.

With a nod of his head, the deliveryman offered Lila what looked like a rectangular, brown Etch A Sketch.

"Would you sign here for the flowers, please?" the man requested.

Though she was strongly tempted to refuse the

flowers, Lila didn't want to create problems for the deliveryman, so she did as he had said.

Then he indicated the flowers. "Where do you want them?" he asked her.

"Be nice, Lila," Lucie cautioned, as if she could see that her friend was tempted to tell the man exactly where she wanted him to put the roses.

Resigned, Lila told the deliveryman, "I'll take them."

When she did, she realized that this vase felt even heavier than the last one had. Looking closer, she saw that the vase appeared to be cut crystal.

"Have a nice day," the deliveryman told her cheerfully, retreating.

"With those roses, how could she do otherwise?" Lucie asked, calling after him.

"You like them so much, here, you take them," Lila said, trying to hand the vase over to the other woman.

But Lucie raised her hands up high, putting them out of reach and thus keeping the transfer from being carried out.

"You know what this means, don't you?" she asked Lila.

"That the price of roses is being driven up even higher?" Lila asked sarcastically.

Lucie shook her head. She looked very pleased with this turn of events.

"No. It means that you might think you're done with this guy from your past, but he clearly is *not* done with you."

Lila had another take on the situation. "Maybe he's

just not used to taking no for an answer," she countered, frowning, then insisted, "All these flowers don't mean anything."

"You know, you still haven't answered my question," Lucie said, watching as Lila placed the flowers on the windowsill beside the other vase.

Lila didn't bother fussing with the newest arrangement. Instead, she sat down at her desk again, still trying to focus on the budget that was due. "What question is that?"

Slowly, enunciating each word for emphasis, Lucie repeated, "What are you afraid of?"

"I thought I answered that," Lila told her. "I believe I said I was afraid of not getting my budget done in time."

Lucie's eyes met hers. "You know I'm just going to keep after you until you tell me what's up with you and this guy."

And she knew very well that Lucie would, Lila thought. This had to stop. It was bad enough she was trying to get Everett to back off and leave her alone. She did *not* need her friend championing Everett's cause as well.

"Lucie, I love you like a sister—but butt out," she told Lucie in no uncertain terms.

"Sorry," Lucie replied, looking at her innocently. "That doesn't compute."

Lila rolled her eyes. "*Make* it compute," she told Lucie and with that, she ushered the woman out and closed the door to her office because, all distractions and two dozen roses aside, she really *did* have a budget to hand in before the end of the week. Which meant that she had no time to think about Everett Fortunado and his attempts to get her to give him another chance to shatter her heart.

The roses on the windowsill were beginning to drop their petals. They fell sporadically, drifting like soft pink tears onto the industrial beige floor covering in her office.

There was something sad about watching the flowers wilt.

Or maybe she felt that way because, despite the two separate deliveries of long-stem roses, she had not heard from Everett since she'd left him in the restaurant on their one and only lunch date—if it could actually have been called that.

Lila told herself that she was relieved. If Everett didn't call, then she didn't have to come up with an excuse not to see him.

But amid all that so-called relief, she had to admit that there was just the slightest tinge of disappointment as well. She really hadn't thought that Everett would give up so easily, or so quickly.

But he obviously had.

He'd moved on and he was off her conscience—not that she'd ever done anything to feel guilty about when it came to Everett, she silently insisted. Everett, on the other hand, had a lot to atone for—

What was wrong with her? she suddenly upbraided herself. Why was she wasting time thinking about Everett or trying to figure out why he'd behaved the way he had? She didn't have time for all that, she admonished herself. Less time than usual.

She was in the middle of a very real health crisis.

Everyone at the Fortune Foundation was. They had been stricken by an unseasonable, full-fledged flu epidemic that was laying everyone low. As a result, they were understaffed, with almost a third of both the volunteers and employees alike calling in sick.

Being short-staffed when it came to the workers was one thing. But now two of the doctors who regularly volunteered their services, making the rounds and tending to the people in her district, had fallen sick and were out of commission as well.

What that meant in the short run was that there weren't enough doctors to administer the flu vaccines or to treat the people who were down with it.

This directly affected Lila, who oversaw the department that made certain poor families in her area had access to flu shots and to medical care.

She needed replacement for the sick doctors. STAT.

Lila had spent half the morning on the phones, calling every backup physician she could think of in the area. All the calls yielded the same results. The doctors were either up to their ears in patients—or they were sick themselves.

The cupboard, Lila thought, exasperated, was appallingly bare. There weren't any doctors in or around Austin left to call.

Frustrated, she closed her physicians' file on the computer. The people whose trust she had painstakingly worked to gain and whom she had gathered into the fold now needed help, and they were counting on her to come through. They weren't going to believe her when she said that she couldn't find any doctors to make house calls.

But it was true. She was totally out of doctors to call. Totally out of options…

Except for one, she suddenly realized as the thought zigzagged through her brain.

She hated to do this. Hated to have to call him and sound as if she was begging.

But this wasn't about her, Lila reminded herself. This was about the sick people who were counting on her. People who were in desperate need of medical care. Otherwise, some of them, the very young and the very old, might not make it.

Telling herself not to think about what she was doing, Lila took out the card Everett had handed her during the less than successful lunch. The card with his phone number on it.

Not his cell phone. She didn't want this to sound personal, although *that*, she had a feeling, might get the fastest results.

Lila squared her shoulders and rejected the thought about using Everett's cell phone number. She was going to try his office phone number first—and pray that she got through that way.

Tapping out the number on her landline, Lila found herself connected to a recording with a list of menu options.

Feeling unusually short-tempered, Lila nearly hung up at that point. But she forced herself to stay on. This was about the kids, she reminded herself. The kids, not her. She needed to try every available possibility.

After dutifully listening to the selections, she pressed "Number 4 for Dr. Fortunado."

That connected her to yet another recording, which asked her to leave her name, phone number and a brief message. The recording promised her a return call within twenty-four hours. It didn't sound reassuring, but she supposed that it was better than nothing.

The second the "beep" went off, Lila began talking.

"Everett, it's Lila. I'm sorry to bother you like this, but we've been hit really hard with this flu epidemic. I'm down two doctors, not to mention a number of staff members. Every backup physician I've called is already handling too many patients—if they're not sick themselves. I'm totally out of options, otherwise I wouldn't be bothering you. I know you're an internist and not a family practitioner, but to put it quite simply, I'm desperate. A lot of the people I interact with are down with this flu and I need help.

"If you're too busy to return this call, I'll understand. However, I hope you'll consider it. You can reach me in my office, or on my cell." She proceeded to recite both numbers slowly. "I hope to hear from you soon, but like I said, if you decide you can't help, I'll understand."

With that, she hung up and desperately tried to think of some other course of action. Maybe she could try physicians' assistants in the area. The way she saw it, it was any port in a storm at this point.

But she just ran into wall after wall.

Lila was beginning to think that the situation was hopeless.

And then her phone rang.

Snatching the receiver up, she cried, "This is Lila Clark," as she literally crossed her fingers, hoping that one of the many, *many* doctors she had called today was calling back to tell her that after due consideration, they had found a way to spare a few hours to work with the needy families.

"Lila," the deep voice on the other end of the line said. "It's Everett."

Chapter Six

As the sound of his voice registered, Lila felt as if everything had suddenly ground to a standstill all around her.

But maybe her imagination was playing tricks on her, or she had just heard incorrectly and *thought* it was Everett calling her. Someone else might have said that wishful thinking was to blame, but she refused to call it that.

Rousing herself, Lila asked in a small, stilted voice, "Everett?"

"Yes."

She exhaled a shaky breath before saying his name, as if to make certain that it really was him calling. "Everett."

Had he gotten her message? Lila wondered. Or was

this just a coincidence and he was calling because she hadn't acknowledged the roses he'd sent her? Taking nothing for granted, Lila replied, "I called you earlier today—"

"Yes, I know," he responded. "About a flu epidemic you're having in Austin. That's the reason I'm calling back. If you still need me, I can be there by tomorrow morning."

Relief swept over her, drenching her like a huge tidal wave and stealing her breath. Lila was certain she now understood how lottery winners felt.

"Oh, I need you," she said with feeling, and then she realized how that must have sounded to him. Mortified, Lila immediately backtracked. "That is… I mean—"

She heard Everett laugh softly. That same old laugh that used to make her skin tingle and had warm thoughts flowing all through her, fast and heavy.

"That's okay, I know what you meant," Everett assured her. "Are you really that short-handed out there?"

Looking at the mounting stack of calls on her desk, almost all requesting help, she stifled a groan. "You have no idea."

"Well, you can give me a tour and let me see what you're up against when I get there tomorrow," he told her.

She knew that Everett had his own practice and that he was going to have to make arrangements on his end in order to accommodate her, even for one day. It didn't take a genius to know that that he was really going out of his way for her.

"I can't begin to tell you how much I appreciate this, Everett," Lila began.

Everett cut her short. "I'm a doctor," he replied simply. "This is what I do." She heard papers being moved around on his end. "I should be able to get in by eight. Where should I meet you?"

This was really happening, she thought. Everett was actually coming to her rescue, despite the way everything had ended between them the last time they saw one another. Relief and gratitude mingled with a sharp twinge of guilt within her.

"Why don't we meet at the Fortune Foundation?" she suggested to him. "And we can go from there."

Lila went on to give him the address of the building, although that would have been easy enough for him to look up if he wanted to. She told him which floor she was on as well as the number of her office.

"I can wait outside the building for you if that'll be easier," Lila added.

"That won't be necessary," Everett assured her. "They taught me how to count in medical school."

Had she just insulted him somehow? Afraid of saying something wrong, Lila felt as if she was stumbling over her own tongue. "Oh, I'm sorry. I didn't mean to—"

"Lila," Everett raised his voice as he cut into her words. When she abruptly stopped talking, he told her, "Stop apologizing."

She took a deep breath, trying to center herself and regroup. None of this was easy for her. Not when it came to Everett. "Um, I guess I'm just not used to asking for favors."

Everett read between the lines. "Don't worry. I'm not going to ask you for a favor back if that's what you're thinking," he assured her. There was another moment of awkward silence on her end and then he said, "All right, if I'm going to be there tomorrow morning, I've got a few things to see about between now and then. See you tomorrow," he told her.

Everett hung up before she had a chance to thank him again.

Lila slowly returned the receiver back to its cradle. "Well," she murmured, still feeling somewhat numb as she continued to look at the receiver, "that at least solves some of my problem."

She was still one doctor down, but one out of two was a lot better in her opinion than none out of two, she told herself. She could definitely work with one.

In the meanwhile, she needed to get the list of patients prepared for the doctors who *were* coming in so that they could start making those house calls.

Lila looked down at the various names and addresses she'd already jotted down. The number of people who were just too ill to get to a local clinic on their own was astounding, and growing rapidly. Some of the people, she thought, were probably exaggerating their conditions, but she couldn't really blame them. The free clinics were always positively jammed from the moment they opened their doors in the morning. Waiting to be seen by a doctor was exceedingly challenging when you weren't running a fever. Sitting there with a fever of a hundred or more and feeling too weak to win a wrestling match against a flea was a whole different story.

If she were in that position, she'd ask to have the doctor come to the house, too.

Oh, who are you kidding? You could be at death's door and you'd drag yourself in to see the doctor because you wouldn't want to inconvenience anyone.

Lila smiled to herself as she gathered her things together to meet with the physicians who were volunteering their time today.

The silent assessment rang true. She'd rather die than to surrender to her own weakness, Lila thought, going out the door.

Lila was exhausted.

Having stayed late, reorganizing supplies and hustling all over the city to beg, borrow or threaten to steal more vaccine serum as well as arranging for more lab tests to be done, she had finally dragged herself home after midnight.

Too tired to eat, she still hadn't been able to get right to sleep—most likely because part of her kept thinking about having to interact with Everett after she had summarily rejected him the last time they had been together.

But she had finally dropped off to sleep somewhere around 1:00 a.m., only to wake up at 4:30 a.m., half an hour before her alarm was set to go off.

She lay there for several minutes, staring at the ceiling, telling herself that she had half an hour before she needed to get up, which meant that she could grab a few more minutes of sleep.

She gave up after a couple more minutes, feeling

that there was no point in trying to get back to sleep. She was wired and that meant she was up for the day.

With a sigh, she got up, showered and dressed. A piece of toast accompanied her to her car, along with a cup of coffee that would have been rejected by everyone except a person who felt they had no extra time to make a second, better cup of coffee.

Sticking the thick-sludge-contained-in-a-cup into a cup holder, Lila started the car.

There had to be a better way to achieve sainthood, she thought cryptically to herself as she drove to the Foundation in the dark.

The streets were fairly empty at that time in the morning. The lack of light just intensified the pervasive loneliness that seemed to be invading every space in her head.

Snap out of it, damn it, she ordered. *He's a doctor and you need a doctor in order to help out. And that's all you need.*

However, ambivalent feelings about seeing Everett again refused to leave her alone. They continued to ricochet through her with an intensity that was almost numbing.

He's not Everett, she silently insisted. *He's just an available doctor who's willing to help you. That's what you have to focus on, not anything else, understand? Don't you dare focus on anything else.* She all but threatened herself.

It helped.

A little.

Arriving in the parking lot located behind the Fortune Foundation building, she found that there were only a few vehicles that pockmarked the area at this hour. Apparently the Foundation had a few early birds who liked to come in and get a jumpstart on the day and the work they had to do.

As she made her way toward the entrance, she saw that one of the cars, a navy blue high-end sedan, had someone sitting inside it in the driver's seat.

As she passed the vehicle, the driver's side door opened and Everett stepped out. A very casual-looking Everett wearing boots, jeans and a zippered sweatshirt with a hood.

She almost hadn't recognized him.

Her heart suddenly began to hammer very hard when she did.

"I got here early," he told her, nodding at Lila by way of a greeting. "Traffic from Houston wasn't too bad this time," he explained. He saw the way she was looking at what he was wearing. He looked down at his attire himself, just to be sure that he hadn't put anything on inside out. "I didn't want to look intimidating," he explained. "Someone told me that three-piece suits make some people nervous."

The way he said it, she felt as if he was implying she was the nervous person.

You've got to stop reading into things, she upbraided herself. Out loud she told him, "You look fine. We need to go in," she said, changing the subject as she turned toward the building. "I need to get a few things before we head out."

Everett nodded, gesturing toward the main doors. "You're the boss," he told her.

That almost made her wince. "This'll work better if you just think of me as your tour guide," she said, avoiding looking at him.

Holding the door open for her, Everett followed her into the building. "You told me that you manage the department," he recalled.

"I do," she answered cautiously, wondering where he was going with this.

"Then that would make you my boss for this," Everett concluded. "At least for now."

This had all the signs of degenerating into a dispute. But Everett *was* doing her a favor by coming in today and he was getting no compensation for it. She didn't want to pay him back by arguing with him.

"Whatever works for you is fine with me," Lila told him loftily.

He smiled at her as they headed toward the elevators. "I'll keep that in mind."

Was he just being agreeable, or was that some sort of a veiled warning, she wondered. This was all very exhausting and they hadn't even gotten started, Lila thought.

The next moment, as she got into the elevator, Lila told herself that any way she looked at it, this was going to be one hell of a long day.

But then, she had her doubts that Everett was going to be able to keep up. Making house calls to all the people on her list was going to turn into a marathon as well as an endurance test, at least for Everett.

And maybe her, too.

Getting what she needed from her office, Lila led the way back out of the building. "We'll use my car," she told him.

"Fair enough," Everett answered agreeably. "You know your way around here a lot better than I do."

"At least in the poor sections," she answered. They had barely gotten out on the road when she said, "Be sure to let me know when you've had enough."

He thought that was rather an odd thing to say, seeing as how they hadn't even been to see one patient yet. "And then what?" he wanted to know.

She spared him a glance as she drove through a green light. The answer, she thought, was rather obvious. "And then we'll stop."

"For the day?" he questioned.

"Well, yes." What else did he think she meant? They weren't talking about taking breaks.

"You made it sound like you needed me for the long haul," he said. And to him, that meant the entire day—with the possibility of more after that.

"I do." However, she didn't want to seem presumptuous and she definitely didn't want to totally wear him out. "But—"

"Well, then that's what you've got me for," Everett said, interrupting. "The long haul," he repeated.

Was he saying that to impress her, or did he really mean it, she wondered.

"I just wanted to warn you," she said as they drove to a run-down neighborhood. "This isn't going to be what you're used to."

He looked at her then. "No offense, Lila, but we haven't seen each other for a very long time," he reminded her. "You have no idea what I'm used to."

Everett was right, she thought, chagrined. She had no idea what he been doing in the years since they had seen one another. She knew, obviously, that he had achieved his dream and become a doctor. She had just assumed that he had set up a practice where he tended to the needs of the richer people in Houston. It never occurred to her that he might concern himself with even middle-class patients, much less those who belonged to the lower classes: the needy and the poor. And she had no idea that he ever volunteered his time to those less fortunate.

"You're right," she admitted quietly. "I don't. I just know that your parents had high hopes for you and that you weren't the rebellious type."

Everett was only half listening to her. For the most part, he was taking note of the area they were now driving through. It appeared seedy and dilapidated. It was light out now, which made the streets only a tad safer looking.

He tried to imagine what it was like, driving through here at night. "How often do you come out here?" he wanted to know.

"As often as I need to. I usually accompany the doctors who volunteer at the Foundation. It wouldn't be right to ask them to come here and not be their go-between."

"Go-between?"

She nodded. "Some of the doctors have never been

to places like this before. They're uneasy, the patients they've come to treat are uneasy when they see the doctor. I'm kind of a human tranquilizer," she told him. "It's my job to keep them all calm and get them to trust each other enough so they can interact with one another," she explained.

"A human tranquilizer, huh?" he repeated with a grin, trying to envision that. "I kind of like that."

She laughed as she brought her small compact car to a stop in front of a ramshackle house that looked as if it was entering its second century.

"I had a feeling you would." Pulling up the hand brake, she turned off the ignition. "We're here," she announced needlessly. "You ready for this?" she asked, feeling somewhat uneasy for him.

Everett looked completely unfazed. "Let's do it," he told her, getting out on his side.

Lila climbed out on the driver's side, rounded the hood of her car and then led the way up a set of wooden stairs that creaked rather loudly with each step she took. Like the house, the stairs had seen better years and were desperately in need of repair.

Reaching the top step, she approached the front door with its peeling paint and knocked.

"The doorbell's out," she explained in case Everett was wondering why she hadn't rung it. "I've been here before," she added.

"That was my guess," Everett responded.

A moment later, the front door opened rather slowly. Instead of an adult standing on the other side, there was a small, wide-eyed little boy looking up at them. He was holding onto the doorknob with both hands.

In Everett's estimation, the boy couldn't have been any older than four.

Chapter Seven

Lila thought that Everett had dropped something when she saw him crouching down at the door of their first house call—single mother Mrs. Quinn. The next moment, she saw that what he was doing was trying to get down to the level of the little boy who stood across the threshold.

"Does your mom know you open the door to strangers?" Everett asked the boy.

The little boy shook his head from side to side, sending some of his baby-fine, soft blond hair moving back and forth about his face. "No. Mama's asleep next to my little brother."

"You're very articulate," Everett told the little boy. "How old are you?"

"Four," the boy answered, holding up four fingers so

that there would be no mistaking what he said. "What's ar-tic—, ar-tic—" Giving up trying to pronounce the word, he approached it from another angle. "What you said," he asked, apparently untroubled by his inability to say the word.

"It means that you talk very well," Everett explained. Then he rose back to his feet. Glancing toward Lila so that the boy would know she was included, he requested, "Why don't you take us to see them? I'm a doctor," he added.

That seemed to do the trick. The little boy opened the door further, allowing them to come in. "Good, 'cause Mama said they need a doctor—her and Bobby," the four-year-old tacked on.

Impressed at how well Everett was interacting with the boy, Lila let him go on talking as she and Everett followed him through the cluttered house.

"Is Bobby your brother?" Everett asked.

This time the blond head bobbed up and down. "Uh-huh."

"And what's your name?" Everett asked, wanting to be able to address their precocious guide properly.

"Andy," the boy answered just as he reached the entrance to a minuscule bedroom. "We're here," he announced like the leader of an expedition at journey's end.

There was a thin, frail-looking dark-haired woman lying on top of the bed, her eyes closed, her arm wrapped around a little boy who was tucked inside the bed. The woman looked as if the years had been hard on her.

Andy tiptoed over to her and tried to wake her up by shaking her arm.

"Mama, people are here. Mama?" he repeated, peering into her face. He looked worried because her eyes weren't opening.

Lila finally spoke up. "Mrs. Quinn?" she said, addressing the boys' mother. "It's Lila. I brought a doctor with me."

The young woman's eyelashes fluttered as if she was trying to open them, but the effort was too much for her. She moaned something unintelligible in response to Lila's announcement.

Before Lila could say anything either to the woman or to Everett, he took over.

Moving Lila aside, he felt for the woman's pulse. Frowning, he went on to take her temperature next, placing a small, clear strip across her forehead.

"No thermometer?" Lila asked.

"This works just as well," he assured her. Looking at the strip, he nodded. "She's running a low-grade fever." Checking the boys' mother out quickly, he told Lila, "I can't give her a flu shot because she already seems to have it. But I can lower her fever with a strong shot of acetaminophen."

As Everett spoke, he took out a syringe and prepared it.

Andy's eyes followed his every move, growing steadily wider. "Is my Mama gonna die?" he asked, fear throbbing in his voice.

"No, Andy. I'm going to make your mom all better. But you're going to have to be brave for all three of you," Everett told him. "Think you can do that?" he asked, talking to him the way he would to any adult.

The boy solemnly nodded his head. He held his breath as he watched his mother getting the injection.

"Good boy." Everett moved on to the woman's other son. "Looks like he's got it, too," he said to Lila. Turning to Andy, he asked him, "Andy, do you know how long your mom and brother have been sick?"

Andy made a face as he tried to remember. He never took his eyes off the syringe, watching as the doctor gave his brother an injection next.

"Not long," Andy answered. "We were watching *Captain Jack* yesterday when Bobby said he didn't feel so good. Mama carried him to bed and she laid down, too."

Everett turned to look at Lila. *"Captain Jack?"* he questioned.

"It's a syndicated cartoon," Lila told him. "I think it airs around eight or so in the morning. One of the women in the office has a little boy who likes to watch it," she explained in case he wondered why she would know something like that.

"So Mrs. Quinn could have been sick for a couple of days?" Everett questioned, attempting to get a handle on how long mother and son had been down with the illness.

Lila was about to narrow it down a little more. "Mrs. Quinn called my office yesterday, but I didn't have anyone I could send."

Everett nodded, taking the information in. "You can only do as much as you can do," he told her. He knew

Lila would beat herself up but it wasn't her fault. She couldn't make doctors appear out of thin air.

He performed a few tests on Mrs. Quinn and Bobby, and then he turned in Andy's direction. "It's your turn, Andy."

Andy looked totally leery as he slanted a long glance in the doctor's direction. "My turn for what?" he asked in a small voice.

"You get to be the one in your family to get a flu shot," Everett told him.

"But I don't want a shot. I'm not sick," Andy cried, his voice rising in panic.

"No, you're not," Everett agreed. "And if you let me give you a flu shot, you'll stay that way. Otherwise…" His voice trailed off dramatically.

Andy tried to enlist Lila to help him. She was just returning into the bedroom, bringing bottles of drinking water she'd brought with her in her car.

"But won't a flu shot give me the flu?" the boy asked, anticipatory tears of pain already gathering in his eyes.

"No, it acts like a soldier that keeps the flu away," Everett told him. "You don't want to get sick like your mom and your brother, do you?" Everett asked. "Someone's got to stay well to take care of them."

Andy looked torn, and then he sighed. "I guess you're right."

"Good man," Everett congratulated the little boy with hearty approval.

Lila set down the bottles of water as well as several pudding cups and bananas she'd brought in. "Attaboy," she said to Andy. "If you like, I'll hold you on my lap while Dr. Everett gives you that shot."

She didn't wait for the boy to answer. She gathered him up in her arms and held him on her lap.

"Okay, Dr. Everett. Andy's ready." She felt the little boy dig his fingers into her arm as Everett gave him the flu injection. She heard Andy breathe in sharply. "You were very brave," she commended the boy.

"I'll say," Everett said, adding his voice to praise the boy. As he packed up his bag, he looked around, concerned. "Is there anyone who can stay with the kids until Mrs. Quinn is well enough to take care of them?" he asked Lila in a low voice. "I don't like the idea of just leaving them this way."

"Mrs. Rooney comes by to stay with us sometimes whenever Mama has to go out," Andy said, looking from the doctor to Lila as if to see if they thought that was good enough.

"Do you know where Mrs. Rooney lives?" Everett asked Lila.

"I think that's the woman next door," she told him before Andy could respond. Shifting Andy off her lap, she rose to her feet. "I can go and knock on her door," she volunteered.

"We'll go together," Everett told her. When she looked at him quizzically, he said, "You shouldn't be out there alone."

In a low voice, she told Everett, "I've been dealing with people in this neighborhood and places *like* this neighborhood for several years now. You don't have to worry about me."

"No," Everett agreed. "I don't 'have to.' But since I'm here, I'd feel better going with you," he told her, adding, "Humor me."

Instead of answering him, she looked at Andy, who was rubbing his arm where he had received his vaccination. "Andy, do you know if Mrs. Rooney does live next door?" she asked.

Sniffing as he blinked to keep big tears from falling, Andy nodded. "Uh-huh, she does."

Lila smiled at Everett. "Problem solved. I'll just pop in next door and ask the woman to keep an eye on this family."

She glanced at her watch. They had spent more time here than she'd anticipated. She was glad that it had gone so well for Everett, but they did need to speed things up.

"And then we're going to have to get a move on," she told Everett. "Otherwise, we're not going to get to see all the people on my list unless we work through the night and possibly into the next morning."

He hadn't thought that there were going to be *that* many houses to visit. But as far as he knew, Lila had never been one to exaggerate.

"Then you'd better find out if Mrs. Rooney is willing to stay with Andy and his family," he urged.

That went off without a hitch.

After getting the woman to stay with the Quinn family, Lila drove herself and Everett to the second name on her list.

Again she was treated to observing Everett's bedside manner. She was completely amazed by how easily he seemed to get along with children. Not only get along with them but get them to trust him and rather quickly.

She smiled to herself as she recalled worrying that he might frighten the children because he'd be too stiff or too cold with them, but that definitely didn't turn out to be the case. Right from the very beginning, she saw that Everett knew exactly how to talk to the children.

Moreover, he acted as if he actually *belonged* in this sort of a setting.

Talk about being surprised, she mused.

As they drove from one house to another, Lila found herself wondering what these people who had so little would think if they knew that the man who was administering their vaccinations, writing out their prescriptions and listening so intently to them as they described their symptoms was actually a millionaire's son with a thriving, fancy practice back in Houston.

She laughed quietly to herself. They'd probably think that she was making it up because Everett seemed so down-to-earth, not to mention so focused on making them feel better.

As she continued observing Everett in setting after setting, Lila could feel her heart growing softer and softer.

It became harder for her to regard Everett in any sort of a cold light and practically impossible for her to keep the good memories at bay any longer.

Everett had grown into the good, decent man she had, in her heart, always felt that he was destined to become.

* * *

"How many more?" Everett asked her as they drove away from yet another house.

He and Lila had been at it for a straight twelve hours, stopping only to pick up a couple of hamburgers to go at a drive-through. They ate the burgers while driving from one patient to the next.

Keeping her eyes on the road as she drove, Lila smiled at his question. She didn't have to pull out her list to answer him. "That was the last house on my list."

"No more left?" Everett questioned, thinking that she might have accidentally overlooked one or two more patients.

"Nope, no more left," Lila told him. She flashed him a relieved grin to underscore her words.

"Wow." Everett leaned his head back against his headrest. "I was beginning to feel like we were going to go on with these house calls forever."

She laughed. "Does feel that way, doesn't it?" She spared him a glance as she came to a stop at a light. "Bet you're sorry now that you returned my call yesterday."

"No," Everett responded quite seriously. "I'm not."

After twelve hours of work on very little sleep, all she should be thinking about was getting some rest, nothing else. So why in heaven's name did she suddenly feel what amounted to an all-consuming hot tingle passing over the length of her body just because Everett had said that he wasn't sorry he'd called her back?

What was wrong with her?

Punchy, she was punchy. That had to be it, Lila decided.

Talk, damn it. Say something! she ordered herself.
The silence was getting deafening.

Clearing her throat, Lila said, "Well, I have to admit
that you surprised me today."

"Oh?" Everett responded. "How so?"

Lila was honest with him. She felt it was the best
way. "I didn't think you had it in you to just keep going
like this. And I really didn't think you knew how to
talk to children."

"Why?" he asked. "Children are just short adults."

Lila laughed, shaking her head. "You would be surprised how many doctors don't really know how to talk
to fully grown adults, much less to little children," she
told him.

"That's right," Everett recalled. "When we started
out today you told me that you were there to act as the
go-between." He continued to look at her profile, curious. "So I guess I passed the test?"

The light turned green and Lila pressed down on
the accelerator. Once they were moving again, she answered, "With flying colors." Again she felt she had to
tell him how surprised she was by his performance. "I
didn't think that you'd keep at it long enough to see all
the people on the list." She struggled to stifle a yawn.
The long day was catching up to her. "But it's kind of
late now," she told him needlessly.

"It is," he agreed.

She glanced at the clock on the dashboard, even
though she already knew what time it was. "Too late
for you to be driving back to Houston tonight," she
told him.

"Are you offering to put me up?" he asked, doing his best to keep a straight face.

That startled her. "What? No, I just—"

"Take it easy," he laughed. "You don't have to worry. I've already talked to Schuyler. She's expecting me. I'm spending the night at her place."

"So that means that you're not going back until sometime tomorrow?" Lila asked.

He laughed again. "I can see the wheels turning in your head. No, I'm not going back to Houston until the day after tomorrow. So, if you want me to make a few more house calls with you tomorrow, I'm available."

That would be a huge help. She was still down a few volunteer doctors and she still hadn't found any more replacements.

"Don't toy with me, Everett," she told him, casting a glance his way.

His eyes were smiling at her. "I wouldn't dream of it."

Her heart fluttered. She forced herself to face forward. "All right. If you don't mind putting in some more time, then yes, absolutely. I could *really* use you for however much time you can spare."

"All right, then, same time tomorrow?" he asked as she pulled into the Foundation's parking lot.

"Make it eight-thirty," she told him.

"I'll be there," he promised, getting out of her car.

"If you decide to change your mind," she began, feeling obligated to give him a way out. After the day he had put in today, she didn't want to force him to come in tomorrow.

But Everett cut her off. "I won't," he told her just before he walked over to his own car.

Lila caught herself smiling. She knew he meant it.

Chapter Eight

When Lila got up the next morning, she felt absolutely
wiped out. If possible, she was even more tired than the
day before. It was as if her get-up-and-go had physically gotten up and left.

"You're just burning the candle at both ends," she
told the tired-looking reflection staring back at her in
the bathroom mirror. "And maybe a little in the middle as well."

The shower did not invigorate her the way it usually did.

Dragging herself over to her closet after her shower,
Lila pulled out the first things she found and got
dressed. She was staring down the barrel of another
grueling day, but at least she had a doctor for part of it,
she thought. And after Everett left for Houston, maybe

she would get lucky and be able to scrounge up another volunteer physician to conduct the house calls that were left on the list.

Determined to make herself look a little more human than what she saw in her mirror, Lila patiently applied her makeup. She succeeded in making herself look a little less exhausted—or at least less like someone who had recently been run over by a truck. The last thing she wanted was to have Everett take one look at her this morning and breathe a sigh of relief that he had dodged a bullet thirteen years ago.

Lila was still struggling to pull herself out of what was for her an atypical funk when she drove to the Foundation. This just wasn't like her, she thought. No matter how tired she felt, she never dragged like this, as if there was lead in her limbs.

C'mon, snap out of it! she silently ordered.

Just like the day before, when she drove into the parking lot, she found Everett sitting in his car, waiting for her.

When Everett saw her car approaching, he quickly got out of his vehicle. The cheery greeting on his lips didn't get a chance to materialize because he took a closer look at her as she got out of her car.

"Are you feeling all right, Lila?" he asked her.

So much for makeup saving the day, Lila thought. "I'm just running a little behind," she answered, deliberately being vague. Changing the subject, she asked, "Do I have you for half a day—or less?"

Rather than give Lila a direct answer, Everett told her, "Why don't we play it by ear and see?"

Lila put her own spin on his words. Everett was setting the stage so he could bail whenever he felt as if he'd had enough. Not that she blamed him, she thought. The man had already given a hundred and fifty percent of his time yesterday, far more than she had the right to expect, and she couldn't be greedy.

The hell she couldn't, Lila caught herself thinking. After all, this wasn't about her. This was about all those people who were counting on her to find a way to keep them healthy—or get them healthy—and at the very least, that involved having a doctor pay them a house call.

"Okay," Lila said with all the pseudo enthusiasm she could muster as she opened the passenger door for Everett. "Let's get started."

"How do you do this every day?" Everett wanted to know after they had made more than half a dozen house calls.

"Doctors used to do this all the time," she told Everett.

It took him a moment to understand what Lila was referring to. He realized that they weren't on the same page.

"I'm not talking about the house calls," Everett told her. "I'm talking about seeing this much poverty and still acting so cheerful when you talk to the people."

"I'm being cheerful *for* their sake. An upbeat attitude brings hope with it," she told him. "And hope and perseverance are practically the only way out of these neighborhoods," Lila maintained.

Everett was more than willing to concede the point. "You probably have something there." And then he blew out a breath, as if mentally bracing himself for round two. "How many more people are on that famous list of yours for today?" he wanted to know.

It was already closer to one than to noon. Did he know that, she wondered. They'd been at this for hours and she'd assumed that no matter what he'd said on the outset, she just had him for half a day.

"Don't you have a plane to catch or a car to drive?" she asked.

"Trying to get rid of me?" he asked her, an amused expression on his face.

"No, on the contrary, trying not to take you for granted and start relying on you too much," Lila corrected. And in a way, that was true. That had been her downfall all those years ago. She'd just expected to be able to rely on Everett forever. And look how that had turned out, she thought. Determined to pin him down, she asked, "How long did you say you could work today?"

"I didn't, remember?" he reminded her.

"Right. You said, quote, 'why don't we play it by ear and see,'" Lila recalled.

"Well, it still seems to be going, doesn't it?" he observed, his expression giving nothing away. "Who's next on the list?" he asked, redirecting her attention back to the immediate present.

Eyes on the road, Lila put one hand into the purse

she kept butted up next to her and pulled out the list of patients that she'd put right on top. All she needed was a quick glance at the page.

"Joey Garcia's next," she answered. "Joey's the baby of the family," she added, giving Everett an encapsulated summary of his next patient. "He's got two big sisters and two big brothers and he always gets everything after the rest of the family's gotten over it.

"However, according to my records," she said, trying to recall what she had entered on her tablet, "I don't think anyone in the family has had the flu *or* gotten the vaccine this year."

"Well, I guess we're about to find out, aren't we?" Everett speculated as she pulled the car up before another house that looked as if it might have been new over fifty years ago.

Lila got out on her side and immediately found that she had to pause for a moment. She held onto the car door for support. Everything around her had suddenly opted to wobble just a little, making her head swim and the rest of her extremely unsteady.

Realizing that she wasn't with him as he approached the house, Everett looked back over his shoulder. "Something wrong?"

"No." Lila refused to tell him she'd felt dizzy, especially since the feeling had already passed. She didn't want to sound whiny or helpless and she definitely didn't want him fussing over her. "Just trying to remember if I forgot something."

Everett thought that sounded rather odd. What could she have forgotten? "Did you?"

"No," she answered rather abruptly. "I've got everything."

He played along for her sake. She didn't look as if she was herself today.

"I don't know how you manage to keep track of everything," he told her as they approached the Garcias' front door.

"It's a gift," Lila told him wryly. She forced a wide smile to her lips as she fervently wished that she'd stop feeling these odd little waves of weakness that kept sweeping over her.

Taking a deep breath, she knocked on the front door. It swung open immediately. The next moment, she was introducing Everett to a big, burly man who appeared to be almost as wide as he was tall.

"Mr. Garcia, this is Dr. Everett Fortunado. He'll be giving you and your family your flu vaccinations," Lila told Juan Garcia and the diminutive wife standing next to him.

The couple went from regarding Everett suspiciously to guardedly welcoming him into their home.

"The children are in the living room," Mrs. Garcia said, leading the way through what amounted to almost railroad-style rooms to the back of the house.

As he walked into the living room, Everett was immediately aware of five pairs of eyes warily watching his every move.

Everett did his best to set the children at ease, talking to them first and asking their names. He explained exactly what he was about to do and what they could expect, including how the vaccine felt going into their arms.

When he was done, he surprised Lila by handing out small candy bars to each child. "For being brave," he told them.

"That was nice of you," Lila said as they left the Garcias' house twenty minutes later.

Everett shrugged. "Candy makes everything better." He got into the car. "I thought you said they called you."

"Well, sometimes I call them," Lila replied. She could feel Everett regarding her quizzically as she pulled back onto the street. "Mr. Garcia is very proud. He doesn't like accepting help. He's also out of work. I thought he and his family could do with a little preventative medicine so that if a job *does* come up, he won't be too sick to take it. He's a day laborer when he's not driving a truck," she explained. When Everett didn't say anything, she elaborated on her statement. "The man has five kids. If they all came down with the flu, it would be guaranteed pure chaos. This was a pre-emptive strike."

That was one way to look at it, Everett thought. Obviously Lila was focused on doing good deeds. "So when did you get fitted for the wings and halo?" Everett asked her.

"I didn't," she answered crisply. "They were left behind by the last department manager." She kept her eyes on the road, not trusting herself to look at him. Sudden movements made her dizzy. "I just try them on for size occasionally."

"Oh." He pretended as if what she'd just said made

perfect sense. "So, how many more house calls do we have left?" he asked, getting serious again.

This time Lila didn't have to consult her list. "We've got two more."

"Just two more?" he questioned. Yes, they'd been at this for a long time, but he'd just expected to keep going until almost nightfall again, the way they had yesterday.

"Just two more," Lila repeated. "And then you're free."

"Free, eh?" he echoed. He studied her profile. "How about you?"

"How about me what?" she asked. Had she missed a question? Her brain felt a little fuzzy and she was having trouble following him.

"Are you free?" Everett asked, enunciating each word clearly.

"Free for what?" she asked. She was still having trouble following him.

"Free for dinner," he asked, then quickly added, "I thought that maybe, since we've developed this decent working relationship, you wouldn't mind grabbing some dinner together."

Lila pressed her lips together. All she'd been thinking about the last few hours was going home and crawling into bed. But she was not about to tell Everett that. She didn't want to have to listen to a lot of questions.

So instead, sounding as cheerful as possible, she said, "I guess I do owe you that."

"I don't want you to have dinner with me because you 'owe' me," he told her. "I want you to have dinner with me because you want to."

Potato, po-tah-to, she thought. He'd come through for her, so she supposed that she could humor him. "I want to," she answered quietly.

"Great," he said. "Let's go see these last two patients."

The visits took a little longer than he'd come to anticipate, mainly because the second one involved more than just dispensing flu vaccinations to the two older children and their parents. Everett found himself tending to a pint-size patient with a sprained wrist that he didn't even know he had.

Afraid of being laughed at by his brothers for being clumsy, when it was his turn for the vaccine, little Alan had tried to hide his swollen wrist.

Drawing him over to Everett, Lila had accidentally brushed against the boy's wrist and saw him wince, then try to pretend he was just playing a game with her. The truth came out rather quickly.

"Never try to hide something like that," Lila told him as Everett bandaged the boy's wrist and then fashioned a makeshift sling for him. "They just get worse if you ignore them," she told him.

Alan solemnly nodded his head.

"He's been moping all day," Alan's mother told them as they were packing up their supplies. "Now I know why. Here," she said handing Lila a pie, which, by its aroma, had just recently left the oven. "This is my way of saying thank-you."

Lila declined. "As a Foundation worker, I can't accept payment," she told the other woman.

"Then take it as a friend," Alan's mother told her. "One friend to another. You will be insulting me if you don't accept it," the woman insisted.

The way she felt, Lila was not up to arguing. Pulling her lips back into a thin smile, she expressed her thanks, saying, "Dr. Everett will take it home with him. Maybe your gift will encourage him to return to Austin again soon."

The woman was obviously pleased to play her part in coaxing the good-looking doctor back.

"Maybe," she agreed, flashing a bright, hopeful smile at Everett.

"I wouldn't have thought of that," Everett told Lila when they were back in her car again. "That was quick thinking," he complimented her.

Lila was hardly aware of shrugging. "I didn't want to hurt her feelings, but I didn't want to set a precedent, either. Having you take it seemed like the only logical way out."

"Still wouldn't have thought of it," he told her.

"Sure you would have," she countered. "You're the smartest man I know."

No I'm not, he thought. He could cite a time when he'd been downright stupid.

Like thirteen years ago.

Everett studied her quietly as she drove. In his opinion, Lila had blossomed in the intervening years. She was no longer that stricken young girl who'd told him she never wanted to see him again. She'd become a self-assured woman who obviously had a mission in life.

A mission she was passionate about, and that passion made her particularly compelling and exciting.

He found himself being attracted to Lila all over again and even more strongly this time than he had the first time around.

"Can you clock out once we get back to the Foundation?" he asked suddenly, breaking the heavy silence in the car.

"This actually is the official end of my day, so yes, I can clock out."

"And we're still on for dinner?" he asked, not wanting to come across as if he was taking anything for granted. He knew that winning Lila back was going to take time and patience—and he very much intended to win her back.

"If you still want to have dinner with me, then yes, we're still on," she answered cautiously. She made a right turn, pulling into the parking lot. "Are you sure this won't interfere with you getting back to Houston? I feel guilty about keeping you away from your practice for so long."

"Nothing to feel guilty about," he assured her. "The choice was mine. And my practice is part of a group. We all pitch in and cover for one another if something comes up."

"And this qualifies as 'something?'" she asked him, a touch of amusement entering her voice.

"Oh, most definitely 'something,'" Everett assured her.

My lord, she was flirting with him, Lila realized. She really wasn't herself.

The next moment, there was further proof. "Lila, you're passing my car," Everett pointed out.

Preoccupied and trying to get a grip on herself, she hadn't realized that she had driven right by the navy blue sedan.

"Sorry," she murmured. "Just double-checking the schedule in my head."

"Schedule?" he questioned. But she'd said there was no one left on today's list, didn't she? Was there some secondary list he didn't know about?

"The list of patients," she clarified.

"Did we miss anyone?" he asked, wondering if she was going to find some excuse to turn him down at the last minute.

She wished she didn't feel as if her brain had a fog machine operating right inside her head. It was getting harder and harder for her to think straight.

"Lila?"

She realized that Everett was waiting for her to answer him. "Oh, no, we didn't. We saw everyone on the list. I was just thinking about tomorrow," she lied. "Let's go have dinner."

"Sounds good to me," he replied, silently adding, *Anything that has to do with you sounds good to me.*

Chapter Nine

"**O**n second thought, maybe I should drive," Everett said to her just as Lila started her car up again.

Putting her foot on the brake now, Lila looked at Everett, confused.

"Why?" she wanted to know. "I know the city better than you do. You said so yourself."

"True, but I've been able to find my way around without much trouble and I don't mind driving. To be honest, you look like you're rather tired and you don't want to push yourself too hard," Everett stressed.

He was right. She *was* tired, Lila thought, but her pride kept her from admitting it. Her self-image dictated that she was supposed to be untiring, with boundless energy.

"Is that your professional opinion?" she asked.

"Professional and personal," Everett replied quietly.

There was that calming bedside manner of his again, Lila thought. But she wasn't a patient, she reminded herself.

"Tough to argue with that," she responded. "But you'll have to drive me back here after dinner so I can pick up my car."

Everett had already taken that into account. "No problem," he assured her. Getting out of her car, he took a few steps, then stood waiting for her to follow suit.

After a moment, Lila sighed, surrendering. Since she hadn't pulled out of the parking space yet, she left her car as it was and got out.

Crossing to his car, Everett unlocked it and then held the passenger side door open for her. After Lila got in, he closed the door and got in behind the wheel. He looked at her and smiled just before he started his car.

Was that smug satisfaction she saw, or something else? Lila wondered. "What?" she asked him.

"I thought you'd put up more of a fight," he confessed as he started up his vehicle. Within moments, they were on the road.

Lila lifted one shoulder in a careless shrug. She realized that her shoulder felt heavy for some reason, like someone was pushing down on it. After dinner, she was heading straight for bed, she promised herself.

"I guess I'm more tired than I thought," she told Everett.

He accepted her excuse. "You in the mood for Chinese or Italian?" he asked, offering her a choice of the first two restaurants he thought of. He favored both.

"The Italian place is closer," Lila told him.

And in this case, he thought, closer seemed to mean better, otherwise she would have cited a different criterion first.

"Italian it is." He spared her one quick glance, coupled with a grin. "Now all you have to do is give me the address."

Lila dug in just for a second. "I thought you said you knew your way around."

"I do," he assured her, then added, "Once I have an address."

She laughed shortly. "That's cheating," Lila accused.

"I'd rather think of it as being creative," he told her, then asked again, "The address?"

She was much too tired to engage in any sort of a war of resistance. With a sigh, she rattled off the address to the Italian restaurant.

Everett immediately knew where it was. "You're right, that is close," he acknowledged.

They were there in less than ten minutes. As luck would have it, someone in the first row of the parking lot was just pulling out and Everett smoothly slipped right into the spot.

Shutting off his engine, he quickly came around to Lila's side.

Aware that Everett had opened the door for her, she felt a little woozy and it took her a moment to focus and swing her legs out. She really would have rathered that Everett wasn't holding the door open for her so he wouldn't see just how unsteady she was.

"You know, I have learned how to open my own door," she told him defensively.

If she was trying to antagonize him, Everett thought, he wasn't taking the bait.

"I know," he responded cheerfully. "I've seen you. But I like doing this," he told her, putting out his hand to her. "It makes me feel like a gentleman."

The wooziness retreated. Lila wrapped her fingers around his hand with confidence. Maybe she was worrying for no reason.

"Then I guess I'll humor you," she said, "seeing what an asset you were yesterday and today."

His smile sank deep into her very soul as he helped her out of the vehicle. "Whatever works."

Closing the door behind her, they crossed to the restaurant.

The homey, family-style restaurant was beginning to fill up, but there were still a number of empty tables available. The hostess seated them immediately and gave them menus.

"Do you come here often?" Everett asked Lila when they were alone.

"Often enough to know that they have good food," Lila answered.

Everett nodded. "Good, then I'll let you do the ordering," he told her, placing his menu on the table.

That surprised her. "Well, you certainly have changed," she couldn't help observing. When he raised an inquisitive eyebrow, she said, "There was a time when you took charge of everything."

He couldn't very well argue the point. He remembered that all too well.

"I've learned to relax and take things light," he explained. "Somebody once told me I'd live a lot longer that way—or maybe it would just seem longer," he added with a laugh.

As their server approached the table Lila asked, "Were you serious about my doing the ordering for you?"

"Very."

Lila proceeded to order. "We'll have two servings of chicken Alfredo," she told the young woman. "And he'll have a side dish of stuffed mushrooms."

"And you?" the young woman asked, her finger hovering over her tablet.

"No mushrooms for me," Lila answered.

"And what would you like to drink?" the server asked, looking from Lila to the man she was sitting with.

"I'll have a glass of water," Lila answered, then looked at Everett, waiting for him to make a choice himself. She remembered he liked having wine with his meals, but maybe that had changed, too, along with his attitude.

"Make that two," Everett told the server, then handed over his unopened menu to her.

Lila surrendered hers after a beat.

"I'll be back with your bread and waters," the server told them.

"Sounds more like a prison diet than something from a homey-looking restaurant," Everett commented.

"That's probably what she thought, too," Lila said. "She looked like she was trying not to laugh." She looked around the large room. More patrons had come in moments after they did. "Certainly filled up fast," she observed, saying the words more to herself than to Everett.

"Worried about my being seen with you?" Everett asked, amused.

"No." She was actually thinking about how all those bodies were generating heat. "Does it seem rather warm in here to you?"

"Well, when you have this many bodies occupy a relatively small space, it's bound to feel somewhat warm," he speculated. And then he smiled. "You remembered I liked mushrooms," he said, clearly surprised.

"I remember a lot of things," she said, and then the next moment regretted it. "Like quadratic equations," she added glibly.

Everett laughed. And then he looked at her more closely. There was a line of perspiration on her forehead, seeping through her auburn bangs and pasting them to her forehead. "It's not warm enough in here to cause you to perspire," Everett observed.

"Maybe you make me nervous," Lila said flippantly.

"If that were the case, then you wouldn't have agreed to dinner," he pointed out. The woman he knew wouldn't do anything she didn't want to.

Lila shifted in her chair, growing progressively more uncomfortable. "It seemed impolite to turn you down after you went out of your way to be my white knight."

Her terminology intrigued him. "Is that what I am? Your white knight?" he asked.

"Did I say white knight?" she asked, as if she hadn't heard herself call Everett that. "I meant Don Quixote, not white knight. I always manage to get those two mixed up," she said.

"I've been called worse," he said with a tolerant laugh.

Their server returned with their glasses of water and a basket of garlic breadsticks. "I'll be back with your dinners soon," she told them, placing the items on the table and withdrawing.

Everett noticed that Lila immediately picked up her glass of water. Drinking, she practically drained the entire contents in one long swallow.

Seeing that Everett was watching her, Lila shrugged self-consciously. "I guess I was thirstier than I thought."

"I guess you were," he agreed good-naturedly. Something was up, but he wasn't about to press. He didn't want to ruin their dinner. Spending time with Lila like this was far too precious to him. Having taken a breadstick, he pushed the basket toward her. "Have one. They're still warm."

He watched her take a breadstick, but instead of taking a bite, she just put it on her plate and left it there, untouched.

"What's wrong?" he asked. "You always loved breadsticks, especially garlic breadsticks."

"I still do," she answered defensively. And then she relented. "I guess I'm just not hungry."

Something was definitely off. "I've been with you

all day. You haven't eaten since you came in—that's assuming that you *did* eat before you came in this morning."

Lila shrugged, then grew annoyed with herself for doing it. She wished that he'd stop asking questions. Most of all, she wished that she was home in bed.

"I'm not hungry," she snapped. "What do you want me to say?"

This was *not* like her. His eyes met hers. "The truth," Everett told her simply.

"I don't know what you're talking about," Lila retorted, irritated. "I'm just not hungry. That's not a crime," she protested.

It felt as if her emotions were going every which way at the same time.

"Look, maybe we should—"

Without thinking, Lila started to get up—which was when the world decided to launch itself into a tailspin all around her. She grabbed the edge of the table, afraid that she would suddenly go down and find herself unceremoniously sitting on the floor. The table wobbled as she grabbed it and she stifled a cry, sitting down again.

Everett reached across the table and put the back of his hand against her forehead. Lila pulled her head away. She regretted the movement immediately because the spinning in her head just intensified.

Her forehead was hot, Everett thought. That and the sharp intake of breath he'd just heard her make gave him all the input he needed.

"Dinner is canceled," he told her. "I'm taking you home and putting you to bed."

"If that's your idea of a seductive proposition, you just washed out," she informed him, struggling very hard to keep the world in focus.

"No, that's my idea of putting a sick woman to bed where she belongs." He looked around and signaled to the server. The latter was just approaching them with their orders. "Change of plans," he told her. "We have to leave."

Without missing a beat, the young woman told him, "I can have these wrapped to go in a few minutes."

Everett was about to tell the woman that they wouldn't be taking the meals home with them, but then he had a change of heart. Lila was going to need something to eat once she was feeling better. As for him, he *was* hungry and he could always take the food to eat later once he had Lila situated.

"There's an extra tip in it for you if you can get it back here in two minutes," Everett told her.

Taking his words to heart, the server was gone before he finished his sentence.

"You're making a scene," Lila protested weakly.

"No," he retorted. "I'm trying to prevent making a scene. You're sick, Lila. I should have seen the signs. But I was so eager just to have dinner with you, I missed the fact that you were steadily growing paler all day."

Just then, the server returned. She had their dinners and breadsticks packed in two rather large paper sacks.

"Your salad is packed on top," she told him.

"Great." Taking out his wallet, Everett handed the young woman a twenty, then put a hundred-dollar bill on the table. "This should cover it," he told the server.

When he turned to look at Lila, his concern grew. She was almost pasty. "Can you walk?"

"Of course I can," Lila retorted just before she stood up—and pitched forward.

Thanks to his quick reflexes, Everett managed to catch her just in time. Had he hesitated even for just half a second, Lila's head would have had an unfortunate meeting with the floor.

The server stared at them, wide-eyed. "Is she all right?" she asked, clearly concerned.

"She will be," Everett told her. He had perfected sounding confident, even when he wasn't. "I think she just has the flu," he added. In one clean, swift movement, he picked Lila up in his arms as if she was weightless. Turning toward the server, he requested, "If you could hand me her purse."

The woman had already gathered Lila's purse. "Don't worry, I'll take it and your dinners and follow you to your car," she volunteered. Looking at Lila, who was unconscious, she asked again, "You're sure she'll be all right?"

Reading between the lines, Everett told her, "Don't worry, it wasn't anything she had here." Then he made his way to the front entrance.

Seeing them, the hostess at the reservation desk hurried to open the front door for them, holding it open with her back. "Is everything all right?" she asked Everett.

"She has the flu. She'll be fine," he answered crisply. "You do know how to make an exit," he whispered to Lila in a hushed voice. Speaking up, he said, "The car's right in front," directing the server who was hurrying alongside of him.

Still holding Lila in his arms, Everett managed to reach into his pocket and press the key fob to open the car doors.

The server moved quickly to open the passenger door for him, and Everett flashed a grateful smile at her. "Thank you."

The server waited until he buckled Lila into her seat, then handed the purse and the dinners she was holding to him.

"Are you sure you don't want me to call the paramedics for you?" she asked one last time, eyeing Lila.

"Very sure," Everett answered. "I'm a doctor. She's been out in the field, visiting sick people for the last two days and it looks like she came down with the flu for her trouble." Closing the door, he looked at the young woman and tried to set her mind at ease one last time. "Thanks for all your trouble—" he paused to read her name tag "—Ruth."

The young woman grinned broadly when he addressed her by her name. "My pleasure, Doctor." With that, she quickly hurried back into the restaurant.

Everett's attention was already focused on Lila. She was still unconscious. How the hell could he have missed all those signs? he thought, upbraiding himself again.

"I'm sorry, Lila. I should have realized what was wrong this morning in the parking lot."

And then it suddenly occurred to him that he had no idea where Lila lived. Getting her purse, he went through it until he found her wallet with her driver's license in it. Looking at it, he repeated her address out loud in order to memorize it.

"Let's get you home, Cinderella."

Chapter Ten

Everett was able to locate the development where Lila lived with only a minimum of difficulty.

Finding her house was a little trickier. Driving slowly and trying to make out the addresses painted on the curb, he finally drove up toward her house.

Pulling up into her driveway, he turned off his engine and then sat in the car, looking at Lila. She hadn't come to once during the entire trip from the restaurant to her house.

"Okay, I got you here. Now what?" he wondered out loud. "The logical step would be to get you *into* the house, wouldn't it?" Everett said as if he was carrying on a conversation with the unconscious woman sitting next to him. "But for that to happen, I'm going to need either a roommate who's living in your house or a key to the front door."

He looked back toward the house. There weren't any lights on, which meant that either Lila lived alone, or if she did have a roommate—which she hadn't mentioned—the roommate was out.

He opened her purse again. This time he was rummaging through the purse looking for her keys. He found a set of keys at the very bottom of her purse. There were five keys on the ring.

"You sure don't make things easy, do you, Lila?" he asked.

He decided he needed to find the right key and open the front door before carrying her out of his car. If he was lucky, she might even wake up by the time he discovered which of the keys fit the front door lock. And awake, she might be able to walk—with some help—to the house. That would eliminate some complications, like nosy neighbors, he thought.

Everett went up the front walk to her door and patiently started trying out keys.

The very last key turned out to be the one to open her front door.

"It figures," he murmured.

Everett went inside the house and flipped on the first light switch he found. The darkness receded.

At least he could find his way around, he thought.

Leaving the front door standing open, he pocketed the key ring and went back to the car.

Lila was still unconscious.

Unbuckling her seat belt, Everett found that the clothes she was wearing were all practically soaked.

"You're sweating this flu out," he told her. "As a doctor, I know that's a good thing. But I'd still feel a lot better if you opened your eyes." He looked at her, half hoping that the sound of his voice would somehow make her come around. But it didn't. "Nothing, huh?" He sighed.

The next moment, Everett took her purse and slung the straps onto his shoulder. Then he lifted her up carefully and carried her to her front door.

"If any of your neighbors are watching this, Lila, we should be hearing the sound of police sirens approaching very shortly. For both our sakes, I hope you have the kind of neighbors who keep their curtains drawn and mind their own business, at least this one time."

The wind had caused the door to close a little but he managed to shoulder it open.

Like a groom carrying his bride over the threshold, he carried Lila into the house. Once inside, he closed the door with his back, making a mental note to lock it as soon as he found some place to put Lila down.

Looking around, Everett found himself standing in a small, sparsely decorated living room.

"You never were one for a lot of possessions," he commented, scanning the room.

He saw a tan sectional sofa facing a medium-size flat-screen TV mounted on the opposite wall. Crossing over to it, Everett gently placed Lila on the sofa, leaving her there for the moment. Going back, he locked the front door and then walked around the single-story house, orienting himself. Like the living room, everything was in place and neatly arranged.

"Anyone here?" Everett called out, although he took the darkened state of the house to indicate that it was empty.

He continued to make his way through the house, looking into each room. There were two bedrooms located in the back across from one another. One was larger than the other. He took the smaller one to be a guest bedroom. Looking into it, he found that it was empty. There were no clothes in the closet.

Apparently, Lila did live alone.

His smile vanished after a moment. This wasn't good, he thought. She was sick and she needed someone here to take care of her.

With a sigh, he went back to the living room. She was right where he'd left her—and still unconscious. He thought of his medical bag in his trunk.

"First things first," he told himself. Picking Lila up again, he said to her, "I need to get you out of these wet clothes and into bed." He caught himself smiling as he carried her to what he had determined to be her bedroom. "There was a time that would have meant something entirely different. But don't worry, I've got my 'doctor hat' on and you have nothing to worry about."

As attracted as he still was to her, his first thought was about her health. He wanted to get Lila well again.

Bringing Lila into the larger bedroom, he managed to move aside the comforter and put her down on the queen-size bed. He took off her shoes and then began going through the drawers of her bureau, looking for a nightgown or something that looked as if she wore it to bed.

Moving a few things aside, he froze when he came across an old college jersey.

His old college jersey.

He remembered when he'd given it to her. He'd told her that when she wore it, she'd be close to him. Taking it out now, he looked at the jersey for a long moment, then at her.

"You actually kept it," he said in disbelief. "And judging by how faded it is, you've been wearing it. Maybe this isn't as hopeless as I thought," he murmured under his breath, referring to his plan to get back together with her.

Moving quickly, Everett removed the rest of her clothes and slipped the college jersey on her. Done, he tucked Lila into bed as if he was tucking in a child. He refused to allow himself to become distracted. Right now, Lila was his patient, not the only woman he had ever loved.

"I'll be right back," he told her even though she was still unconscious and couldn't hear him. "I'm going to bring in the food and get my medical bag out of the trunk."

He was back in a few minutes, leaving the to-go bags on the kitchen table for the time being. He had something far more important on his mind than food, despite the fact that his stomach kept rumbling in protest over being neglected.

Opening up his medical bag, Everett took out his stethoscope and several other basic instruments he never went anywhere without. Then he gave Lila a quick but thorough exam to confirm what he pretty much already suspected.

Her pulse was rapid, her temperature was high and, at one point, as he conducted his examination, she began to shiver.

"Chills," he noted. "And you were already displaying signs of fatigue this morning. You, Lila Clark, are a regular poster child for the flu," he concluded. Setting aside his stethoscope, he frowned. "I bet with all that running around you were doing, you forgot to get yourself immunized for the flu, didn't you?"

Mentally crossing his fingers, he looked through his bag and found that he had thought to pack some extra acetaminophen. Taking out a fresh syringe, he removed the plastic casing and gave her an injection.

"That should help lower your fever," he told Lila. He frowned thoughtfully. "But you still can't be left alone, not like this."

There was a chair over in the corner by the window and he dragged it over to her bed. Sitting down, Everett studied her for a few minutes, reviewing his options. He was due back in Houston tomorrow, but there was no way he was about to leave her in this condition.

The injection he gave her should lower her fever, but things didn't always go the way they were supposed to. If Lila took a turn for the worse, there was no one here to take her to the hospital. Or do anything else for her, for that matter.

Even if he didn't feel the way he did about her, he couldn't just abandon her.

Everett made up his mind. He might not have been there for Lila thirteen years ago, but he could be here for her now.

Stepping out into the hallway, he took out his cell phone and placed a call to one of the doctors he worked with. He found himself listening to an answering machine telling him to leave a message. He'd hoped to talk to the other man directly, but that wasn't an option right now.

"Ryan, it's Everett. I'm in the middle of some sort of flu epidemic here in Austin and I'm going to be staying here a few more days. I'm going to need you and Blake to cover for me at the office. I appreciate it and I owe you—big time. Any questions, you have my cell."

With that, he terminated the call.

Coming back into the room to check on Lila, Everett called Schuyler next. His sister answered on the second ring.

"Schy, it's Everett. I'm going to be staying in Austin a few more days."

"Oh?" Schuyler really didn't sound all that surprised, he thought. "Did you and Lila manage to patch things up?" she asked.

He wasn't about to get into that right now. That was a personal matter and it was officially on the back burner until Lila got well.

"It's not what you think," Everett was quick to tell his sister.

"Okay, if you're not trying to romance Lila into taking you back, then why are you going to be staying in Austin a few more days?" Schuyler wanted to know.

"You know that flu epidemic I came here to help treat?"

"Yes, I got my vaccination, Ev," she told him, thinking that was what her brother was going to ask her.

"Good, but that wasn't what I was about to tell you," Everett said.

"Okay, then what were you going to tell me?" Schuyler asked gamely.

"Lila came down with the flu," he told his sister simply. "She lives by herself and there's no one to take care of her."

"My Lord," Schuyler cried. "If I saw this story on one of those movie-of-the-week channels I'd shut off the TV."

"I didn't ask for your evaluation," Everett told her impatiently. "I just wanted you to know that I was still in town—and why."

After a moment, Schuyler said, "You're serious. Then she's really sick?"

Did Schuyler think that Lila would pretend to be ill—and that he'd just blindly fall for it?

"Schuy, I'm a doctor. I know what 'sick' looks like. Right now, Lila's not only displaying all the signs of the flu, she's unconscious."

Schuyler's tone of voice changed immediately. "Anything I can do?"

He thought of Lila's car. It was still at the Foundation's parking lot where Lila had left it. He knew that Lila would undoubtedly prefer to have the car close by when she regained consciousness—if for no other reason than there might be something in it that she needed.

"As a matter of fact, there is," Everett told her. "If you and one of your friends could swing by here tomorrow morning to get the keys, could you pick up Lila's car from the Foundation's parking lot and drive it over to her house?"

"I think I liked you better when you didn't feel it was seemly to ask for favors," Schuyler told him.

He knew she was kidding. He also knew he could count on his sister.

"I'm growing as a person," Everett quipped.

"That's not how I see it," she told him. "All right, where's 'here'?" his sister asked.

He thought he heard her shuffling papers on the other end and then he heard Schuler say, "Okay, give me Lila's address."

He did, and then he said, "I assume you know where the Fortune Foundation is located."

"You know, you can be very insulting, big brother," Schuyler told him.

"Not intentionally," he told her, then added, "Thanks for this, Schuy."

"Yeah. I just hope you're not going to wind up regretting this, that's all," she told him, sounding concerned.

She was worried and he appreciated that. But there was no need for his sister to feel that way. "Schuy, Lila's sick. I'm a doctor. I'm supposed to take care of sick people."

Schuyler barely stifled a laugh. "You don't think this a little above and beyond?" she questioned.

"I'm an 'above and beyond' kind of doctor," Everett answered, doing his best to make light of the concerns his sister was displaying.

"Not funny, Ev," Schuyler informed him. "I worry about you," she stressed.

"And I said I appreciate that. I also appreciate you picking up that car and bringing it back to Lila's house for me," he said, bringing the conversation back to what he was asking her to do.

Schuyler sighed. "What time do you want me to come by?"

There was no reason to push. "Whenever it's convenient." He glanced toward Lila's room. "It doesn't look as if I'm going to be going anywhere for at least a while."

"I'll still call you first," she told Everett. It was obvious that she wasn't going to take a chance on walking in on something.

Everett was just about to end the call when he heard his sister say his name. Bringing the cell phone closer again so he could hear her, he asked, "Did you just say something?"

"I just had a last-minute thought," she told him.

"And that is?"

His sister hesitated for a moment. "I don't suppose I can talk you into hiring someone to look after Lila, can I?"

He knew she was just thinking of him, but he wished she would stop. He wanted to do this and his mind was made up.

"I'll see you in the morning, Schuyler," he said just before he terminated the call.

Putting the phone back into his pocket, he returned to Lila's bedside.

When he touched her forehead, it seemed a little cooler to him. Taking out the thermometer he'd used earlier, he laid the strip across her forehead and watched the numbers registering.

He removed the strip and put it back into his medical bag.

"You still have a fever," he told her. "But at least it's a little lower. Although not low enough," he stressed with a frown. "You can't go out and do your angel-of-mercy bit until that fever is gone and you're back to your old self again."

Lila moaned.

He knew it wasn't in response to what he'd just said, but he pretended that there was a semblance of an exchange going on between the two of them.

Lila had a small TV in her bedroom. Nothing like the one in the living room, but at least it would be something to fill the silence and distract him, he thought.

Turning on the TV, he put the volume on low, sat down in the chair next to Lila's bed and made himself as comfortable as possible.

He knew he could make use of the guest room and lie down on the bed there, but he preferred proximity over comfort. He wanted to be there for her if Lila woke up in the middle of the night and needed him. One night in a chair wouldn't kill him.

Besides, how many nights had he gone without sleep when he was an intern at the hospital? That certainly hadn't done him any harm, Everett reminded himself—and neither would spending a night sitting up and keeping vigil in a chair.

Everett doubted that he would get any sleep in the guest room anyway. He knew himself. He'd be too busy straining his ears, listening for any strange noises that would indicate that Lila was awake.

No, he decided, trying to make himself as comfortable as possible in the chair. Staying in Lila's room this way was better. He'd be right here, able to hear her make the slightest sound when she woke up. And he figured she *had* to wake up soon.

"I know you need your rest so I'm not going to worry about this yet. But I'd take it as a personal favor if you opened those big blue eyes of yours soon, Lila. *Very* soon."

The only response he heard was the sound of Lila breathing.

Chapter Eleven

"What are you doing in my house?"

The raspy voice was hardly louder than a hoarse whisper, but it was definitely unnerving and accusatory in nature. Catching Everett off guard, it made him jump in his chair and almost caused him to knock it over.

Coming to, Everett realized that he must have finally dozed off for a few minutes.

It took him a moment longer before it hit him that it was Lila who'd asked the question.

Fully awake now, he got up and stood over Lila's bed. Her eyes were open and she looked bewildered. Relief washed over him as he took her hand in his. "You're awake!"

"And you didn't answer my question," Lila responded, annoyed with herself because she couldn't seem to speak any louder. "What are you doing in my house?" she asked again.

Bits and pieces were slowly beginning to dawn on her. She looked down at herself. "And where are my clothes?" Her eyes narrowed as she looked up at Everett angrily. "You undressed me," Lila choked out. It was not a question.

Everett wasn't about to deny the obvious, but she needed to understand why he'd removed her clothes. "You had a high fever and you were sweating. Your clothes were soaked straight through."

Frustration robbed her of the little voice she had so she couldn't immediately respond. She struggled to sit up.

All Everett had to do was put his hand gently on her shoulder to keep her down, which he did. "Don't exert yourself," he told her.

Who the hell did he think he was? He couldn't tell her what to do, Lila thought angrily. Her head was throbbing and she couldn't remember anything. But one thing was obvious.

"You took off my clothes," she accused again.

"I already explained why," Everett told her patiently.

She couldn't make any sense out of what he'd told her. "But we were in the restaurant," she protested, desperately trying to piece things together. It felt as if there was a huge gaping hole in her brain and facts were just falling through it, disappearing without a trace.

Maybe if he gave her a summary of the events, Everett thought, it might calm her down.

"You passed out in the restaurant," he told her. "I

brought you to your house and carried you to your room. Your clothes were all wet, so I got you out of them and into that jersey."

She looked down again, doing her best to focus on what she was looking at. The jersey seemed to swim in front of her eyes. "You went through my things," she accused.

"Just in order to find something to put on you," he answered simply. Maybe he should have let it go at that, but he couldn't help saying, "You kept my jersey."

She wasn't about to get into that—and she wouldn't have had to if he hadn't gone rummaging through her drawers, she thought angrily.

"You had no right to go through my things," she said defensively.

This was going nowhere. He wasn't about to get sucked into a circular debate about what he'd done and why he'd done it.

"Lila, you have the flu. The best thing for you right now is to rest and drink plenty of fluids. Arguing is not part of that formula. Now I'll get you some water—or tea if you'd prefer. Your job in this is to take care of the 'rest' part."

Lila made a disgruntled face. "I don't like tea," she told him.

"Water it is," he responded, heading out to the kitchen.

A couple of minutes later Everett came back with a large glass of water. He propped her up with one hand beneath her pillows while he held out the glass to her with the other.

Lila took the glass with both hands and began to drink with gusto.

"Sip, don't gulp," he cautioned.

"I know how to drink water," she informed him, her voice still raspy. However, she grudgingly complied with his instructions. Getting her fill, she surrendered the glass.

Taking it from her, Everett slowly lowered her back down on the bed.

Lila's head felt as if it was floating and there were half thoughts darting in and out of her brain. Her eyes shifted in his direction.

"Did you enjoy it?" she asked.

His back was to her as he put the glass down on the bureau. Turning around, Everett looked at her quizzically. He had no idea what she was referring to. "Did I enjoy what?"

"Undressing me."

Her voice was even lower than it had been before and he could hardly make out what she was saying. He filled in the blanks.

"I did it in my capacity as a doctor," Everett answered.

Confusion furrowed her brow. Nothing was making sense. "Meaning you didn't look?"

Everett had deliberately divorced himself from his feelings while he'd gotten her out of the wet clothes and into the jersey. But not enough to be completely unaffected by what he was doing. However, he wasn't about to tell her that. That would have been deliberately buying trouble in his opinion.

Instead, he said, "Only to make sure I didn't rip anything."

Her eyes narrowed further as she tried to look into his. "I don't think I believe you," she whispered.

The next moment, her eyes had closed and within a few seconds, she was asleep again.

"That's okay," he whispered back, gently pushing her hair away from her face and tucking her back under the covers. "I wouldn't believe me either if I were you."

He'd gotten her out of her clothes and into the jersey as quickly as he could, but that didn't mean that doing so hadn't stirred something within him even though he had tried his damnedest to block out those thoughts and feelings.

He *had* been functioning as a doctor, but he was remembering as her lover and that image was really difficult to shake.

The next time Lila opened her eyes and looked around, she saw that she was alone.

It had all been a dream, she thought with a twinge of disappointment.

She struggled into an upright position, her body aching and protesting every movement she made.

She stifled a groan. She felt as if she'd been run over by a truck. A truck that had deliberately backed up over her then taken off after running her over again.

She struggled to focus, her head throbbing, impeding her thoughts.

How did she get here? The last thing she actually

remembered was being in the restaurant—sitting opposite Everett.

Everett had been part of her dream, she realized.

All these years and she was still having dreams about Everett. Strange dreams.

She needed to get up, she thought.

Just as she was about to throw back her covers, Everett walked into the room carrying a tray.

He smiled, pleased to see her up. "You're awake."

Lila's mouth dropped open as she stared at him. "I didn't dream you."

He set the tray down on the bureau for the moment.

"You dreamt about me?" he asked. He was practically beaming.

She became instantly defensive. "What are you doing here?"

"We went through this last night," he reminded her patiently. "Don't you remember?"

"I thought that was a dream." She was repeating herself, Lila thought. She held her head. It was really throbbing. "I feel awful."

"Well, if it makes you feel any better, you don't look awful," he told her. "But you are sick."

"No, I'm not," she protested. She tried to throw the covers off again and found that the single movement was exceedingly taxing to her strength. What the hell had happened to her? "I have to get ready for work," she told Everett defiantly, wanting him to leave.

Everett carefully drew her covers back up. "No work for you until you get well," he told her, leaving no room for argument.

Didn't he understand? "I've got people counting on me," she told him.

"And if you turn up, you'll be *infecting* those people." She tried to get up again and this time, he held down her hands just enough to keep her where she was. "Are you familiar with the story of Typhoid Mary?"

Was that what Everett thought she was? A woman who wantonly infected people? "That's not funny."

"I'm not trying to be funny, Lila," he told her. "But I am trying to get through to you. You're sick." Everett told her, enunciating every word slowly. "You have the flu."

She felt like hell warmed over, but she still protested, "No, I don't."

His eyes met hers. "Which one of us went to medical school?" he asked her in a quiet, tolerant voice that only served to infuriate her.

She blew out an angry breath. "You did," she said grudgingly.

Everett smiled. She had made his point for him. "You have the flu," he repeated.

"I can't have the flu," she insisted. She looked up at Everett, her eyes pleading with him.

This had to be good, he thought. "Why?"

Exasperation throbbed in every syllable. "Because I just can't."

Everett decided to play along as if she had a valid argument that needed exploration. "Did you get vaccinated?"

"No," Lila admitted, mumbling the word under her breath.

A triumphant look slipped over his face. "Okay, all together now: You have the flu."

Defeated, Lila sank back onto her pillow as if all the air had been suddenly pumped out of her.

"I really have the flu?" Lila asked him, silently begging him to come up with another explanation.

Rather than answer her immediately, Everett decided to back himself up with evidence. "What's your throat feel like?"

She didn't have to think before answering. "Sandpaper."

"And your head?" he asked, giving her a chance to contradict his diagnosis.

It was getting harder and harder for her to focus because of the pain. "Like there're twelve angry elves with steel hammers in it trying to beat their way out."

"Add that to the chills I observed last night and the high fever—which by the way is going down—and you have more than your fair share of flu symptoms."

"The flu," Lila repeated in despair, saying it as if it was the mark of Cain on her forehead. "Isn't there anything you can do for me?" she asked, almost pleading with him.

"I'm doing it," he told her. "I'm nursing you back to health with bed rest, liquids and I have here a bowl of chicken soup that's guaranteed to cure what ails you," he quipped.

He'd found a folding TV tray tucked away in one of the closets and he set it up now next to her bed. When he was satisfied that it was stable, he put the bowl of soup on it along with a large soupspoon.

"See if you can hold that down," he told her.

Lila looked down into the bowl of soup as if she was trying to make up her mind about it. "Chicken soup?" she repeated.

"Highly underrated, by the way," he told her. "Apparently, our grandmothers knew something about its healing powers that we didn't. Seriously," he told Lila. "Try taking a few spoonfuls," he urged, helping her sit up and placing two pillows at her back to keep her upright.

The spoon was in her hand, but it remained motionless for now. "Where did you get the soup?" she asked. She knew she didn't have any canned soups in her kitchen cabinets.

"I had Schuyler bring it," he answered. He'd called his sister this morning and added that to his first request. "Along with your car," Everett said.

"My car?" Lila repeated. And then it suddenly came back to her. "My car's at the Foundation." Panic had entered her voice.

"Not anymore. Schuyler and her fiancé swung by this morning to pick up the keys to your car. They already drove it over. It's right outside in your driveway," he told her.

Lila looked at him in wonder. "You took care of everything," she marveled.

Everett grinned. "What can I say? I'm an overachiever."

Lila smiled at his choice of words. "I remember that about you," she said with almost a fond note in her voice.

When she sounded like that, he could feel himself

melting. Now wasn't the time. "Eat your soup before it gets cold," he urged.

"And loses its magic healing powers?" she asked in an amused voice that was finally beginning to sound more like her.

"Something like that."

Lila nodded. "All right, I'll eat—if you tell me exactly what happened last night," she bargained.

"I already told you," he said. Seeing that she wasn't about to budge until he'd told her the whole story without skipping anything, Everett sighed. "But I'll tell you again," he said, resigned. "We were at the restaurant and you suddenly passed out."

She visualized that now and became horrified. "In front of everybody?"

"Just the people looking our way," he quipped. "I didn't take a head count," he said, doing his best not to get her agitated.

"Nobody called the paramedics, did they?" Lila asked. The last thing she wanted was for this to get around. She wanted to be able to do her job when she got back, not have to constantly be answering a lot of questions because there were rumors circulating about her. Rumors always had a way of escalating and becoming exaggerated.

The thought of having to deal with that made her feel more ill.

"Well, you frightened the server, but I told her I was a doctor and that seemed to satisfy her. So I picked you up and carried you to my car. Our waitress followed us with your purse and the dinners she packed up to go—

which, by the way, are in the refrigerator waiting for you once you get your appetite back."

"How did you know where I lived?" Lila asked suddenly. She hadn't told him her address.

"I got it from your driver's license in your purse," he told her. "Which, before you ask, is where I found the keys to your house. And the car," he added, "so that Schuyler could drive it here. Okay," he informed her, "that about catches us up."

Turning, he was about to return to the kitchen when she cried, "Wait."

Now what? He did his best not to sound impatient. "I told you everything," he stressed.

"Weren't you supposed to go back to your practice in Houston today?" she asked, remembering he'd said something to that effect.

He looked at her pointedly. Was she trying to get him to make some sort of a declaration about the way he felt about her, or was this just an innocent question? "My plans changed."

"You don't have to stay here on my account," she protested.

"Lila, right now a pregnant cat could beat you at arm wrestling with one paw tied behind her back. You have the strength of an overcooked noodle. You need to rest and you need someone to take care of you while you're resting. I'm volunteering."

She shook her head and almost instantly regretted it. Her head started swimming and she waited for it to steady itself again. "I can't let you do that."

"I don't recall asking for permission," he told her.

"I've got more vacation time coming to me than any two people in my office combined and I'm electing to take some of it now. Now don't argue with me. Eat your soup and lie back, watch some mindless TV and rest. Doctor's orders," he added when she opened her mouth to protest. "Understood?"

Looking somewhat subdued, which both surprised and worried him, Lila repeated, "Understood."

Chapter Twelve

She remembered.

Although Lila tried very hard not to, over the course of the next few days she began to remember why she had fallen in love with Everett to begin with. Not because he was so devastatingly handsome—which he still was, perhaps even more so—but because he was so kind.

Kind and thoughtful and caring.

She'd witnessed those traits in action while accompanying Everett on the house calls they'd paid together before she'd gotten ill, and now she was witnessing it up close and personal while he was taking care of her and nursing her back to health.

In essence, Everett was very quietly waiting on her hand and foot. He made sure she drank plenty of fluids.

He prepared a soft, bland diet for her, then slowly sub-stituted food with more substance when he felt she could handle it. The progression took close to a week because he told her he didn't want to rush things and risk her having a setback.

By the end of the fourth day of her convalescence, Lila had gotten comfortable enough with him to allow herself to share a few old stories about people they had known back in high school.

Since she had left Houston thirteen years ago, he was in a far better position to tell her what some of the people they had grown up with were doing these days.

"Remember Jack Logan?" Everett asked, bringing up another name as they were sharing a lunch of soup and sandwiches in her room.

It took Lila a moment to put a face to the name. "Oh, you mean the guy who expected every woman to faint at his feet just because he looked their way?" She re-membered that Jack was always telling everyone he had big plans for himself. "Whatever happened to him?"

Everett smiled, remembering how brash and abrasive Logan had been. "He still lives in Houston and works at the airport as a baggage checker."

As she recalled, that didn't exactly match up to Logan's lofty goals. "Is he still a lady-killer?"

He looked at Lila and answered her with a straight face. "Only if he fell on top of one. I saw him recently. He must have gained over a hundred pounds since graduation."

Lila tried to stifle a laugh, but she couldn't help her-self. Somehow, that seemed like poetic justice. Logan had always been cruelly critical of anyone he felt wasn't as good-looking as he was. His remarks were always particularly hurtful about women he viewed to be over-weight, even if they were carrying only a few extra pounds.

"He was always such an egotist," she said when she stopped laughing.

"That part hasn't changed," Everett told her. Finishing his meal, he wiped his mouth and put down his napkin. "I think he just sees his expanding weight as there being more of him to be impressed with." He looked at Lila's plate. "Are you finished?" he asked, nodding at her tray.

"Yes." As Everett removed the tray, she told him, "You know, you really don't have to wait on me hand and foot like this."

For the time being, Everett placed the tray aside on the bureau. He could take both trays to the kitchen the next time he left the room.

"Well, I'm here and there's not that much else to do," he reasoned. "So, to my way of thinking, I might as well make myself useful."

"That's another thing," she said, picking up on the fact that he was still in Austin. "I'm keeping you from your practice."

His eyes met hers for a long moment. And then he said, "Maybe I like being kept."

Lila felt herself growing warm and she didn't think that she was having any sort of a relapse. At least not the kind that involved the flu.

She did her best to steer the conversation in the initial direction she'd intended.

"What I'm saying is that you don't need to take care of me anymore. I'm getting better all the time."

"That's because of all the excellent care you've been getting."

Lila smiled, shaking her head. Everett had always had a way with words. "I won't argue with that."

"Good," Everett said with finality. He had brought her that day's TV schedule earlier for her to look through. He picked it up now and thumbed through it. "Now what would you like to watch this afternoon?" he asked. Watching TV after lunch had become a ritual for them the last few days, something he felt that they both looked forward to. "There're some pretty good old movies on the Classic Channel and I found a station that's streaming a lot of those old sitcoms you used to like watching." He named a couple of specific programs.

Hearing them cited, Lila looked at him in surprise. "You remember that?" she marveled.

"I remember a lot of things," he told her. He had committed a great many things to memory about her, Everett thought.

Lila could feel her heart racing even though she fiercely ordered it not to. She'd been this route before and she knew exactly where it ended. Nowhere, leaving her with an ache in her heart. She did *not* want to go there, not again.

But somehow, she just couldn't seem to convince herself to turn away, to choose a different path. She tried to assuage her conscience by telling herself that this was only for a little while.

Lila shrugged in response to his question. "I don't know, you pick something," she told him. The next moment, she threw back her covers and swung her legs down. "I'll be right back."

"Where are you going?"

"I need to use the bathroom," she informed him with as much dignity as she could muster.

All the other times she'd felt the need to go, Everett had taken her arm and walked her to the bathroom as if they were out for an evening stroll. It was obvious to him that this time around, Lila was attempting to assert her independence. Not that he could blame her. In her place, he'd try to do the same thing.

Everett took a step back, allowing her space so she could get out of bed. However, he still kept a watchful eye on her.

On her feet now, he could see that Lila was still rather unstable. She took a single step and her right knee buckled.

Everett's arms were around her instantly, keeping her from landing on the floor. When he drew her back up, her body slid ever so slightly against his.

It was only for a second, but it was enough. Enough to send sparks flying between them and throwing old longings into high gear.

Everett caught his breath, silently ordering himself to remain steady instead of pulling her closer to him and kissing her the way he wanted to.

Instead of making love with her the way he desperately wanted to.

Only extreme self-control kept him from acting on the impulses that were urgently telegraphing themselves throughout his whole body.

"I know you wanted to do this alone, but maybe I should just walk with you to the bathroom this one more time," he suggested.

"To keep me from doing a pratfall?" she asked ruefully.

Her ego stood as much of a chance of being hurt as her body, so he tactfully rephrased what she'd just asked. "So you don't risk bruising anything if you do happen to fall," he told her. "So, is it okay?" he asked, waiting for her to give him the go-ahead on this.

She sighed and then smiled at him. She realized Everett was trying to spare her feelings. "Well, the old saying is that pride always goes before a fall and I don't want to fall, so I guess I'll have to just tuck away my pride and let you walk me to the bathroom one more time."

Everett laughed softly. "Good call," he congratulated her. "You'll be doing solo runs again before you know it," he promised.

Sitting on the edge of Lila's bed, Everett set aside his stethoscope. He'd just finished giving Lila her latest examination.

"Well, your fever's gone," he told her. "You're keeping your food down and your color's definitely back. And when you talk, you no longer sound like someone who starts their mornings with a shot of scotch and a cigarette. Although I have to say that I was getting kind of used to hearing that sexy voice. I might actually miss it," he admitted, smiling fondly at her.

"Well, I won't," Lila assured him with feeling. "I thought I sounded like some kidnapper placing a ransom call." She looked at him hopefully. "Does this mean that I'm being cleared for work?"

Everett nodded. He closed his medical bag and set it on the floor.

"Our little unofficial holiday is over," he told her, then in case there was any doubt, he added, "Yes, I'm clearing you for work."

Lila didn't take her eyes off him. "And you'll be going back to Houston?"

"I will," Everett confirmed. He knew he had to be getting back, but there was a part of him that didn't want to leave.

If he were honest with himself, he'd admit that he'd used nursing Lila back to health as an excuse to spend more time with her.

The last thirteen years had been filled with work, at times almost nonstop. He knew now that he had been trying to fill the emptiness—the gaping void that losing her had created—with work. Work and the occasional woman. None of them ever measured up to Lila simply because no one had ever even come close to making him feel the way Lila had.

The way she still did.

"But I'll still be coming back to Austin a lot," he told her, never breaking eye contact. "To see Schuyler and help her out with some things," he added, not wanting to scare Lila off. He paused for a moment, then, despite the advice Schuyler had given him, he asked, "Is it all right if I call you when I'm in town?"

After the way that he had put himself out for her, she hadn't expected Everett to ask permission to call her. She assumed he'd think he'd earned the right to call her any time he wanted to.

"How can I say no to the man who nursed me back to health?" she asked, trying to sound as if she was amused by his question.

"I'm not asking you to see me as the man who nursed you back to health," Everett pointed out. "I'm asking you to see me—" he paused for a moment, looking for the right phrasing "—as an old friend."

The silence between them grew until she finally said to him, "I couldn't say no to that, either."

"Glad to hear it," he told her.

He let out the breath he'd been holding. Honestly, he really hadn't known what Lila would say in response to his question. He wouldn't have put it past her feelings of self-preservation to tell him that seeing each other again wouldn't be a good idea.

But now that she had agreed, he saw that there was something far greater than self-preservation going on between them.

He could feel it.

And it was not just on his end. Nor was it just wishful thinking.

There was something tangible and real pulsating be-

tween them, ready to spring to life at the slightest bit
of encouragement.

But even with all that, Everett knew he had to tread
lightly. One wrong step and it could all crumble right
beneath him, sending him plummeting head first into
an abyss.

"Hi, are you free for dinner tonight?"

"Everett?" Lila was immediately alert. She'd answered her cell phone just as she'd walked in her front
door, thinking it was someone at the Foundation working late, calling with a question.

But it wasn't.

"I didn't expect to hear from you this soon," she said.

It had been six days since she had gone back to work
and he had returned to Houston.

"Well, I'm only in Austin for a few hours," he explained, "so I thought, if you're free, you might want
to get together."

There it was, she thought. Her way out. He was handing it to her.

If you're free.

That was all she had to say to him. That she wasn't
free. That her evening was already spoken for and she
had somewhere else to be. And knowing Everett, he
would accept that, murmur his regrets and that would
be that.

The problem was, she didn't want to take this way
out that he was handing her on a silver platter. She
wanted to see him. The truth of it was, after seeing him
every day for almost a week, she missed him.

She knew that she shouldn't feel this way. Knew that she needed to cut Everett out of her life before he became a habit. But then on the other hand, this *was* only going to be dinner. And dinner would last for a few hours at most, nothing more. She knew that Everett was far too conscientious to lie to her, especially for some ulterior motive. If he said he was only here for a few hours, then he *was* in Austin only for that time.

Those few hours might as well be spent with her, she thought in a moment of weakness.

"I am free," she heard herself saying, sealing her fate, at least for the next few hours. "We can do dinner if you like. And I promise not to pass out this time," she added with amusement, remembering the last time they were in a restaurant together.

"Oh." He pretended to sound as if he was sorry to hear that. "Too bad," he told her. "I was looking forward to playing the hero, sweeping you into my arms and carrying you to my car."

"I think being the hero once would be enough for any guy."

"Oh, I don't know," Everett speculated. "It's kind of addictive if the hero has the right damsel in distress to save."

That definitely conjured up an image, Lila thought. "I never envisioned myself as a damsel in distress," she told Everett.

"I wouldn't have thought of you as one, either," he admitted. "I guess the world is full of surprises." Then he changed topics. "Well, like I said, I'm only in Austin for a bit, so where would you like to go?"

"Seeing what happened the last time when we went to the Italian restaurant, how about Chinese food?" Lila suggested.

"Sounds good to me," he told her. He would have said the same thing if she had suggested strolling through the park, eating ice cream cones. He just wanted to see her. It had been six long days during which time he had forced himself not to call her just to see how she was doing. Or to hear the sound of her voice. He didn't want Lila to feel as if he was crowding her, or worse, as if he was stalking her.

But it hadn't been easy.

He had spent six days *with* her when she'd been ill with the flu and he had quickly gotten used to seeing her everyday. *Not* seeing her was hell now, but he couldn't behave like some privileged adolescent who was accustomed to having his every whim indulged—no matter how much he wished.

This was too important for him to risk messing up again. So he treaded lightly.

"If it's okay, I can be at your place in half an hour. Or is that too soon? Do you need more time?"

"Actually, I need less if you're close by. I just got home from work and I still look very businesslike, so I don't need to change."

He preferred the temptress look he'd seen on her, but to remain safe, he thought that it was best to go along with the business suit.

"You always look good no matter what you have on." *And sometimes even better the less you have on*, he added silently. "I'll be there in fifteen minutes."

Chapter Thirteen

Lila felt as if she had suddenly blinked and just like that, found herself going back to square one all over again. She was experiencing feelings of excitement and wariness and that in turn had created knots in her stomach.

Big ones.

But not quite big enough for her to call Everett and tell him that she'd changed her mind about having dinner with him.

Despite saying that she didn't need any extra time to get ready because she was still dressed for work, Lila impulsively flew into her bedroom for a quick change of clothes. She didn't want to look as if she was going to a business meeting. She wanted to look as good as she could possibly look.

Like a woman who was going out to dinner with a man who had once owned her heart.

Not that she planned on letting him own it again, she maintained as she quickly pulled the pins out of her hair. Instantly, the changed hairstyle made her appear more carefree. Her auburn hair cascaded around her face instead of being neatly pulled back, out of the way.

Her practical attire gave way to an attractive, form-flattering dress. She had just slipped on a pair of high heels that could have never, by any stretch of the imagination, been called sensible, when she heard the doorbell ring.

The sound instantly had her heart accelerating.

Showtime, she thought.

Hurrying to the front of the house, she stopped just short of the front door in order to catch her breath. She pulled herself together, doing her best to look as if she was totally nonchalant about the evening that lay ahead of her.

Everett would probably see right through her, she thought. Even so, she felt that she still had to keep up the charade.

Taking in one more deep breath and then slowly releasing it, she opened the door.

"When you say fifteen minutes, you really mean fifteen minutes," she said as she smiled up into Everett's handsome face.

"A man's only as good as his word," he responded. "You know, we don't have to leave right away if you're not ready yet."

"Do I look like I'm not ready yet?" she asked.

Despite her coy bravado, Lila couldn't help wondering what it was that Everett saw when he looked at her. Had he been hoping she'd be wearing something more appealing? Sexier?

Don't borrow trouble, she warned herself.

Everett's eyes slowly washed over the length of her. There was nothing but approval evident in his eyes. "You look, in a word, perfect," he pronounced.

Lila smiled at the compliment, secretly pleased although she tried her best to appear indifferent. "Then I guess I'm ready." Taking her purse, she walked out of the house, then paused to lock up.

Everett's Mercedes was waiting in her driveway.

"By the way," Everett said as he held the passenger door open for her, "I know you said we were going to a Chinese restaurant, but if I'm driving, you need to tell me the address."

She waited for Everett to get in on his side. Once he buckled up, she gave him the address, adding, "It's about half a mile past the Foundation. A lot of people from work like grabbing lunch at Gin Ling's."

Everett thought for a second. "I think I know which restaurant you mean," he told her. He remembered seeing it when he'd driven to the Foundation. "That's the one that's built to look like a pagoda, right?"

"Right."

Gin Ling's was doing brisk business when they arrived. They had to wait a few minutes to be seated.

Thinking that Everett might grow impatient, Lila

told him, "We can go somewhere else if you don't want to wait."

Everett made no move to take her up on the suggestion. "Do you like eating here?" he asked her.

She wouldn't have suggested coming here if she hadn't. That wasn't the point. "Yes, but—"

"Then we'll wait," he told her, adding, "I'm not in any hurry. I like making the most of the little downtime I get."

There was a reason why she had mentioned the idea of going to another restaurant. "I just don't want to make you late."

Everett looked at her as if he wasn't quite following her. "For what? I don't have a plane to catch," he reminded Lila. "I'm driving back to Houston."

"Doesn't all that driving make you tired?" In his place, she'd find driving back and forth between Austin and Houston exhausting after a while.

However, Everett shook his head. "On the contrary. Driving relaxes me."

Relaxing made her think about falling asleep at the wheel—not that Everett would ever admit that he was in danger of doing that. But she didn't want to think that he ran the risk of having something happen to him because of her.

"Still," she told him, "I don't want you so relaxed that you just slide right out of your seat."

"Never happen," Everett assured her. Still, her comment made his heart lighter.

She was clearly worried about him, he thought, and that felt particularly encouraging. Because that meant that there were still feelings there. Feelings he intended to stoke and encourage.

"Don't worry," he said. "I like staying in one piece as much as the next man. If I ever feel too tired to drive back, I'll rent a motel room and sleep until I feel up to driving. And, don't forget, there's always Schuyler," he reminded her.

A hostess came to show them to their table. Lila fell into place behind the woman with Everett following right behind her.

"Sorry, I was just remembering how stubborn you could be," Lila told him as they were being shown to a cozy booth.

"Not stubborn," Everett corrected, waiting for her to slide in before taking his own seat opposite her. "Determined."

Lila smiled. "Right. Determined," she repeated, humoring him.

"So how was going back to work?" Everett asked her after their server had brought them a pot of tea and then departed after taking each of their orders.

"Wonderfully hectic as always," she told him.

But Everett was more interested in the state of her health. "You didn't have any relapses or feel any ill effects from the flu?"

"No. I didn't expect that there would be," she told him honestly, smiling at Everett. "I always knew that you would be a fantastic doctor."

Everett maintained a straight face as he nodded. "I haven't mastered walking on water yet," he deadpanned, "but I'm working on it."

About to bring the small cup of tea to her lips, Lila stopped just short of completing the action, staring at him.

Everett laughed. "Well, you were making it sound as if I'd done something extraordinary," he told her. "I just took it a step further."

"You went out of your way for a patient—which was what I was," she reminded him. "Not every doctor would have stayed with a patient for almost a week because there was no one to take care of her."

"Not just any patient," Everett pointed out, "but a patient I was once nearly engaged to."

"And that near-engagement ended badly," she reminded him. Before he could say anything in response, she went on to tell him, "You had every right in the world to call the paramedics, then have them take me to the hospital while you walked away."

He inclined his head like a man conceding a point. "Okay. You got me. I'm a magnificent doctor—who was hoping for a second chance at dinner," he added as if that had been his sole motive behind seeing to it that she got well. "In order to do that, I had to make sure that you stayed alive. The best way to do that was to see to it myself." He shrugged. "I don't delegate very well."

She paused to sample the egg roll appetizer that had been brought to the table and then laughed.

"When did you get so good at twisting around words to make them back you up?" she wanted to know.

"It comes with the medical degree," Everett responded.

"No, it doesn't," Lila countered. She felt herself

verging on impatience at the way he was so dismissive of his own abilities.

"Okay, then let's just say it's an inherent talent. A gift," he emphasized. "Born out of necessity," he added. "Satisfied?" He studied her across the table.

"No," Lila answered honestly. "But I guess that it'll have to do for now."

She was rewarded with a smile that seemed to come from deep inside of Everett. She could feel her heart flutter in response.

They talked for another hour, long after the main course and the fortune cookies had come and gone and the pot of tea had been refilled.

"I think we'd better get going. It looks like our server wants the table." She looked toward the reception area and saw why. "There's a line going all out the door now."

Everett found himself reluctant to leave. "I'm sure I can find a way to make it up to him if you want to stay a little longer. Would you like a few more appetizers?" he asked.

Lila laughed. "If I so much as look at another one, I'll explode."

"Okay, that's a no," he acknowledged. "So I guess you're ready to go?"

Lila nodded. "I've got another day at work tomorrow and you, you've got a long drive ahead of you," she reminded him. "I can call a cab for myself if you'd like to get started on that drive home," Lila offered, watching Everett's expression for any indication that he did want to leave.

Everett regarded her thoughtfully. "If I didn't know any better, I would venture to say that you were trying to get rid of me."

"No," Lila denied, saying the word with feeling. "I'm not."

He grinned at her. "Good, because it's not working. I'm going to be taking you home. The few extra minutes that it'll take me isn't going to make a difference as far as my trip is concerned," he assured her. Raising his hand, he signaled to the server.

True to his word, Everett left an extra large tip on the table for the man. Large enough to prompt their server to call after them as they left, saying, "Please come again!"

Lila and Everett exchanged looks and grinned at one another just before they walked out of the increasingly crowded restaurant.

"I had a really nice time tonight," she told Everett once she was at her door.

Everett nodded, doing his best to look solemn as he reviewed their evening.

"Well, you made it all the way back home without passing out, so the way I see it, it was a successful evening," he said dryly.

Lila shook her head. "You're not going to let me live that down, are you?" she asked.

"In time, maybe," he conceded.

Key in hand, Lila stopped just short of putting it into

the lock. She knew she was stalling, but she couldn't help herself.

"Does that mean you want to do this again?" she asked Everett.

"Absolutely," Everett answered with certainly. He paused for a moment, debating whether or not to say what was on his mind or quit while he was ahead. After a beat, he made up his mind to continue. "Lila, I just want you to know that I intend to rebuild what we once had," he told her. He saw the wary look that came over her face even though he could tell she was trying to appear unaffected by his words. "I didn't say that to scare you, Lila. I want to be fair about this. I'm not going to go behind your back, or spring something on you. This is all going to be aboveboard and honest. I just really want to make the most of this second chance."

"Second chance?" Lila repeated.

The fact that she wasn't immediately dismissing what he'd just said told Everett that at least to some extent, she felt the same way he did. This *was* their second chance. Or more accurately, *his* second chance.

"I think that Fate threw us together like this for a reason, Lila, and I'm not about to ignore that," he told her.

He could see that she still looked wary.

"Don't worry," he reassured her quickly. "I don't plan on throwing a sack over your head and running off with you to some isolated cabin in order to wear you down until you see things my way. I told you that I'm patient and that's not just when it comes to getting a table in a restaurant. I will go as slow as you want me to go, but

I have a feeling that in the end, you'll agree with me that we were meant to be together."

As he talked, standing so close to Lila, he was overwhelmed by an urge to kiss her. But he instinctively knew that doing so at this moment would spook her and he couldn't afford the setback that would create. Kissing Lila might satisfy the need he had just to feel her lips against his, but it very well might cost him in the end. He'd be winning the battle but losing the war, so to speak.

So, difficult as it was, he was determined to hold himself in check and wait.

He had no other choice. He had told Lila the truth. Patience was at the very core of his psychological makeup. He intended to wait as long as he had to in order to win Lila back.

"Are you sure that you're up to driving all that distance?" Lila asked him, breaking into his thoughts.

The fact that she worried about him touched Everett again. It proved to him that he was right. In the long run, they were going to wind up together. Fate wouldn't be that cruel to him, to bring her back into his life like this only to ultimately have him lose her a second time. He just had to stay strong and keep his wits about him.

"I'm fine," he told her. "And I'm going to be back sometime next week for a day. I'll see you then," he promised. "Now go inside and lock the door so I can get going."

Lila was about to point out that she got inside her house on her own every night without supervision, or having anything happen to her, but she let it go. She didn't want to ruin the evening. Everett was being protective and there was something to be said for that, she told herself. Besides, being this close to him was practically setting her on fire, which she could not afford.

So she unlocked her door under his watchful eye and then went in, closing the door behind her.

"Now lock it," he told her after a beat, raising his voice to be heard.

"Yes, sir," Lila called back, humoring him. She turned the lock. "It's locked," she announced.

"Good night, Lila."

"Good night, Everett."

And then, after a couple of beats, she heard Everett's car starting up. He was leaving.

Why did that have such a mournful sound to her, she asked herself. After all, she *wanted* him to leave. Everett might be confident about their future together, but she wasn't.

He'd also been confident about their future when they were younger. *Very* confident. And look how that had ultimately turned out, she reminded herself. That big, wonderful future he had been so sure stretched out before them had shriveled up and died before it had ever had a chance to actually take root and thrive.

And history, she reminded herself as she went into her bedroom to change out of her dress, had a terrible habit of repeating itself.

Lila closed her eyes and shivered. She couldn't bear to go though that kind of heartbreak a second time.

She wasn't strong enough.

Chapter Fourteen

Lila had vacillated about whether or not to invite Everett to the Fortune Foundation fund-raiser for the better part of a week. And now the event was tonight. That meant it was too late for her to change her mind again and invite him.

Just as well, Lila told herself. She'd attend the black-tie gala solo, just as she had initially planned when she'd first gotten the invitation.

Before Everett had popped up back in her life.

The only problem was, she felt conflicted.

Ever since Everett had gone out of his way and nursed her through that bout with the flu, she'd been sorely tempted to invite him—just as a show of gratitude, of course. However, she felt that if they attended the function together, that would be like practically announcing to the world at large that they were a couple—again.

And it was much too premature for that sort of speculation to make the rounds.

Because they weren't a couple anymore and they might never *be* a couple.

So, as she wavered back and forth, Lila fell back on her old stand-by: Why borrow trouble?

Consequently, she was going alone.

It wouldn't be the first time, she thought. And given what her life was like, it undoubtedly wouldn't be the last.

The way she felt at the moment, Lila had a premonition that she was destined to be alone for the rest of her life. Her dreams about Everett had been just that: dreams. And sooner or later, people were destined to wake up from dreams.

To boost her spirits, Lila bought herself a brand-new dress. It was a gown really, she thought, looking herself over from all angles in her wardrobe mirror as she prepared to leave.

The floor-length baby-blue silk gown swirled around softly as she moved and made her feel like she was a princess.

A princess without a kingdom—or a prince, Lila added ruefully—but a princess nonetheless.

"At least for one night," Lila whispered to her reflection.

Taking a deep breath, she gathered up her wrap and her purse. She checked her purse one last time to make sure she had her invitation. It was right where it had been the last four times she'd checked, tucked against her wallet.

She was ready.

"Nothing left to do but drive Cinderella over to the ball," Lila murmured to her reflection.

She smiled to herself as she locked the door and got into her car.

Where are the singing mice when you need them? she wondered wryly, starting up her vehicle.

The Fortune Foundation's fund-raiser was being held on the ground floor ballroom of Austin's finest hotel. Everything about the evening promised to be of the highest, most expensive quality.

After slipping into her purse the ticket that the valet who'd taken her car had given her, Lila went into the hotel.

She didn't need to look at the signs to know which ballroom the fund-raiser was being held in. All she had to do was follow the sound of music and laughter. It was evident that the crowd was having a good time.

The sound quadrupled in volume the second she opened one of the doors to the Golden Room.

She stood there just inside the doors, acclimating herself and looking around what seemed like a cavernous ballroom. There were people absolutely everywhere.

"You made it!"

Surprised, Lila turned to her right and found herself looking at Lucie. Her friend easily hooked her arm through hers.

"I was beginning to think you'd decided to take a pass on this," Lucie said as she began to gently steer Lila in what seemed to be a predetermined direction.

"I didn't think the Foundation allowed us to take a pass," Lila answered honestly. Not that she would have. Her sense of duty and loyalty was just too strong.

"Well, I don't know about 'allowed,'" Lucie replied, considering the matter, "but I do think that there would have been a lot of disappointed people here if you hadn't shown up."

Lila laughed. "I really doubt that," she told Lucie.

"I don't," Lucie retorted. Her eyes were sparkling with humor as she added, "Especially one someone in particular."

Lila stared at her. Lucie had managed to completely lose her. Her brow furrowed as Lila asked, "What are you talking about?"

"Come." The woman tugged a little more insistently on Lila's arm. "I'll show you. By the way, I like the gown. Light blue's a good color for you. It brings out your eyes," she added with approval.

"It's new," Lila confessed, having second thoughts and thinking that maybe she shouldn't have indulged herself like this.

Glancing at the gown one more time, Lucie nodded. "I had a feeling."

"Why? Did I forget to remove a tag?" Lila asked nervously, looking down at her gown and then trying to look over her shoulder to see if there were any telltale tags hanging from the back.

"No, you didn't forget to remove a tag, silly. It just

has that first-time-off-a-hanger look." Looking past Lila, Lucie raised her hand and waved.

"Who are you waving at? Chase?" Lila asked, referring to her friend's husband. Scanning the immediate area, Lila tried to get a glimpse of the rancher.

"Chase is off talking to Graham about that pet project of theirs, the center for military equine therapy," Lucie said. She was talking about Graham Fortune, the man who not only had taken over Fortune Cosmetics but also owned the successful Peter's Place, a home where troubled teens were helped to put their lives together. "No," Lucie told her, a very satisfied smile playing on her lips, "I was waving at the person I said would have been disappointed if you'd decided not to attend tonight."

Before Lila could ask any more questions, she suddenly found herself looking up at someone she'd never expected to see.

Everett. In an obligatory tuxedo.

At that moment Lila realized Everett in a tuxedo was even more irresistible than Everett in jeans.

Face it, the man would be irresistible even wearing a kilt.

"What are you doing here?" Lila asked when she finally located her tongue and remembered how to use it.

"You know, we're going to have to work on getting you a new opening line to say every time you see me," Everett told her with a laugh. "But to answer your question, I was invited."

Lucie stepped up with a slightly more detailed explanation to her friend's question. "The invitation was the Foundation's way of saying thank-you to Everett for his volunteer work."

"Disappointed to see me?" he asked Lila. There was a touch of humor in his voice, although he wasn't quite sure just what to make of the stunned expression on Lila's face.

"No, of course not," Lila denied quickly. "I'm just surprised, that's all. I thought you were still back in Houston."

"I was," Everett confirmed. "The invitation was express-mailed to me yesterday. I thought it would be rude to ignore it, so here I am," he told her simply, as if all he had to do was teleport himself from one location to another instead of drive nearly one hundred and seventy miles.

"Here you are," Lila echoed.

Everything inside her was smiling and she knew that was a dangerous thing. Because when she was in that sort of frame of mind, she tended not to be careful. And that was when mistakes were made.

Mistakes with consequences.

She was going to have to be on her guard, Lila silently warned herself. And it wasn't going to be easy being vigilant, not when Everett looked absolutely, bone-meltingly gorgeous.

As if his dark looks weren't already enough, Lila thought, the tuxedo made Everett look particularly dashing.

You're not eighteen anymore, remember? Lila reminded herself. *You're a woman. A woman who has to be very, very careful.*

She just hoped she could remember that.

"Since your last name practically sounds like Fortune," Lucie was saying to Everett, flanking him on the other side, "maybe you'd like to meet a Fortune or two—or twelve," she teased.

He turned to look at Lila. "Is that all right with you?"

The fact that he asked surprised her. "Why would I object?" she asked, puzzled.

Bending over, he whispered into her ear. "I thought, looking like that," he paused to allow his eyes to skim over her from top to bottom, "maybe you'd want me all to yourself."

She wasn't sure if it was what he said, or his warm breath in her ear that caused the shiver to run rampant up and down her spine.

Whatever it was, it took everything Lila had not to let it get the better of her. She knew where that sort of thing led her. To heaven and then, eventually, to hell as a consequence.

That wasn't going to happen again, she silently swore.

Clearing her throat, Lila ignored the last part of what he'd said and crisply answered, "Yes, it's fine with me."

Lucie smiled. "Then let the introductions begin," she announced, taking charge.

Lucie led off with her husband, Chase. The latter was a genial man who struck Everett as being very down-to-earth, considering the fact that he was an extremely wealthy man.

It was while Everett was talking to Chase that he was introduced to Graham Fortune Robinson. Graham,

Everett was told, was one of Jerome Fortune/Gerald Robinson's eight legitimate offspring. Again, rather than behaving as if he was spoiled or indifferent, or extremely entitled—all traits that Everett had seen displayed by many of the wealthy people he'd grown up with—Graham Fortune came across as only interested in the amount of good he could do with the money he had.

The man, like so many of the other Fortunes who were there that evening, had a keen interest in philanthropy, Everett concluded.

While he was being introduced to and talking with various members of the Fortune clan, Everett found himself exploring the subject that was so near and dear to Schuyler's heart: that perhaps there was some sort of a family connection between the Fortune family and his own. Was "Fortunado" just a poor attempt by someone in the previous generation to either connect to the Fortunes, or to clumsily try to hide that connection?

Everett's radar went up even higher when, after Lucie said that her connection to Graham went beyond just bloodlines, Graham joked that it seemed like everyone was related to him these days.

Everett forced himself to bite his tongue in order to refrain from asking Graham if, by that comment, he was referring to the Fortunados.

The next moment, Graham cleared up the possible confusion by saying that he was referring to the fact that numerous illegitimate Fortune offspring had been located over the past couple of years. Apparently, many years ago the prodigious patriarch Jerome Fortune had deliberately disappeared. When he had resurfaced, he had changed his name, calling himself Gerald Robinson. And, in addition to going on to amass a wealthy portfolio of his own, Gerald/Jerome had amassed a sizeable number of offspring, both legitimately with his wife, Charlotte, and illegitimately with a whole host of women whose paths the man had crossed.

"How did he manage to keep track of all those kids?" Everett marveled, still trying to wrap his mind around the fact that one man had wound up fathering a legion of children.

"Quite simply, he didn't," Graham answered. "But according to one story I've heard, his wife—and my mother—did. She got it into her head to look up every one of her husband's progeny. Some of my siblings think she wanted to be prepared for any eventuality," Graham explained. "Supposedly, she has everything she found written down in a big binder or something along those lines."

Graham smiled. "My personal theory is that when she collected enough data to make that binder really heavy, she was going to use it to hit my father upside the head and teach him a lesson for tomcatting around like that."

Lila nodded, saying in all seriousness, "If you ask me, the man certainly had it coming, spreading his seed around like that without any thought of how this was affecting anyone else in his family—especially those children."

"Yes, but then on the other hand, if he hadn't done it, there would be a lot less Fortunes in the world and so far, all the ones I've met have been really decent people whose hearts are in the right place," Everett pointed out.

Graham smiled his approval at Everett's comment. "I couldn't have put it better myself. I've come to like every one of my siblings." He shrugged and held up his wineglass as if in a silent toast to them. "It's not everyone who has a family big enough to populate a medium-size town."

Everett touched his glass to Graham's. He felt as if he could go on talking about the various members of the Fortune family all night. But suddenly, everyone in the ballroom was being asked to stop what they were doing.

"Can I have everyone's attention for a moment?" a tall, imposing man with a booming voice said into a microphone. He was standing before a podium at the front of the ballroom. "This is the time in our evening where we all temporarily suspend the festivities and are asked to dig deep into our hearts—and our pockets," the MC added with a laugh. "In other words, it's time for us to donate to the Fortune Foundation so it can go on doing all those good works and helping all those people who are not nearly as fortunate—no pun intended—as we all are."

The man's piercing blue eyes seemed to sweep around the entire ballroom. No easy feat, Lila thought, watching from the sidelines.

"Now don't be shy," the MC continued. "Give as much as you're able. No donation is too small, although bigger is always better. But even a little is better than nothing. So, like I said, open your hearts and get those checkbooks out. Remember, it feels good to give. And when you do, you'll find that you'll get back in ways you never even suspected were possible."

Listening, Lila opened up her purse and took out her checkbook. She was about to start writing out what she viewed to be a modest amount—although it was all she could afford—when Everett put his hand on hers, stopping her.

She looked at him, puzzled. Why wasn't he letting her write the check?

"I'll take care of it for both of us," he told her. The next moment, as she watched, she saw Everett write out a check for the sum of one hundred thousand dollars.

At the last second, she remembered to keep her mouth from dropping open.

Chapter Fifteen

The MC, David Davenport, looked at the check that had just been passed to him by one of the aides collecting donations from the guests. Holding the check aloft, Davenport scanned the crowd until he made eye contact with Everett.

"Is this right?" the MC asked Everett, astonished. "Your pen didn't slip?"

Everett's mouth curved slightly as he smiled at the man in front of the room. "My pen didn't slip," he assured the MC.

Davenport, a distinguished-looking, gray-haired man in his fifties, instantly brightened. "Ladies and gentlemen, I'm proud to announce that we have a new record," he told the gathering. "Dr. Everett Fortunado has generously donated the sum of one hundred thousand dollars to the Fortune Foundation."

A hush fell over the entire ballroom. It lasted for almost a full minute and then people began clapping. The sound swelled until the entire ballroom was engulfed in appreciative applause.

Everett wasn't really sure just how to react to the applause. He hadn't made the donation because he wanted to garner any sort of attention. He'd written the check because he felt it was his obligation to share the good fortune he had always felt so privileged to grow up experiencing.

When the applause finally died down, Davenport proceeded to try to utilize the moment to the Foundation's advantage.

"All right, people, let's see if Dr. Fortunado's generosity can motivate some of you to do your fair share as well." The MC looked around. It seemed as if he was making eye contact with everyone there. "Remember, this is for those deserving mothers and fathers and children who so badly need our help in order to make it through the hard times."

Everett stood back and watched as more of the fundraiser's attendees began writing out checks. There seemed to be chatter going on all around him.

Except at his side.

From the moment he had written out the check, Everett noticed that Lila had fallen completely silent. She hadn't said a single word to him during the entire time that the checks were being written and collected on all sides of them.

Nor, he observed, did Lila say anything during the buffet dinner that followed, despite the fact that he had intentionally stayed close to her during the whole time. He had broached a number of topics in an effort to engage her in conversation and had only received single-word replies.

Finally, unable to take the silence any longer, he drew Lila aside to a little alcove, away from the rest of the ballroom, and asked her point-blank: "Is something wrong?"

Lila had been trying to reconcile the mixed feelings she'd been having ever since she'd watched Everett writing out a check for such an exorbitant amount. Because she didn't want to cause a scene or start an uproar, she'd been doing her best just to squelch the suspicions that had been growing in her head. That involved keeping her mouth shut and not saying anything, although it wasn't easy.

But her doubts weren't going away, and rather than taking a hint and keeping quiet, Everett was pressuring her for an explanation.

Finally blowing out a frustrated breath, Lila asked him bluntly, "Are you trying to buy me?"

Dumbfounded and more than a little confused, Everett could only stare at her. He wasn't even sure if he had actually heard Lila correctly.

"What?"

Lila pressed her lips together, then ground out, "Are you trying to buy my love by giving that huge sum of money to the Foundation?"

Stunned, he told her, "I made that donation because

the Foundation is a worthy cause that does a great deal of good work. I thought you'd be happy about my contribution." He looked at her, not knowing where this had come from. Not for the first time, he felt as if he was walking on eggshells around her.

"Why do you have to dissect every single move I make and search for an ulterior motive?" he wanted to know. "Can't I just be generous because I want to be? Because it makes me feel good to do something decent for people who weren't born as lucky as I was?" He saw tears suddenly shimmering in her eyes and immediately felt a pang of guilt because he knew he was responsible for those tears. "Hey, I didn't mean to make you cry—"

Lila shook her head, halting his apology. Taking a deep breath to center herself, she said, "You didn't. You're right. You did something selfless and I just took it apart, looking for hidden reasons behind your donation when you were just being a decent guy." She blew out a shaky breath. "I guess I've just gotten to be really mistrustful."

And that was on him, Everett thought. He'd done this to her—taken a sweet, optimistic young woman and crushed something inside of her all those years ago. He had to find a way to fix this, he told himself.

But how?

How did he convince Lila that his feelings for her were genuine? That all he wanted was to be able to show her that he loved her and that he was willing to make things up to her for the rest of his life?

Desperation had him making the next move in his

desire to reach her, to communicate to her just how sincere he was.

Since he had taken her away from the rest of the guests in the ballroom by drawing her into a recessed alcove to talk to her, he knew they'd be safe from any prying eyes.

Framing Lila's face with his hands, Everett bent his head and did what he had been longing to do since he had first seen her in that sandwich shop in Austin.

He kissed her.

The moment his lips touched Lila's, Everett realized just how much he had missed her.

How much he really wanted Lila.

A little voice in his head told him he should stop kissing her, but he couldn't. Instead, Everett deepened the kiss.

And just like that, the captor became the captive.

At that moment, he knew that he would have walked through fire just to have Lila back in his life the way she had been all those years ago: loving and untainted by uncertainties and doubts.

Lila's breath caught in her throat. A split second before Everett had kissed her, she suddenly knew that he would. Knew too that with all her heart she wanted him to kiss her.

And then he did.

Just like that, all those years they'd spent apart melted away. She was instantly responding to Everett just as she had back then.

Except that now Lila was responding as a woman, not as a starry-eyed young girl.

Lila could feel every inch of her body heating as she fell deeper into the kiss. She wrapped her arms around Everett, savoring the taste of his lips urgently pressed against hers.

Longings, locked away for so long, came charging out, demanding attention as they carelessly trampled reason into the dust.

Her heart was pounding wildly when he drew his lips away. She found herself struggling in order to pull air into her lungs.

She looked up at Everett in wonder, desire mounting within her.

He hadn't meant to get this carried away, to let the moment get out of hand like this. He'd only wanted to kiss Lila again, to silently communicate to her that his feelings for her were as strong as ever.

Stronger.

"I'm sorry, Lila," Everett began. "I didn't mean to get—"

But Lila quickly cut short his apology. She didn't want Everett to be sorry for kissing her. Didn't want to have him withdrawing from her. Not when she was suddenly having all these unresolved feelings ricocheting throughout every inch of her being.

She wanted more.

Needed more.

"Let's get out of here," Lila breathed.

She didn't mean that, Everett thought, even as he asked, "Now?"

"Now," she echoed adamantly.

Everett stood there for a moment arguing with himself, trying very hard to convince himself to do the right thing.

Another man would have talked her out of it, pointing out what it might look like if someone saw them leaving before the fund-raiser was over. Another man would have taken her by the hand and led her back into the ballroom proper.

But another man hadn't spent every day of the last thirteen years missing Lila so much that there were times he literally ached.

Now that there was a glimmer of hope that they could get back together, that he could win her back, he could admit that to himself. Admit that the reason that every possible relationship that had loomed before him over the years had fallen through was because all the women in those would-be relationships hadn't been able to hold a candle to Lila.

So instead of doing the noble thing and trying to talk Lila out of what she'd just suggested, Everett took her hand in his. And together they made their way out of the ballroom. And then out of the hotel.

Once outside, as the cooler evening air slipped over them, Everett looked at Lila for some sign that she'd had a change of heart about leaving. He didn't detect any, but because he absolutely wanted her to have no regrets, he asked, "You're sure?"

"I'm sure," Lila answered breathlessly. All she wanted was to be alone with him. To be with him in every way possible.

"We both drove here separately," Everett reminded her. While he feared that if she drove herself she might change her mind, he knew that if Lila left her car here at the hotel, someone from the fund-raiser would take note of that.

Questions would be asked and gossip would spread. He didn't want Lila subjected to any sort of talk or speculation as to why her car was still in the parking structure while she herself was nowhere to be found. He wanted to protect her from that sort of thing at all costs.

Although she didn't want to be more than a foot away from him right now, Lila didn't see any actual problem. "So? We can both drive our cars to my house. My driveway can accommodate two vehicles," she told him.

Lila could feel her heart hammering with every word she uttered as a tiny voice in her head, barely audible above the beating of her heart, was telling her to take her car and make good her escape.

But she didn't want to escape. One taste of Everett's lips and it was all she could do not to beg for more right here, right now.

When the valet came up to them, they both handed him their tickets.

"Bring the lady her car first," Everett told him.

The valet nodded. "Be right back," he promised, heading into the parking structure quickly.

"Think anyone noticed you left?" Everett asked her as they waited.

"If they notice anyone's gone, it would most likely be you," Lila told him. "After all, you're the man of the hour after that huge donation."

When the valet brought her car up and held the door

open for her, she handed him a tip and then slid into the driver's seat.

She looked up at Everett, said, "I'll see you," and then drove off.

I'll see you.

Her words echoed in his brain. She hadn't said "I'll see you *later*." Just "I'll see you." Did that mean she'd had a change of heart and decided that she'd almost made a terrible mistake?

Now who's overthinking everything? Everett admonished himself.

He put the original question on hold when the valet brought up his car.

"You car handles like a dream," the valet told him enthusiastically and a bit enviously as he got out of the vehicle. Backing away, he left the driver's door open for him.

Everett inclined his head, a grin curving his mouth. "She likes to be babied," he told the valet as he handed him a ten-dollar bill and got in.

The valet's eyes widened as he looked at the bill. "Thanks!"

Everett pulled away, eager to catch up to Lila's car. But it felt like he was catching every single red light between the hotel and her house.

He really hoped that by the time he got there Lila hadn't reflected on her impulsive decision and changed her mind about the night ahead.

If she did, he would have no choice but to go along with her decision. He would never force himself on her, but he decided that he was going to do everything in his power to convince her that they were meant to be together.

Because they were.

It was hard to stay focused on the road. All he could see in his mind's eye was Lila. Lila, offering herself to him. Lila, making love with him.

Lila, who was and always had been the center of his universe.

How had he allowed himself to let her go? Everett silently asked himself. He wouldn't have tied her up in the attic, but he could have tried to talk her out of breaking up with him, could have tried his damnedest to convince her to give him another chance.

Well, this is your chance, Everett, he thought as he turned onto Lila's block. *Don't blow it.*

Chapter Sixteen

What if Everett didn't come?

What if he did?

Lila pressed her hand against her stomach, trying to quiet the butterflies that seemed to be wildly crashing into one another in her stomach. She'd never felt so confused before.

Back in the ballroom alcove, when Everett had kissed her, awakening all those old feelings, she'd wanted him right then and there. But now she'd had a little time to distance herself from that kiss, doubts had begun creeping in. It was as if she was playing a tennis match with herself in her brain.

Where *was* he?

Granted she'd flown through every light and gotten home in record time, moving as if her car was being propelled by a gale, but she hadn't left *that* much ahead of Everett.

He should have been here by now.

Unless he'd changed his mind and decided to go straight to his sister's house instead.

Or maybe he'd just decided to head back to Houston from the fund-raiser instead of coming over to her house.

To her.

Had she come on too strong?

But after he kissed her like that, unearthing all those old memories, she just couldn't help herself. Any thoughts of hanging back or taking it slow had just incinerated right on the spot. All she could think of was how much she'd missed being in Everett's arms, of having him hold her as if she was something very precious.

She felt as if she was losing her mind.

Lila looked out her window and saw only her car in the driveway.

He'd had a change of heart, she thought, letting the curtain drop back into place.

With a gut-wrenching sigh, she turned away. Served her right for giving in to her emotions like some silly schoolgirl and—

She jerked her head up, listening. Was that—?

Yes, it was. It was the sound of a car pulling up in her driveway.

All those doubts that were surfacing took a nosedive and she threw open the door before he had a chance to ring the doorbell.

"There are way too many red lights in this city," Everett told her.

Grabbing hold of his shirt, Lila pulled him over the threshold and into her house, slamming the door shut right behind him.

"I don't want to talk about red lights," she said just before she rose up on her tiptoes and sealed her mouth to his.

It was more than a couple of minutes later that they managed to come up for air—temporarily.

"Right," Everett breathlessly agreed, devouring her with his eyes. "No talking about red lights."

"No talking at all," Lila countered.

As she sought out his lips again, sealing hers to them, she began to systematically remove Everett's tuxedo, separating it from his body so quickly she worried that she'd wind up ripping something.

If she did, she could fix it, she assured herself. She knew her way around a needle. But right now, she wanted to relearn her way around his body.

It had been a long, long time since she'd been intimate with him. Since she'd been intimate with *anyone*, because after she had left Everett, she'd never met anyone to take his place, or even come close to qualifying as a candidate for that position. Without love as an ingredient in the mix, lovemaking just didn't seem right to her.

As she was eagerly removing his clothing, Everett was doing the same with hers.

Lila could feel his hands moving along her body. Locating her zipper, he pulled it down her back in one swift movement, then peeled away the silky gown from her skin.

It fell to the floor like a sinking blue cloud, pooling about her high heels.

Lila caught her breath as she felt his strong hands tugging away her bikini underwear, then gliding over her bare skin, swiftly reducing her to a pulsating mass of desire.

With urgent movements, she hurried to return the compliment until they were both standing there in her living room, nude—except for one thing.

She was still wearing her high heels.

Lila quickly remedied that, kicking the shoes off and instantly becoming petite.

"Damn," Everett whispered against the sensitive skin of her throat as he pressed kiss after kiss along it, "I can't tell you how many times I've dreamed about doing this."

The feel of his warm breath sliding along her skin caused all her desires to intensify. Her mushrooming needs almost engulfed her as they seized control over every single facet of her being.

Her mind in a haze, Lila felt her back being pressed against the sofa. She didn't even remember how they got there.

Everett was taking inventory of every single inch of her body with his mouth, creating wonderful sensations as he moved.

Doing wonderful things.

She was eager to return the favor, but for the moment, she couldn't find the strength to do anything but absorb every nuance of what was happening. She was utterly immersed in the deliciously wicked feelings that were erupting all over her as his lips and tongue left their mark everywhere, branding her.

Making her his.

Lila twisted and arched, savoring and absorbing every wondrous salvo wildly echoing throughout her body.

And still he continued, moving lower and lower by pulsating increments.

Anticipation rippled through her like shockwaves as she felt first his breath, and then his mouth moving down to the very center of her core.

His tongue teased her ever so lightly, skimming along the delicate, sensitive area, all the while raising her response higher and higher, creating a fever pitch within her until finally, delicious explosions erupted simultaneously all through her, undulating over her like a series of earthquakes.

Lila cried out his name, pulling him to her until he was right above her, melting her soul with the intense look of desire and passion in his eyes.

She felt him coaxing open her legs with his knee. What there was left of her shallow breath caught in her throat.

The next moment, he entered her and they were sealed to one another, creating a single heated entity.

Everett began to move his hips so slowly at first, she thought she had only imagined it. But then the movements began to increase, growing stronger. Taking her with them.

And then they were no longer on her sofa, no longer in her house. They were somewhere else, completely isolated from the world. A place where only the two of them existed.

The only thing that mattered was Everett and this insanely wondrous sensation that they were sharing. Their bodies danced to music that only the two of them could hear.

The tempo increased, going faster and faster until suddenly they found themselves racing to the top of the world, to a place that was both new and familiar at the same time.

Lila could feel her heart slamming against his. Could feel Everett's heart echoing hers to the point that she thought their two hearts would forever be sealed together as one.

And then she felt the fireworks exploding, showering a profusion of stars all around her until that was all there was.

A world filed with stars.

She clung to Everett then, clung to the sensation that they had created together. She clung to it for as long as she could and bathed in the euphoria that came in its wake.

She held onto the sensation—and Everett—for as long as possible. But even so, it receded no matter how hard she fought to hang onto it.

Sorrow began to wiggle its way into the spaces the euphoria had left behind.

Everett shifted his weight off her, moving so that he was lying beside her.

He tightened his arm around her, exulting in the feeling of warmth generated by holding onto her. He glanced down at his chest and was mildly surprised that he wasn't glowing or giving out some sort of light like a beacon that guided the ships through the night at sea.

She was back, he thought. He'd won Lila back. And the lovemaking between them was so much better now than it had been before. The sex might have been familiar at its roots, but it had also felt wonderfully brand-new.

The woman in his arms was so much more now than she had been all those years ago.

How did he get so lucky? Everett silently marveled. Lying here next to Lila, reliving the lovemaking they had just shared, he found himself wanting to take her all over again.

Wanting her with a renewed fierceness that was impossible to ignore.

Propping himself up slightly, Everett leaned over her face and kissed one eyelid, then her other eyelid.

Then her mouth.

He lingered there, deepening the kiss until it all but consumed both of them, feeding something in his soul.

And then hers.

She looked up at him with wonder. "Again?" she questioned.

Lila saw laughter entering his eyes as Everett told her, "Honey, I am just getting started."

Something came over her.

Lila seized the moment and just like that, turned the tables on him. It was her turn to be the seducer rather than the seduced. This relationship didn't have a prayer of working if only one of them gave while the other received, she thought.

So, just as he had done before, Lila began to prime his body, ever so lightly gliding both her lips and her tongue along all the sensitive, seducible areas of his body.

Priming him until he verged on the edge of full readiness.

She moved with purpose along Everett's chest, gliding the tip of her tongue along his nipples just as he had done to her.

And then she slid her tongue along the hard contours of his chest, moving steadily down to his belly, teasing it until it quivered beneath her hot, probing mouth.

Raising her eyes, she met his. A wicked look entered them as she proceeded to work her way lower along his anatomy until she had reached his hardening desire.

With an air of triumph, she went on to make him hers by branding him.

She did it, once, then twice—then suddenly, she felt his hands on her forearms, stopping her. He drew her away and brought her back up to his level by pulling her body along his.

Arousing both of them even more.

The next second, he raised his head and captured her mouth with his own, kissing her over and over again until he had reduced her to the consistency of a rain puddle that was about to go up in the steam of a hot summer sun. At that moment, he deftly switched their places. He was above her and she was back under him.

And just as before, they united, forming one whole.

This time he moved urgently right from the start. There was no gentle increase in tempo. There were just the swift, direct movements that were intended to bring them swirling up to journey's end.

And it did.

So quickly that it stole away their breath, leaving them gasping and panting in the aftermath of the crescendo that had brought all the stars raining down on them.

As before, the euphoria that sealed around them in the aftermath was wondrous. And, also as before, it slipped away much too soon, leaving Lila exhausted and slowly making her way back to reality.

With painstakingly slow movements, Lila shifted her head so that she was looking at the man next to her without alerting him to the fact that she was.

It was happening. Happening just as she had been afraid that it would.

She could feel it.

She was falling in love with Everett all over again. And she was totally powerless to prevent it, she thought with a sliver of panic that was beginning to grow inside of her.

Why had she done this?

Why had she allowed it to happen? She could have stopped it from ever taking place—*should* have stopped it from taking place not once, but twice, she ruefully reminded herself. She had allowed the evening—and herself—to spin completely out of control and now she had consequences to face.

She didn't like this feeling, this feeling of being unable to stop her life from spinning out of control.

Lila could feel herself growing more and more afraid. Afraid of what she'd done. Afraid of where she just *knew* it was going to lead—to the same unhappiness she'd experienced thirteen years ago.

How could something that had felt so right in the moment be so very wrong in the long run?

But it was, she thought.

It was.

What made her think that just because they'd managed to recapture the rapturous happiness of lovemaking it was destined to end any other way for them than it already had once before?

Those that do not learn from history are doomed to repeat it.

And that was her, she thought ruefully. She was doomed to repeat the mistakes she'd made once. In fact, she already had repeated those mistakes.

Well, she *could* learn from her mistakes, Lila silently insisted. And she intended to start right now, before it was too late and things spun further out of control, setting the stage for Everett to break her heart all over again.

Summoning her resolve, not to mention her courage, Lila turned toward the man lying next to her on the sectional sofa.

She struggled into an upright position.

Everett shift toward her. "Want to take this to your bedroom and do it again?" he asked her with a warm, inviting smile.

"No," she said with such finality that it froze Everett in place. "I want you to leave."

The blissful happiness he'd just been experiencing broke up into tiny slivered shards. He felt as if he'd just been blindsided.

Everett stared at her. "Did I do something wrong?" he asked, trying to understand why she had made this unexpected U-turn.

"Things are moving too fast, Everett," she told him. Her tone left no room for any sort of attempts to change her mind. "You need to go."

Chapter Seventeen

Everett sat up. "You're really serious?" he asked, unable to believe that Lila actually meant what she'd just said to him.

He'd been with a number of women since he and Lila had broken up and although he'd never gotten to the serious relationship stage with any of those women, none of them had ever kicked him out of bed, either, figuratively *or* literally.

His confidence shaken, Everett had no idea how to react to this totally unfamiliar situation.

Lila had already gotten up off the sofa, wrapping a crocheted throw around herself in lieu of clothing. Her insides were quaking, but she held her ground.

"Yes, I'm serious," she insisted, her voice rising in pitch. "*Very* serious."

Well, he'd tried his best and for a little while there, he thought that he'd succeeded in winning Lila over. But obviously, he'd miscalculated, Everett told himself. He was willing to do anything to win Lila back except for one thing: he was not about to beg. A man had to have some pride, he thought fiercely.

Nodding his head, he quickly pulled on his discarded tuxedo slacks. Securing them, he grabbed the rest of his things and held the clothes against his chest in a rumpled ball of material. He didn't even bother putting on his shoes. Instead, he just picked them up and held them in his other hand.

"All right then," he told her, heading for the door. "I'd better go."

Lila stood like a statue, saying nothing.

Everett let himself out the door, leaving it wide open. As he walked to his car in the driveway, he heard the front door close with finality behind him, obliterating any hope that at the last minute Lila would change her mind and either come running after him or at least call him back into the house.

Forcing himself not to look back, Everett opened his car door and got into his vehicle. He felt so totally stunned and deflated that he could hardly breathe as he started up his car and pulled out of Lila's driveway.

He stopped at the first all-night gas station he came to. Ignoring the convenience store clerk's curious looks, he asked for the restroom key. Taking it from the man, he let himself into the single stall bathroom.

The conditions in the restroom were far from ideal, but he managed to put on the rest of his clothes. He wanted to avoid having Schuyler ask him a barrage of questions if he walked in wearing only the tuxedo slacks.

He loved his sister dearly, but he just wasn't up to fielding any of her questions, however well intentioned they might be. He just wanted to quietly get his things from her guest room and drive back to Houston.

But as luck would have it, a swift, clean getaway was just not in the cards for him.

Despite the hour, Schuyler was up and heard him coming in. Everett had barely closed the front door and walked in before his sister walked out of the kitchen and managed to waylay him at the foot of the stairs.

"What are you doing back so soon?" she asked him in surprise. "I wasn't expecting you back until around midmorning."

He offered her a careless shrug in response. "Fundraiser ended so I came back."

Schuyler furrowed her brow, as if something didn't sound right to her. "Why didn't you go get a nightcap with Lila?"

"I didn't want to drink and drive," Everett answered. He looked longingly up the stairs. So near and yet so far, he couldn't help thinking.

Schuyler's furrowed brow gave way to an all-out, impatient frown.

"Damn it, Ev, I'm trying to politely tiptoe around the subject but you're making me have to come flat out and ask." She paused, waiting for her brother to jump in and say what she was waiting for him to tell her. But he remained silent. Huffing, Schuyler asked, "Why aren't you over at Lila's place, picking things up where the two of you left off back in college?"

"It's complicated, Schuy," Everett told her.

"That's what people say when they don't want to deal with something," she insisted. She pinned her brother with a penetrating look that went clear down to the bone. "Do you care about this woman?" she asked him point-blank.

Still smarting from his rejection, he *really* didn't want to get into this with his sister. "Schuyler, go to bed."

They had always talked things out before and Schuyler apparently refused to back off now that she had broached the subject. "Do you care about this woman?" she repeated, enunciating each word slowly with intentional emphasis.

He could see that Schuyler wasn't about to let this go until she had an answer from him. So he gave her one. A short one.

"No."

Schuyler's eyes narrowed, looking deep into his. "You're lying."

Everett did his best to separate himself from any emotion. He really didn't want to shout at his sister. "No, I'm not."

"Yes, you are," Schuyler retorted. When he tried to turn away, she grabbed hold of his shoulder, making him face her. "You have this 'tell' when you lie. There's a tiny nerve right under your left eye that jumps every time you don't tell the truth."

"Then why even bother asking me?" He came close to biting off his question.

"So you can hear the words out loud for yourself," she told him. "Ev, when you first told me you were going to win Lila back, I didn't think you had a chance in hell of doing it. I thought you'd eventually come to your senses and forget the whole thing."

She shook her head, amused by her preconceived notion. "But you're not the type to forget the whole thing and you managed to bring me around to your way of thinking. A guy like that doesn't just give up out of the blue."

Taking his hand, Schuyler tugged on it, making him sit down on the bottom step. She sat down beside him, just the way they used to do as kids whenever they wanted to talk about things.

"What happened?" she asked him.

After a short internal debate, Everett gave her an abbreviated version, mentioning his donation to the Foundation in passing, but not the amount.

He told his sister about going back with Lila to her place, but left it for her imagination to fill in the details of what transpired there. He ended by telling his sister that Lila had suddenly pulled back, saying that things were going too fast and that he needed to go home.

"And...?" Schuyler asked, waiting for him to tell her more.

"And I came home," Everett said with a shrug. "Or to your house," he corrected. "I wanted to change out of this monkey suit, get my suitcase and go back to Houston."

"And nothing else happened?" she questioned, studying his face closely.

"Nothing else happened," he echoed flatly. He just wanted to get his things and hit the road, putting this night—and Lila—behind him.

Schuyler's mouth curved in a tolerant, loving smile. "You do realize that your shirt is inside out, don't you?" his sister asked. "Did you wear it that way at the fundraiser?"

He glanced down. Damn it, leave it to Schuyler to catch that, he thought, annoyed. "Yup. The whole fundraiser," he told her stubbornly.

"I see," Schuyler replied, watching the nerve just beneath his eye flutter. "Well, maybe nobody noticed," she said loftily. "Or maybe Lila did and that's why she told you things were moving too fast and sent you away." Schuyler's smile widened. "She didn't want to be associated with someone who couldn't dress himself properly."

"Schuyler—" There was a warning note in Everett's voice.

Schuyler held up her hands, warding off what he was about to say.

"I'm just teasing you," she told him. And then her tone changed. "Why don't you stay here for what's left of the night and then go talk to Lila in the morning?" she suggested. "Things always look better in the morning," she added kindly.

"No," he told his sister, his mind made up. "I need to be getting back. I've let a lot of things slide lately and I need to do some catching up."

"That's not the Dr. Everett Fortunado I know," Schuyler told him, rising to her feet when he did. "You can juggle more balls in the air than any two people I know."

"Not this time," he answered as he started up the steps. "This time those balls are all falling right through my hands."

"Want me to help you pack?" she offered, calling up the stairs.

"No, I've got this," he told her, glancing over his shoulder.

Schuyler stood there, arms akimbo, and murmured loud enough for him to hear, "No, I don't think that you do."

"That was some hefty donation that your boyfriend made on Friday," Lucie said the following Monday morning as Lila passed her open door.

Lila made no answer, merely shrugging in response as she stepped into her office.

Lucie didn't take the hint. Instead, she followed her friend into Lila's office. When Lila sat down at her desk, Lucie peered at her a little more closely.

"You look awful," she observed. Then a small smile lit her eyes. "Didn't get any sleep all weekend, huh?"

"No," Lila answered, deliberately not taking Lucie's bait. Her tone flatly denied any further dialogue between them.

But Lucie wasn't about to take the hint. "So how was it?" she asked with a grin.

Lila spared her friend a glance. Lucie was now firmly planted on the edge of her desk. "How was what?"

"You know…" But since Lila gave no indication that she did, Lucie further elaborated. "Getting back together with Everett."

"We're not back together," Lila answered, biting off each word. They all had a bitter taste, but that would pass, she told herself. It *had* to.

"Why the hell not?" Lucie cried. When Lila looked at her sharply, Lucie said, "Anyone at the fund-raiser could see he was crazy about you. When you two left early, I was sure you were going back to your place— if you made it that far," Lucie added.

This time Lila's head shot up. She was really hoping that no one had noticed them leaving the fund-raiser. So much for hoping.

"What's that supposed to mean?" she wanted to know.

Lucie sighed.

"Lila, there were so many sparks flying between the two of you that you'd make an electrical storm seem like an afternoon at the library in comparison." She gave Lila a deep, penetrating look, as if willing the truth out of her. "You can't tell me that you two didn't get together after you left the fund-raiser."

"All right," Lila replied grudgingly. It wasn't in her to lie. "We did."

Getting up off the desk, Lucie closed Lila's door, then crossed back to her desk, coming closer. "And?" she coaxed.

Lila shifted uncomfortably in her chair, but it was

clear that Lucie wasn't going anywhere until she heard all the details.

"And then I sent him away," she said, jumping to the end without elaborating anything in between.

Lucie stared at her. "You're joking."

"No, I'm not," Lila replied firmly. "I sent him away."

"Why in heaven's name would you do that?" Lucie cried incredulously.

"Because things were moving much too fast between us," Lila blurted out, frustration bubbling beneath her statement.

Leaning forward, Lucie took her friend's hands into hers. "Lila, honey," she began gently, "it's been thirteen years. After all that time, things were not moving fast. They were barely crawling by at a turtle's pace." She squeezed Lila's hands as she looked deeper into her eyes, as if trying to understand, to read Lila's thoughts. And then it must have hit her, because she sharply drew a breath. "You got scared, didn't you? He made you have all those feelings again and it scared you."

Lila looked away. Lucie had homed in on the truth.

But there was no running from the truth. She knew that now.

With a sigh, she nodded. And then she looked up at Lucie. "How did you do it?" she asked, silently begging the other woman for guidance.

"Do what?" Lucie asked.

"With Chase," Lila said, hoping that Lucie had some sage, magical knowledge to impart. Some words of wisdom that could somehow guide her through this densely wooded area she found herself stumbling through.

"How were you able to pick up where you left off with Chase?" The two hadn't just been high school sweethearts, they'd eloped and had been married—for all of five minutes.

"Very easy," Lucie answered her nonchalantly. "I didn't."

Lila stared at her. She didn't understand. "But you two were just recently married."

"Actually, we'd been secretly married as teenagers and never had it annulled, but didn't find out until recently. We had to get to know each other as adults, not as the impulsive kids we once were. And that's what you have to do," Lucie told her in all honesty. "You and Everett have to do the work and get to know each other all over again—from scratch," she insisted. "You have to take into consideration that Everett, in all likelihood, may very well *not* be the person he was at sixteen or eighteen or twenty."

Lucie circled to the back of the desk and put her arm on Lila's shoulder.

"And while we're at it, why do you assume that history has to repeat itself?" she questioned gently. "What if Everett really means what he says and wants to get back together with you not for a romp or a weekend of lovemaking, but for good?"

Lila rose from her chair and paced about the small office. She couldn't come to grips with the desperate feeling she was experiencing in her gut.

"Even if Everett's serious, even if he wants things to be different this time around, the past is still standing between us like a giant roadblock," Lila insisted.

"By the past you mean the little girl that you gave up." It wasn't a question. Lucie was reading between the lines. She knew the truth about Lila's past. In a moment of weakness, Lila had entrusted her with her deepest secret.

"Yes," Lila cried, struggling not to cry. "It still haunts me," she admitted. "Holding her in my arms and then giving her up—some nights I still wake up in a cold sweat, remembering how that felt. To have her and then not have her, all in the blink of an eye," Lila confessed sadly.

"Does Everett realize how you feel?" Lucie asked.

Lila pressed her lips together and shook her head. "I don't know," she answered. "I never said anything about it."

"Did you *ask* him if he knew?" Lucie pressed. "Or say anything at all about what giving her up did to you?"

"No," Lila admitted in a low voice, avoiding Lucie's eyes.

"Then for heaven sakes, *talk* to him about it," Lucie urged. "Tell him how you felt giving up your baby. How you *still* feel."

"I can't," Lila said. "I just can't. Lucie, I know you mean well, but just please, please leave me alone right now. It'll work out."

It will, Lila told herself as Lucie walked out of her office.

It had to.

Chapter Eighteen

"All right, I'm here," Everett declared when his sister opened her front door to admit him into her house several days later. "I got Blake to take over a few of my patients, had the rest of them rescheduled and drove right out because you sounded as if this was urgent." His eyes swept over her and she certainly didn't look as if she was in the throes of some sort of an emergency. "Now what's this all about?"

Instead of answering his question, Schuyler said, "I can't tell you here." Getting her purse, she took out her car keys. "In order to explain, I need to take you some place first."

Everett looked at his sister suspiciously. This wasn't making any sense to him. "Where?" he wanted to know.

Again she avoided giving him a direct answer.

"You'll understand everything once we're there," Schuyler told him, hurrying toward her spacious garage.

Fetching her red BMW, she pulled up next to her brother. "Get in," she told him, leaning over and throwing open the passenger door.

Since he'd all but raced out of Houston, driving at top speed until he'd reached Austin because he was extremely concerned about Schuyler, he went along with her instructions.

"You're being awfully mysterious about all this," he accused.

"The mystery will be cleared up before you know it, big brother," Schuyler promised, mentally crossing her fingers.

Everett suddenly sat up a little straighter in the passenger seat as a thought occurred to him.

Looking at her now, he asked, "Hey, Schuy, you're not pregnant, are you?" As the question came out of his mouth, he began grinning so widely, his lips almost hurt. He'd thought his sister would get married first before starting a family, but that didn't negate his happiness for her. "Wow, that's terrific. How far along are you?" he asked excitedly. "What does Carlo think about this? Have you picked a godfather yet?"

Apparently overwhelmed, Schuyler took a second to speak. "Hey, slow down," she said then. She slanted a look in his direction before turning back to the road. "So you like the idea of babies," she said, obviously referring to his exuberant reaction.

"Of course I do. How far along are you?" he asked her again.

"I'm not," Schuyler told him.

Everett looked as if his bubble had been pierced, sending him twisting in the wind. "Wait, I don't understand. Then you're not pregnant?" he asked, more confused than ever.

"No," Schuyler answered. "I never said I was. *You* jumped to that conclusion," she pointed out. "Let me have my wedding first, then we'll see about babies."

Everett slumped back against his seat. "Okay, then I don't understand," he said, confused. "What's this all about?"

Schuyler bit her lower lip, stalling. "I already told you—"

"No, you didn't," he insisted, trying to keep his voice even. He didn't like games, especially not at his expense.

"Just hang on a little longer and you'll see what this is all about."

Everett sighed. "Well, since you've kidnapped me, I guess I don't have a choice."

"I didn't kidnap you," Schuyler informed him. "You got into the car of your own free will."

That's not how he saw it. "You just keep telling yourself that," he said. Laying his head back against the headrest, Everett closed his eyes. Running around and not getting much sleep was finally beginning to catch up with him. "Wake me whenever we get to wherever it is that we're going," he told her.

"We're here," Schuyler announced not five minutes later.

"Well, that didn't take long," Everett commented.

Sitting up, he looked around as his sister got out of the car.

Schuyler had driven them to the Fortune Foundation.

Alert, not to mention annoyed, Everett glared at his sister when he got out. "Hey, why are we here?"

"You'll find out," she said cheerfully.

Neither his mood nor the look that he was giving her over the hood of her car improved.

"Schuyler, just what the hell are you up to?" he demanded.

"You'll find out," his sister repeated. She gave him what she no doubt hoped was an encouraging look. "Just give it a few more minutes."

But Everett didn't move an inch. "And if I don't?"

"Then you'll never know how things might have turned out." When he still didn't move, Schuyler looked at him plaintively. "Do it for me, Everett. Please," she implored.

"Damn it, Schuyler, you owe me," Everett snapped, finally coming around the sporty red vehicle.

Schuyler inclined her head and gave him a wink. "We'll see."

Lila was engrossed in drawing up the following week's schedule for the volunteer doctors when Lucie walked into her office.

"Save whatever you're working on, Lila," Lucie told her. "I need your full, undivided attention right now."

Surprised by Lucie's serious tone, Lila looked up. "What's going on?"

Instead of answering her, Lucie looked over her

shoulder and beckoned to someone. Just who was she summoning to Lila's office?

Totally stunned, Lila was immediately on her feet when she saw him.

Everett was the last person she'd expected to see here. After practically throwing him out of her house, she'd never thought she would see him again.

She fisted her hands, digging her knuckles into her desk to keep her knees from giving way.

She shot an angry look at her friend. "Lucie, what have you done?" she demanded.

"Saved two really nice people from a lifetime of loneliness and heartache," Lucie answered. Then she stepped out of the way, allowing a bewildered-looking Everett to enter Lila's office. But not before she gave a big grin and a high five to a well-dressed woman behind him.

Schuyler, Lila recognized.

Peering into the office around her brother, Schuyler declared, "I hereby officially call this intervention in session."

With that, she stepped away from the doorway.

Following her out, Lucie told the two people who were left in the room, "And don't come out until you've resolved this properly." And then she closed the door behind her.

"This your idea?" Lila asked Everett.

"Hell, no," he denied. "I think Schuyler cooked this up."

"Not without Lucie's help," Lila said accusingly. Furious, she let out a shaky breath. And then she turned toward Everett. She was furious. "You know you can leave," she told him.

"I know." Lord, but he had missed her, he thought now, looking at Lila. "But since I'm here...maybe we should talk."

"About what?" Lila wanted to know. "What is there left to say?" Restless, uneasy, she began to pace within the limited space. "I trusted you once and got my heart broken for my trouble."

Her accusation hurt. But this wasn't one-sided. "I could say the same thing," Everett countered.

Her eyes narrowed as she looked at Everett, stunned. "You?" she questioned. What was he talking about?

"Yes," he informed Lila. "I'd trusted you, too. Trusted that you'd be with me forever—and then you walked out. It wasn't easy for me after we broke up. I might have gone on with my studies—because that was what I was supposed to do—but there was this huge, empty, jagged hole in my chest where you used to be."

His dry laugh was totally mirthless as he continued. "I think I must have picked up the phone a hundred times that first year, wanting to call you and tell you about something that had happened in class or at the hospital, before I realized that I couldn't. That you wouldn't be there to answer the phone." His eyes met hers. "Nothing meant anything without you," he told her.

Lila stood there looking at him. The inside of her mouth felt like cotton and she struggled not to cry. She'd held her feelings in too long. For thirteen years, to be exact. Now she could hold them in no longer.

"I still think about our baby all the time," she admitted.

Everett felt her words like a knife to his heart. More than anything, he wished he could go back in time to make things right. To do things differently. "Do you regret giving her up?"

"Yes," she answered so quietly, he had to strain to hear her. And then Lila took a deep breath. "No."

She blinked hard, telling herself she wasn't going to cry. Forbidding herself to shed a single tear. Tears were for the weak and she wasn't weak. She'd proven that over and over again.

"I know that our daughter has had a good life. The people who adopted her send me letters and photographs every once in a while, to let me know how she's doing." Lila smiled sadly. "Emma's a beautiful girl and she's doing really, really well in school."

Everett looked at her in surprise. He'd had no idea this was going on. "Her name is Emma? And you've stayed in contact with the family?" he asked.

Lila nodded. "Yes. Not knowing what was going on with Emma was killing me so it took a bit of doing but I managed to get in contact with the family that adopted her. Emma's parents are good people. They understood how hard it was for me to give up the baby. As a matter of fact, they're grateful to us for giving them what they call 'the most precious gift of all,'" Lila said. "Over the years, I've kept track of her through emails and pictures from her parents."

It was a lot for Everett to take in. Numerous questions rose in his head.

"How is she doing? What grade is she in now?" Everett asked.

"You actually want to know?" Lila asked him, astonished. "I mean, after the baby was born, you seemed really eager to put the whole incident behind you and forget about it. About her."

Her words stung, but he knew they were true. He'd been young and he'd just wanted to pretend that none of it had happened because it was easier to erase the guilt that way.

"I was," he admitted. "I'm not proud of it now, but it was the only way I could deal with it at the time, to just bury it and put it all totally out of my mind." Everett put his hands on her shoulders now, looking into Lila's eyes. "I'm sorry I wasn't more understanding, Lila. I didn't realize that you were hurting. I only knew that I was."

Lila struggled to wrap her mind around what he was telling her. She'd never suspected any of this. "You were hurting?"

Everett nodded. "She was my little girl, too," he told Lila.

"Oh, Everett, I wish you had told me," she cried.

So much time had been lost because of a failure to communicate. So much heartache could have been avoided if he had only verbalized his feelings to her.

If he'd just given her a clue…

"I wish I had told you, too," Everett said with all sincerity. And then he looked at her hopefully. "You wouldn't have a picture of Emma with you, would you?" he asked.

Lila opened up a drawer, took out her purse and

pulled out her cell phone. She pressed the photo app and scrolled through a few photos until she came to the one she was looking for.

"This is Emma," she told Everett, holding out her phone to him.

Everett looked at the young girl on the screen. He could feel his heart swell as he stared at the image. Emma looked to be on the verge of her teen years and she had a mouth full of braces.

She was the most beautiful girl he had ever seen.

"She has your smile," he said, taking in every detail of the photo. And then he looked up at Lila. "I can't believe how beautiful our daughter is." With a sigh, he handed the phone back to Lila.

Lila closed her phone and put it back in her purse. "Emma's not our daughter anymore, Everett," she told him quietly.

Everett nodded. "Right. Have you ever seen her in person?"

Lila shook her head. "No. I wanted to, but I don't want to confuse Emma. One mother and father is enough for her right now at her age. Besides, her parents know how to get in contact with me. They have my cell number. Someday, when she's older, if Emma wants to meet me, they'll let me know and I'll be there in a heartbeat. But for right now, all I want is for Emma to grow up happy and well adjusted."

"You're a strong, brave woman, Lila," Everett told her with admiration. He hadn't realized until this moment just how strong and brave she really was.

Lila shrugged. "You do what you have to do in order

to survive. And you make the best of the situation," she added. "The alternative is much too dark."

He nodded. "You're right. It is." He paused for a moment before looking at her and saying, "Would it surprise you if I told you that I think about Emma, too? That over the last few years, I've found myself thinking about her a lot. Wondering where she was, what she's doing. If she was happy. If she ever wondered about her birth parents and thought they—we—gave her up because we didn't love her."

"She knows we gave her up to give her a better life," Lila told him.

"You're just speculating," he said.

"No, I know that Emma knows that because her adoptive parents told me they told her that when she was old enough to begin asking questions."

Everett was quiet for a long moment. And when he finally spoke, what he said really surprised her. "I really wish I could meet our daughter."

It took Lila a moment to fully absorb what he had just said.

"Do you really mean that?" she asked Everett, astonished to hear him voice the same feelings that had been haunting her for years.

"Yes," he told her honestly. "I do."

She pressed her lips together, thinking over the feasibility of what he had just told her. "Well, I'm not sure how Emma's parents would feel about that, but I could certainly let them know that you're back in the picture and that you would like to meet Emma whenever it's convenient for them—and for her."

He nodded. It was a difficult situation all around and he fully understood that.

"I'd really appreciate that," he told her. He paused, trying to find the right words to convey what he wanted to say to her. "Lila…" Everett started, then stopped, his brain freezing up on him. This was a great deal harder than he'd anticipated.

"Yes?" she asked, wondering what else there was left for him to say. He'd already gladdened her heart by telling her that he not only thought about Emma, but actually wanted to meet her. That meant a great deal to her.

His eyes met hers. "Can you ever forgive me for not being there for you?" he asked softly.

Lila blinked. She could have been knocked over with the proverbial feather. Staring at Everett, she realized that he was being sincere.

"Oh Everett, I really wish I had known that you were hurting, too and that you felt the way you did. It would have helped me deal with everything that happened so much better." She smiled at him, fighting back tears again. "We really should have communicated more honestly with one another."

Everett stepped closer, letting himself do what he'd wanted to since he'd walked into this office. He enfolded Lila in his arms. "You're absolutely right. I should have talked with you, told you what I was feeling. But I just closed myself off, trying to deal with what was going on. I was blind and didn't realize that you were going through the same thing, too, and could have used my support." He'd been such a fool, Everett thought, regret riddling him. "Can you find it in your heart to forgive me?" he asked again.

Now that she knew that Everett had experienced the same doubts and emotions about their daughter that had haunted her, all of Lila's old feelings of anger and resentment vanished as if they had never existed. All Everett ever had to do was tell her what he'd gone through.

Forgiveness flooded her. "Yes, of course I can," she told him.

Relief mingled with love, all but overwhelming Everett. He kissed Lila, temporarily disregarding where they were and the fact that the people she worked with could easily look over and see what was happening.

And she kissed him back.

Everett forced himself to draw back. Still holding her in his arms, he looked down into her eyes. "From now on," he promised, "I'm putting all my cards on the table."

"Are you planning on playing solitaire or poker?" she asked Everett, a smile curving the corners of her mouth.

"Definitely not solitaire," he answered. "But any other game that you want. Oh, Lila, we've wasted much too much time and we'll never get any of that time back," he told her. His arms tightened around her. It felt so good to hold her against him like this. He felt he'd never let her go. "But we can have the future."

"And by that you mean...?" Her voice trailed off.

She wanted him to spell everything out so that there would be no more mix-ups, no more misunderstandings to haunt either one of them. She wanted to be absolutely certain that Everett was talking about what she *thought* he was talking about.

"I mean that I'm planning on being very clear about my intentions this time around. I know what I want," he told her, looking deep into her eyes. "All you need to do is say yes."

But she wasn't the same person she'd been thirteen years ago. She knew how to stand up for herself, how not to allow herself to be swept away.

She surprised him by telling Everett, "I never say 'yes' unless I know exactly what it is that I'm saying yes to."

"To this," Everett told her, pulling something out of his pocket. When he opened his hand, there was a big, beautiful heart-shaped diamond ring mounted on a wishbone setting in the center of his palm. He'd brought it with him for luck—and just in case.

Lila stared at it, momentarily speechless. When she raised her eyes to his face, she could barely speak. "Is that—?"

She couldn't bring herself to ask the question, because the moment she did—and he said no—a little of the magic would be gone. And she really couldn't believe that the ring she was looking at was the one she'd fallen in love with so many years ago.

But Lila discovered that she needn't have anticipated disappointment, because Everett nodded.

"Yes," he told her, pleased by her reaction, "it is. It's the one you saw through the window in that little out-of-the-way shop that day when we were back in college. You made me stand there while you made a wish and just stared at it, like it was the most beautiful thing you'd ever seen."

She smiled, remembering every detail. "I was being silly and frivolous," she admitted.

"No, you were being honest about your reaction," he corrected.

She continued looking at the sparkling diamond in his hand, completely mesmerized. "But how did you...?"

Everett anticipated her question and was way ahead of her. "After I dropped you off home, I doubled back to the store to buy the ring. The store was closed for the night by then, but I kept knocking on the door until the owner finally came down and opened it. Turns out that he lived above the store," he told her. "Anyway, I made him sell me the ring right then and there. I hung onto it, confident that I would give it to you someday." He smiled ruefully. "I just never thought it was going to take quite this long," he confessed.

Taking a deep breath, he held the ring up to her and said in a voice filled with emotion, "Lila Clark, will you marry me? I promise if you say yes, I will never leave you again."

Lila could feel her heart beating so hard in her chest, she was certain it was going to break right through her ribs. The wish she'd made that day in front of the shop window was finally coming true.

"I don't plan to keep you on a leash," she told him, so filled with love she thought she was going to burst. "But yes, I will marry you."

Thrilled, dazed, relieved and experiencing a whole

host of other emotions, Everett slipped the engagement ring on her finger.

The second he did, he swept her into his arms and kissed her again, longer this time even though he could see that they had attracted an audience. It didn't matter to him.

Lila's colleagues were watching them through the glass walls of her office and cheering them on, his sister and her cohort in front of the pack.

He looked down into Lila's eyes. "We can have more kids," he told her. "An entire army of kids if that's what you want. And they'll never want for anything. We can have that wonderful life that we used to just talk about having."

"A better one," she interjected.

"Absolutely," he agreed, hugging her to him again. "The sky's the limit," he promised. "But there's just one more thing."

"Oh?" Lila refused to be concerned. She'd been down that route and this was a brand-new route she was embarking on—with Everett beside her. She knew that she could face anything as long as he was with her. "What's that?"

"I don't want any more secrets between us," Everett said.

"Neither do I," Lila agreed wholeheartedly. "Is there something you need to tell me?"

"More than just you," Everett answered. "If we're going to start with a clean slate, there is something else I need to do."

Now he was beginning to really make her wonder,

but she wasn't about to shrink away from his revelation. Because whatever it was, they would face it together. Conquer it together.

"Go ahead," Lila said, thinking that he was going to confess something serious to her.

Instead, Everett opened her office door and called out, "Schuyler, Lucie, would you mind stepping back in here?"

The two women obligingly filed back into Lila's office.

"Okay," Schuyler said to her brother, "make your announcement, although we both saw you put that huge rock on Lila's finger so this is going to be a little anticlimatic."

"It's not what you think," Everett told his sister.

Schuyler exchanged looks with Lucie, obviously confused. "All right, enlighten us then," she said.

"I'm through sneaking around," he told his sister. "This is what we talked about when I first came to Austin, thinking I was picking you up to bring you home."

"What is he talking about?" Lucie asked, looking at Everett's sister.

Everett turned toward Lucie. "Lucie, I think it's time I told you who we really are. Or at least who we *think* we are."

Lucie looked from Everett to Lila, her brows furrowed. "Lila?"

But Lila shrugged, as mystified as Lucie was. "I have no idea what he's talking about," she admitted.

Everett laced the fingers of one hand through Lila's hand as he went on to make his revelation. Nodding toward his sister, he told Lucie, "As you know, our last name is Fortunado."

Lucie waited for more. "Yes?"

"What you might not know, and I've recently come to find out—thanks to Schuyler's detective work—is that the Fortunado family might actually be descendants of Julius Fortune, Jerome Fortune's father," he added for clarity.

"You know," Lucie told Everett, a smile spreading across her face, "I'm not half surprised. With all of Jerome's illegitimate offspring coming to light lately, it stands to reason he learned the art of seduction from his father." She reached out and placed a hand on Everett's shoulder. "In that case, I have some people I would *really* love for you to meet."

"People who could substantiate my suspicions?" Everett wanted to know.

"Oh, more than substantiate, I think," Lucie said with emphasis.

Instead of eagerly asking her friend to make the meeting happen, the way Lila thought he would, Everett turned to look at her. She saw a wicked sparkle in his eyes. Her pulse instantly began to accelerate.

"That really sounds wonderful, Lucie, and I'd appreciate the introduction," he told her without so much as a glance her way. His eyes were solely on Lila. "But I'm afraid the meeting is going to have to wait for now."

"Oh? Why?" Lucie asked.

"Because," Everett began, raising Lila's hand to his lips and brushing a kiss lightly against her knuckles, "my fiancée and I have plans for this afternoon. Plans," he said, "starting right now. So if you'll please excuse us…"

The request was merely a formality. Everett was already leading Lila out of the office and toward the hallway and the elevator beyond. He was vaguely aware of Schuyler's squeal of joy behind them and the sound of Lucie's laughter as she applauded.

All that and more blended into the background and then faded away as he stepped into the elevator car with Lila. They had a lot of catching up to do. And he planned to start this minute by taking her into his arms and kissing her as the elevator doors closed, locking the rest of the world out.

* * * * *

SMALL TOWN
MARRIAGE MIRACLE

JENNIFER TAYLOR

CHAPTER ONE

'I feel terrible about what's happened, Emma. You came home for a rest, not to be faced with this.'

'It doesn't matter. Really it doesn't.'

Emma Roberts smiled soothingly as she led her aunt, Margaret Haynes, over to a chair. She sat down beside her, seeing the strain that had etched deep lines onto the older woman's face. Her aunt had aged a lot since the last time Emma had seen her and she couldn't help feeling guilty. She should have realised that something was wrong and returned home sooner than this.

'Now tell me what the consultant said,' she ordered gently.

'He said that it's imperative your uncle has a coronary artery bypass done as soon as possible. If Jim waits any longer, there will be no point doing it.'

'Wait? Do you mean that Uncle Jim has been putting off having it done?' Emma queried in surprise.

'Yes. I'm afraid he has.' Margaret Haynes sighed. 'His angina has been getting worse for some time now. Even his medication doesn't always help when he has a really bad attack. I kept nagging him to have the bypass done, but you know how stubborn he can be.'

Emma smiled. 'I do indeed. Once Uncle Jim gets an idea into his head, it's impossible to shift it.' She sobered abruptly. 'But from what you've said, it sounds as though the situation is extremely urgent now.'

'It is.' Margaret gave a little sob. 'I thought I was going to lose him yesterday. He was in such terrible pain…'

'Shh, it's OK. He's going to be fine,' Emma assured her. She put her arm around the older woman's shoulders, wishing she were as certain of the outcome as she was trying to appear. Her aunt and uncle had brought her up after her parents had died and she loved them dearly. The thought of anything happening to Uncle Jim was almost more than she could bear.

'Of course he will. I'm just being silly, aren't I?' Margaret blew her nose. 'The consultant told me that he has high hopes the operation will be a complete success, so I have to remember that and not get upset. I certainly don't want your uncle to see me weeping and wailing.'

'It's the last thing he needs,' Emma agreed, admiring her aunt's steely determination. 'Uncle Jim will need plenty of rest after he's had the operation, though. I hope he understands that.'

'Oh, I shall make sure he does,' Margaret said firmly. 'He'll be in hospital for about twelve days and after that I intend to take him away to the cottage. Jim will need at least six weeks to recover from the operation and I won't be able to keep him out of the surgery for that length of time if we're at home.'

'Which is where I come in,' Emma said quickly, stifling a small pang of regret. Maybe she had been looking forward to a much-needed rest after a gruelling six months spent working overseas, but this was an emergency. If she ran the practice while her uncle recuperated, he would be less likely to worry. It was a small price to pay for all the love her aunt and uncle had lavished on her over the years.

'I'll take charge of the surgery while you're away,' she began, but her aunt shook her head.

'Oh, no, you don't need to do that, dear. Daniel will be here, so if you could just help out if it gets really busy, that would be more than enough.'

'Daniel?' Emma repeated, somewhat at a loss.

'Yes. I'm sure I told you last night when you phoned that Daniel had agreed to step in earlier than planned… Or did I? I was so worried, you see…'

'Daniel who?' Emma put in hurriedly before her aunt could drift off at a tangent again.

'Daniel Kennedy.'

Emma swung round when a deep voice answered her question. Her green eyes widened when she saw the tall, dark-haired man who was standing behind her. Just for a moment shock stole her ability to speak as she stared at him in dismay. It had been five years since she'd last seen him, and a lot had happened during that time, yet all of a sudden it felt as though she was right back to where she had been all those years ago—madly in love with the man she wanted to spend her whole life with. The thought scared her witless.

'Hello, Emma.' Daniel smiled at her but there was a wariness about the look he gave her, Emma realised, as though he wasn't sure how she would feel about seeing him again.

He was right to wonder, too, Emma thought grimly as she rose to her feet. Maybe she *had* believed at one time that Daniel was the man for her, but she didn't believe it any longer. The truth was that Daniel had used her, slept with her and then cast her aside when he had discovered she'd been getting too serious about him. It had taken her a long time to accept what he had done, but nowadays she was under no illusions. Daniel had never truly cared about *her*. He'd only ever cared about himself.

Emma took a deep breath. Maybe she hadn't expected to see him here, but she would deal with it. She was no longer the naïve and trusting young woman she had been back then. She had grown up now and she had seen too much of the world to be dazzled by a man like Daniel Kennedy ever again!

Daniel felt as though his smile had been pasted into place. He had been dreading seeing Emma again for a number of reasons, although he wasn't about to delve into them right then. He held out his hand, playing the role of old friend to the best of his ability even though he knew it wasn't true. He and Emma had been a lot more than friends at one time.

'It's good to see you again, Emma. How are you?'

'Fine, thank you.'

She shook his hand and a frisson ran through him when he felt the coolness of her skin. Just for a moment he was reminded of all the other occasions when he had touched her. Her skin had been cool then but it had soon warmed up as he had stroked and caressed her. The memory sent a surge of heat coursing through him and he hurriedly blanked it out, knowing how foolish it was to go down that route.

'This must have come as a shock to you?'

'It has.' She glanced at her aunt and drew him aside. 'Aunt Margaret just told me that Uncle Jim has been putting off having the bypass done. Is that true?'

'Yes, it is.' Daniel sighed. 'You know how dedicated Jim is. I expect he was worried about what would happen to the practice if he took any time off.'

'That's so typical of him. He puts everyone else's needs before his own.' She gave him a hard look. 'Did you know that he was delaying having surgery?'

'No. I knew Jim had angina, of course, but he never admitted how bad things had got until last week,' Daniel answered truthfully. 'I suspect he only told me then because he needed my help. He'd finally agreed to have his op at the end of the month and he wanted me to cover for him.'

'Really?' Emma frowned. 'I don't understand why he asked you to take over the practice. He knew I was coming home, so why didn't he ask me?'

'I can't answer that. You'll have to ask Jim, although I suggest you leave it until after he's had his operation.' He shrugged when he saw her mouth tighten. It was obvious that she didn't appreciate his advice but he refused to let it deter him. 'Jim needs peace and quiet more than anything else at the moment. What he doesn't need,

Emma, is for us to be conducting some sort of personal vendetta.'

'Don't flatter yourself,' she snapped back. 'The days when I cared enough to fight with you, Daniel, are long gone.'

'Good. Then it won't cause any problems if I'm in charge of the practice in your uncle's absence.'

'The only problem I have is understanding why you've agreed to do it. I mean, working in the middle of nowhere is hardly a step up the professional ladder, is it, Daniel?'

Daniel flinched when he heard the scorn in her voice. It didn't make it any easier to know that he only had himself to blame for it either. He'd been so desperate to convince her that there was no future for them that he had led her to believe that all he was interested in was his career. Now he was reaping the consequences.

'It's all good experience,' he said quietly. 'Plus, I'm very fond of your aunt and uncle. I'm happy to help in any way I can.'

'How very altruistic of you.' She smiled but her green eyes were chilly. 'Of course a cynic would wonder if there was an ulterior motive to your generosity. Still, I'm sure the truth will come out at some stage.'

She turned away before he could reply, not that he could think of anything to say in his defence. Emma wouldn't believe him if he told her that he wasn't interested in personal advancement and never had been. All of a sudden he bitterly regretted those claims he had made about going into private practice one day, but what else could he have done? Accepted what she'd been offering him, knowing that it could ruin both their lives?

Daniel's heart was heavy as he excused himself and made his way along the corridor. There was a coffee machine at the bottom of the stairs and he fed some coins into it. It disgorged a stream of insipid-looking liquid into a plastic cup but he didn't care how it looked or tasted even. He took it over to the window and stood there staring out across the town. Avondale was a pretty little market town in the middle of the Yorkshire Dales. During the summer months, the population virtually doubled thanks to a steady influx of tourists, but at this time of the year there were few tourists willing to brave the inclement weather. He had first come to the town to do his GP training and that was how he had met Emma. She had just completed her rotations and was enjoying a well-deserved break before she took up a junior registrar's post in Scotland with a top surgical team.

Daniel knew that competition for surgical posts was always fierce, and that it was particularly hard for a woman to break into that field. Whilst most consultants paid lip service to the idea of equality between the sexes, far too many refused to accept a woman as part of their team. The old prejudices were still rife: what was the point of training a woman when she would only leave to have a family? That Emma had overcome such narrow-minded thinking and secured a prestigious post for herself proved how hard she must have worked. He was impressed. He was also deeply attracted to her.

Almost before he'd realised what was happening,

Daniel had fallen in love with her and she with him. It had been a gloriously blissful time for them both until Emma had announced one day that she had changed her mind about going into surgery. She no longer wanted such a demanding career, she'd claimed. She wanted a private life, time for them, so she would stay in England and train as a GP instead. That way they could be together.

Daniel had realised immediately that he couldn't allow her to sacrifice her dreams for him. Although she might truly have believed that she was happy to give up her plans to become a surgeon, he knew how much it meant to her and that it would drive a wedge between them eventually if she didn't fulfil her goals. He had seen it happen to his own parents, watched as his mother's resentment at forsaking her career had eaten away at their marriage, and he had sworn the same thing would never happen to him.

For Emma to succeed in her chosen field, Daniel knew that she would need to focus all her attention on her training for the next few years. Even though he could have found a job in Scotland easily enough, he realised that it wasn't the answer. She would be working long hours and wouldn't have time to devote to a relationship. He would be a distraction for her, a hindrance, and he couldn't bear the thought that she might fail because of him. Although it was the hardest decision he had ever made, he decided that he had to give Emma up rather than run the risk of her ending up hating him.

He sighed as he recalled her shock when he had told her curtly that he had no intention of making a commitment at that stage in his life. He had plans for the future and they were far more important than their relationship. The contempt in her eyes as she had told him that she understood had devastated him. He had almost weakened at that point and admitted that he'd lied, but somehow he had managed to hold back. She had packed her bags and left that same night and he hadn't seen her again until today.

The sound of footsteps made him look round and he felt pain stab his heart when he saw her coming along the corridor. She must have come straight to the hospital from the airport because her clothes were crumpled after the long flight, her red-gold hair lying in tangled waves around her shoulders, but that didn't matter. She was still the most beautiful and most desirable woman he had ever seen. It was only when she drew closer that Daniel could see the lines of strain that tugged down the corners of her mouth.

He knew from what Jim Haynes had told him that she'd been working overseas for the past six months and could imagine how hard it must have been, working under the most gruelling conditions. However, he also knew that it wasn't the work or the shock of learning that her uncle was ill that made her look so drawn. It was seeing him again that was the problem. In that second Daniel realised that he had to make the situation as easy as possible for her. He couldn't bear to think that he might end up hurting her again as he had hurt her once before.

Emma took a steadying breath as she stopped in front of Daniel, but she could feel her heart racing. Seeing him again had been a shock—she had admitted that—but she could handle it. She certainly didn't intend to go to pieces just because the man she had once mistakenly thought she'd loved had reappeared in her life.

'Aunt Margaret has gone in to see Uncle Jim,' she said coolly. 'They'll be doing the bypass later today and she wants to sit with him until it's time for him to go to Theatre.'

'The sooner it's done, the better.'

There was a roughness to Daniel's voice that troubled her until she realised how stupid it was to let it worry her. Daniel Kennedy was part of her past, nothing more than a memory she had long since relegated to the darkest reaches of her mind.

'Definitely.' She glanced along the corridor, giving herself a moment to absorb that thought. When she turned to face him again, she was pleased to discover that she didn't feel a thing. 'I'm not sure how long it's going to take, but there doesn't seem any point you hanging around here.'

'It isn't a problem.' He checked his watch and shrugged. 'I don't need to get back to the surgery for another couple of hours yet, so I'll stay a bit longer.'

'There's no need. Aunt Margaret will be fine.' Emma stood up straighter, determined to get her own way. 'I'm more than capable of looking after her.'

'I'm sure you are.' He smiled, his hazel eyes skimming over her face before they came to rest on her mouth, and despite her resolve, Emma felt a little flutter of awareness in the pit of her stomach. She took a quick breath, determined that it wasn't going to grow into anything bigger. The days when one of Daniel's smiles could turn her insides to jelly were long gone!

'You always were very good at looking after other people, Emma, but you need to think about yourself for once. You've had a long journey to get here and you must be tired. Why not let me stay with your aunt while you go home and get some sleep?'

'I don't need you to tell me what to do!' she shot back, terrified by the speed of her response. One minute she'd had herself under control and the next….

She shivered as a wave of fear swept over her. She couldn't bear to think that Daniel still had an effect on her. Five years ago she would have done anything for them to be together, but he had made it clear that all he'd cared about was his career. It had been a devastating blow but it had taught her a valuable lesson: she would never make the mistake of falling in love again.

'I am not trying to tell you what to do. I'm just making a suggestion. It's entirely up to you whether you stay here or go home.'

His tone was reasonable in the extreme and she felt her face heat. She knew she was overreacting and she hated to think that Daniel might read anything into it. She didn't care about him any longer, but if she carried on this way, he would never believe that.

'I apologise. I shouldn't have jumped down your throat like that.'

He shrugged. 'It doesn't matter. It's little wonder that you're stressed after everything that's happened. All this coming on top of the journey you've had would be a lot for anyone to cope with.'

It was on the tip of her tongue to deny it until she realised that she was in danger of digging an even deeper hole for herself. Did she really want to admit that it was seeing him again that was causing her to behave so irrationally?

'Probably.' She glanced at her watch and came to a swift decision. 'If you're happy to stay then maybe I will go back to the house. I need to unpack and get settled in.'

'It's fine by me,' he agreed equably.

'Right, that's what I'll do, then. I'll just let Aunt Margaret know what's happening first.'

'I'll come with you.' He shrugged when she glanced sharply at him. 'I'd like to see Jim before he goes down to Theatre, set his mind at rest that the practice is in safe hands. You know what a worrier he is.'

'That's true.' Emma headed back along the corridor, very conscious of the fact that Daniel was just a step behind her. She paused outside the door to the private room where her uncle had been taken and glanced at him. 'It would be best if Uncle Jim didn't have to worry about anything at the moment, so I suggest we call a truce.'

'That's fine by me.' He smiled at her and Emma felt her breath catch when she saw the warmth in his eyes. She had never expected him to look at her that way and it threw her for a moment. It was an effort to concentrate when he continued. 'I don't want to fight with you, Emma. It's the last thing I want, in fact.'

'Me too,' she replied stiffly.

'Then we'll agree to set our differences aside, shall we?'

'Yes.'

She turned away, struggling to contain the emotions that were welling up inside her. It had been months since she'd even thought about Daniel, although in the beginning the memory of what had happened had tormented her. She had kept going over everything he'd said, reliving the pain of discovering that she had meant less to him than his precious career had done. Only by immersing herself in her work had she got through that terrible period and she refused to place herself in the same position again.

She squared her shoulders. No matter what Daniel said or did, no matter how convincing he sounded, she would never trust him again.

CHAPTER TWO

BY two o'clock Emma had finished unpacking and put everything away. She looked fondly around the room that had been hers since childhood. It had changed very little over the years and she found it reassuring to see her collection of stuffed toys on top of the wardrobe and the shelves of books she'd read while she had been growing up. She had moved house several times in the past few years and although it had never bothered her, it was good to know that there was somewhere permanent she could return to.

She sighed softly as she stowed the canvas hold-all in the bottom of the wardrobe because if Uncle Jim was forced to give up the practice, there would need to be a lot of changes made. The surgery was attached to the house and it was unlikely that her aunt and uncle would want to carry on living here. Nothing was truly permanent and she had to get used to the idea, even though she hated the thought of not being able to call this place her home.

Emma closed the wardrobe door and headed downstairs to make herself a cup of tea. She glanced at the clock as she filled the kettle. Uncle Jim should be leaving

Theatre soon, so she would drink her tea then go back to the hospital to keep her aunt company. It would give Daniel time to get back for evening surgery.

'I wouldn't say no to a cup of tea, if you're making one.'

As though thinking about him had somehow conjured him up, Daniel suddenly appeared. Emma looked round in surprise when she heard his voice. 'What are you doing here? I thought you were going to stay at the hospital until I got back.'

'I was, but your aunt insisted that she'd be all right by herself.' He grimaced. 'I tried to persuade her to let me stay but she wouldn't hear of it. I think she was worried in case I was late for evening surgery.'

Emma sighed. 'She's as bad as Uncle Jim. Their lives revolve around the practice and have done for years. It isn't right that it should come first, especially not at the moment.'

'It certainly isn't.' He pulled out a chair and sat down. 'They need to concentrate on making sure that Jim makes a full recovery and that's where we come in.'

Emma wasn't sure she appreciated that *we*, although she didn't correct him. She poured boiling water into the pot then went to fetch the milk out of the fridge. The days when she and Daniel had been a couple were long gone and she, for one, wouldn't wish them back again.

'So what do you suggest?' she asked, adopting a deliberately neutral tone to conceal the pain that thought had aroused, oddly enough.

'Basically, what we agreed on today. We make sure we do nothing to cause your aunt and uncle any concern.' He shrugged. 'Margaret told me that she's hoping to take Jim to their cottage on the coast while he recuperates, but he'll refuse to go if he thinks you and I are at loggerheads.'

'I can assure you that I have no intention of causing a disruption,' Emma said sharply, trying to ignore the squirmy feeling in the pit of her stomach. It was one thing to agree to a truce but it could be something entirely different to stick to it. Could they really maintain a wholly professional relationship when they had once been lovers?

The fact that she should be experiencing such doubts when she was determined not to let Daniel affect her in any way annoyed her and she glared at him. 'I said it before but obviously it didn't sink in so I'll repeat it. I don't *care* enough to fight with you, Daniel. OK?'

'Good.' He smiled calmly back at her. 'It should make life a lot simpler for all of us.'

Emma didn't say anything as she poured the tea. Daniel obviously believed her and that was all that mattered. She certainly didn't want him to suspect that she had doubts, not that she really did. She had moved on from the days when splitting up with him had left her feeling utterly devastated.

Of course it must have been easier for him to get over their break-up, she thought as she placed the cups on the table. He had never invested as much of himself into their relationship as she had done. Although he had told her at the time that he loved her, it patently hadn't been true. He would never have chosen his career over her if he'd felt even a fraction of the love she had felt for him.

She frowned. It made his decision to work in Avondale all the more difficult to understand. Taking time off to come here didn't make sense when he was so keen to pursue his ambitions. *Did* he have an ulterior motive? It was what she had accused him of earlier in the day, although she hadn't seriously believed it. Now she found herself wondering if it was true. As she knew to her cost, Daniel's career meant more to him than anything else.

Daniel wasn't sure what was going through Emma's mind, but he could tell that it wasn't anything pleasant. He bit back a sigh because he had a nasty feeling that it had something to do with him. Once again he found himself wishing that he hadn't misled her five years ago, even though he knew that he'd had no choice. He had loved her far too much to let her sacrifice her dreams for him.

'Are you still working in London?'

He looked up when she spoke, trying to control the surge his pulse gave as his eyes alighted on her face. Although he had been out with a number of extremely attractive women since they'd parted, he had never been tempted to have a long-term relationship with any of them. A few dates and that was it: *finito*. In fact, he'd gained a bit of a reputation amongst his friends as being a 'love them and leave them' kind of guy. He always laughed off the accusation by claiming that he simply hadn't met the right woman, but now he realised the truth was far more complicated. He had never met anyone who could match up to Emma.

It was an unsettling thought and he tried not to dwell on it as he answered her question. 'Yes. It's a busy practice, lots of variety, and I get on well with the rest of the team so I've not been tempted to leave.'

'And they don't mind you taking time off to work here?'

'No. They were very sympathetic, in fact,' Daniel replied, wondering what was behind her sudden interest.

'It must have caused a problem when you had to drop everything without any warning, though,' she persisted. 'Didn't you say that Uncle Jim had asked you to cover from the end of the month originally?'

'That's right. Fortunately, our practice manager was able to juggle the timetable and fit it in.' He shrugged. 'It's worked out quite well, actually. I had some leave owing, so I'm using it up.'

'Really?' Her brows rose. 'You had six whole weeks of leave stored up?'

'One of the senior partners was pregnant last summer and we couldn't get locum cover for part of her maternity leave,' he explained. 'I offered to carry my leave forward. It's lucky I did as it turns out.'

'Hmm, very lucky indeed.'

Daniel frowned when he heard the scepticism in her voice. He wasn't sure what had caused it and before he could ask, the telephone rang. He stood up before he was tempted to explain that it wasn't the first time he hadn't taken his full holiday entitlement. It always seemed like a waste of time, taking time off, when he could be working. Although he had never been driven by personal ambition, he wanted to learn all he could so he could help the people who relied on him for their care. That aim had become even more important since he and Emma had parted.

'I'll get that,' he said briskly. It wouldn't help the situation to dwell on how much his life had been influenced by what had happened between him and Emma. 'It's probably Ruth checking that there'll be a surgery tonight. Morning surgery had to be cancelled so I expect it will be busy this evening.'

'I'll give you a hand when I get back from the hospital,' Emma offered.

'That would be great.' He smiled at her, relieved that she was willing to do her bit to maintain the peace. 'Thanks.'

He went out to the hall to take the call. As he'd expected, it was the practice receptionist, Ruth Hargreaves. He assured her that surgery would go ahead as scheduled and hung up. There was no sign of Emma when he went back to the kitchen but he heard a car starting up and looked out of the window in time to see her driving away. She hadn't bothered saying goodbye but why should she? So far as Emma was concerned, she would do what had to be done and that was it. She wasn't going to suddenly want to become his best friend and he didn't blame her. He had hurt her badly and the worst thing was knowing that he could never atone for what he had done. Even if he told her the truth, and even if by some miracle she believed him, it was far too late to get back what they'd had.

* * *

The waiting room was packed when Emma got back shortly after five p.m. Aunt Margaret had decided to stay the night at the hospital so Emma had come back on her own. Ruth was on the phone when she went in, looking unusually harassed. Emma waited until the receptionist finished the call.

'Problems?'

'Oh, just the umpteenth person phoning to see if we're open.' Ruth rolled her eyes when the phone rang again the second she put down the receiver. 'That'll be another one. I'm sorely tempted to take the wretched thing off the hook!'

'I don't blame you.' Emma smiled sympathetically. 'I'm helping out tonight so you can send the next patient in to me when you get the chance.'

'Will do.'

Ruth snatched up the receiver as Emma made her way along the corridor. There were two consulting rooms and she guessed that Daniel would be using the one her uncle normally used. She made her way to the other room and switched on the light. The room hadn't been used very often since her uncle's partner had retired some years ago. Although Uncle Jim had tried to find a replacement, few doctors had been keen to relocate to the area. The younger ones thought the town too quiet to consider living there permanently, while the older ones weren't willing to cope with the difficulties of the job.

As well as caring for the townsfolk, the practice provided care for the people living on the outlying farms. Some home visits could be extremely difficult to reach, especially during the winter months. The few candidates who had applied for the post had soon lost interest when they'd discovered what the job had entailed, so in the end her uncle had given up advertising and run the surgery single-handed. However, if the number of patients in the waiting room was anything to go by, it really needed more than one doctor to run the practice.

It was something that needed thinking about in view of her uncle's health, Emma decided. However, there was no time to worry about it right then. A knock on the door heralded the arrival of her first patient, a young woman who looked vaguely familiar. Emma smiled at her.

'Please sit down. I'm Dr Roberts. I'm helping out while my uncle is in hospital.'

'Oh, I remember you!' the young woman exclaimed. 'You were in the same class at school as my sister— Cathy Martindale. Remember her?'

'Of course I do.' Emma laughed. 'No wonder you look so familiar. You're very like Cathy. How is she, by the way?'

'She's fine. She lives in Leeds now with her husband and her two little boys.'

'Tell her I was asking about her, will you?' Emma picked up the folder of notes that the girl had brought in with her. 'So, Judith, what can I do for you today?'

'It's my periods, Dr Roberts. They're so heavy and irregular that they're causing me a real problem. I also suffer the most awful pain in my tummy and lower back each time it happens.'

'I see. How long has this been going on?' Emma asked.

'About a year now. I came off the Pill eighteen months ago because my husband and I want to start a family. My periods were very erratic after I stopped taking it, but I thought everything would settle down once the drugs were out of my system. Instead, it's just got worse.'

'Have you had any other symptoms? Pain on having intercourse, perhaps?'

'Yes.' Judith blushed. 'I've never had a problem before, but recently I dread making love with David because it's so uncomfortable.'

'Which doesn't help when you're hoping to have a baby,' Emma said sympathetically, standing up. 'I'll just check your blood pressure and then I'd like to examine you, if that's all right?'

'Oh, yes, of course it is.' Judith sounded relieved as she slipped off her coat. 'I've been putting off coming for weeks, to be honest. Dr Haynes is lovely, but I felt so embarrassed about having to explain it all to him. I couldn't believe my luck when Ruth told me I'd be seeing you tonight!'

'Good.' Emma laughed, although she couldn't help wondering how many other women were delaying making appointments because they felt uncomfortable about discussing their problems with an elderly male doctor.

She checked Judith's BP, which was fine, then asked her to undress and lie on the couch while she examined her. She gently palpated her abdomen and then performed an internal examination but could find nothing to indicate what was causing the problem. Judith had had a smear test the previous month and that had come back clear.

'And there's been no other symptoms at all?' she asked after Judith had got dressed again. 'Not even something that is apparently unrelated?'

'No…well, apart from the fact that I've had several bouts of diarrhoea. It's not something I've ever suffered from before, but it's happened a few times lately. Either that or I get constipated,' Judith added, grimacing.

'I see.' Emma frowned thoughtfully as she considered what she'd heard. 'It's possible that you're suffering from endometriosis, although I wouldn't like to make a final diagnosis without sending you for some tests first. However, the symptoms you described could point towards it being that.'

'Endometriosis?' Judith repeated. 'What's that? I've never heard of it.'

'It's when tiny pieces of the lining of the womb, the endometrium, are shed during menstruation but don't pass out of the body. Instead they travel up the Fallopian tubes into the pelvic cavity and attach themselves to the pelvic organs. They continue to respond to your menstrual cycle so each month they bleed, but because the blood can't escape, it causes cysts to form. And they're the cause of most of the pain and discomfort.'

'How weird!' Judith exclaimed. 'And you think that's what is wrong with me?'

'I think it's worth investigating further.' Emma brought up the relevant document on the computer and filled in the patient's details. She glanced at Judith. 'You need to be seen by a gynaecologist so I'll organise an appointment for you. Basically, what it means is that your pelvic cavity will need to be examined. It's done by using a laparoscope, which is a special instrument that's passed through the wall of the abdomen. There's a tiny camera on the end of it so the gynaecologist can see what's going on inside you.'

'It sounds horrible,' Judith said, shuddering.

'It'll be fine,' Emma assured her. 'And it will be worth having it done if it means we can sort out this problem you have.'

'If I do have this endometriosis, how will you treat it?'

'It depends how severe it is. Drugs can be very effective in some cases. In others, where the cysts are very large, surgery to remove them is the best option. Pregnancy can also suppress the condition.'

'So I can still have a baby?' Judith asked anxiously.

'Yes, although it's only fair to warn you that endometriosis can affect your fertility. However, let's find out if my diagnosis is correct before we worry about that.' Emma tried to sound as positive as she could but she could tell that Judith was upset by the thought that she might not have the baby she longed for.

Emma saw her out and buzzed for her next patient. The evening flew past and before she knew it, it was time to pack up for the night. She collected up the files she had used and took them into the office. Ruth looked up from the computer and smiled at her. She had worked at the practice for many years and had watched Emma growing up so there was no question of her standing on ceremony.

'I bet you're sorry you came home now, aren't you, love?'

'It did cross my mind,' Emma replied, jokingly. She held up the files. 'You'd think we should be able to do away with all this paperwork now that we have computers to help us.'

'I wish!' Ruth replied cheerfully. 'The trouble is that computers have a nasty habit of breaking down, so we need the files as back-up.'

'I suppose so.'

Emma looked round when she heard footsteps in the corridor, feeling her pulse surge when Daniel appeared in the doorway. She had been too stressed about seeing him again to take much notice earlier in the day, but all of a sudden she found herself taking stock of the changes the past few years had wrought. Although he was still extremely good looking with those craggy, very masculine features and that thick dark hair, there were lines on his face that hadn't been there five years before, an underlying sadness in his hazel eyes that surprised her. Daniel looked as though he had suffered some kind of sorrow in his life and she couldn't help wondering what had happened. Was it possible that he had fallen in love and been let down?

The thought sent a shaft of pain searing through her. Emma bit her lip to contain the cry that threatened to emerge. That Daniel might have experienced the same kind of unhappiness as she had done when they'd parted should have filled her with a certain satisfaction, but it didn't. All she felt was an overwhelming sense of grief that he might have loved some other woman more than he had loved her.

'I hope it isn't always as busy as that?' He grinned at Ruth. 'Sure you didn't ring round all the patients and ask them to call in tonight so you could put me through my paces?'

'How did you guess?' Ruth winked at Emma. 'Drat! We've been found out.'

'I…um…it looks like it.' Emma did her best to respond to the teasing comment but it wasn't easy. The thought of Daniel loving another woman was more painful than it had any right to be. She was over him and it shouldn't matter, but it did. She took a quick breath to control the pain when she saw him look at her in surprise. 'We're only joking, Daniel.'

'That's good to hear.' He smiled coolly. 'I'd hate to think you had it in for me, Emma.'

Emma flushed when she heard the irony in his voice. She turned away, busying herself with placing the files she'd used in the tray. By the time Daniel added his, it was brimming over. 'Do you want me to put these away so you can have a clear run in the morning?' she offered.

'There's no need. Dr Haynes took on a part-time receptionist at Christmas,' Ruth explained. 'There was some sort of wretched tummy bug doing the rounds and I was snowed under with all the extra paperwork. Claire comes in three mornings a week and helps with the filing, et cetera. We'll soon get everything sorted out between us.'

'Oh, right. That's fine.' Emma placed the referral letter she'd printed in the tray for posting. 'There's just the one letter that needs sending as well.'

'And I've got another one here.'

Daniel leant past her and dropped his letter on top of hers. Emma tried not to flinch when his shoulder brushed against her but he must have felt the small involuntary jerk she gave. He stepped back, his face betraying very little as he told Ruth that he would lock up and set the alarm.

Emma took it as her cue to leave. She murmured a general goodbye and hurriedly left. Although the surgery was attached to the house, it was completely self-contained and she had to walk round to the front door to let herself in. She hung her coat in the hall then made her way to the sitting room to turn on the gas fire. Although the central heating was switched on, the house still felt chilly.

She sighed. It probably felt chilly because her body hadn't adjusted to the change in temperature yet. When she'd left South Africa early that morning the temperature had been in the high 30s, so it was bound to be a shock to her system to be plunged back into the tail end of a British winter. Still, she would soon adapt…

Emma looked round in surprise when she heard the front door open. It slammed shut and a moment later she heard footsteps crossing the hall. Her heart was already racing when Daniel appeared, even though she had no idea what he wanted.

'Oh, good. You've got the fire going. It's a lot colder

up here than it is in London,' he observed, crossing the room to warm his hands.

'I suppose it is,' Emma agreed uncertainly. She frowned when she realised that he wasn't wearing a coat. He'd had it on earlier so why had he taken it off? A horrible suspicion started to rear its head and she stared at him in alarm. 'What are you doing here, Daniel?'

'At this precise moment, I'm trying to warm up. But give me a couple of minutes and I'll make myself useful.'

'Useful?'

'Uh-huh. I'll cook dinner tonight. It doesn't seem fair to expect you to do it after the day you've had.'

'Cook dinner?' Emma took a quick breath when she realised that she was repeating everything he said. 'Why on earth would you want to cook dinner?'

'Because we both need to eat,' he replied reasonably. He glanced at her, the light from the fire reflecting in his eyes so that she found it impossible to read his expression. 'We can work out a rota if you prefer, but tonight I'll cook.'

He straightened up and headed for the door but Emma knew that she couldn't let him leave before she found out what was going on. 'Why do we need a rota? Surely you'll be having dinner wherever you're staying? Most of the guest houses will provide an evening meal if you ask them to.'

'Your aunt hasn't told you, then?' He stopped and

turned, and she could see the concern on his face. It made her feel even more alarmed.

'Told me what?' she snapped.

'That I'm staying here.'

CHAPTER THREE

'EVERYTHING happened so fast that there was no time to arrange accommodation before I left London. I was going to sort something out when I got here, but Margaret insisted that I stay at the house.'

Daniel shrugged but he could tell from the frozen expression on Emma's face that the news had come as a shock to her. 'I can't see that it will cause a problem, Emma, but if you aren't happy with the arrangement then, of course, I'll find somewhere else.'

'There's no need,' she said stiffly. 'If Aunt Margaret invited you to stay, I'm certainly not going to object.'

'Fine. If you change your mind, though, just let me know.'

Daniel managed to maintain an outward show of indifference as he left the sitting room, but he sighed as he headed for the kitchen. Emma's reaction to the news that they would be sharing the house was upsetting but what did he expect? It might have been different if her aunt and uncle had been there, but she probably didn't relish the idea of them being on their own. All he could do now was monitor the situation and find somewhere else if it looked as though it was going to create friction.

It was the logical solution, although it didn't make him feel good to know that he was *persona non grata* so far as Emma was concerned. He tried not to dwell on it as he made a start on dinner. He was just mashing the potatoes to go with the lamb chops and green beans he had cooked when Emma appeared.

'I'll set the table.'

She busied herself with place mats and cutlery, glasses for water and condiments. Daniel suspected that it was displacement activity, aimed at taking her mind off the thought of eating with him. He couldn't help feeling sad as he remembered all the other meals they had shared—impromptu picnics in the country, lunches in one of the local pubs. It hadn't mattered what they'd eaten or where because they'd always enjoyed it. Just being together had added extra zest to the food.

'Remember that meal we had at the Golden Goose?'

Emma's voice cut into his thoughts and he felt a tingle run through him. That she had been recalling the good times they'd had seemed too much of a coincidence, yet why should it be? It wasn't the first time their thoughts had been so in tune. Maybe there was still some kind of connection between them.

Daniel hurriedly quashed that thought. He couldn't allow himself to think like that; it was too dangerous. 'Not really,' he replied offhandedly.

He spooned mashed potato onto the plates, ignoring the flicker of hurt that crossed her face. He was doing this for her sake. They couldn't go back and they couldn't go forward either. Not together. Leaving aside the fact that Emma no longer loved him, the old objections were as valid today as they had been five years ago. He knew from what Jim had told him that Emma was determined to make consultant one day. If that was to happen then he knew that she needed to remain completely focused. If she failed to achieve her goal, she would regret it just as much as she would have done if she'd given up surgery all together.

Daniel's heart was heavy as he carried the plates over to the table. Even if Emma was prepared to give them a second chance—which she wasn't!—there was no future for them. 'I hope this is all right for you. There's no gravy, I'm afraid. I've never mastered the art of making decent gravy.'

'It's fine. Thank you.'

Her tone was painfully polite and it cut him to the quick to know that she was deliberately distancing herself from him. He didn't react, however, as he pulled out a chair and sat down because there was nothing he could do that would help. Emma sat down as well and began to eat. Apart from the faint clatter of cutlery, the room was silent and Daniel could feel the tension mounting as the minutes passed. He searched his mind for something uncontroversial to say, but all he could come up with was work. Still, it was better than nothing.

'How did you get on tonight?'

'Fine, thank you.' Emma forked a little potato into her mouth. She chewed and swallowed it then looked at him. 'How about you?'

'Oh, yes, fine. Thanks.' Daniel inwardly groaned when he heard the stilted note in his voice. This was hardly the best way to improve the atmosphere, was it?

He cleared his throat and tried again. 'I was surprised by how busy it was, to be honest. I know morning surgery had to be cancelled, but even so I didn't expect that many patients to turn up. Did you?'

'No.' She scooped a little more potato onto her fork then hesitated. Daniel held his breath, hoping that she would find something else to say. If the next few weeks weren't to be an ordeal for them both, Emma needed to meet him halfway.

'To be frank, I don't know how Uncle Jim copes on his own. It was obvious from the number of people we saw tonight that it needs more than one doctor to run this practice.'

Daniel felt like punching the air in relief, but managed to control the urge. Two sentences didn't make a conversation. And they definitely didn't make up for past hurts. 'I agree. The workload is way too much for one person, especially when that person has health issues of his own,' he agreed soberly, trying to ignore the pang of guilt he felt. He had never set out to hurt her, far from it. He'd done what was necessary to safeguard her happiness and he had to remember that, even though it was hard.

'We have to find a way to make Uncle Jim understand that.' Emma sighed. 'It won't be easy, though. You know how independent he is and admitting that he needs help will be extremely difficult for him. Then there's the problem of finding someone suitable who's willing to work here. That will be another major hurdle.'

'Jim told me once that he'd not had much luck finding a replacement after his partner retired,' Daniel said quietly.

'No. There were very few applications when the post was advertised, so he wasn't exactly spoiled for choice. And the couple of candidates he interviewed changed their minds when they discovered what the job actually entailed.' She shrugged. 'It takes a certain type of person willing to go out to a call at one of the farms in the middle of winter.'

'Not many doctors are as dedicated as Jim is, but he has to face facts. He's not getting any younger. Even without this operation, he would have had to think about at least scaling back even if he doesn't intend to retire. Quite frankly, he can't go on working as hard as he's been doing.'

'We know that, but convincing Uncle Jim is another matter. The practice means everything to him,' she added worriedly.

'I know it does, Emma, but somehow we have to make him see that he needs to think about himself for a change. And about your aunt, too. She must be worried sick about him.'

'She is.' Tears welled to her eyes and she looked away.

Daniel reached out and laid his hand over hers, hating to see her looking so upset. 'We'll work something out, Emma. Promise.'

He gave her hand a gentle squeeze, his heart lifting when he felt her fingers curl around his for a moment before she pulled away. Picking up her cutlery, she started eating again and he knew that the all too brief moment of togetherness had passed. They finished the meal as it had begun, in silence. Daniel knew there was no point trying to draw her out again, even if he'd had the heart to try. Emma was deliberately shutting him out and although it hurt like hell, he understood why. She didn't trust him after what had happened and he couldn't blame her.

Emma refused both dessert and coffee. Her nerves were stretched so tightly by then that she would have been sick if she'd consumed anything else. She stacked her plate and glass in the dishwasher then went upstairs to her room. Daniel had mentioned something about watching television in the sitting room, but she had no intention of joining him. Dinner had been enough of an ordeal.

She sighed as she lay down on the narrow single bed. The thought of having to spend the next few weeks making stilted conversation wasn't appealing, but what choice did she have? If she asked Daniel to find some-where else to live it would only arouse her aunt and un-cle's suspicions that things weren't right between them. Although Aunt Margaret and Uncle Jim knew that she and Daniel had spent a lot of time together five years ago, they had no idea just how serious the relationship had been or, rather, how much it had meant to *her*. As far as the older couple were concerned, it had been nothing more than a summer romance and she didn't intend to disabuse them of that idea. She and Daniel would have to muddle through as best they could, although one thing was certain—if he tried to touch her again, she would make it clear that he was overstepping the mark.

Emma tried to ignore the tingle that shot up her arm as she recalled the warm grip of his fingers. She got up and went to the bookshelves, selecting a well-worn copy of *Black Beauty*, a childhood favourite. Curling up on the bed, she proceeded to reacquaint herself with the familiar characters. She must have drifted off to sleep at some point because the next thing she knew, the telephone was ringing.

She got up and hurried out to the landing, but Daniel had beaten her to it. He had already lifted the phone off its rest and was holding it to his ear. Emma felt her breath catch when she discovered that all he was wearing was a pair of pyjama pants resting low on his narrow hips. His chest was bare, the thick, dark hair out-lining the solid strength of his pectoral muscles before it arrowed down to disappear tantalisingly beneath the waistband of his pants. It was only when he dropped the receiver back onto its rest with a clatter that she managed to drag her gaze away.

'That was Harry Groves from High Dale Farm. Apparently, his wife has gone into labour and the mid-wife is at another call. Harry has phoned for an ambulance but it will be at least an hour before it gets there,' Daniel explained. 'I said I'd go over there straight away.'

'High Dale Farm is right up in the hills. It's a long drive even from here, so no wonder the ambulance will need time to get there,' Emma agreed worriedly.

'Is it marked on the map?' Daniel asked, referring to the Ordnance Survey map they kept in the surgery.

It showed the location of every farm in their catchment area, with the roads leading to it marked in red.

'It should be. It's certainly one of the most difficult places to find if you don't know the area.' Emma hurried back into her room and slipped on her shoes. 'I'll fetch it while you get dressed.'

'Thanks. Oh, and can you bring me a printout of Mrs Groves's most recent notes? I don't want to go unprepared.'

'Will do.'

Emma ran down the stairs. There was a set of keys for the surgery on the hook by the door and she picked them up then snatched her coat off the peg. Although it was the end of March, the air felt frosty as she made her way to the surgery and let herself in. Once she'd turned off the alarm, she found the map and checked that the farm was marked on it. She groaned as she traced her finger along the route. As she'd thought, it was one of the most difficult places to reach.

After printing out a copy of Sarah Groves's notes, she ran back to the house. Daniel had started his car and was ready to leave by the time she got there. Emma hurried round to the passenger side and opened the door. 'Turn left as soon as we leave here, then right at the crossroads.'

'You don't need to come, Emma. So long as I have the map, I should be able to find the place.'

Emma shook her head as she slid into the seat. 'You can't map-read and navigate these roads. They're little more than cart tracks in places.'

She fastened her seat belt, hoping that he wasn't going

to argue with her as she really didn't feel like a confrontation at this time of the night. It was a relief when he put the car in gear and headed out of the drive.

'Seeing as you're here, can you read through Mrs Groves's notes,' he suggested as soon as they were on the road. 'Her husband said that it had been a textbook pregnancy so far, but I'd like to be sure. There's a torch in the glove box. You can use that instead of turning on the interior light.'

Emma nodded as she found the torch. It would make it easier for Daniel to see where he was going if he didn't have to contend with the glare from the interior lights. She shielded the end of the torch with her hand as she quickly read through the notes that had been made when Sarah Groves had last visited the surgery.

'There's nothing here to indicate a problem,' she told Daniel as they reached the crossroads and turned right. 'She was seen last week and her BP was fine. Nothing showed up in her urine sample either, and there was no sign of oedema.'

'How many weeks is she? I asked the husband but he was in such a state he couldn't remember.'

'Thirty-five,' Emma told him, checking the woman's chart.

'That's not too bad, is it? I know that technically a baby is considered premature if it's born before thirty-seven weeks, but it should be a decent enough weight by this stage.'

'I wonder why she's gone into labour. Did the husband say if she was bleeding?'

'No. I did ask him, but he was almost incoherent

and didn't seem to be taking much in. He just kept asking how soon I could get there.' She felt him glance at her. 'You're wondering if there's a problem with the placenta?'

'Yes.' Emma felt a shiver run down her spine when he correctly interpreted her thoughts. Once, the fact that they'd been so much in tune had delighted her, but now it filled her with alarm. She didn't want to share that kind of closeness with him ever again.

'It's one of the causes of premature labour so we certainly can't rule it out.' He slowed down and peered through the windscreen. 'There's another junction coming up. Which way now?'

'Straight on for about ten miles then we'll need to turn off the main road and head into hills,' she told him, checking the map.

'That's when the fun really starts, is it?' he asked with a laugh as he picked up speed again.

'It will be fine.'

'Spoken like someone who's used to tearing around the back of beyond. Jim told me that you've done several stints overseas in the last couple of years. How did you get into that sort of work?'

'Richard suggested it. He worked for an aid agency when he was a junior registrar and said it was invaluable experience.'

'Richard?'

'Richard Walker, my boss,' she explained.

'You obviously get on well with him,' he observed, and she frowned when she heard the edge in his voice.

She had the impression that something had displeased him, but had no idea what it could be.

'Yes, I do,' she said a shade defensively. 'All the team think very highly of him, in fact.'

'I see.' He changed gear then glanced at her and there was no sign of anything other than friendly interest on his face. 'Working overseas must be challenging, I imagine.'

'Sometimes.' She shrugged. 'It all depends where you're working. If you're based at a clinic, like the one I've just worked in, then it tends to be easier. The facilities are better, and there's usually more staff to help out than if you're working at a field hospital.'

'And do you enjoy surgery as much as you thought you would?'

Emma frowned. She had the strangest feeling that her answer was important to him and couldn't understand why. Why should it matter to Daniel if she was happy or not? He certainly hadn't cared about her happiness five years ago, had he?

The thought pierced a hole right through the protective shell she had built around her heart. It was an effort to respond when it felt as though it was in danger of cracking wide open. It was only pride that gave her the strength to carry on, pride plus a desire not to let him know how badly he had hurt her.

'Yes, I do. It's everything I hoped it would be.' She laughed wryly. 'I suppose I should thank you, Daniel. If you hadn't been so committed to your own career, I might have turned down the chance to become a surgeon and that would have been a huge mistake. I don't doubt that in time I would have come to regret my decision.'

CHAPTER FOUR

DANIEL drew up in front of the farmhouse and switched off the engine. Emma hadn't faltered as she had directed him along a series of increasingly narrow tracks. He knew that he would have had a much harder time finding the farm without her help but, contrarily, wished that she had stayed at home. At least then he wouldn't have to face up to the realisation that he had been right all along. Their relationship would never have survived if she had given up her dreams to be with him.

'I'll let Harry know that we're here.' She got out of the car and ran over to the house. The door was open and she didn't waste time knocking before she hurried inside.

Daniel got out and took his case out of the back. He also lifted out the pack of medical supplies that Jim kept ready for just such an emergency as this. There was no sign of Emma when he let himself into the house but he could hear voices coming from upstairs so headed in that direction and soon found himself in the main bedroom. A fair-haired man in his thirties, whom he assumed must be Harry Groves, was holding the hand of the woman lying on the bed. She was very pale and obviously in a great deal of pain. Emma was in the process of checking her pulse so Daniel left her to deal with that while he introduced himself.

'I'm Daniel Kennedy. I'm covering for Dr Haynes while he's in hospital.'

'So Emma said,' Harry replied. He looked anxiously at the door. 'Did you pass the ambulance on your way here?'

'No, but it may have taken a different route from us.' Daniel smiled reassuringly at the couple. 'Can you tell me exactly what's happened?'

'I started having pains after tea but thought it was because of the way the baby was lying,' Sarah Groves explained. 'I lay down on the settee for a while and that seemed to help, but then the pains started again, worse than ever. That's when I discovered I was bleeding. I told Harry to phone the midwife, but she was out at another call so he phoned for an ambulance.' Her voice shook. 'When they said it would take over an hour for it to get here, he rang the surgery.'

'You did exactly the right thing,' Daniel said soothingly. He glanced at Emma, hoping his feelings didn't show. Maybe it was foolish to feel upset but he couldn't help it. In a tiny corner of his heart, he had nurtured the hope that their love could have overcome any obstacle. Even though he hadn't been prepared to take that risk, it had been something to cling to, but now he could see how stupid it had been. His relationship with Emma would have ended the same way as his parents' had done if they had stayed together.

'We need to know how much longer the ambulance is going to be,' he said with a heavy heart.

'I'll get onto Ambulance Control and see if they can give us an update,' Emma offered immediately.

She left the bedroom and Daniel turned his attention to Sarah again, relieved to have something to focus on apart from his aching heart. 'Has the bleeding stopped now?'

Sarah shook her head, her pretty face clouded with worry. 'No. In fact, I think it's got worse in the last ten minutes or so.'

'I'll just take a look, if that's all right with you.'

Daniel drew back the bedding, struggling to hide his dismay when he saw the bright red pool that had collected on the sheets. He fetched the foetal stethoscope from the pack of emergency medical supplies and listened to the baby's heartbeat. It was slightly slower than it should have been but not worryingly so, which was a relief. He had just finished when Emma came back and he could tell immediately that it wasn't good news when she beckoned him over to the door.

'What's happened?' he demanded.

'Apparently, the ambulance has had a puncture. They're waiting for the breakdown truck, so Ambulance Control has dispatched a second vehicle.'

Daniel rolled his eyes. 'Which means we're starting from scratch. It could be another hour before an ambulance gets here.'

'It looks like it.' Emma looked at Sarah. 'How is she?'

'She's lost a lot of blood. I'm going to set up a drip,

which should help, but I'm not happy with the way things are going.'

'How about the baby?'

'Foetal heartbeat is slightly slower than I would like it to be. We'll need to keep a close check on what's happening.'

'It looks like a placental abruption, doesn't it?'

'Yes, that's my guess too. At least part of the placenta has become detached from the wall of the uterus.' He sighed. 'If we were able to perform an ultrasound scan then we could tell how bad the abruption is, but at the moment we're batting in the dark.'

'What's going on, Doctor? I may not have seen a human baby being born before but I've delivered umpteen lambs and I know this isn't normal.'

Daniel turned when Harry came to join them. The farmer was obviously worried and Daniel led him out onto the landing. The last thing he wanted was to upset Sarah any more. 'The bleeding could be a sign that the placenta has become partially detached from the wall of the uterus.'

'But why?' Harry demanded. 'Sarah's been fit as a fiddle up to now, so why on earth should this have happened right out of the blue?'

'It's impossible to say. These things just happen sometimes and there's no explanation as to why.'

Daniel glanced back into the room. Emma was bending over the bed while she inserted a cannula into the back of Sarah's hand. Her face was set with concentration, even though she must have performed the procedure many times before. Daniel felt a wave of emotion wash over him as he watched her. He might regret having to let her go but he knew that he would do the same thing all over again. He simply couldn't bear it if Emma ended up hating him for ruining her life.

Emma could feel Daniel watching her but she didn't look up. She felt too emotionally raw to take that risk. Had Daniel ever regretted breaking up with her? she wondered as she taped the cannula into place. Had he ever missed her? Even though she knew how stupid it was, she couldn't help wishing that he'd felt *something*.

Sarah moaned softly, clutching her stomach, and Emma quickly returned her thoughts to what was going on. 'Are the pains coming at regular intervals?' she asked, placing her own hand on the woman's distended abdomen.

'I don't know…they seem to be coming closer together,' Sarah murmured.

Emma kept her hand on Sarah's abdomen and felt it tense as her uterus contracted. There was no doubt in her mind that Sarah was in labour. She reached for the foetal stethoscope and checked the baby's heartbeat, frowning when she discovered how slow it was. It was a sign that the baby was in distress and that they needed to take immediate steps to help it. She beckoned Daniel over to the bed.

'The baby's heartbeat has dropped. We need to deliver it as soon as possible.'

'A Caesarean section, you mean?'

'Yes. I know it's not ideal to do it here, but we don't have a choice,' she said, hoping he wouldn't disagree with her. 'Even if the ambulance arrives in the next few minutes, it will take at least another hour to get Sarah to hospital. That's way too long in my opinion.'

'You're right, we can't afford to wait that long.' His dark brows rose. 'It's been ages since I did my obstetrics rotation. I assisted with a couple of sections then but I've not done any since. How about you?'

'I did one a couple of weeks ago,' Emma told him.

'Great! You lead and I'll assist.'

It was all arranged with the minimum of fuss. Although it made sense for her to take the lead in view of her surgical background, Emma was a little surprised that Daniel had suggested it. It certainly didn't gel with the idea of him wanting to cover himself with glory, did it?

There was no time to dwell on the thought, however. Emma unpacked the emergency medical supplies while Daniel explained what they were going to do. Sarah and Harry were naturally concerned, but once Daniel had told them that their baby was in distress, they agreed to go ahead. In a very short time, everything was organised.

Emma draped the bed with clean sheets while Daniel attended to the anaesthetic. Harry showed her where the bathroom was so she could scrub up. Daniel did the same and then they helped each other glove up. Harry had elected to stay with his wife so once Emma had swabbed Sarah's abdomen with antiseptic solution, she set to work, knowing there was no time to lose.

Daniel handed her a scalpel, standing back as she made a horizontal incision just above the bikini line.

Any qualms she may have had about carrying out the procedure soon disappeared as she focused on what needed doing. Within a very short time she was able to lift the baby out of Sarah's womb and hand it to Daniel, who wrapped it in a clean towel and carried it over to the chest of drawers that was doubling as an examination table. There was a moment when they all held their breath and then the baby cried, a tentative sound at first that soon grew louder.

'Congratulations!' Emma smiled at the couple. 'You have a lovely little boy.'

'A boy?' Harry repeated. He appeared completely shocked after what had happened and stared at her in confusion. 'We decided that we'd wait until the baby was born to find out what it was, but we were convinced we were having a little girl. Are you sure it's a boy?'

'Oh, yes, there's definitely no mistake about that. He's got all the necessary bits and pieces,' Emma replied with a laugh. She delivered the placenta and checked that there were no bits missing from it then set about stitching up the wound. Daniel brought the baby over to the bed while she was doing so.

'So who gets first go at holding him?' he asked.

'Sarah,' Harry said promptly. He bent and kissed his wife tenderly on the cheek. 'If it wasn't for Sarah, we wouldn't have this little fellow.'

Daniel placed the tiny mite in his mother's arms, smiling as he watched Sarah pull back the folds of towel to perform the age-old ritual of counting his fingers and toes. Emma looked away when she felt a lump come to her throat. Once upon a time she had imagined just such a scene, only the baby whose toes were being counted had been hers and Daniel's. That was how much she had loved him, enough to want to give him a child.

Tears stung her eyes as she busied herself, stitching up. Even though she was over him, it still hurt to recall how much she had once loved him. She had wanted the whole lot with Daniel—marriage, motherhood, years and years of happily-ever-after as a family.

Would she ever have a family now? she wondered suddenly. Ever experience the joy of holding her own child in her arms?

She tried to picture it but it was impossible to imagine a life not dictated by her work. It made her question if she was right to devote every waking minute to her job, and it was worrying to be beset by doubts. For the past five years her work had been what had kept her centred, what had given meaning to her life, but all of a sudden she found herself wanting more, a life that wasn't shaped by the demands of her profession, and it was unsettling. However, the worst thing of all was that it was being around Daniel that had triggered such thoughts.

It was an effort to push it to the back of her mind as she finished off. She made Sarah comfortable and then Daniel helped her clear everything away. By the time they'd finished, the ambulance was pulling up outside. Sarah was reluctant to leave the house at first until Emma gently explained that she and baby Thomas needed to be checked over in the hospital's maternity unit. Although little Thomas appeared to be fit and healthy, technically he was premature, and Sarah herself had lost a lot of blood: it would be foolish to take any risks at this stage.

She and Daniel waited while the family were loaded on board the ambulance then they got into the car and followed it back to the main road. It roared away, taking the opposite direction from where they were heading.

'All in all, I'd say that was a good night's work, wouldn't you?'

Daniel's voice echoed with satisfaction and nothing else. If he'd experienced even a fraction of the anguish she had felt earlier then it certainly wasn't apparent, Emma thought sickly as she murmured her agreement. Maybe they had never discussed having children but in her mind the two were linked—when you loved someone, you wanted to have a child with them. It proved beyond any doubt that Daniel's feelings for her hadn't been what he had claimed. Although she should have felt glad that she was rid of him, oddly enough it hurt to have yet more proof of the way he had lied to her.

Daniel knew that he would remember that night for a long time to come. Seeing little Thomas make his appearance in the world had touched him in a way he had not expected it to. All he'd been able to think about was how wonderful it would have been if he'd been watching his own child—his and *Emma*'s son—being born.

He glanced at her as they reached the outskirts of the town but she wasn't looking at him. Her eyes were closed, although he didn't think she was asleep. Had she been moved by tonight's events, wondered how it would have been if it had been their child? He doubted it. Emma had made her feelings perfectly clear when she had told him that she was glad they had parted. She certainly wasn't wasting her time by thinking about what might have been!

A feeling of dejection swept over him as he drew up in front of the house. He'd known it would be difficult to see Emma again when he had agreed to run the practice, but he had never imagined that he would feel this wretched. The only way he could hope to get through the coming weeks was to forget what had happened in the past and focus on what was happening at the present moment. And the one thing that was crystal clear was that Emma had moved on.

Daniel followed her into the house and headed straight for the kitchen to make himself a cup of tea in the probably vain hope that it would give him a much-needed boost. He hadn't expected Emma to join him and looked round in surprise when he heard her follow him into the room. 'Would you like a drink as well?'

'Please. I don't know if it's the excitement of what happened tonight or the fact that all that travelling has upset my body clock, but I'm too wide awake to sleep.' She tossed her coat over a chair and went to the cupboard. 'I wonder if there's any hot chocolate... Ah, yes, there it is.'

She stood on tiptoe to try and reach the jar of drinking chocolate but it was just out of her grasp. Daniel crossed the room and lifted it down off the shelf. 'Here you go, shorty,' he said without thinking.

'I'm not short, just tidily packaged,' she retorted, as

she'd done so many times when he had teased her about her height.

Daniel felt the blood rush to his head. He remembered only too well what came next, how he would apologise for the supposed slight with a kiss. His eyes flew to Emma's face and his blood pressure zoomed several more notches up the scale when he saw that she too remembered what had used to happen. Whether it was that or the fact that his emotions were already in turmoil he didn't know but all of a sudden he found himself bending towards her until he was close enough to feel the moistness of her breath cloud on his lips.

'Emma.'

He wasn't sure if he actually spoke her name out loud or not. He was beyond hearing by that point, beyond everything including reason. What did it matter if he had just resolved to forget about the past? It wasn't a sin if he changed his mind, was it? All he wanted was to feel her lips under his once more, taste their sweetness, savour their warmth and softness. One kiss was all he asked for, just one kiss to stave off the pain that was gnawing away at his heart. Surely it wasn't wrong to allow himself this one brief moment of pleasure?

His head dipped until merely a millimetre separated them. Daniel could feel the heat of her skin now, smell the scent of the soap she'd used. Memories crowded his mind but he no longer needed to recall the past when he had a chance to create a whole new delicious present...

His mouth touched hers and the shock of the contact almost brought him to his knees. He could feel the blood rushing through his veins like liquid fire, feel the heat that invaded every cell in his body, and groaned. His hands lifted as he went to draw her closer so that he could feel the soft curves of her body moulding themselves against the hardness of his, but he never got the chance. With a tiny cry of alarm, Emma pushed him away and ran from the room.

Daniel leant back against the worktop, needing its support as all the strength suddenly drained from his body. He desperately wanted to go after her but he knew it would be the wrong thing to do. Maybe he could persuade her to let him kiss her again—possibly even do more than kiss her—but it wouldn't be fair. Perhaps there was still some vestige of attraction between them, but it didn't alter the fact that he could so easily ruin her life even now. Emma needed to focus on her job now more than ever or she could end up losing everything she had worked so hard for. Nothing was worth that risk, certainly not his own selfish desires.

Emma slammed the bedroom door, scarcely able to believe what had happened. She wanted to blame Daniel for it but she was too honest to claim that she hadn't been partly at fault. She had wanted him to kiss her, wanted it so much that her cheeks burned with shame. Hadn't she learned anything from past experiences? Did she really want to find herself right back where she'd been five years ago, her life in tatters, her heart broken?

She pressed her fist against her mouth to stem the sob that threatened to escape it. She refused to cry, refused to risk her hard-won composure by breaking down. So what if she had been tempted for a moment? She had come to her senses in time, hadn't she? If anything, it proved that she could handle this situation. Daniel's kiss may have been tempting but she had realised the risks, assessed the damage it could cause, and taken steps to stop what was happening. She should be proud of herself for what she had done.

The thought steadied her. She quickly undressed and got into bed, pulling the quilt up to her chin. It was gone midnight and she needed to get some sleep if she hoped to be fit enough to help out at morning surgery...

The sound of footsteps climbing the stairs made her eyes fly open. She hadn't thought to ask Daniel which room he was using and found herself holding her breath as she waited for him to reach the landing. The house was large and there were a number of empty bedrooms, including the room next to hers.

Her breath whooshed out in relief when she heard his footsteps fade. He was obviously using the guest room, which was on the opposite side of the house. For some reason, she felt safer knowing that he wasn't sleeping in the room next to hers. She had resisted temptation once tonight and she didn't intend to put herself to the test again. She might not like the idea, but she had to face the fact that she might not have the strength to hold out a second time.

CHAPTER FIVE

'THAT'S excellent news. Thank you for letting me know... Yes, of course. I'll pass on your message.'

Daniel replaced the phone and leant back in his chair. Morning surgery had ended and he'd been getting ready to go out to some house calls when Harry Groves had phoned to tell him that Sarah and baby Thomas had been given a clean bill of health by the consultant at the hospital. Harry had asked him to pass on the news to Emma, which he would do, but he needed a few minutes' breathing space before he sought her out.

He sighed as he tipped back his chair and stared at the ceiling. The memory of what had happened the previous night had continued to haunt him. He kept remembering that kiss and how sweet it had been, even though he knew how stupid it was. He had made a mistake by kissing her and he had no intention of repeating it, so it would be better if he put it out of his mind; however, it was proving to be easier said than done. Every time his thoughts wandered, he could feel Emma's mouth under his and it was driving him mad!

'Ruth said there's quite a lot of calls to do today, so do you want me to help?'

The sound of Emma's voice almost made him tip over the chair. Daniel hurriedly returned it to all four legs as he turned towards the door. He'd made a point of leaving the house extra early that morning so it was the first time he'd seen her that day. Now he found his senses running riot as he took stock of her slender figure encased in a neat grey skirt and a crisp white blouse. It may not have been the sexiest of outfits, granted, but it definitely did something for him.

'No, it's fine.' Daniel dragged his unruly thoughts back into line again and prayed they would stay there. That sort of thinking wasn't going to help one jot. 'I imagine you want to visit your uncle this afternoon, so I'll do the calls.'

'Well, if you're sure?' She gave him a moment to reconsider then shrugged. 'I'll do them tomorrow, then. OK?'

'Fine, although don't feel that you have to. After all, Jim asked me to cover for him.'

He'd only meant to point out that she wasn't under any obligation to work in the surgery. Although he appreciated the offer, she had come home for a holiday and it seemed a shame that her plans should be scuppered. However, that obviously wasn't how she took it. Daniel's heart sank when he saw the mutinous set to her mouth.

'I'm very much aware of that, thank you. Don't worry, Daniel, I don't intend to step on your toes. So far as my aunt and uncle are concerned, you're the knight in shining armour who's come to rescue them. Let's just hope they still feel the same way in a few weeks' time.'

'Meaning what precisely?' he demanded, stung by the comment.

She shrugged. 'That I still find it hard to believe it was purely altruism that brought you here. There has to be something in it for you, personally or professionally, otherwise why would you give up so much of your free time to work in the back of beyond?'

'I see. So what do you think I'm hoping to gain from it?' he asked, refusing to let her see how much it hurt to hear her judge him so harshly. Maybe it was his own fault that she had such a low opinion of him, but if she had loved him—as she'd once claimed—surely she shouldn't have been so willing to believe the worst?

'I don't know. I haven't worked that out yet.' She gave him a cool smile. 'But when I do, you'll be the first to know.'

She left the room, leaving the door wide open. Daniel listened to the sound of her footsteps receding along the corridor and sighed. He could go after her and tell her that she was wrong, that his motives were of the very highest order, but she wouldn't believe him. She wanted to think badly of him, wanted to bury any feelings she'd had for him under a blanket of mistrust. It shouldn't be that difficult, not after what he had done. She must be ninety-nine per cent certain that he was a rat of the first order, but obviously she was keen to add that precious last one per cent to the score. And finding out that he had an ulterior motive for offering to cover for Jim would be the perfect way to round up the total, so help him.

Emma went back to the house and made herself a sandwich. She took it up to her room, unwilling to stick around in case Daniel decided to have his lunch before he did the calls. She was still smarting from their most recent confrontation and needed time to calm down before she saw him again.

She sighed as she took a bite of the bread. It would take more than a few hours to soothe her feelings where Daniel was concerned. Every time she spoke to him, she felt so churned up inside that it was hard to maintain an outward show of composure. Maybe it was always difficult to relax with someone you'd once been heavily involved with—she really didn't know.

Although she'd been out with several different men in the last few years, she had never had a serious relationship with any of them. She had told herself that she was too busy with her career to worry about that side of her life but it wasn't true. Her experiences with Daniel had put her off, made her wary of getting involved with anyone again. However, she couldn't allow the past to continue influencing her or she would never be truly free of him. She had to put what had happened behind her. And mean it.

Emma finished her lunch, wondering if this might prove to be a turning point. Discovering that Daniel was working here had been a shock but it could turn out to be a good thing. Seeing him again had awoken a lot of feelings she'd thought were dead and now she would be able to dispatch them for ever. And if she did find out that he had his own agenda for agreeing to cover for her uncle then so much the better. It would put the final nail in the coffin of their relationship.

* * *

Daniel got through the house calls faster than he'd expected. He checked his watch after he left his final call and realised that he had time to drop into the hospital. It would only take him ten minutes or so to drive there and he would like to see how Jim was faring.

He started his car, refusing to speculate as to how Emma would feel about him joining her at her uncle's bedside. She'd made it perfectly clear yesterday that she hadn't wanted him there, but it was hard luck. He just wanted to reassure the older man that everything was going smoothly, or at least everything to do with the running of the *practice*. So far as his relationship with Emma, well, it would be better not to mention that.

He managed to find a parking space close to the main doors, which was a minor miracle. Hurrying inside, he made his way to the lift and pressed the button. It arrived promptly and he was about to step inside when he heard someone calling his name. Glancing round, he spotted Emma crossing the foyer, carrying two cardboard containers of coffee. She glared at him as she drew closer.

'What are you doing here?'

'I came to see how Jim was doing,' he replied evenly, putting out his hand to stop the lift doors closing.

'He's fine,' she said shortly, stepping inside. 'I had a word with his consultant and he's very happy with how things went.'

'That's good to hear.' Daniel stepped into the lift. Pressing the button for their floor, he turned to her. 'Your aunt must be very relieved.'

'Of course.' Her tone was clipped. 'What Uncle Jim

needs now is plenty of rest. What he doesn't need is a lot of people visiting him.'

'I agree. However, he'll be able to rest more easily once he's sure that everything is running smoothly at the surgery.'

'I've already assured him that everything is fine.' She tipped back her head, a hint of challenge in her eyes. 'It doesn't need both of us to give him a progress report, Daniel. I'm perfectly capable of doing that by myself.'

'I'm sure you are, but knowing Jim he will still worry in case you're keeping something from him.' He shrugged. 'Jim knows that I'll tell him the truth.'

'Tell the truth and shame the devil. Is that the maxim you live by, Daniel, or only when it suits you?'

'I do my best to be truthful at all times,' he said quietly.

A flash of hurt crossed her face. 'Really? Then all I can say is that there must be more than one version of the truth in your world.'

The lift came to a halt and she got out before he could reply, although what he could have said was open to question. Daniel's heart was heavy as he followed her because he knew what she was alluding to. Five years ago he had told her that he'd loved her, but he'd also told her that his career had meant more to him than she would ever do. No wonder she was so reluctant to believe him.

Jim Haynes was in the intensive care unit where his heart and other bodily functions were being closely monitored. He was awake and looked remarkably chirpy for someone who had undergone major surgery in the past twenty-four hours. He smiled with genuine pleasure when he saw Daniel. 'Ah, good to see you, Daniel. At least I know you won't fuss over me like these two insist on doing.'

Daniel laughed. 'I shall try my very best not to fuss, I promise you.' He pulled up a chair and sat down, trying to ignore the fact that Emma was sitting next to him. He had to stop being so aware of her and treat her as he would any colleague, politely and civilly. If he could stick to that there wouldn't be a problem.

'Good.' Jim frowned. 'So how is everything at the surgery? Emma insists that it's all going swimmingly but I doubt if she'd tell me even if it weren't. The main thing is, are you coping?'

'Yes, we are.' Daniel leant forward, feeling heat flash along his veins when his arm brushed against Emma's. Even though he was wearing a jacket he could feel the contact in every cell. He cleared his throat, keeping his gaze centred on the other man so that it wouldn't wander in her direction. It would be silly to check if she had felt that same flicker of awareness run through her.

He gave Jim a complete rundown about what had been happening. He sensed that Emma wasn't happy about him going into so much detail but he guessed that it would worry Jim more if he tried to gloss over how busy it had been. He realised he was right when he saw the frown disappear from the older man's face after he finished.

'Excellent. It's good to know the practice is in such safe hands,' Jim declared. 'Now I can let Margaret whisk me away to the cottage to recuperate without having to worry about what's going on here.'

'How did you know that I was planning on taking you to the cottage?' Margaret demanded. 'I've never even mentioned it!'

'After forty years of marriage, my dear, I can read you like an open book,' Jim told her, winking at them.

Everyone laughed at that and then Daniel stood up. 'I don't want to tire you out so I won't stay any longer. Take care of yourself, Jim, and do what your doctor orders.'

'Oh, I shall.' Jim raised his eyes to the heavens. 'I don't have a choice with this pair standing guard over me!'

Daniel was still laughing as he left ICU. He made his way along the corridor, pausing when he heard Emma calling him. He waited for her to catch him up, wondering what misdemeanour he was guilty of this time. He was already steeling himself for another tongue-lashing when she came to a halt.

'I just wanted to say that you were right. Uncle Jim did need to hear it from you that everything was all right at the surgery.'

'Oh…right…thank you.'

Daniel was so shocked that he couldn't think of anything else to say. She gave him a tight little smile then turned and hurried away. He carried on walking, only realising that he must have walked straight past the lifts when he came to the end of the corridor and could go no further. He turned around and went back the way he'd come, thinking about what Emma had said.

Maybe he was reading too much into it but it was good to know that she thought he'd done something right for a change.

He groaned as he punched the button to summon the lift. How pathetic was that? A few words of praise from Emma and all of a sudden the world seemed like a much brighter place!

Emma was home well in time for evening surgery. Her aunt had returned with her but only to pack a bag. Margaret Haynes had decided to stay at a friend's house close to the hospital to save her having to make the journey back and forth. It meant that Emma and Daniel would be on their own again that night and for many more nights to come.

Emma washed her hands and then made her way round to the surgery, determined that she wasn't going to waste her time worrying about it. They were both adults and more than capable of sharing the house for the next few weeks. She was due back in Scotland in just over a month's time so it wasn't as though the situation was going to last indefinitely. Obviously, if she'd needed to take over the practice while her uncle recuperated, she would have had to arrange compassionate leave, but with Daniel here that wouldn't be necessary. He would be able to run things until Uncle Jim was well enough to return to work.

She frowned, wondering once again why Daniel had agreed to give up so much of his time to help. Although she knew that he had got on well with her uncle while he'd been doing his GP training, she hadn't realised the two men had kept in touch. Her aunt and uncle had never mentioned Daniel over the years and she certainly hadn't asked about him. She had wanted to expunge the whole unhappy episode from her life rather than dwell on it. It made her feel uneasy all of a sudden to wonder if Daniel had ever asked about her.

Emma quickly dismissed the thought as she pushed open the surgery door. Daniel had demonstrated his lack of interest five years ago in the most effective way possible!

'I'm afraid evening surgery doesn't start until four.'

Emma glanced up when she realised someone was speaking to her. She smiled at the young woman behind the reception desk. 'You must be Claire.'

'That's right. How did you know…? Oh, you must be Emma!' The other woman blushed. 'I'm so sorry. Ruth told me that you'd probably be coming in tonight, but I was expecting someone *much* older.' She clapped her hand over her mouth, obviously wishing she hadn't said that, and Emma laughed.

'Thank you. I shall take that as a compliment. Believe me, some days I feel as old as Methuselah, so it's nice to know that I don't actually look it!' She glanced around the waiting room. 'Is Ruth not in tonight?' she asked, neatly changing the subject to spare Claire's blushes.

'Yes, but she might be a bit late. A filling fell out of one of her teeth and the dentist could only fit her in this afternoon as he's on holiday for the rest of the week,' Claire explained. 'She asked me if I'd hold the fort until she gets here. I hope that's all right.'

'Of course it is.' Emma smiled at her. 'If you have

any problems, give me a buzz. I used to work on the reception desk when I was a student and I might be able to help.'

'Thanks. That's really kind of you.' Claire beamed at her. 'Daniel told me the same thing, to buzz him if I got stuck. It's the first time I've manned the desk on my own, so it's a relief to know that I can call on you two.'

'No problem.'

Emma drummed up a smile, although she could feel her hackles rising. Trust Daniel to try and worm his way into the receptionist's good books, she thought sourly, then realised how two-faced that sounded when it would appear she had done the same thing. However, her offer had been a genuine one, she assured herself as she made her way to the consulting room, aimed at making life simpler for all of them. Whereas Daniel's had undoubtedly been a way to curry favour.

She sat down at the desk, refusing to admit that she was being unfair to him. Maybe she didn't have any proof, but everything Daniel did, he did for a reason. Look at the way he had pursued her five years ago. At the time, it had seemed that their feelings had arisen so spontaneously that she had never questioned if his were genuine. Even after they'd parted she had clung to the belief that he had genuinely felt something for her, although obviously not enough to put her before his precious career. It had taken a while before she had accepted that he had merely used her feelings for him to get her into his bed.

Emma bit her lip. It might have happened a long time ago, but it still hurt to know that she had been nothing more to him than a convenient and willing bedmate.

CHAPTER SIX

THE week came to an end and Saturday arrived. As Daniel made his way downstairs, he couldn't help wishing there was a morning surgery that day. At least if he was working, he could stay out of Emma's way.

He sighed as he went into the kitchen. To say that relations between him and Emma were strained was an understatement. She only spoke to him when it was absolutely necessary and even then it was hard to get more than a dozen words out of her. He had hoped that her attitude towards him might be softening after he'd been to visit her uncle, but obviously not. He wished he could think of a way to ease the situation but it was impossible when every time he tried to talk to her, she cut him dead.

He filled the kettle with water and popped some bread into the toaster, wondering for the umpteenth time how he could gain her trust. He wasn't a threat to her, yet she insisted on treating him like some kind of pariah, and it was very hard to take. He knew that he had hurt her but he'd been hurt too; it didn't seem fair that he should have to suffer when he had been trying to do what was right.

Daniel gave himself a brisk mental shake. Feeling sorry for himself wouldn't help. What he needed was something to take his mind off the situation and put him in a more positive frame of mind. It was a glorious day and a good long walk in the hills should blow away a lot of cobwebs.

He made himself a pot of coffee then sat down at the table to eat his breakfast. He had almost finished when Emma appeared and he sighed when he saw her stop as soon as she spotted him sitting at the table. Even the local axe murderer would receive a warmer welcome than him! He dropped the last piece of toast back onto his plate and stood up.

'Just give me a couple of seconds to wash my dishes and I'll get out of your way.'

'There's no need,' she said sharply. 'You're perfectly entitled to finish your breakfast.'

'Thank you.' It was impossible to keep the sarcasm out of his voice. 'However, I seem to have lost my appetite all of a sudden.'

He carried his dishes over to the sink. He knew that Emma was still standing in the doorway and felt pain stab through him. Had it reached the point now where she couldn't even bear to be in the same room as him?

The thought seemed to set light to his temper and he turned on the tap with far more force than was necessary. A jet of water hit the edge of his cup and bounced back up, soaking the front of his T-shirt. Daniel cursed under his breath as he hastily turned off the water. That was all he needed!

'Here.'

A hand suddenly appeared, offering him a towel. Daniel took it, trying to hide his surprise at such a conciliatory gesture. He mopped the front of his T-shirt then glanced round. Emma was standing beside him and for the first time in days she wasn't giving off the usual icy vibes. She looked up and his breath caught when he saw that her lips were twitching.

'That tap's always been a nuisance. I've had the odd soaking over the years,' she told him, struggling to contain her amusement.

'I doubt if you've been as wet as I am,' he replied drolly, shaking his head so that beads of water flew out of his hair.

'No, I haven't.' She gave a choked little gurgle. 'I know I shouldn't laugh, but if you'd seen the expression on your face...'

She burst out laughing and Daniel felt the cold knotty feeling that had been building up inside him for days suddenly start to unravel. He grinned at her, his hazel eyes sparkling with amusement.

'Think it's funny to see someone almost drowning, do you?'

'Yes... I mean, no. Of course not.' She bit her lip, doing her best to behave with suitable decorum.

Daniel chuckled wickedly. Turning on the tap, he scooped up a handful of water. 'I wonder how funny you'd find it if you were on the receiving end of an impromptu shower?'

'Daniel, you wouldn't!'

'Oh, wouldn't I?' He let a few drops of water dribble

onto her bare arm, grinning when he heard her squeal in alarm. 'Are you sure about that?'

'Yes, I am.' She stared up at him and he could see the conviction in her eyes. 'You wouldn't be that cruel!'

'No, I wouldn't.' He opened his hand and let the water flow into the sink, feeling the knotty feeling start to build up inside him again. 'It's good to know that you don't think I'm completely rotten to the core, Emma.'

She didn't say anything to that and he didn't wait around while she thought of something either. He left the kitchen, taking the stairs two at a time as he headed for his room. Why in heaven's name had he said that, let her know how much it hurt to be treated as an outcast? It wouldn't achieve anything, definitely wouldn't improve her opinion of him. The last thing he wanted was for it to appear as though he was looking for sympathy!

He cursed roundly, stopping dead when he heard a knock on the door. Striding across the room, he flung it open, too angry with himself to care about putting up a front. 'Yes?'

'I just wanted to say that I'm sorry.'

Her voice was so low that it was a moment before Daniel realised what she had said. He frowned, unsure where this was leading. 'You're sorry?'

'Yes. About the way I…I've behaved recently.' She tipped back her head and looked him squarely in the eyes. 'I agreed to call a truce and I haven't kept to that. I apologise.'

'I know how difficult this situation is, Emma,' he said quietly, more touched than he cared to admit. 'I find it hard, too.'

'Do you?' She looked at him in surprise and he sighed.

'Yes. I can't just forget what happened five years ago. You meant a lot to me, Emma.'

'Did I?'

'Of course you did.' He frowned when he saw the uncertainty on her face. Surely she must know how he had felt, even though he had pushed her away? He had never tried to hide his feelings—how could he have done? She had meant the whole world to him and all of a sudden it seemed important she understood that.

'I cared a lot about you, Emma,' he said quickly, wishing that he didn't have to use such a milk-and-water term to describe how he'd felt. Claiming he'd cared barely touched on the way he had really felt about her but what else could he say? Admitting that he had loved her with every fibre of his being wasn't what she wanted to hear. His heart ached as he repeated it with as much conviction as he dared. 'I really and truly cared about you.'

'But not as much as you cared about your career.' She smiled and his heart filled with sadness when he saw the bleakness in her eyes. 'Don't worry, Daniel, I understand. And as I said the other day, it's probably a good thing that we parted. Oh, I won't pretend that it didn't hurt at the time because it did. A lot. But I'm both older and wiser, and I can see the problems it would have caused if we'd stayed together.'

'You would have regretted giving up your dreams of becoming a surgeon?' he said flatly.

'Yes. I love my job and I'm good at it, too.' She gave a little shrug. 'It was the right decision for both of us.'

'I'm glad you think so,' he said roughly. Maybe he should have been relieved to hear her say that, but all he felt was a terrible emptiness. He couldn't help wishing that he had been brave enough—or foolish enough—to take a chance and see what would happen, and it shocked him to find himself entertaining such a crazy idea. It was an effort to concentrate when she continued.

'I do. I have a job I love, good friends and a nice home. I have everything I want, in fact.'

'How about love and marriage?' he asked, then could have bitten off his tongue for asking such a personal question. Emma's love life had nothing to do with him.

'Not on my agenda at the present time. It's hard enough for a woman to establish herself in surgery without adding a husband and a family to the equation, although I haven't ruled them out completely.' She shrugged. 'If they happen at some point down the line, that's fine, but if not then I can live with it. How about you? Is there anyone special in your life?'

'No. My job seems to take up most of my time, too,' he said, not willing to admit that he had never considered the idea of marriage after they had parted.

'Still determined to set up in private practice one day?' She smiled but he could tell from her tone what she thought of the idea.

'Maybe.' He shrugged, unable to add to his guilt by deliberately misleading her again. 'Who knows what could happen in the future?'

'Who, indeed? But I'm sure you'll do everything in your power to achieve your ambitions, Daniel, won't you?'

Daniel's heart sank when he heard the suspicion in her voice. It seemed that their brief moment of harmony was over and they were back to where they had started, with Emma mistrusting his motives. Suddenly, he couldn't bear it any longer. He had to set matters straight and to hell with the consequences. 'Look, Emma, you're completely—'

He never had a chance to finish because at that moment the phone rang. Emma excused herself and went to answer it. Daniel guessed from what she said that it was her aunt calling so went back into his room. He found himself a sweater and a waterproof jacket because the weather was very changeable at this time of the year. Emma was still on the phone when he headed to the stairs; she gave him a curt little nod as he passed her then turned away, concentrating on what her aunt was saying.

Daniel left the house and walked into the town centre; there was a footpath beside the church that led up into the hills. He set off at a brisk pace, hoping the fresh air and exercise would soothe him, but it was hard to enjoy the peace and quiet when his mind was in turmoil. He hated to think that Emma was so suspicious of him but what could he do? He had forfeited her trust when he had told her that his career had meant more to him than she had done, and it was doubtful if he could win it back. Although it hurt like hell, he had to accept that Emma would never trust him again.

Emma found it hard to settle after she'd spoken to her aunt. Aunt Margaret had told her that two of her uncle's friends were planning on visiting him that afternoon. As the number of visitors to the IC unit was strictly limited, Emma had immediately offered to wait until the following day. Now she had a free day ahead of her and suddenly found herself wondering what to do. Although there were jobs that needed doing in the house, she felt too restless to spend the day indoors. Maybe a walk would help to work off some of her excess energy.

She fetched her jacket and found an old pair of walking boots in the hall cupboard. Although she wasn't planning on going too far, she found herself taking all the usual precautions that her aunt and uncle had drummed into her over the years. The weather in the Dales could be very changeable and it was better to be prepared rather than come unstuck.

She made some sandwiches and a flask of coffee and packed them into a small haversack. After adding a map and a compass, she checked that her mobile phone was charged. Although reception was patchy in the Dales, it could come in useful. As she let herself out of the back door, she could feel her spirits lifting. It had been ages since she'd been for a good long tramp across the hills and she was suddenly looking forward to it.

The air was cool as she set off across the stile that led to the lower slopes of the hills. There were dozens of footpaths criss-crossing the area, but Emma didn't hesitate. She'd done this walk many times before and remembered the route even though it had been at least five years since she'd last been along it. She and Daniel had come this way one Sunday morning and had had a picnic at the top of the hill. And after they had finished eating they had made love, right there in the open with only the blue sky above them.

Emma blinked when she realised that she couldn't see properly. Running her hand over her eyes, she wiped away tears. She wasn't going to cry, certainly wasn't going to waste the day by thinking about the past. It was the present that mattered, nothing else. As she'd told Daniel, she liked her life the way it was and was glad that she hadn't given up her dreams for him.

She walked for almost two hours then decided to stop for a break when she reached Pilgrim's Point, a local beauty spot. Finding a sheltered area in the lea of the huge rock that marked the spot, she unzipped her jacket and laid it on the ground then sat down. Uncapping the flask, she poured herself a cup of coffee, sighing appreciatively as she inhaled the fragrant aroma. Without the usual traffic fumes to clog up her nose, everything seemed to smell so much better.

She had almost finished the coffee when she heard someone coming along the path close to where she was sitting. It was a popular route with walkers and she wasn't surprised that someone else had decided to take advantage of the weather. Glancing round, she caught a glimpse of a figure heading towards her before he disappeared into a dip in the land, but it was enough for her to recognise him. What on earth was Daniel doing here? Surely he hadn't followed her, had he? Emma's temper was already creeping up the scale when Daniel reappeared. He stopped dead and she saw the surprise on his face when he spotted her.

'Emma! What on earth are you doing here? I thought you were going to visit your uncle this afternoon?'

'Some friends of Uncle Jim's are visiting him so I decided to go for a walk instead,' she replied curtly. Although it was obvious from his reaction that he hadn't followed her, she still felt annoyed. She had been hoping for a few Daniel-free hours and it was irritating to have him turn up like this. She glowered at him. 'I was hoping to enjoy a bit of peace and quiet on my own.'

'Don't let me stop you,' he said calmly, but she saw the hurt in his eyes and immediately felt awful about being so rude. Maybe there wasn't any love lost between them nowadays but that was no excuse for the way she was behaving.

'You're not.' She gave a little shrug, unable to bring herself to actually apologise. 'I just stopped for a drink.'

Daniel sniffed the air. 'Ah, so that explains it. I thought I could smell coffee as I was coming along the path but decided I was hallucinating.' He smiled at her and her heart lifted when she saw the warmth in his eyes. 'I don't think any of the coffee-house chains has set up an outlet in the hills yet, have they?'

'Not so far as I know. It must be an oversight on their behalf,' Emma said, chuckling.

'Oh, I'm sure they'll realise that they're missing a trick,' he assured her. 'Give it a few more months and I expect you'll be able to buy your double cappuccino with hazelnut syrup on the slopes of Mount Everest!'

Emma laughed out loud. 'It wouldn't surprise me. It never fails to amaze me just how many coffee shops there are. Every town and city seems to be awash with them.'

'I have a theory about that,' Daniel said gravely. He bent towards her and lowered his voice. 'I think they're a front for alien invaders. I mean, think about it. All those hissing and gurgling machines can't just be making cups of coffee, can they? They're probably powering up the spaceships that are hidden in the basements.'

It was so ridiculous that Emma couldn't stop laughing. She clutched her aching sides. 'Don't! I feel sick from laughing so much.'

'Sorry.' Daniel didn't sound the least bit repentant. He grinned down at her. 'I won't tell you my theory about burger bars, then.'

'Oh, please, don't! I don't think I can take any more.' Emma wiped her streaming eyes and smiled up at him, feeling her breath catch when her gaze met his. Why was Daniel looking at her that way? she wondered dizzily. He didn't love her; he never had loved her. And yet there was something in his eyes that made her heart start to race…

'Looks like the weather is about to change.'

He turned to stare across the hills and the moment passed. Emma shuddered as she looked at the black clouds that were amassing on the horizon. Had she imagined it or had Daniel really been looking at her as though she meant the whole world to him?

She took a shaky breath when she realised how ridiculous that idea was. Daniel might care about her but only in the sort of impersonal way he would care about any woman he'd had a relationship with. She would be a fool to imagine it was anything more than that.

Emma stood up abruptly and shrugged on her jacket. Although the sun was still shining, she felt chilled to the bone and knew that it had little to do with the impending storm. Picking up the flask, she offered it to him. 'There's some coffee left if you want it.'

'Thanks.' He took the flask from her with a smile that held nothing more than gratitude. Unscrewing the lid, he filled the cup and offered it to her first. 'Do you want some more?'

'No, thank you. I've had more than enough.'

Emma could hear the edge in her voice and hated it because of what it represented. She wanted to remain indifferent to Daniel, to not allow him to affect her in any way, but it was proving impossible to achieve that. It worried her that she was so responsive to his every mood. If she was over him then she shouldn't care how he felt about anything. Including her. The thought was too much to deal with on top of everything else.

'I think I'll head back,' she informed him coolly. Bending down, she picked up the haversack and went to swing it over her shoulder, stopping abruptly when he put out his hand.

'I know this is really cheeky but those aren't sandwiches, are they?' He pointed to the package sticking out of her bag and Emma nodded.

'Yes, I thought I might have my lunch while I was out.'

'But you've changed your mind?' he suggested.

Emma could tell that he suspected he was the reason for her change of plans and shrugged. The last thing she wanted was for Daniel to think that he could exert any sort of influence over her. 'I'd prefer to get home before the rain starts.'

'Of course. But if those sandwiches are going spare, I wouldn't mind them. I'm afraid I'm not as well prepared as you are.'

He gave her a tight little smile and Emma knew immediately that he hadn't believed her excuse. She handed him the sandwiches, refusing to dwell on the thought. Let him think what he liked—she didn't care!

'Thanks. I'll see you later, I expect.' He sat down in the spot she'd recently vacated and opened the package. Emma watched as he selected a thick ham and cheese sandwich and bit into it with relish. If he was at all disturbed about ruining her plans for the day, it certainly didn't show, she thought bitterly.

'Actually, I'm going out this evening,' she said abruptly. Although she hadn't planned on going out, the thought of spending the evening with him was suddenly more than she could bear, and she hurried on. 'I don't know when I'll be back, so I'll see you tomorrow.'

'Right. Have fun.'

Whether or not he believed her was open to question and Emma didn't waste any time worrying about it. She made her way back along the paths until she reached the stile. It had started to rain now, a fine drizzle that obscured the view of the hills. As she stepped down from the stile, she couldn't help wondering if Daniel would be all right. Although he had enjoyed walking in the area when he'd done his training here, it was easy to get lost. Maybe she should have made sure that he got back safely?

She took a deep breath. Daniel had made it clear five years ago that she had no rights where he was concerned. He wouldn't thank her for worrying about him now!

CHAPTER SEVEN

DANIEL finished the sandwiches and wadded the cling film into a ball. Tucking it into his pocket, he drained the last dregs of coffee from the cup. The clouds were fairly scurrying across the sky now and he guessed it wouldn't be long before the rain started. Maybe he should follow Emma's example and head back?

He sighed as he set off along the path. Once again he'd thought he was making headway with her and once again he'd been mistaken. It was a case of one step forward and two back, and it was difficult to explain how frustrated he felt. Maybe it was foolish to hope that she would accept him as a friend after what had happened in the past, but he couldn't bear to think that she would continue to think so badly of him.

Daniel's heart was heavy as he climbed out of the dip. The path skirted an area of loose shale and he picked his way around it, wary of slipping. The first drops of rain started to fall as he cleared the area and he picked up speed, hoping to avoid getting soaked. Although it would have been quicker if he'd taken the path Emma had used, he wasn't sure if he could remember the way.

The last thing he needed to round off the day was to get himself lost!

He must have gone about a mile or so when all of a sudden he heard someone shouting. He stopped and looked around but it was difficult to see now that the rain was falling in earnest. Cupping his hands around his mouth, he shouted as loudly as he could, 'Hello! Where are you?'

'Over here,' the reply came back immediately.

Daniel turned towards the direction from where the sound seemed to be coming and frowned when he caught a glimpse of a figure frantically waving to him. What on earth was going on?

He hurriedly changed course, his heart sinking as he got closer and discovered there were actually two people, both teenage boys, and one of them was injured. 'What happened?' he demanded, crouching down beside the injured boy.

'We were just messing about, having a sword fight with a couple of sticks, when Jack slipped. I thought he was kidding at first when he didn't get up, but then I saw all the blood...' The boy gulped, obviously too shaken by what had happened to continue.

'I see.' Daniel didn't press him for any more details as he carefully eased the boy's blood-soaked T-shirt aside so he could examine the puncture wound in his chest. Although it wasn't very large, it was obviously deep and had bled copiously. He could hear the boy struggling to breathe and placed his hand over the wound. Even if the lung itself wasn't damaged, this type of injury—where air was being drawn directly into the chest cavity—could cause it to deflate

'How long ago did it happen?' he asked, glancing up.

'I'm not sure. Half an hour, maybe longer—I seem to have been shouting for ages.' The boy wiped his eyes with the back of his hand. 'I didn't know what to do. I tried to get Jack to stand up but he couldn't, so I thought about going for help. But even if I'd managed to find someone, I wasn't sure if I'd be able to find my way back here.'

'You don't have a mobile with you?' Daniel queried, dragging over a haversack and using it to support the boy's head and shoulders. He inclined the teenager's body towards the injured side so that the sound lung was uppermost then dug in his pocket and took out a clean handkerchief plus the piece of crumpled cling film. Sealing the wound to stop any more air entering the chest cavity would help the boy to breathe more easily.

'Yes, but there's no signal out here. I've tried it dozens of times but my phone just won't work!'

'Typical.' Daniel sighed as he placed the handkerchief over the hole in the boy's chest. 'Can you hold that there while I unravel this piece of cling film?' he instructed. Once he had smoothed out the plastic wrapping, he placed it over the handkerchief, pressing it tightly against the boy's damp skin. He was pleased to hear that the teenager's breathing sounded a little less laboured after he'd finished.

Standing up, he stripped off his jacket and laid it over

the boy. Hypothermia was a very real concern in a situation like this and he needed to do whatever he could to avoid it. Once he was sure the boy was protected from the rain, he turned to his friend again. 'What's your name, son?'

'Ryan.'

'OK, Ryan. I'm Dr Kennedy. I work at the surgery in Avondale—do you know it?'

Ryan shook his head. 'No.'

'So can I take it that you don't live round here?'

'No. We're on a school trip. We're staying at the outward bound centre near Malham.'

'I see. So is there anyone who's likely to be looking for you right now? Your teachers, for instance?

'No. They don't know we're out here,' Ryan mumbled, looking sheepish.

'What do you mean, they don't know you're out here?'

Ryan shrugged. 'Most of the teachers have gone to Settle with the rest of the group. They're going on a train ride. Jack and I weren't allowed to go because we smuggled some beer into our dormitory last night. A couple of the boys were sick and things got a bit messy, so we had to stay behind to clean up as a punishment.'

'Surely you weren't left on your own?'

'No, one of the teachers stayed with us, but he had to go to the office to deal with a query.' Ryan looked even more uncomfortable. 'Jack and I decided to sneak out while he was gone and that's how we ended up here.'

'And found yourself in an even bigger mess from the look of it,' Daniel declared, sighing. He quickly considered their options but it was obvious what needed to be done. 'We can assume you'll be missed at some point but it could take a while before the alarm is raised and even longer before they send someone out to look for you. Quite frankly, we can't afford to wait around too long so here's what we're going to do. I'm going to stay here with Jack while you go for help. It's better if I stay with him in case anything happens.'

'But what if I can't find my way?' the boy exclaimed.

'You'll be fine,' Daniel assured him, hoping he wasn't being overly confident. 'I'll take you back to the main path and show you which way to go. So long as you stay on the path and don't wander off it, you'll be perfectly all right. It brings you out into the centre of Avondale and once you're there, just ask anyone you meet to help you.'

'But how about finding my way back here?' Ryan asked anxiously. He glanced around and shuddered. 'All this countryside looks the same to me.'

'Have you got a watch?' Daniel unfastened his own watch when the boy shook his head and handed it to him. 'Put that on and use it to time how long it takes you to reach the town. That should give the search and rescue team a rough idea of where we are. You can also tell them that we're about a mile or so from a large rock and that Dr Roberts at the surgery can probably help to pinpoint our location if they ask her. Think you can remember all that?'

'I think so.' Ryan took a deep breath. 'Do you want me to go now?'

'Yes. Oh, and also tell them that we'll need an ambulance on standby and that they should inform the hospital to be prepared for a serious chest trauma. OK?' He smiled when Ryan nodded. 'Good. Let's get going, then. The sooner we get your friend to hospital, the better.'

Daniel led the boy back to the path and pointed him in the right direction, repeating his instruction to stay on the path and not wander off it. He frowned as he watched him set off, hoping he was doing the right thing by sending him for help, but what choice did he have? He couldn't go because he needed to stay with Jack.

He sighed as he made his way back to the injured boy. What was that saying about the road to hell being paved with good intentions? Although his intentions may have been good five years ago, look how badly things had turned out then. Hopefully, there would be a happier outcome this time.

Emma decided to go to the cinema in the end. Although it was a bit of trek to the nearest town that boasted a cinema, it would be worth it. If she set off early, she could do some shopping first and then watch the film. She may as well go for a meal afterwards too. Then she could keep out of Daniel's way for the rest of the day.

She groaned as she stepped into the shower. She couldn't continue avoiding him. Whether she liked the idea or not, she and Daniel were going to have to get along for the next few weeks both in and out of the surgery. Maybe there was a lot of history between them but the key word in that statement was *history*. Their relationship was in the past and it shouldn't have any bearing on what happened at the present time. She'd been out with other men in the past few years and remained on good terms with them too. If she could get it into her head that Daniel was just someone she had once dated, she could put it behind her.

She got dressed and went downstairs. She was just unhooking her jacket off the hall peg when she heard a car pull up outside and frowned. She wasn't expecting visitors and had no idea who it could be. Opening the door, she blinked in surprise when she saw one of the local search and rescue vehicles parked outside. Although her uncle had been a member of the team for many years, he had been forced to retire when his health had started to deteriorate. She couldn't imagine what they were doing here and waited expectantly as Mike Harding, the team leader, hurried towards her.

'Looks as though we've arrived in the nick of time,' Mike observed jovially. A pleasant man in his forties who ran the local pub with his wife, April, he'd been leading the local team for the past ten years. 'I take it that you were on your way out?'

'I was,' Emma agreed. 'I was just about to head off to the cinema, in fact. Why? Is there a problem?'

'Seems like it.' Mike pointed towards a boy sitting in the front passenger seat. 'According to that young fellow, his friend is out in the Dales somewhere, injured, and Dr Kennedy is with him.'

'Daniel!' Emma exclaimed. 'Are you sure?'

'As sure as I can be. The lad came stumbling into the pub about ten minutes ago and told us that his friend was hurt and that there was a man with him who said he was a doctor.' Mike shrugged. 'April asked him to describe him and she said that it sounded very much like Dr Kennedy.'

'She's probably right,' Emma said slowly. 'Daniel did go for a walk this morning. In fact, I met him while I was out.'

'And where was that?' Mike said quickly. 'Apparently, Dr Kennedy told the lad to tell us that he was about a mile from a large rock and that you'd know where it was.'

'He must mean Pilgrim's Point,' Emma told him. 'I was sitting there when I saw Daniel.'

'Great!' Mike beamed at her. 'It doesn't half help when folk are able to narrow down the search area. I'll get on the radio and let the others know where we're heading.'

Emma followed him back to the car, waiting quietly as he put through a call to the rest of the team. 'Do we know how badly injured the other boy is?' she asked as soon as he finished.

'Chest injury, apparently. Your Dr Kennedy told the lad to tell us to have an ambulance on standby and to inform the hospital to prepare for a serious chest trauma.'

Emma felt her face heat. He wasn't *her* Dr Kennedy; he never had been hers in any way, shape or form. It was on the tip of her tongue to point that out until she realised how silly it was to make a fuss. She was supposed to be trying to think of Daniel as just another ex-boyfriend!

'It might be best to have the air ambulance on stand-by,' she suggested, confining her thoughts to the matter at hand.

'We've already done that,' Mike informed her. 'Air Ambulance Control has logged the request, although they can't guarantee another call won't come in in the meantime.'

'Of course not,' Emma agreed, shivering as she glanced towards the hills. The rain was much heavier now, a heavy blanket of clouds overhead stealing the light from the day. Although it was barely the middle of the afternoon, it looked more like evening. She knew that the longer Daniel and the boy were missing, the greater the risk of them not being found before night fell. The thought spurred her to a swift decision.

'I'm coming with you.' She held up her hand when Mike started to protest that it wasn't necessary. 'No, I want to come. I'll be able to help with the boy if nothing else. Give me two minutes to change and I'll be right with you.'

She ran back into the house, quickly exchanging her lightweight jacket for something more suitable. Her walking boots were on the mat where she'd left them and it took only seconds to slip them on. She knew the team carried basic medical supplies as a matter of course so didn't need to worry about that. Within a couple of minutes she was back at the Land Rover.

'Ready,' she told Mike as she climbed into the rear seat. She could feel her tension building as they drove into the centre of the town. The rest of the team was gathered outside the church. There were about a dozen altogether, all of them volunteers.

Emma nodded hello then stood to one side while Mike spread an Ordnance Survey sheet on the bonnet of the car. He ringed Pilgrim's Point in red then turned to the boy. Emma bit her lip when Ryan explained that it had taken him just over two hours to reach the town. It was already three o'clock, which meant it would be going dark before they got back to where Daniel was waiting and that was assuming they could pinpoint his location. Finding people lost in the Dales wasn't easy, as any member of the team would confirm.

She took a deep breath as Mike folded up the map. The thought of Daniel being at risk was more than she could bear, even though she refused to ask herself why.

Without a watch to refer to, Daniel had no idea how much time had passed since Ryan had gone for help. It seemed to be hours since the boy had left yet he knew that it was probably his mind playing tricks. As he checked Jack's pulse again, he found himself praying that help would arrive soon. The boy had lapsed into unconsciousness a while ago and there was no doubt that his condition was deteriorating. He needed to be admitted to hospital as quickly as possible if he was to have any chance of pulling through.

The thought had barely crossed his mind when the boy suddenly stopped breathing. Daniel quickly rolled him onto his back and checked his airway. Once he was sure it was clear, he pinched Jack's nostrils closed and breathed into his mouth, sharply, four times to inflate his lungs. He then checked his pulse and was relieved to find that his heart was still beating. He breathed into his mouth again and continued doing so for several more minutes until Jack started breathing for himself again.

After placing the boy in the recovery position, Daniel stood up, groaning as he stretched his aching limbs. He was soaking wet, thanks to the rain, and freezing cold too. He jumped up and down to try to generate some warmth in his body, flapping his arms as well for good measure. It helped a bit but he knew that the effects wouldn't last. Night was drawing in and the temperature would drop even lower then. What wouldn't he give to be sitting in front of a roaring fire with Emma curled up beside him…?

He blanked out that thought. He was feeling miserable enough without making himself feel even worse because the chances of Emma ever curling up beside him were nil!

Although Emma must have walked along the route dozens of times before, she had never attempted it in such appalling weather. The rain was beating down now, turning the path into a sea of mud in places, so that it was difficult to keep her footing. It didn't help either that some of the streams had burst their banks, forcing them to wade ankle deep through icy-cold water. It was only the thought of Daniel and the injured boy waiting for them that kept her going. They had to find them.

'OK, let's stop for a moment while we get our bearings.' Mike called the group to a halt, waiting until they

had formed a circle before he continued. 'By my reck-
oning, we should be fairly close to where young Ryan
here said he left his friend so we'll split up into groups
and see if we can find him and the doc.'

Everyone nodded. Within a very short time they had
formed four groups. Mike turned to Emma. 'You and
the lad can come with me. They can't be far from here
so let's hope we can find them pretty soon.'

He didn't add anything else as he started walking
again but he didn't need to. Emma knew that once it
got dark, the chances of them finding the pair were
very slim. She and Ryan followed the others along the
track, scouring the land to right and left in the hope of
spotting them. They came to a slight rise in the ground
and Ryan suddenly stopped.

'I remember this bit!' he exclaimed excitedly.

'How far is it from where you left your friend?' Mike
demanded.

'Not very far, I think…ten, twenty metres, something
like that,' the boy told him.

'Right then, let's start shouting and see if they can
hear us.' Mike cupped his hands round his mouth.
'Hello! Can you hear us? Are you out there, Doc?'

Emma held her breath. Ryan seemed so certain that
surely he couldn't have been mistaken? Mike shouted
again but there was still no reply and her heart sank.
They carried on for another few minutes and then Mike
stopped and repeated the process. When a voice suddenly shouted back she didn't know whether to laugh
or cry because she felt so overwhelmed with emotion. It

was all she could do to stumble after the others as they hurried towards where the sound had come from.

'Am I glad to see you,' Daniel began, standing up. He suddenly caught sight of her and Emma saw the shock on his face. It was blatantly obvious that he hadn't expected to see her and all of a sudden she felt uncomfortable about her reasons for being there.

Crossing the narrow strip of ground that separated them, she crouched down beside the injured boy, busying herself with doing his obs while Daniel conferred with Mike. Although she could hear what was being said, it seemed to be happening at one step removed from her. It was only when Daniel crouched down beside her that everything snapped back into focus.

'I'll set up a drip,' she said crisply, starting to rise, but he caught her hand and stopped her.

'I didn't expect you to come, Emma.'

'No?' She gave a little shrug, hoping it would convince him that her reasons had had little to do with him. 'I thought you might need help, that's all. With the boy.'

'That was good of you. Thank you.'

His voice was low but she could hear the note it held and her heart reacted immediately to it. She stood up abruptly and hurried over to where Mike had left the bag of medical supplies. Saline, antiseptic wipes, cannula… She mentally listed all the things she needed because it was safer to concentrate on them than on anything else, far safer than letting herself think about the way Daniel had looked at her just now.

She took a deep breath, held it until she felt dizzy,

then let it out as slowly as she could, but the thought didn't flow away with it. It seemed to be stuck in her head, neon bright and incredibly scary: Daniel had been pleased to see her, surprised but pleased. What did it mean?

CHAPTER EIGHT

DANIEL could feel his heart thumping as he helped Emma set up the drip. It had been a shock to see her and there was no point denying it. Had she come purely to offer her services as a doctor, or because she had been worried about him?

His heart beat all the harder at that beguiling thought and he gritted his teeth. He was doing it again, letting himself hope for the impossible, and it was stupid to behave this way. Emma's reasons for being here had nothing to do with him and everything to do with their patient!

He stood up abruptly and turned to Mike. 'That's about all we can do for him. The sooner we get him to hospital, the better his chances will be.'

'The air ambulance is on its way,' Mike informed him. 'The problem is that it can't land out here in the dark—it's way too dangerous. We're going to have to carry the lad to the nearest stretch of road and have him picked up from there.'

'How long's that going to take?' Daniel demanded, his heart sinking at the thought of there being a further lengthy delay.

'Fifteen minutes max,' Mike assured him.

'But it takes a lot longer than that to get back to town,' Daniel protested.

'It does, but I expect the team will use a different route to get him to the road,' Emma said quietly beside him.

Daniel spun round, feeling his senses reel when he realised how close she was. Normally, she kept her distance, both physically and mentally, but she was standing so close to him now that he could feel the warmth of her skin. It was hard to concentrate when every cell in his body was so acutely aware of her.

'Do you mean to say that I could have got help here sooner if I hadn't sent Ryan into the town?' he demanded, the force of his reaction making him sound—and *feel*—distinctly tetchy.

'I doubt it. The nearest road to here is fairly isolated. There's very little traffic uses it, especially at this time of the year, so the chances of Ryan being able to flag down a car were pretty remote. You did the best thing by sending him back to town to get help,' she replied calmly, although Daniel couldn't help noticing that she avoided meeting his eyes.

Was she equally aware of him as he was of her? he wondered, then had to swallow his groan when his heart set off again, pounding away as though possessed. When Mike came over with a foil blanket for him to wrap around himself, he barely managed to nod his thanks. Forget about feeling cold and wet—it would be a miracle if he didn't have a heart attack at this rate!

It took them just under the allotted time to stretcher

the injured boy to the pick-up point. The police were already there and had set up a landing site for the helicopter in a nearby field. It arrived a couple of minutes later and Daniel handed over his patient, briefly explaining to the crew what had happened and what he had done. Five minutes later, it was on its way again. The police had also contacted the outward-bound centre where the two boys were staying and one of the teachers had come to collect Ryan. From the glum expression on the teenager's face as he got into the car, Daniel guessed that he wasn't expecting much of a welcome when he got back.

'That's it, folks. Let's just hope the lad will be all right, eh?'

Mike voiced everyone's opinion as they headed over to the vehicles. A couple of the reserve team had driven over to collect them and Daniel had to admit that it was a relief not to have to walk all the way back to town. Now that the adrenalin rush was dying down, he felt too cold and stiff to welcome the thought of a long walk home.

He slid into the back of one of the vehicles, moving over when Emma got in beside him. Another member of the team climbed in beside her so it was a bit of a squash. Daniel held himself rigid as they set off but it was impossible to avoid touching her as they swung around the bends.

'Sorry,' he murmured when once again he found himself cannoning into her.

'That's OK.'

She gave him a tight little smile then stared straight ahead, making it clear that she wasn't keen to start a conversation. He wasn't either, mainly because he didn't want anything he said to be misconstrued. He sighed wearily. When had life become so complicated that he had to watch every word he said?

Emma couldn't wait to get home. Sitting beside Daniel was sheer torture. Every time they rounded a bend, his shoulder brushed hers or his thigh pressed against her thigh and she didn't appreciate the feelings it aroused inside her. It was a relief when the car drew up outside the house.

Daniel got out and offered her his hand but she pretended not to see it. Sliding across the seat, she got out and thanked the driver. The car drove away with a toot of its horn, its taillights rapidly disappearing into the darkness. Emma headed towards the front door, feeling her tension mounting when she heard Daniel's footsteps crunching on the gravel behind her. All of a sudden she was achingly aware of the fact that there were just the two of them. She would have given anything to open the door and find Aunt Margaret at home but it wasn't going to happen so she had to make the best of things. Unlocking the front door, she summoned a smile.

'I'll put the kettle on while you get out of those wet clothes. Do you prefer tea or coffee?'

'Coffee, please.' Daniel grimaced as he stepped into the hall. 'I'm soaking. I'd better take my clothes off here rather than drip water all through the house.'

He shed the foil blanket then dragged his sodden sweater over his head. Emma just caught a glimpse of a broad, muscled chest before she hastily turned away.

'I'll get the coffee on,' she murmured, hurrying along the hall as though the hounds of hell were snapping at her heels. She filled the kettle then took off her wet coat and carried it through to the back porch so it could drip. When she chanced a wary glance along the hall there was no sign of Daniel, just a heap of sodden clothing lying neatly on the mat.

She ran upstairs to her room and changed into dry jeans then went back down and gathered up Daniel's clothing to take it through to the kitchen, putting his sweater and jeans straight into the washer. His boots were soaked so she stuffed them with newspaper and left them in the corner to dry. By the time she'd done all that, he reappeared, shaking his head as he came into the kitchen.

'You shouldn't have cleared up after me, Emma. I'd have done it myself.'

'It wasn't a problem,' she said lightly, not wanting him to attach any significance to her actions. She had done it purely because she liked order in her life, not because she'd wanted to help him, she assured herself. She headed towards the kettle then stopped when he waved her aside.

'*I'll* make the coffee. It's the least I can do.'

Emma opened her mouth then hurriedly shut it again. Arguing about who should make the coffee would be extremely childish. Walking over to the cupboard, she lifted out the biscuit tin and set it on the table. When Daniel brought over the tray, he looked hopefully at her.

'I hope there's some chocolate biscuits in there.

There's nothing like comfort food when you're feeling cold and miserable.'

'There should be.' Emma took the lid off the tin and nodded. 'You're in luck. There's a new packet of chocolate digestives—your favourites.'

'So you remember which biscuits I like?' His tone was even but she felt the blood rush up her face when she realised how revealing that had been. If she had erased him from her life then why on earth would she remember his taste in food?

'Yes,' she said firmly, knowing there was no point lying. She looked him straight in the eyes. 'I'm hardly likely to forget, bearing in mind the amount of biscuits you consumed when you worked here.'

'Hmm, I suppose not.' He grinned. 'I *could* claim that I'm a reformed character and only eat them in exceptional circumstances but that would be cutting off my nose to spite my face.' He helped himself to a biscuit. 'All I can say is that it's my only vice, or the only one I'm willing to admit to!'

He chuckled as he bit into the biscuit and Emma felt a little flurry of heat run through her veins. She had forgotten how endearing he could be when he was poking fun at himself.

The thought troubled her and she picked up the pot, quickly pouring coffee into two mugs. She didn't want to think about Daniel's good points, certainly didn't want to remember the reasons why she had fallen in love with him. She needed to focus on the way he had treated her. She had been willing to give up her dreams for him but it hadn't been enough. His career had meant far more to him than what she could have given him.

Pain lanced her heart and she took a gulp of her coffee then coughed when the hot liquid shot down the wrong way. Putting the mug down on the table, she tried to catch her breath but it felt as though her lungs had gone into spasm.

'Are you all right?' Daniel leant forward and looked at her in concern. 'Emma?'

Emma tried to answer but there was no way that she could force out even a single word and she saw him leap to his feet. Moving swiftly behind her chair he slapped her on the back and with relief she felt the constriction loosen. Sucking in a deep breath, she finally managed to speak.

'I'm all right now.'

'Sure?' He went over to the sink when she nodded and filled a glass with cold water and gave it to her. 'Take a couple of sips of this.'

Emma obediently sipped the water then set the glass on the table, feeling embarrassed about having caused such a fuss. 'Some of the coffee must have gone down the wrong way.'

'Easily done,' he said lightly, sitting down again. He slid the biscuit tin across the table. 'Aren't you going to have one?'

'I'm not sure if I should risk it after what just happened,' she said wryly.

Daniel laughed. 'Go on—live dangerously. Anyway, I'm a dab hand at the Heimlich manoeuvre if the need arises.'

Emma grimaced as she selected a biscuit. 'Let's hope it doesn't come to that.'

'Fingers crossed,' he said, suiting his actions to his words.

Emma chuckled as she bit into her biscuit. Daniel had a real gift when it came to putting people at ease. Some of the doctors she had worked with seemed to enjoy feeling superior, but Daniel wasn't like that. He cared too much about other people to want them to feel uncomfortable around him.

The thought surprised her because it didn't gel with the image she had held of him for the past few years. If Daniel was the single-minded, ambitious man she had believed him to be, surely he wouldn't care about anyone else's feelings?

'Penny for them.'

Emma looked up when he spoke, feeling her heart lurch when she saw the way he was watching her so intently. Why did she have the feeling that he really wanted to know what was troubling her? She had no idea but it was that thought which made her reply without pausing to consider the wisdom of what she was doing. 'I was just thinking what a contradiction you are.'

'Really?' His brows rose as he picked up his mug of coffee. He took a sip of the hot liquid then placed the mug carefully back on the table. 'In what way?'

'Well, you've never made any bones about the fact that you're very ambitious, have you, Daniel? And yet in some respects you don't fit that bill.' She shrugged when he looked quizzically at her. 'You genuinely seem to care about people and it's rare that the two go hand in hand.'

'Of course I care. I wouldn't have gone into medicine if I hadn't.'

Emma frowned when she heard the edge in his voice, wondering if she had touched a nerve. 'One doesn't always follow the other,' she pointed out. 'I've worked with a number of doctors who openly admitted that they decided on medicine purely because it seemed like a good career choice.'

'They're the exceptions. Or I hope they are.' He stared down at the mug he was holding. 'In my opinion you can't do this job properly unless you genuinely want to help people.'

'So how does your desire to help people equate with wanting to go into private practice? Surely you could help far more people by working for the NHS?'

'Rich people get sick too, Emma.' He glanced up and she was surprised when she saw the sadness on his face because she wasn't sure what had caused it. 'Having money doesn't protect you from all the usual ailments.'

'I know that.' She leant forward, suddenly impatient to get to the bottom of this mystery. The more she thought about it, the stranger it seemed that Daniel of all people should be so keen to follow this course. 'And I'm not suggesting that people who can afford it shouldn't have the right to choose to pay for their treatment. But setting yourself up in private practice doesn't seem like something you would want to do. I just can't understand it, if I'm honest.'

Daniel wasn't sure what to say. If he admitted that he'd never had any intention of going into private practice, he would have to tell her the truth. How would she feel if he admitted that he had deliberately misled her? Hurt, angry, upset; she was bound to feel all of those things. But would she understand that he had been trying to protect her, stop her doing something she would regret?

'What's to understand?' he said shortly, knowing it was a risk he wasn't prepared to take. 'Everyone has their aims in life, including you. What made *you* decide to become a surgeon?'

'Because I saw how surgery could improve people's lives when I did my rotations,' she said simply. 'That's why I chose it.'

'There you are, then. You chose your path and I chose mine. It's as simple as that.' He stood up abruptly, pushing back his chair so fast that the legs scraped across the tiles. 'I think I'll have an early night. Hopefully, a good night's sleep will ease some of the kinks out of my aching muscles.'

'Of course. I'll see you in the morning, I expect.'

'If I manage to drag myself out of bed.'

Daniel summoned a smile but it was a poor effort, he knew. He left the kitchen and headed upstairs to his room. Switching on the bedside lamp, he sank down on the bed, wishing with all his heart that he could have done things differently five years ago. Letting Emma go had been the hardest thing he had ever done yet he was more convinced than ever that it had been the right thing to do. Maybe they would have had a few years of happiness together, but eventually she would have regretted giving up her dreams to be with him.

He took a deep breath. No matter how hard it had been, it would have been so much worse if Emma had ended up hating him.

Emma spent a couple of hours watching television after Daniel retired to his room. The plans she'd made to go to the cinema had been put on hold because she couldn't be bothered getting ready to go out. However, by the time the old grandfather clock in the hall struck nine, she was bored stiff. She switched off the set and made her way upstairs. She reached the landing and paused to listen but there was no sound coming from Daniel's side of the house. Obviously, he was fast asleep, worn out after his exertions that day.

Emma went to her room and collected her toilet bag then made her way to the bathroom. She felt too restless to sleep and was hoping that a long, hot soak in the bath would help her relax. Turning on the taps, she added a generous dollop of bubble bath to the water then stripped off her clothes. Water had been in short supply where she had been working recently and it was a luxury to be able to fill the bath almost to the brim.

She slid into the scented bubbles with an appreciative groan and closed her eyes. Whether it was the warmth of the water or the silence, she soon drifted off to sleep only to awake with a start when the bathroom door suddenly opened. Emma's eyes shot open as she stared at Daniel in dismay.

'What are you doing? Get out!'

'I'm sorry. I had no idea you were in here. The door wasn't locked,' he began, then stopped.

Emma saw him swallow and looked down, feeling her heart leap when she realised that all the bubbles had melted away while she'd slept. Without them to conceal her, her body was naked to his gaze and she could tell that the sight was having an effect. Water sloshed over the side of the bath as she scrambled to her feet and reached for a towel off the rail, but Daniel was ahead of her.

'Here.' He passed her a towel then turned away while she wrapped it around herself.

Emma stepped out of the bath, shaking her wet hair out of her eyes. She felt both cold and shivery, and it owed little to the fact that she'd been lying in the cooling water for too long. Daniel wanted her: she had seen it in his eyes, seen the desire that had filled them just now. The thought should have repulsed her but it didn't—just the opposite, in fact. Heat suddenly scorched along her veins when she realised with a jolt of shock that she wanted him too….

Afterwards, she was never sure what happened next, whether she made some sort of small betraying sound or it was sheer coincidence that he turned at that moment. There was a second when their eyes locked and held before he slowly reached out and touched her cheek.

'Emma.'

Her name sounded so different when he said it that way, his deep voice throbbing with hunger and need. Emma wasn't aware of moving yet all of a sudden she was standing in front of him, so close that she could feel the tremor that passed through his body. When his hand lifted to her face again, she didn't move, just stood there while his fingers grazed along her jaw, gliding so lightly over her skin that it was hard to know for sure if he was actually touching her.

'Your skin's so soft,' he whispered as his fingers came to rest a millimetre away from her mouth.

Emma knew that if she dipped her head the barest fraction she would feel them on her lips and the thought was the sweetest kind of torment. She wanted him to touch her mouth but she wasn't sure where it would lead if he did. Could she allow Daniel to touch her, caress her, *make love* to her, and not feel anything except desire? Maybe it was what she needed to finally get him out of her system. Although she had been out with other men since they had split up, she had never wanted to sleep with any of them. In the beginning she had been too wary of getting hurt to risk getting involved and, more recently, she had been so busy in work that she'd had no time for a private life—or so she had told herself. Now Emma found herself wondering if the truth was far more complicated: she had never really drawn a line under her affair with Daniel so that she could move on.

This could be the perfect opportunity to do so, but still she hesitated. Her feelings for Daniel were so muddled up. Although sleeping with him might give her the closure she needed, it might achieve just the opposite result. What if she found that the old feelings she'd had for him, the ones she had thought were dead and buried a long time ago, were still very much alive? It was the uncertainty that scared her, the thought that she might regret whichever decision she made for the rest of her life.

CHAPTER NINE

DANIEL could feel his heart racing. It wasn't just this desire he felt to take Emma in his arms and make love to her that was causing it to happen but fear as well. For the past five years he had kept his emotions strictly under wraps. It hadn't been difficult. He had never had a proper relationship with another woman since they had split up and had never wanted one. Although he dated frequently, he steadfastly avoided commitment. Whenever he made love to a woman, it was a purely physical experience: he had remained emotionally detached. However, he knew he wouldn't be able to do that with Emma.

Fear turned his guts to ice and he froze. Emma was standing stock still as well and he sensed that she was fighting her own inner battle about what should happen. He was already preparing himself for the inevitable rejection when her head dipped just a fraction. He sucked in his breath when he felt her mouth brush his fingers. Heat surged through his veins, melting away the fear that had filled him only moments before. He wanted her so much, wanted to bury himself in her softness and sweetness while they made love. Maybe it was madness and maybe he would regret it later but right now he needed this more than he had needed anything in his life!

He drew her into his arms and it was like coming home. Her body felt so sweetly familiar as it nestled against him, each soft curve fitting so perfectly that he didn't have to think how he should hold her—he just did. He could feel her breasts pressing against his chest and closed his eyes as a wave of pure pleasure swept over him. She felt so right in his arms that the years they'd spent apart might never have happened.

'Daniel?'

Her voice was low, the uncertainty it held filling him with tenderness. Bending, her touched her mouth with his in a kiss that was meant to reassure and calm her fears. However, the moment his lips tasted hers desire took over. He pulled her to him, letting her feel the effect she was having on him, and felt her tremble. There wasn't a doubt in his mind that she was equally affected and his heart overflowed with joy. Even after everything that had happened, Emma still wanted him!

He kissed her again with a passion that immediately had her clinging to him. When her lips opened, inviting him to deepen the kiss, he groaned. He was shaking by the time he drew back but so was she. Cupping her face between his hands, he looked deep into her eyes, hoping she could see how much this meant to him.

'I want to make love to you, Emma, more than anything, but are you sure it's what you really want?'

'Yes.' Her voice was still low but there was a conviction in it now that reassured him she knew exactly what she was doing. 'It's what I want too, Daniel.'

'Good.'

He smiled as he bent and kissed her again. When he lifted her up into his arms, she rested her head on his shoulder. He carried her back to her room and laid her down on the narrow single bed then sat down beside her. Reaching out, he tugged gently on the folds of damp towel, feeling his breath catch when they parted to reveal her body to his gaze. Her breasts were high and full, the rose-pink nipples standing erect and proud beneath his gaze. Her waist was narrow, her hips curved, her thighs smooth and firm. Every tiny inch of her was so perfect that for a moment he was overwhelmed by her beauty and couldn't move. It was only when she placed her hand on his that the spell was broken.

He lifted her hand to his mouth and pressed a kiss against her palm. 'You're beautiful, Emma,' he whispered, his voice grating with the force of his desire.

'Am I?' She smiled at him, her green eyes heavy with passion.

'Yes. More beautiful than any woman I've ever known.'

He kissed her palm again then gently placed her hand by her side while his fingers trailed across her wrist and up her arm. He paused when he came to her shoulder. Her skin was still slightly damp from her bath and he allowed himself a moment to savour its warmth and moistness under his fingertips. When his hand moved on, following the line of her collarbone, he heard her murmur and smiled. This was one journey they were both enjoying making together.

His fingers traced the delicate bones until they came

to her throat where once again they lingered. Daniel could feel her pulse beating, could feel it racing, in fact, but as his was racing too it didn't seem strange. Bending, he let the tip of his tongue touch the spot where it beat so strongly and felt her shudder, and shuddered too, more affected by her response than he would have believed. In that second he realised just how different it was making love to Emma than to any other woman. Whatever she felt, he felt too; they were that much in tune.

The thought almost blew him away but there were more delights awaiting him and he wanted to savour them all. His hand glided down her throat, following the lines of her body as it skated over the swell of her breasts, the dip of her waist, the curve of her hips. He could have stopped at any one of those places, and remained there quite happily too, but he was greedy to reacquaint himself with every inch of her delectable body.

Her thighs came next, then her knees and her ankles followed by her feet. As he caressed her toes, Daniel knew that he would never feel this depth of desire for any other woman. It was only Emma he had ever wanted so totally, only Emma he had ever loved so completely.

Emma could feel the desire building inside her as Daniel continued to stroke and caress every inch of her body. He had always been a considerate lover, taking time and care to ensure that she enjoyed their love-making as much as he did. She'd had a couple of brief affairs before she had met him, but nobody had ever made her feel as loved and as cherished as Daniel did. When his hand began its upward journey, retracing the route it had taken, she closed her eyes, relishing the touch of his fingers as they glided over her skin. She knew that she had given in to temptation and that she might regret it later, but at that moment it didn't seem to matter. All she wanted right now was to feel: his hand on her thighs, on her belly, her breasts….

Desire shot through her, red-hot and urgent, when his hand was replaced by his mouth as he took her nipple between his lips and suckled her, and she gasped. She had forgotten how intensely Daniel could make her feel, how he could carry her to a peak of need and then take her even higher. No man had ever done that apart from him. No man ever would.

Pain lanced her heart at the thought but there was no time to dwell on it because his mouth had moved to her other breast. Once again there was that surge of desire that made her stomach muscles clench and her senses reel. When he raised his head, Emma was no longer capable of thinking, only feeling, and he must have realised that. His mouth skimmed up her throat and captured hers in a kiss so raw, so filled with passion that it seemed to consume her totally. She could barely breathe when he drew back but, then, neither could he. They looked at one another for a long moment and she could see the same wonderment in his eyes that she knew must be in hers.

'Emma, I…'

He stopped and shook his head, although whether it was because he couldn't find the words to describe how he felt or because he was reluctant to say them, she wasn't sure, and maybe it was for the best. Even though she had no idea what would happen later, she knew that this wasn't the start of something more. Passion was one thing but love was something completely different and she knew for certain that Daniel didn't love her.

Tears filled her eyes but she blinked them away. She refused to cry. The past was over, the future unknown; it was the here and now that mattered. When Daniel stood up and stripped off his clothes, she focused on the moment, nothing more. And when he lay down beside her and took her in his arms, she let their passion sweep her away to a place where nothing else existed except her and Daniel and the magic they were creating together.

The air was cool when Daniel awoke the following morning. The central heating hadn't switched on yet and the temperature had dropped considerably through the night. Leaning over, he carefully drew the quilt over Emma's shoulders, resisting the urge he felt to kiss her awake. They had made love several times during the night and it wouldn't be fair to wake her when she needed to sleep.

He sighed as he swung his legs out of bed and stood up. Had it been fair to make love to her in the first place? Last night he'd been carried away by his desire for her but it was time to face up to what he had done. He had made love to Emma when he had known in his heart that it was the last thing he should have done. It made no difference that she had been as eager and as willing as he'd been; he should have had the strength to resist temptation. He would never forgive himself if he ended up hurting her through his selfishness.

Daniel's heart was heavy as he made his way to the bathroom. Switching on the shower, he let the hot water pound down on his head and shoulders. However, if he'd hoped that it would wash away some of the guilt he felt then he was disappointed. Last night shouldn't have happened and there was no excuse for his actions. All he could do now was to try and lessen the damage he may have caused.

He went to his room and dressed then made his way to the kitchen. As soon as the kettle boiled he made himself a cup of instant coffee and sat down at the table while he tried to work out how he should handle things. So much depended on how Emma felt about the situation, of course. Would she be stricken with guilt too? He hoped not. Emma wasn't to blame for the fact that he had been unable to control himself!

'Stop it, Daniel.'

The sound of her voice brought his head up. Daniel's heart gave an almighty lurch when he saw her standing in the doorway. She was wearing a thick towelling robe and he knew without having to be told that she wasn't wearing anything under it. Heat scorched along his veins and he cursed soundlessly. He couldn't afford to dwell on thoughts like that when he had to make sure that Emma didn't come to any harm.

'I don't know what you mean,' he said, his voice sounding unnaturally gruff as he tried to work out how to salvage the situation.

'Of course you do.' She came into the room and stood in front of the table. 'You're sitting there, wallowing in guilt because of what happened last night, and it's so typically arrogant of you.'

'Arrogant?' His brows shot skywards and he looked at her in surprise.

'Yes.' Resting her hands on the edge of the table she bent so that she could look straight into his eyes. 'You didn't coerce me into bed, neither did you have your *wicked way* with me. I made love with you because I wanted to. If I hadn't wanted to, it would never have happened. Is that clear?'

'Yes.' He was so stunned by her forthright approach that he couldn't think what else to say but Emma didn't seem to expect him to say anything.

'Good. The last thing I need is you thinking that I'm holding out for a reconciliation.' She gave a sharp laugh. 'Last night was fun and I enjoyed it but that's as far as it went. It certainly wasn't the start of something more.'

'That's how I feel too,' Daniel said thickly. Even though he knew he should be relieved that she felt this way, he couldn't help feeling hurt that their love-making had meant so little to her.

'It seems we're in agreement, then.' She gave him a cool little smile and went to switch on the kettle.

Daniel finished his coffee in a couple of quick gulps and excused himself. Emma was making toast when he left the kitchen, acting as though everything was completely normal, and maybe it was for her. Maybe she'd had a string of lovers in the past few years, men she had enjoyed the odd night of passion with. She'd mentioned her boss, hadn't she? Richard something-or-other. Maybe he was one of them, although there could be a long line of past and present suitors for all he knew. Although he hated the idea, what right did he have to criticise how she lived her life? The truth was that he had forfeited any rights where Emma was concerned five years ago. She was free to do whatever she wished.

The thought was so agonising that Daniel knew he had to get out of the house before he made a fool of himself. Unhooking his coat off the peg, he let himself out of the front door. His car was parked in the drive so he got in and started the engine. When he reached the main road, he headed towards Harrogate purely because it was somewhere to aim for. He wasn't heading *to* somewhere but away from a place where it was too painful to be. The trouble was that no matter how many miles he put between himself and Emma, it didn't stop him thinking about her, definitely didn't stop him wishing that things could have been different.

Emma managed to maintain her composure until she heard Daniel's car driving away. She sank down onto a chair, feeling sick and shaken by what had happened. She had known the moment she had seen him sitting at the table that he had regretted what had happened the night before. It had been pride that had helped her deal with the situation, pride plus the fear of what might happen if he realised how much it had meant to her.

She bit her lip, overwhelmed by a sudden feeling of dread. Making love with Daniel had been everything she could have wished for but she wasn't foolish enough to think that it had meant anything special to him. Maybe he had desired her but that was all it had been. Whilst she had tried to convince herself that it would be the ideal way to draw a line under the past, she doubted if Daniel had viewed it that way. He hadn't needed to because he had got over her a long time ago. There was no way that had he been celibate for the past five years, and last night she had been just another in a long line of women willing and eager to give him pleasure.

The thought of Daniel making love to all those other women was incredibly painful, so Emma tried not to dwell on it. There were just two weeks left of her stay and after that she would return to the life she had built for herself. It had taken her a long time to get over Daniel the last time and she couldn't bear to think that she would have to go through that kind of heartache again, so she would make sure he didn't gain any kind of hold over her. And that meant there must never be a repeat of what had happened last night.

Daniel was snatching five minutes' break in the middle of what had turned out to be an extremely busy Monday morning surgery when Emma knocked on his door.

'Ruth said you didn't have a patient with you at the moment,' she explained as she came into the room.

'I was just taking a breather,' he replied, hoping he sounded calmer than he felt.

He had managed to stay out of her way for the remainder of the weekend. It had been almost midnight when he'd got back to the house and she'd been in bed. There'd been no sign of her when he'd got up that morning either, although he hadn't lingered. He had skipped breakfast and come straight to the surgery, making do with a cup of coffee to tide him over. If he'd had his way he would have avoided seeing her for the rest of the day too, but obviously that wasn't to be. Now all he could hope was that the decision he'd made yesterday to behave calmly and professionally around her for the next couple of weeks would see him through.

'It has been busy,' she agreed evenly. Closing the door, she came over to his desk and handed him a file. 'Would you mind taking a look at this for me? I'm afraid it's got me stumped.'

'Of course.' Daniel took the file and quickly read through the patient's notes. His brows rose when he noted how many times the man had visited the surgery in the past two months. 'Alistair Grant is either an extremely sick man or he's a complete hypochondriac. You could fill a textbook with the variety of symptoms he's presented with recently.'

'Exactly.' She leant across the desk and selected a sheet from the file. 'Uncle Jim sent him for a whole battery of tests last month and they all came back clear.'

'Hmm.' Daniel placed the file on the desk, trying to ignore the leap his heart gave when her hand brushed his as she passed him the test results. Ruthlessly, he battened it down, refusing to allow himself even the tiniest leeway. He was going to treat Emma as a colleague from now on, even if it killed him!

'Does he seem genuine to you?' he asked, sticking determinedly to the matter under discussion.

'It's hard to say.' She grimaced. 'I only met him today so I don't have any real idea of what he's like as a person.'

'So he hasn't lived in Avondale all that long?'

'No. Apparently he moved here three months ago.'

'And almost immediately began visiting the surgery on a regular basis.' Daniel frowned as he picked up the patient's file again and flicked through it. 'How come we don't have any notes from his last GP?'

'He's been working abroad ever since he left university. He told me that he assumed his notes would be still at the practice his parents use but they've been unable to find them. Ruth has contacted the university to see if they were transferred to their medical centre but so far she's not heard back from them.'

'That's a shame. It would have been helpful to see if he had a history of visiting his GP on a frequent basis.'

'It would. To be honest, it's not a situation I've come across before. Most people who are undergoing surgery have been seen by several doctors before they reach us. That tends to weed out any malingerers.'

'Would it help if I had a word with him?' Daniel offered. 'I'm not saying I'll be able to tell if he's making it up, but it might deter him if he knows we're dubious about the claims he's been making.'

'Would you mind? I'd hate to make any hasty assumptions about his credibility and overlook something serious.'

Daniel heard the relief in her voice and immediately stood up. He would do anything to help her, he thought as he followed her to the door. He sighed as they walked along the corridor together. If only he'd thought about that on Saturday night. Making love with Emma may have been wonderful, but it had caused problems for him if not for her. She might be able to chalk it up to experience but he certainly couldn't. Just for a second his head reeled as he recalled how sweetly responsive she had been when he'd held her in his arms before he forced the thought to the deepest, darkest reaches of his mind. He couldn't afford to think about that or he wouldn't be able to function!

Alistair Grant was sitting in the chair exactly where Emma had left him. A thin young man in his late twenties with sandy-coloured hair and a pale complexion, he cut a rather pathetic figure. Emma smiled at him as she went into the room.

'I'm sorry to have left you sitting here, Alistair. This is Dr Kennedy. He would like to have a word with you to see if he can get to the root of your problems.'

'I hope somebody can.' Alistair stood up to shake hands. He sat down heavily again as though he didn't have the strength to remain on his feet for very long. Propping himself against the edge of the desk, Daniel regarded him thoughtfully.

'You seem to have been through the mill recently, Alistair. I've read your notes and you've had a lot of distressing symptoms in the last few months, it appears.'

Emma took her seat behind the desk, leaving it up to Daniel to take the lead. She had to admit that the case had her stumped and she would value his help. She listened attentively while he asked Alistair how his health had been in general over the past year.

'I was fine right up until a few months ago,' Alistair

assured them. 'I never had anything wrong with me before that apart from the odd cold.'

'Dr Roberts told me that you've been working abroad. Were you ill while you were there or did it all kick off when you came back to England?'

'When I moved to Avondale, actually. I'd only been here a couple of weeks when I started feeling really rough—tired and as though I had no energy. Then I started with all these aches and pains, the headaches, etcetera.'

He sounded really despondent and Emma frowned. If he was making it up then he was extremely convincing. By the time Daniel finished talking to him, she could tell that he was as perplexed as she was.

'I have to admit that it's got me baffled, Alistair. I know you've had a whole range of tests done, but I'd like to send you for more blood tests and see what they show up. Where were you working when you were abroad, by the way?'

'South Africa was the last place but I've been all over in the past few years—India, China, various parts of Africa. I'm a civil engineer so I go wherever the job takes me.'

'Are you working here at the moment?' Emma put in.

'Yes. I'm overseeing the building of a new wind farm. We're due to start in a couple of weeks' time so I've been doing a lot of the ground work beforehand.'

'I imagine there was opposition to building a wind farm around here,' Daniel suggested.

Alistair sighed. 'There was. It's taken years to get

the go-ahead and there's a lot of folk who still aren't happy about it. One of the local farmers in particular has caused us a great deal of trouble—dumping loads of manure and old oil drums in the middle of the track to block our access, that sort of thing. Last week he even warned some of the men off with a shotgun. When we called the police, he claimed it was all a misunderstanding and that he was out shooting rabbits.'

'It can't be easy, dealing with that kind of behaviour!' Emma exclaimed.

'It isn't, although it wouldn't be so bad if I felt a bit more up to it,' Alistair stated ruefully.

'Well, let's hope we can get to the bottom of this as soon as possible,' Daniel said encouragingly. 'Bearing in mind where you've been working recently, I'd like you screened for some of the more obscure tropical diseases as well. It could be that you've picked something up overseas and that's what's causing the problem. We'll arrange for a blood sample to be sent to the School of Tropical Medicine in Liverpool and see if they can come up with any answers.'

Emma printed out a form for bloods to be taken at the hospital, adding a request for samples to be sent straight to Liverpool. She handed the form to Alistair who thanked her rather wearily and left. She frowned as the door closed behind him. 'I don't think he's making it up, do you?'

'No. It didn't seem like it to me either,' Daniel agreed. 'Let's hope something shows up in the next lot of tests because it's very puzzling.'

'Fingers crossed.' She reached for the button to buzz

through her next patient, not wanting to appear as though she was keen to detain him. However, he was way ahead of her.

'Let me know when the test results come back, will you?' he asked as he strode to the door.

'Of course.'

Emma summoned a smile but it was galling to know how eager he was to avoid spending any time with her. He had stayed away from the house all day on Sunday, only returning when he'd been sure that she would be in bed. She had heard his car turn into the drive well after midnight and had hurriedly switched off her lamp, afraid that he would think she was waiting up for him.

It was obvious that Daniel was keen to avoid a repeat of what had happened on Saturday night. She was too but for a different reason. She was afraid of getting emotionally involved but that wasn't something he would worry about. Daniel simply didn't want any complications in his life. Maybe he *had* told her that she was more beautiful than any woman he had ever known but talk was cheap: actions said far more. And he had proved beyond any doubt that he didn't care a jot about her.

CHAPTER TEN

THE week wore on and Daniel found to his dismay that he couldn't stop thinking about what had happened between him and Emma. It wasn't so bad while he was working, he could focus on his patients then. However, when he was on his own, that was when the real problem started.

It was as though Emma had invaded his mind and every time he relaxed his guard, thoughts of her popped into his head. He kept remembering in glorious detail how it had felt when they'd made love and it was driving him mad. He longed to tell her how he felt yet he knew he couldn't do it. How could he confess that making love to her had touched his heart and his soul when it was clear that she didn't feel the same way?

In an effort to retain his sanity he spent an increasing amount of time away from the house. Fortunately the weather had improved and with the nights getting lighter, he was able to go walking after evening surgery ended. He became quite familiar with the various footpaths surrounding the town, although he was careful not to stray too far afield. It was while he was out one evening that he came across the search and rescue team tending an injured walker. When Mike Harding asked him if he would take a look at the woman's ankle, Daniel readily agreed.

'It looks to me very much like a Pott's fracture,' he declared after he'd examined her. He glanced at Mike and grimaced. 'When she fell, she broke her fibula and either broke the tibia as well or tore the ligaments, resulting in a dislocation of the ankle. It's a nasty injury.'

'Can you help us put a splint on it, Doc?' Mike asked. 'We certainly don't want to cause any more damage.'

'Of course.' Daniel gave the woman some Entonox™ to help with the pain then helped Mike fit an inflatable splint to support her ankle. He accompanied the team back to their Land Rover, shaking his head when Mike thanked him profusely. 'I was happy to help.'

'I still appreciate what you did, Doc. That's twice in a very short time that we've been glad of your services. How's that young lad doing, by the way? Have you heard?'

'Do you mean Jack? He's been moved from Intensive Care and by all accounts is making an excellent recovery.'

'Which he probably wouldn't be doing if you hadn't been on hand to help him.' Mike shook his head when Daniel demurred. 'No, credit where it's due, Doc. You saved that kid's life and that's a fact. It's just a shame that you aren't going to be here long term. We could do with someone like you to call on, especially as we're coming up to our busiest time of the year. I don't suppose you'd consider moving here permanently, would you?'

'Nice idea, although I'm not sure my colleagues in

London would appreciate me jumping ship,' Daniel told him with a laugh to disguise how touched he felt by the request.

'Pity. You've fitted in really well around here. Everyone's said so. And they don't always take kindly to outsiders, believe me.'

Mike sketched him a wave and drove off. Daniel made his way back to the house, thinking about what the other man had said. Despite the problems with Emma, he had enjoyed working in the town far more than he had expected. Not only had he enjoyed being part of such a close-knit community, he had dealt with a far wider variety of cases than he normally would have seen. With the nearest hospital being so far away, the surgery was the first port of call in an emergency and it had been good to test his skills.

He knew that if circumstances had been different, he would have been tempted to ask Jim Haynes if he was still interested in taking on a partner. There was certainly sufficient work for a second doctor; in fact, he couldn't imagine how Jim was going to cope on his own when he returned to work. However, he also knew how Emma would feel about the idea. He would be the last person she would want working here.

It was a dispiriting thought. Knowing how Emma felt about him hurt, even though he refused to examine the reasons why it was so painful. He knew that she would take care to ensure their paths never crossed in the future and it was hard to accept that once she left, he would never see her again. Even though he knew it was for the best, he was going to miss her.

* * *

Emma found it difficult to put what had happened between her and Daniel behind her. The fact that he never
once alluded to it should have helped but it didn't. She
found it deeply hurtful that he'd been able to dismiss
the fact that they had slept together.

In an effort to make the remainder of her stay in
Avondale bearable, she made a point of keeping out of
his way outside working hours. It wasn't difficult. Daniel
had taken to going for a walk after evening surgery
finished, which meant he was rarely at home. She did
wonder if he was avoiding her too but decided she was
being fanciful. Daniel had demonstrated very clearly
that he had very few feelings for her, so why would he
feel that he needed to keep out of her way?

Another week passed and the surgery was busier than
ever. There was a steady influx of tourists arriving in the
area and they added to the number of people wanting to
be seen. Emma couldn't help wondering how her uncle
was going to cope when he returned to work. Although
he was making excellent progress, according to her aunt,
running a busy practice with all that it entailed was
very different from convalescing. She couldn't bear to
think that Uncle Jim might put his health at risk out of
a sense of duty and decided to speak to Daniel about
it. She managed to catch him on his way out to some
house calls on Friday lunchtime.

'Have you got a minute?'

'Yes, of course. What's up? Problems?'

He put his case on the desk and turned to face her.
Emma felt her heart give a little jolt and swallowed. The
weather had been exceptionally warm that day and he'd

shed his jacket and rolled up his shirtsleeves. The pale blue cotton set off his olive-toned skin and provided the perfect foil for his dark brown hair. He looked big and vital and so gloriously male that she was suddenly aware of her own femininity in a way she hadn't been since the night they had made love.

The thought wasn't the least bit welcome. She hurriedly drove it from her mind and concentrated on what she'd come to say. 'I've been thinking about what's going to happen when Uncle Jim comes back to work.'

'You mean how he's going to manage on his own?' Daniel said immediately, and she looked at him in surprise.

'Yes. How did you know that's what I meant?'

'Because I've been thinking about it too.' He gave her a tight smile. 'It doesn't take a genius to see that he's going to be pushed to keep up with the workload here. Quite frankly, it's way too much for one person.'

'It is. He needs someone to help him, ideally another partner, but I can't see that happening, can you?'

'It could take time to find the right person,' Daniel said slowly. 'And it isn't something we can organise without your uncle's consent.'

'No, it isn't. And if Uncle Jim is as choosy this time round as he was the last time he advertised, it could take for ever.' She sighed. 'It's hard to know what to do, isn't it?'

'How about a locum?' Daniel suggested.

'Do you think we'd find anyone willing to work here, though?'

'I can't see why not. Oh, I know Avondale isn't

exactly a mecca for bright lights and a wild social life, but neither is it the back of beyond. And at this time of the year—when the weather is fine—it might be an attractive proposition for someone.'

'It's worth a try,' she said slowly. 'I don't suppose you know any reliable agencies who provide locum cover? It's not something I've had to deal with.'

'I'll get onto our practice manager and ask her for some phone numbers,' Daniel assured her. 'We often need locum cover so she keeps a list of agencies.'

'That would be great. Thank you. Should we tell Uncle Jim what we're planning when he phones?'

'Oh, yes, I think so, don't you?' He shrugged. 'If I were in his shoes, I'd expect to be kept up to date with what was going on here.'

'I only hope he doesn't object,' Emma said anxiously. 'You know how touchy he can be about his patients, wants to be sure they receive first-class care, et cetera.'

'Leave it to me. I'm sure I can convince him it will be in everyone's best interests if he has help, if only during the summer months.'

'That's probably the best way to sell the idea to him,' Emma agreed. 'Even Uncle Jim will have to admit that it's hard to cope when there are so many visitors in the area.'

'And once he's admitted that, it should be easier to make him see that he needs help at other times of the year as well.'

'Take it one step at a time, you mean?' she said, frowning as she considered the idea and realised that it had a lot of merit.

'Yes.' Daniel sighed. 'Trying to push your uncle into admitting that he isn't up to running the practice on his own any longer will only make him dig in his heels, so we'll take things slowly, let him discover for himself that he needs help.'

'It makes sense. I'd hate it to look as though we doubt his capabilities.'

'Exactly. This way, any decisions that are made about the future of the practice will be his. He won't feel as though he's being pushed into doing something he doesn't want to do.'

'You're right,' Emma agreed, surprised by Daniel's astute assessment of the situation. She knew that her uncle would hate to feel as though he wasn't in charge any more, but it surprised her that Daniel had realised that too.

She turned to leave then stopped when Daniel said suddenly, 'Oh, by the way, those test results for Alistair Grant have come back. I was in the office when they arrived so I had a look at them. I hope you don't mind?'

'Of course not. What did they show? Anything?'

'According to the lab at Liverpool there are traces of pesticide in Alistair's blood.' Daniel shrugged. 'It would certainly explain the wide variety of symptoms he's presented with recently, wouldn't it?'

'It would. Do you think he's been in contact with pesticides while he's been here or did it happen while he was working overseas?' she queried.

'Liverpool seems to think the problem is recent. I've asked Ruth to phone Alistair and get him to make an appointment to see if we can find out how he may have come into contact with the chemicals. If we can't find an answer, I imagine environmental services will need to be alerted to see if they can sort it out.'

'Of course. If it is a local problem then we don't want anyone else being taken ill,' she said worriedly.

'Exactly.' He smiled at her. 'I'll mention it to your uncle when he phones. I'm sure he'd enjoy getting to the bottom of the mystery.'

'I'm sure he would,' she agreed quietly.

Emma sighed as she left the room. She couldn't help wondering how one person could be such a contradiction. On the one hand Daniel genuinely seemed to care about other people's feelings, but on the other hand he didn't seem to care a jot about hers. Even though she knew it was stupid, she couldn't help wishing that he would spare some of that concern for her.

The house calls had taken far longer than he'd expected so that it was after three p.m. by the time Daniel drew up in front of Niths Farm. He switched off the engine and reached for the printout that Ruth had prepared for him. According to the patient's notes, it had been over ten years since Harold Dawson had last visited the surgery. He'd suffered an injury to his left arm following an incident with some kind of farm machinery but had refused to go to the hospital. Jim had stitched his arm, given him a tetanus shot, and that had been it. Harold Dawson hadn't returned to have the stitches removed and had ignored several telephone messages asking him to contact the surgery. Daniel grimaced as he got out of the car. It didn't bode well for what was going to greet him today.

He rapped on the farmhouse door, glancing around while he waited. Although the farm was large, it was very untidy. Bits of rusty old machinery littered the yard and there was a pile of stones heaped up in the corner where one of the barn walls had given way. The whole place had a pervading air of neglect that saddened him. It seemed a shame that what had been once an obviously thriving concern should have been reduced to such a pitiful state as this.

'Aye? And what do you want?'

Daniel swung round when a gruff voice spoke behind him. He summoned a smile as he greeted the elderly man standing in the doorway. 'I'm Dr Kennedy. You phoned the surgery and requested a home visit.'

'I asked to see the real doctor, not some stand-in,' the man replied rudely. He glared at Daniel. 'Tell them I want to see Dr Haynes, no one else.'

'I'm afraid Dr Haynes is away at the present time,' Daniel explained quietly.

'Then I'll wait till he's back.'

He went to shut the door but Daniel put out his hand and stopped him. 'Dr Haynes won't be back for another month. Are you sure you want to wait that long, Mr Dawson?'

The man hesitated while he considered the idea. He scowled as he wrenched open the door. 'Suppose you'd better come in, then, seeing as you're here.'

Daniel sighed ruefully as he followed the old man into a dingy hallway. Not exactly the warmest welcome he'd ever received. Harold Dawson led him down the hall to the kitchen, which turned out to be equally neglected. Daniel's heart sank as he took stock of the piles of dirty dishes on the draining board and the inch-thick layer of grease that coated the top of the old-fashioned range. It didn't appear as though any cleaning had been done in the place for months, if not years. Pushing aside a stack of old newspapers, he placed his case on the table.

'So what exactly is the problem, Mr Dawson? You told Ruth it was something to do with your foot, I believe.'

'That's right, although I wouldn't have bothered phoning if I weren't in so much pain.' The man glared at him. 'I don't hold with all these pills you doctors hand out. Don't do folk no good, in my opinion.'

Daniel forbore to say anything, deeming it wiser not to get embroiled in an argument he was unlikely to win. 'I'd better take a look at your foot.'

Harold Dawson sat down heavily on a chair and started to peel off a filthy sock from his right foot. Daniel shook his head in dismay when he saw the how red and swollen it looked.

'When did this start?' he asked, kneeling down in front of the old man.

'A few weeks ago, mebbe a bit longer,' Harold replied curtly. He winced when Daniel touched the inflamed skin. 'It's real tender so don't you go poking and prodding at it.'

'I'll be as careful as I can,' Daniel assured him. He carefully felt the swollen foot, pausing when he discovered a strong pulse beating beneath the flesh because it confirmed his initial diagnosis. Standing up, he took a bottle of hand gel out of his case, deeming it more hygienic than using the sink to wash his hands.

'It looks to me as though you have immersion foot, Mr Dawson. It's a type of injury caused when feet are allowed to remain wet and cold for a prolonged period. You may have heard of trench foot which so many soldiers in the First World War suffered from? It's the same thing.'

'I've not been standing in any trenches,' Harold retorted scathingly.

'I'm sure you haven't. But if you've been outdoors and got your feet wet and not bothered to change your shoes and socks, that could have caused it.' Daniel tactfully didn't add that from the state of the man's socks there was no *could* about it. It was doubtful if Harold Dawson had put on clean socks or anything else for a very long time!

He took a prescription pad out of his case and wrote out a script for painkillers. 'I imagine your foot's very painful so these will help. You'll also need to bathe your foot in tepid water to cool it and reduce the swelling. Make sure you put on clean, dry socks and that your shoes or boots are dry too.' Daniel handed the man the prescription. 'If you notice any sores appearing, contact the surgery. Skin ulcers can develop and that's something we want to avoid.'

'So that's it, is it?' Harold Dawson slammed the prescription down on the table. 'Take some pills and put on dry socks. I could've worked that out for myself!'

Daniel smiled calmly, resisting the urge to tell

the man that if he'd done that in the beginning there wouldn't have been a problem. 'That's right. It's just a question of taking care of yourself.'

'I don't need any advice from you,' the old man responded belligerently. He shuffled towards the door, making it clear that he expected Daniel to leave.

Daniel picked up his case, knowing how pointless it was to suggest that he arranged for the community nurse to call and check how Harold's foot was healing. If the poor woman received the kind of reception he'd received, she would probably refuse to call a second time, and he wouldn't blame her either. He made a note to speak to Ruth about the old man when he got back to the surgery and headed out to the hall, pausing when there was a loud banging on the front door.

'What the dickens…!' Harold Dawson pushed past him and strode along the hall. Wrenching open the door, he glowered at the young man standing outside. 'You can take yourself off my property right now.'

'Believe me, I'd like nothing better than not to see hide nor hair of you or this place for the rest of my life,' the other man retorted.

Daniel frowned when he realised that the caller was Alistair Grant. It seemed a coincidence that he should turn up here when he needed to speak to him. However, he was less concerned about resolving Alistair's health issues at that moment than he was about defusing the situation.

He hurried to the door, hoping to avert a full-scale row.

'Hello, Alistair,' he said quietly, drawing both men's attention to him. 'I'm surprised to see you here.'

'I'm not here out of choice, believe me, Dr Kennedy,' Alistair replied angrily. He glared at the old man. 'If you don't stop dumping stuff on the road to the construction site then I warn you, Dawson, that the company I work for will take legal action. Carry on with your little games and you'll find yourself in prison. Is that clear?'

'Aye, it's clear enough. But if you think a young pup like you can come to my home and threaten me, think again.'

Daniel's heart sank when he saw Harold Dawson reach behind the front door and pick up a shotgun that had been standing there. He aimed it at Alistair Grant's chest. 'You need to learn some manners, lad, and I'm just the one to teach them to you.'

'Come on, now, let's all calm down,' Daniel said soothingly. He stepped forward then stopped when Dawson swung round and pointed the gun at him.

'I've told you once that I don't need any advice from you.' The old man scowled at him. 'You're no better than he is. Coming in here, thinking you can tell folk what to do. Well, I've had enough, do you hear me? It's 'bout time someone stood up to the likes of you. Inside, both of you.'

Dawson waved the shotgun towards the kitchen. Daniel hesitated but one glance at the old man's face warned him that it would be foolish to refuse to do what he asked. He headed back along the hall, wondering what was going to happen next. Maybe Dawson only wanted to scare them but he didn't think so—it looked far more serious than that.

He put his case on the table as Alistair followed him

into the room, seeing the sheen of perspiration on the younger man's face. It was obvious that he was scared stiff and Daniel didn't blame him. Harold Dawson was on the brink of losing control and there was no knowing what would happen then.

A picture of Emma suddenly appeared in his mind's eye and he felt a shaft of regret so sharp run through him that he winced. He couldn't bear to think that he might die without telling Emma that he loved her.

CHAPTER ELEVEN

'I DON'T suppose you've seen Daniel, have you, Emma?'

Emma paused when Ruth called to her on her way into the surgery that afternoon. It was five minutes to four and she was keen to get to her room before her first patient arrived. 'Not since lunchtime, I'm afraid.'

'Oh, right.' Ruth sighed.

Emma frowned. 'Why? Is there a problem?'

'No, not really. It's just that he usually pops in with his notes after he's finished the house calls, but he's not been in yet this afternoon.'

'Maybe he's running late,' Emma suggested.

'Probably, although there weren't that many calls to do today.' Ruth shrugged when the phone rang. 'Maybe he got held up. You know how some people love to talk—he probably couldn't get away.'

'I expect that's it,' Emma agreed as she carried on along the corridor, although she was surprised that Daniel would have allowed himself to be late. He was a stickler for punctuality and was usually at his desk well before his first appointment was due.

She booted up her computer then glanced through the list that Ruth had left on her desk. It wasn't too long for a change so, hopefully, she could finish on time for once. She buzzed through for her first patient, smiling when Judith Fisher walked into the room.

'Hello, Judith. How are you?'

'I'm all right, Dr Roberts.' The young woman sat down in front of the desk. 'I had an appointment at the hospital on Wednesday. The consultant did a laparoscopy and confirmed that I have endometriosis, like you suspected.'

'At least we know what we're dealing with now,' Emma said quietly.

'I suppose so,' Judith agreed wistfully.

Emma guessed that it had been a blow for Judith to have her suspicions confirmed and tried to focus on the positive aspects of the diagnosis. 'What did the consultant suggest by way of treatment?'

'He's put me back on the Pill to prevent me menstruating. It will help to control the pain and, hopefully, stop the cysts from getting any bigger. He also said that he might surgically remove some of the larger cysts at a later date.'

'And you're worried about how that will affect your chances of having a baby?'

'Yes.' Tears rose in Judith's eyes. 'I don't think I'll ever have a baby now, will I?'

'I haven't received a copy of your consultant's report yet, Judith, so there is no way that I can tell you that everything is going to be all right. However, what I can say is that between sixty and seventy per cent of women who suffer from endometriosis are able to have children.'

'That sounds much better than how the consultant put it.' Judith managed a watery smile. 'He said that thirty to forty per cent of women with endometriosis are infertile.'

'I suppose it's the glass half full or half empty scenario,' Emma said with a chuckle. 'It depends which way you choose to look at the figures.'

'Well, I prefer your way.' Judith sounded more optimistic all of a sudden. 'I have almost a seventy per cent chance of becoming a mum and that's pretty good odds, I'd say.'

'So would I.' Emma smiled at her. 'I know it must be hard but try to remain positive. Once you've completed the treatment, who knows what might happen? And the plus factor is that pregnancy is known to suppress the symptoms of endometriosis.'

'A case of fingers crossed.' Judith laughed as she stood up.

'Exactly.'

Emma was still smiling as she buzzed through her next patient. It was always good to know that you had helped someone be more positive about their life. That was one of the reasons why she loved surgery, of course, although she hadn't realised that she would derive the same pleasure from general practice work. No wonder Daniel enjoyed his job so much.

The thought startled her. Ever since Daniel had announced that he planned to go into private practice, she'd had a jaundiced view of his motives for becoming a GP. Now she could see that she may have misjudged him.

It didn't necessarily mean that it was purely financial gain that drove him.

It was uncomfortable to find her view of Daniel knocked off kilter. Emma found it difficult to push the idea aside as she dealt with her next patient, an elderly man who suffered from chronic bronchitis. She renewed his prescription for an inhaler and gently suggested that he might benefit from oxygen therapy. Once she had explained that oxygen cylinders could be delivered to his home, he happily agreed. She made a note to ask Ruth to contact the nearest supplier and saw him out. She was just about to sit down again when Ruth, herself, hurried into the room.

'I'm sorry to barge in, Emma, but Daniel still hasn't appeared. I'm getting really worried now, because it just isn't like him not to turn up,' the receptionist told her anxiously.

'No, it certainly isn't,' Emma agreed. 'Have you tried his phone?'

'Yes, but it goes straight to voice mail.' Ruth bit her lip. 'You don't think he's had an accident, do you? Some of the roads round here are a bit tricky if you don't know them that well.'

'I'm sure we'd have heard if he had,' Emma assured her, although her heart had started to race at the thought of Daniel lying injured somewhere. She took a deep breath before panic could set in. 'Do you have a list of the calls he was supposed to do this afternoon?' When Ruth nodded, she hurried on. 'Then I suggest you telephone everyone on the list and check what time he visited them. That way we'll have a better idea of where he might be.'

'Good idea!' Ruth exclaimed. She hurried to the door then paused. 'What about his patients, though? There's a real backlog forming.'

'I'll have to see them,' Emma told her. 'I'll see one of mine then one of Daniel's—that will be fairer than making his patients wait till I finish my list.'

Emma picked up the phone as soon as Ruth left and dialled Daniel's phone but the call went straight to voice mail again. She hung up, feeling her stomach churning with nerves. What could have happened to stop him even answering his phone? She had no idea but it was extremely worrying. Maybe they didn't see eye to eye on a lot of things but she couldn't bear to think that he may have been hurt or worse even.

Her heart suddenly seemed to shrivel up inside her. The thought of never seeing Daniel again was more than she could bear.

Daniel heard his phone ring and guessed that it must be Ruth calling to see where he was. He glanced at his watch, realising with a start that it was almost four-thirty. How much longer was Dawson going to keep them here? he wondered, glancing at the old man, who was standing guard by the kitchen door. He had no idea but something needed to be done to resolve this situation soon.

'Look, Mr Dawson, I know you're upset but this is crazy. Keeping us here won't achieve anything,' he said in his most reasonable tone. 'All you'll do is find yourself in a whole load of trouble and I'm sure that isn't what any of us wants.'

'I don't care how much trouble I'm in. It'll be worth it to put a stop to what's going on.' Harold Dawson raised the shotgun and pointed it at Alistair Grant. 'If him and his cronies think they can come here and tear up the countryside then they can think again!'

Daniel saw the colour drain from Alistair's face and quickly interceded. 'If that's the way you feel, you need to talk to someone, see if you can get the decision to build this wind farm reversed.'

'Talk! I've talked till I'm blue in the face and no one's listened to me.' Harold's face flushed with anger. 'No, it's actions that will get their attention, nothing else.'

Daniel opened his mouth to try again to make him see sense when the telephone rang. Harold Dawson lifted the receiver off its rest. Daniel could tell from what the old man was saying that it was the surgery phoning and guessed that Ruth must be checking up on his whereabouts. He was tempted to shout out that he was there but Dawson must have realised he might do that and swung the gun towards him.

'No, the doctor left a while ago. No, I don't know what time it was. I've better things to do than keep a check on folk's comings and goings.'

He went to slam the receiver back on its rest at the same moment that Daniel's mobile phone rang again. He let it go to voice mail once more, knowing it would be foolish to try and answer it. Dawson's mood was far too volatile to risk upsetting him any further. He glanced at Alistair and saw the fear in the younger man's eyes.

'What are we going to do?' Alistair mouthed desperately.

Daniel shook his head. Reasoning with the old man obviously wasn't going to work and using physical force was out of the question when Dawson had that gun. All he could hope was that Emma would call the police when he failed to turn up. So long as she didn't try tracking him down herself, of course.

The air seemed to lock in his lungs at the thought of her following him to the farm and placing herself in danger. He knew if that happened he would have to do something, no matter how risky it was.

He took a deep breath and his mind was suddenly crystal clear. He would give up his life to protect Emma because he loved her.

It was seven o'clock before the last patient left. Emma hurried through to Reception, not needing to ask if there was any news when she saw the worry on Ruth's face. 'Still nothing,' she said helplessly.

'No. I just don't know what to do next, Emma.'

'You've called everyone who'd requested a home visit?'

'Yes, and they all said that Dr Kennedy had left ages ago.' Ruth shook her head. 'Most of them were able to tell me almost to the minute what time he left too. It was only old Harold Dawson who refused to say what time Daniel left his farm but that's typical of him. A really awkward old devil, he is.'

'Harold Dawson from Niths Farm, you mean?' Emma queried.

'That's right. He's always been difficult but he's got worse since his wife died. He doesn't have any family and I doubt he's got any friends either...' Ruth paused and frowned.

'What?' Emma said quickly. 'You've obviously thought of something.'

'It's just that when I was hanging up the phone after speaking to him I could have sworn I heard a mobile phone ringing in the background.' Ruth shrugged. 'It just seems odd. I wouldn't have thought old Mr Dawson would be the sort to bother having a mobile.'

'Maybe he had somebody visiting him,' Emma suggested.

'Could be, although I doubt they'd get much of a welcome. He's not one to mix, believe me.'

Emma sighed. Although it did seem strange, it had nothing to do with what had happened to Daniel so there wasn't time to worry about it right then. She came to a swift decision. 'I'm going to phone the police and report Daniel missing. I'm not sure what they can do but we can't just sit here, wondering what's happened to him.'

'I think you should call them,' Ruth agreed, looking relieved. 'Daniel would have let us know if his car had broken down or if he'd had some sort of minor accident.'

Emma bit her lip as she reached for the receiver. Ruth was right. Daniel *would* have contacted them—if he could. She put a call through to the police station and told them what had happened. They promised to check with the various agencies in case Daniel had been involved in an RTA and get back to her. Ruth insisted on staying while they waited for the police to phone back and went off to make them a cup of tea. Almost as soon as she'd gone, there was a loud banging on the surgery door and Emma felt her spirits soar in relief. That had to be Daniel!

Hurrying to the door, she swung it open. 'And about time too—' she began, then stopped abruptly when she found Mike Harding standing on the step. 'Sorry, Mike. I thought you were someone else.'

Mike grimaced. 'And I'm sorry to turn up like this too but I noticed the lights were still on as I was passing.' He held up his hand, which was covered in a blood-soaked bandage. 'We've been out on a training exercise tonight and I managed to get my thumb caught in one of the ratchets we use to haul people up the hillside. It needs a stitch or two and I was hoping you might do it to save me having to trail off to the hospital.'

'I…um…yes, of course. Come in.' Emma led the way inside. 'Come straight through to my room while I take a look at it.'

Mike followed her along the corridor, glancing round when Ruth came rushing out of the staffroom. He must have seen her face fall because he grinned. 'Obviously, I'm not the person you hoped to see either.'

'No, you're not,' Ruth said bluntly.

Mike's smile faded as he looked from her to Emma. 'Is something wrong?'

'Daniel failed to turn up for surgery this evening,' Emma explained as she ushered him into her room. 'He hasn't phoned and he isn't answering his mobile either.'

'That's odd.' Mike frowned as he sat down and unwound the bandage. 'I wouldn't have thought there was a problem getting a signal in that part of the Dales.'

Emma stopped and stared at him. 'What do you mean, that part of the Dales? Have you seen him?'

'Yes, well not *him* but I've seen his car. It's parked outside old man Dawson's place—Niths Farm. You know.'

'What time was this?' Emma demanded.

'Oh, around six-thirty, give or take a few minutes.' Mike shrugged. 'I did my hand in soon after that so it can't have been much later.'

'But Ruth phoned Harold Dawson way before then and he told her that Daniel had already left!' Emma exclaimed.

'Well, it was definitely Dr Kennedy's car. You don't get many fancy motors like that round here and certainly not at Dawson's place. There was another car there too, now that I think about it, a site vehicle from that wind farm they're building on the edge of Dawson's land.' Mike looked worried now. 'Why on earth did Dawson say the doc wasn't there when he was?'

'I don't know but it needs checking.' Emma picked up a dish and filled it with saline then gently bathed Mike's thumb. She frowned when she saw the deep gash at its base. 'That looks nasty. It's going to need three or four stitches by the look of it.'

She numbed Mike's thumb with an injection of local anaesthetic then set to work. It only took her only a few minutes to complete the job and Mike shook his head in admiration. 'That was quick work. You've done that a time or two, by the look of it.'

'Just a couple of times.' Emma summoned a smile but it was hard to concentrate. She had a nasty feeling about what Mike had told her and wouldn't rest until she had paid Harold Dawson a visit to see what was going on.

'Dr Haynes told me that you'd gone into surgery.' Mike smiled at her as he stood up. 'He's every right to be proud of you.'

Emma merely nodded, her mind too busy churning over possibilities to focus on the compliment. She looked up when Mike sighed. 'If it's hurting I can give you some painkillers,' she offered, feeling guilty for neglecting her patient.

'It's fine. No, it's obvious that you're worried sick about Dr Kennedy, aren't you?'

Emma flushed. 'It just seems strange that he hasn't called us,' she demurred.

Mike gave her an old-fashioned look. 'Hmm. It does. Why don't we drive over there and see what's going on? It's the least I can do after you've saved me a long wait in Casualty.'

'Oh, I couldn't expect you to do that,' she began, but Mike shook his head.

'Of course you can. In fact, I'm going to get onto the rest of the team and tell them what's happened. If the doc's out there, we'll find him. That's a promise.'

He put a comforting arm around Emma's shoulders and she sagged gratefully against him. 'Thanks, Mike,' she murmured huskily.

'No sweat.' He gave her a brotherly hug then went to the door. 'I'll put through that call and see you outside. OK?'

Emma nodded then hurried to find Ruth and tell her what had happened. They agreed that the police should be informed that Daniel's car had been seen, although whether they would act on the information was open to question. Mike had the engine running when Emma hurried outside and as soon as she got into the Land Rover, they set off. It was a good thirty-minute drive to Niths Farm and Emma was on tenterhooks all the way. If Daniel had left the farm, she had no idea where to start looking for him.

They turned down the lane leading to the farm and Mike slowed as they reached the bottom. 'Look,' he said, pointing.

Emma's heart leapt into her throat when she saw Daniel's car parked in the yard alongside another vehicle, which bore the logo of the wind farm's contractors. Obviously he was still there despite Harold Dawson's assurances to the contrary. 'What should we do?' she asked anxiously.

'I don't know, but whatever we decide we need to be careful.' Mike's tone was sombre. 'Old Dawson is a bit of a loose cannon lately. Folk have seen him walking round with a shotgun. Let's not go rushing in until we know what's happening, eh?'

'But Daniel may be in danger!' she protested.

'Yes. And we don't want to make matters worse by forcing Dawson's hand.' Mike picked up the radio receiver. 'I'm going to call the police and get them over here right away.'

Emma opened her door and climbed out of the car while Mike made the call. There were only a few hundred yards between her and Daniel but the distance had never seemed greater. The fact that she had no idea what was happening to him was so painful that she felt tears well to her eyes. Maybe they weren't destined to spend their lives together, as she had once hoped, but that didn't matter. So long as she knew that he was safe and well somewhere in the world, that was enough. In that moment she was forced to acknowledge the truth. She loved him. She loved him with the whole of her heart and she always would.

CHAPTER TWELVE

DANIEL heard the sound of a car stopping in the lane and frowned. Was it possible that someone had come looking for him and Alistair? He glanced at Harold Dawson but the old man seemed oblivious to what was happening outside. Dawson had grown increasingly agitated in the past hour. He had placed the shotgun by the back door and started walking around the kitchen, muttering to himself. Daniel might have been tempted to make a grab for the shotgun if it weren't for the fact that someone could get hurt if there was a struggle. It had seemed safer to bide his time but he might not have that luxury for much longer. He turned to Alistair.

'There's a car stopped in the lane,' he mouthed.

'Do you think it's the police?' Alistair whispered, hopefully.

Before Daniel could answer, Harold Dawson swung round and glared at them. 'Don't you two start thinking you can get up to anything.' He grabbed hold of the shotgun and pointed it at them. 'I won't think twice about using this, I warn you.'

'And what will that achieve, Mr Dawson?' Daniel

said in sudden exasperation. 'You'll end up in prison and the wind farm will still go ahead.'

'At least they'll know they can't trample all over me,' Harold roared. He aimed the gun at the ceiling and pulled the trigger. Daniel ducked as bits of wood and plaster rained down on them. His ears were throbbing from the noise of the explosion so that it was several seconds before he could hear let alone speak.

'Force isn't the answer,' he told the old man grimly. 'The powers-that-be won't give in because you threaten them. You need to go through the proper channels.'

If Dawson was listening he gave no sign of it. Daniel realised that he was wasting his breath trying to reason with him. He glanced towards the window, mentally crossing his fingers that it was the police outside and not some other unsuspecting visitor. His heart turned over at the thought that it might be Emma before he realised how foolish it was to imagine she cared enough to try and find him. Emma may have contacted the police when he hadn't turned up for evening surgery but that would have been all. She certainly wouldn't be spending her time worrying about him.

Emma's heart seemed to stop when she heard the sound of a shotgun being discharged. Mike was speaking to the police on the radio and she saw the shock on his face as he looked up. He hastily finished his call and hung up.

'The police will be here ASAP,' he told her. 'They said that we're not to approach the house and that

under no circumstances are we to try and contact either
Dawson or Dr Kennedy.'

'But we can't just sit here,' Emma protested. 'Anything could be going on inside that farmhouse. We need
to do something!'

'We daren't risk it, Emma. I know it's hard but we
could make matters a whole lot worse if we go rushing
in.' Mike patted her hand. 'Let's wait for the police,
love. They know what they're doing.'

Emma bit her lip. She knew Mike was right but it
was sheer agony to wonder if Daniel might be hurt. It
seemed to take for ever before the police arrived. She
and Mike told them everything they knew, which was
very little. When the police insisted that they back up
the lane, she protested, but the police were adamant.
They couldn't risk there being any civilian casualties.

The time dragged after that. The police used a loud-
hailer to speak to Harold Dawson, trying to persuade
him to let the hostages go. He refused all their pleas,
ending the negotiations by firing the shotgun out of
the window. Armed police officers were deployed to
surround the house and everyone looked very tense.
However, by the time midnight arrived, little progress
had been made.

Emma couldn't imagine what it must be like for
Daniel and the other hostage being caught up in such a
drama. All she could do was hope that Harold Dawson
would come to his senses and let them go. And if he did
then she intended to tell Daniel the truth about how she
felt. She loved him and she wasn't going to lie about it,

wasn't going to pretend any more. She would tell him the truth—and hope that it meant something to him.

Daniel could feel his nerves humming with tension. Ever since Dawson had fired that shot at the police, he had become increasingly unstable. Daniel knew that he was within a hairsbreadth of losing control and had no idea what would happen then. Somehow he had to get the old man talking and hopefully defuse the situation.

'Why exactly are you so against this wind farm being built?' he asked as Harold made another circuit of the room.

'Because it shouldn't be there, that's why.' Harold glowered at him but Daniel tried not to let it deter him.

'You think it will spoil the countryside?'

''Course it will. Who wants to look at dozens of great lumps of metal? My Mary wouldn't. That's for sure.'

'Mary's your wife?' Daniel said quickly, wanting to keep the conversation flowing.

'Was. She died six years ago.' Tears suddenly welled into the old man's eyes. 'She loved the view over those hills, did my Mary. There's a meadow there that's full of wildflowers in the spring and she always said it was the most beautiful place on God's earth. Even when she was so ill that she couldn't get out of bed most days, she'd ask me to take her up there. And now folks like him want to dig it all up and spoil it.'

He jerked his thumb at Alistair, who blanched. Daniel realised that he had hit upon the real crux of the problem. Harold Dawson's desire to stop the wind farm going ahead was all tied up with his late wife. He realised that he needed to tread warily.

'No wonder you're upset about what's happening,' he said quietly. 'It must be difficult to accept that a place which meant so much to your wife is going to change. But do you think Mary would have been happy about what you're doing?'

'What do you mean?' Dawson demanded querulously.

'Keeping us here and threatening us. Shooting at the police.' Daniel shrugged. 'What would Mary say if she knew that was what you were up to?'

Harold Dawson stopped pacing; his expression was reflective. 'My Mary hated guns. She wouldn't even let me shoot rabbits when she was alive. Said it was cruel, she did.'

'Then I doubt if she'd have approved of this, would she?' Daniel held out his hand. 'Why not give me the shotgun, Mr Dawson. Let's stop this now before things get any worse.'

Harold Dawson hesitated then slowly handed over the shotgun. Daniel carefully ejected the cartridges then placed it against the wall and stood up. 'I suggest we tell the police that we're coming out.'

Dawson didn't try to stop them as he and Alistair walked along the hall. Daniel cautiously opened the front door, shouting out that he and Alistair were coming out. Everything happened at great speed after that. The police came running towards them, some of the officers going straight into the house while others hurried him and Alistair away to safety. People were firing questions at him from all directions and he did his best to answer them, but he had caught sight of a figure standing just beyond the police cordon. Emma was here? She had cared enough to come and find him?

His heart sang with joy as he walked straight past the policeman who was trying to speak to him. Emma had started walking too, ducking under the tape, so that they met in the middle of the lane. When he opened his arms, she stepped into them and it was then that he knew everything was going to be all right. How could it not be when the love of his life was here in his arms, her heart beating in time with his?

He bent and kissed her, uncaring that everyone was watching them. He didn't give a damn who knew how he felt so long as Emma knew it. Drawing back, he looked into her eyes, wanting there to be no more misunderstandings, either deliberate or accidental.

'I love you,' he said softly, his voice grating with emotion. He felt the tremor that ran through her, heard the sharp indrawn breath she took, and held her tighter, knowing it must be a shock for her to hear him say that. He had hurt her so much, seemingly thrown away her love, and it was a lot to ask her to believe him now, but he had to try. 'I love you, Emma. I always have.'

'Daniel, I…'

She stopped and swallowed. Daniel could see the uncertainty in her eyes and prayed that she would find it in her heart to give him another chance. He wanted to take her somewhere quiet and explain it all to her, but there was no hope of that right now. He sighed when the officer in charge came over and told him firmly that he needed to speak to him at the police station. It appeared that sorting things out with Emma would have to wait for now.

'I'll have to go,' he told her huskily, smoothing a silky lock of her hair behind her ear. He dropped a kiss on her lips then smiled at her. 'I'll be back as soon as I can. Will you wait up for me?'

'Yes.' She gave him a wobbly smile, her eyes holding his fast for a moment before she turned away.

Daniel watched her walk over to Mike, who put a friendly arm around her shoulders as he led her to his car. He would have felt better if they could have sorted things out immediately rather than wait, but there was nothing he could do. As he allowed the officer to lead him to the waiting police car he sent up a silent prayer that everything would be all right. He just needed Emma to give him a second chance.

It was five a.m. before Emma heard a car turn into the drive. She ran to the window, feeling her heart leap when she saw Daniel getting out of a police car. Hurrying into the hall, she flung open the front door, seeing the lines that fatigue had been etched onto his handsome face.

'I thought they were never going to let me go,' he said as he stepped into the hall. 'I must have gone over what happened a dozen times before they were satisfied that I'd told them everything.'

'Come into the sitting room.'

Emma led the way, waiting until he had sunk down onto a chair before she went back to the door. She had spent the intervening time wondering what would happen when he got back. He had told her that he loved her but was it true? She longed to know yet now that the moment had arrived, she was suddenly afraid. What if Daniel hadn't really meant it, what if it had been merely a reaction to the stress he'd been under? She wasn't sure if she could cope with the disappointment of having her hopes dashed a second time.

'I'll make you a drink,' she said hurriedly. 'What do you prefer—tea or coffee?'

'Neither, thank you. My stomach is awash with the foul brew that passes for tea at the police station.' He gave her a gentle smile as he held out his hand. 'Come and sit down, Emma. We need to talk.'

Emma bit her lip as she slowly sat down on the end of the sofa. She didn't know how she was going to bear it if Daniel told her it had been the stress of the moment that had made him say that he loved her. People said all sorts of things they didn't mean when they were under pressure, after all.

'Emma, about what I said before—' he began, but she didn't let him finish, couldn't bear to hear him say the words that once again would rip open her heart.

'I understand, Daniel. Really I do.' She gave a light laugh and saw him frown.

'You do?'

'Of course. You were under a huge amount of strain. It's perfectly understandable if you…well, if you said something you didn't really mean.'

'So you think that I didn't mean it when I said that I loved you?'

His tone was so devoid of expression that Emma

found it impossible to guess what he was thinking. She shrugged, not wanting him to suspect how difficult this was for her. She loved him so much, had even planned to tell him that, but now she realised how foolish it would be. She simply couldn't bear to put herself in the position of having her heart broken all over again.

'I think it's perfectly natural that you reacted to the stress of the moment. People say the strangest things when they're under pressure.'

'I see. And you're not angry that I said what I did?'

'Of course not! We've all said things we've regretted, Daniel. It's part and parcel of being human, so please don't worry about it.'

'It's kind of you to take that view,' he said gruffly.

Emma frowned when she heard the roughness in his voice. He sounded upset but why should he be when she had offered him the perfect escape route? It was very strange but before she could work out what might be wrong, he stood up.

'I think I'll try and snatch a couple of hours' sleep or I'll be fit for nothing.'

He left the room before Emma could stop him. She followed him into the hall but he had already gone upstairs. She made her way to her room and lay down on the bed, fully clothed. She had done the right thing, she assured herself, given Daniel the let-out he'd needed. He didn't love her and it would have been a mistake to let herself believe that he did. Tears trickled down her cheeks but she didn't try to stop them. She needed to cry out all the disappointment and put it behind her if she was to get on with her life.

The sound of the door suddenly opening made her jump. Pushing herself up against the pillows, she stared at Daniel in surprise. 'Daniel! What is it?'

'I'm probably about to make a complete and utter fool of myself but there is no way that I can let this go.' He came over to the bed and glared down at her. 'I didn't tell you that I loved you because I was under pressure, Emma—far from it. For the first time in a long while I was thinking clearly. Letting you go five years ago was the hardest thing I have ever done. Not a day has passed since then when I haven't wished that I could have done things differently. I love you, Emma. That's the plain and simple truth. It might not be what you want to hear but it's what I need to tell you.'

He spun round on his heel and strode out of the door but there was no way that Emma was prepared to let him leave after making such a mind-blowing statement. She scrambled off the bed and ran after him, catching up with him on the landing. 'Daniel, wait! You can't come barging into my room and tell me that and then just... *storm* back out!'

'Better I do that than commit another sin,' he ground out, his eyes blazing into hers in a way that made a shaft of heat sear through her.

Emma felt her breath catch when she saw the expression in his eyes. It wasn't anger that had driven him to such extremes of emotion, she realised, but desire, desire for *her*. Her hand half lifted in a gesture that could have been interpreted either way, as a rejection or as an invitation. Even she wasn't sure what it meant, but then Daniel took a step towards her so that she could feel the heat of his body burning into hers, and her mind was suddenly crystal clear. She wanted him. Only him.

Her arms wound around his neck at the same moment as he reached out and hauled her towards him so that their bodies collided with a small thud, as though they had been struck by a mini-earthquake. Emma could feel the aftershocks rippling through her, tiny flurries of sensation that made her feel wonderfully alive. As her fingers buried themselves in the crisp dark hair at the nape of Daniel's neck, she murmured softly—sounds, not words—because forming anything as difficult as a word was beyond her, but Daniel seemed to understand what she meant anyway.

His mouth found hers, his lips parting hers so that he could plunder her mouth, and she groaned. There was nothing gentle about the kiss, nothing tender. It was as though every scrap of raw passion had been distilled into this one kiss, so that she was breathless when it ended, her body throbbing, her mind numb, her heart awash with emotions.

'Emma, my sweet, sweet Emma.'

His voice was hoarse as he gently laid her down on the carpet and started to undo the buttons down the front of her shirt. Emma would have loved to help him but her hands wouldn't respond. They were locked around his neck, her fingers still buried in his cool crisp hair, and they refused to let go. She just lay there as he finished unbuttoning her shirt and parted the edges, lay there still as he reached beneath her and unclipped her bra. It was only when he lifted her right breast free of the lacy cup that the spell was broken and she was able to move but even then her hands remained locked around his neck as she drew his head down, inviting him to suckle her.

She gasped as a wave of intense pleasure rushed through her when his lips closed around her nipple. There was no slow build-up of passion, no need for caresses or time. She wanted him, right there, right now, this minute.

He lifted his head and must have seen how she felt because he shuddered. Emma could feel the tension in his body as he stripped off her clothes then shed his own. He made love to her there on the floor, his body pressing hers down into the carpet, but even though everything was heat and passion, there was tenderness, too. And it was that more than anything else that convinced her that Daniel had been telling her the truth. He did love her. Her heart soared at the thought.

Daniel could feel his heart pounding as he slowly came back down to earth. Making love with Emma had always been the most wonderful of experiences and this time they had reached new heights. Propping himself up on his elbows, he stared down into her face, feeling his love for her swamp him.

'Wow! I'm not sure how that came about but it was definitely something else,' he murmured, buzzing her lips with a kiss.

'It was.' She smiled as she cupped his cheek with her hand. 'A definite wow in my book too.'

'I'm glad to hear it.' Daniel laughed throatily. 'At least I don't have to apologise for not finding somewhere more comfortable.'

'Oh, it's comfy enough.' She wriggled a little and his breath caught when he felt her body moving beneath his. Even though it was only moments since they had made love, he could feel himself responding. 'Although I may need to check my backside for carpet burns.'

'If you do find any, I'll be more than happy to administer a little first aid,' he assured her, grinning.

'I'll let you know,' she told him, laughing.

Daniel kissed her lightly on the mouth then rolled to his feet. Although he could have happily stayed there all day, they needed to talk and they couldn't do it there. He offered her his hand, unable to resist pulling her into his arms when she stood up.

'I didn't plan for that to happen, Emma, but I'm glad that it did.' He raised her chin so that he could look into her eyes. 'I know you think that I was under a lot of pressure earlier but I'm not under any pressure now and I still feel the same. I love you and that's why I made love to you just now. I only hope that somehow, some way, I can make you believe me.'

'I do believe you, Daniel.' She gave a little shrug when he gasped. 'You couldn't have made love to me like that and not cared.'

'No, I couldn't,' he agreed, his heart overflowing with emotion. He kissed her on the lips then led her to her room and gently steered her through the door. 'We need to talk and I won't be able to concentrate if you're in that state of undress. Put something on and come downstairs. We'll talk then.'

She didn't say anything as she went into her room and closed the door. Daniel went back to his own room and quickly dressed, hoping he hadn't made a mistake by suggesting they waited. Would Emma start to have second thoughts while she was away from him? He hoped not but even if she did, he would convince her that he was telling her the truth. What would happen then was up to her, of course, and his stomach sank at the thought that his future was hanging in the balance. He might love Emma with his whole heart and every fibre of his being, but he had no real idea how she felt about him.

CHAPTER THIRTEEN

EMMA could feel her stomach churning as she made her way down the stairs. Now that the rush of euphoria had started to fade, she'd had time to think and there were a lot of questions that needed answering, the main one being that if Daniel had loved her five years ago then why had he let her go? Maybe he had been keen to further his career but surely he must have known that she would have supported him? After all, she had offered to give up her own dreams of becoming a surgeon so they could be together—how much more proof had he needed about her commitment to him? It was all very puzzling so it was little wonder her heart was racing as she went into the sitting room.

'That was quick.'

He stood up and came over to her, taking her hand to lead her over to the sofa. He had switched on the gas fire and the room felt warm, too warm, in fact. Emma sank down onto the cushion, feeling slightly faint, although maybe it was the ambiguity of the situation that was causing her to feel like this rather than the temperature. She needed answers and she needed them now.

'Look, Daniel, I...'

'I know how difficult...'

They both spoke at once and both stopped. Emma bit her lip in an agony of frustration. They would get nowhere if they carried on this way.

'You first.' Daniel sat back in his seat and regarded her gravely. 'What were you going to say?'

'Just that I don't understand why you pushed me away if you loved me, as you claim to have done.'

'The simple answer is that I was afraid,' he said quietly.

'Afraid?' Emma looked at him in confusion. 'What of?'

'Of hurting you. Of ruining your life.' He stared down at the floor for a moment and his expression was bleak when he looked up. 'Of you ending up hating me.'

Emma didn't know what to say. She stared at him in silence, too shocked by the statement to dispute it. Daniel sighed heavily as he reached for her hand and linked his fingers through hers.

'I decided it was better if I drove you away rather than run the risk of that happening, Emma. Maybe I was wrong but I did it with the best of intentions. I did it for you and I hope you will believe that.'

'It's hard,' she said shakily. 'You hurt me so much, Daniel. At the time I didn't know if I would ever get over what you'd done, and now you tell me that you did it for me—'

She broke off, unable to disguise her scepticism. She hated to think that he might be lying to her but what else could she think? She had offered him her love and he had rejected it in the cruellest way possible. How could that have been to her advantage?

She went to stand up, not sure if she could sit there and listen to any more, but he pulled her back down beside him. His tone was urgent now, the look he gave her filled with desperation.

'I'm not explaining this very well, so it's no wonder that you're confused. But what I said was true. Sending you away seemed like the only thing I could do to protect you.'

'Protect me? From what? I loved you, Daniel. I wanted to be with you and told you that. Surely you must have known I was telling you the truth?'

'Of course I did!' He gripped her hand so hard that she winced and he swore softly, under his breath, as he released her. Standing up, he went over to the window and stood there, staring out across the garden. And when he spoke his voice echoed with so much pain that it brought tears to her eyes.

'I knew you loved me, Emma, and that was what scared me, the fact that you loved me so much you were willing to give up your dreams to be with me.' He turned and she could see the regret in his eyes. 'I couldn't let you do that, my darling. It was too great a risk, you see.'

'No, I don't see. I don't understand what you mean, Daniel.' She leant forward beseechingly. 'I would have been happy to give up my plans to become a surgeon if it had meant we could be together.'

'I know you mean that but can't you see that it would have driven a wedge between us eventually?' He came back and knelt in front of her. 'You admitted only the other day that you would have regretted giving up surgery, so how long do you think it would have been before you'd blamed me for making that decision?'

She started to demur but he shook his head. 'No, I've seen it happen before, Emma. It was the reason why my own parents' marriage failed. My mother was just starting out as a barrister when she met my father. He was in the diplomatic service, which meant he was posted overseas for long periods of time. It would have been impossible for Mum to pursue her career after they married so she gave up the law.'

'But surely she must have thought it all through, weighed up the pros and cons before she made her decision?'

'Of course she did, and I suppose she thought that being with Dad was more important than anything else.' He shrugged. 'Sadly, it didn't work out that way. Mum became increasingly resentful about giving up her career. My childhood was one long round of arguments about it, in fact. It was a relief when I was sent to boarding school because it meant I didn't have to listen to my parents fighting.'

'It must have been horrible for you,' she said quietly, and he shrugged.

'It wasn't a happy time. Mum was bored and frustrated, and Dad felt guilty because if it hadn't been for him, her life would have been very different. The sad thing was that they really loved one another in the beginning but it wasn't enough.'

'And you believe it wouldn't have been enough for us either?' Emma said flatly.

'No, I don't think it would have been. I think that in time you'd have regretted giving up so much for me.' He squeezed her fingers. 'I knew how much surgery meant to you, you see. That's why I discounted the idea of moving to Scotland to be with you while you did your training.'

'You would have done that for me?'

'Yes, willingly, if it had been the right thing to do. The problem was that I knew you would need to devote all your time and energy to your work. Surgery isn't an easy option and I would have been an unnecessary distraction.' He sighed. 'That's why I told you that my career meant more to me than our relationship. I wanted to protect you, Emma, and, if I'm honest, I wanted to protect myself as well. I couldn't have stood it if one day I'd seen resentment in your eyes when you looked at me because you'd failed to achieve your ambitions.'

Daniel took a deep breath. He had no idea how Emma was going to react to what he had told her and the strain made him feel as though every nerve had been stretched to breaking point. He literally jumped when she finally spoke.

'Why didn't you tell me all this, about your parents and everything, five years ago?'

He looked up but it was impossible to guess what she was thinking and his nerves seemed to tighten that bit more. 'Because I was afraid that you would persuade me that none of it mattered, that what had happened to my parents would never happen to us,' he told her simply.

'Maybe it wouldn't have done. Maybe we could have worked things out somehow. The trouble is that you weren't prepared to give us a chance, were you?'

'I wasn't prepared to take any risks,' he corrected, his heart sinking when he heard the bitterness in her voice.

'But it wasn't just your decision, Daniel. It was mine too, only I wasn't allowed to decide what *I* wanted. You took things out of my hands and that was it.' She stood up abruptly. 'Maybe I can't say for certain that our relationship would have lasted, but I would have liked the chance to try and make it work. You denied me that opportunity and no matter how well intentioned your motives were, you didn't have the right to do that. You didn't trust me, Daniel. That's what it all boils down to. And that hurts more than anything else.'

She left the room and Daniel heard her footsteps walking along the hall. He wanted to go after her and beg her to believe that he had done it for her benefit but he knew how pointless it would be. She needed time to come to terms with what he had told her, time to work out how she felt about him now that she knew the truth.

He put his head in his hands as a wave of despair washed over him. He had to face the fact that Emma might not be able to forgive him for what he had done. He might lose her again for telling her the truth, just as he had lost her before for trying to protect her.

It was a busy morning. As well as having to deal with an exceptionally long list, Emma was summoned to the police station at lunchtime to make a statement about what had happened the previous evening.

She stuck determinedly to the facts. How she had felt when she'd realised that Daniel was missing wasn't the issue and the police didn't need to know about that. However, when she left the station an hour later she felt both physically and emotionally drained. Recalling the moments when she'd thought Daniel had been hurt had brought back all the horror.

She made her way to the nearest coffee shop and sat down at a table, wondering what she was going to do. She loved Daniel so much, but discovering that he hadn't trusted her to know her own mind five years ago hurt unbearably. The fact that he had chosen to end their relationship rather than try to make it work made her wonder if he really understood what love meant. Maybe he'd thought he'd loved her then as he thought he loved her now, but did he? Really? Was he even capable of the depth of love she felt for him?

By the time she left the coffee shop, her head was throbbing from trying to work it all out. It had started to rain heavily and the traffic was moving at a snail's pace as she drove through the town. Emma grimaced as she glanced at the dashboard clock. She was going to be late for evening surgery if she didn't get a move on.

She managed to pick up speed once she left the town. There were a lot of cars on the road, probably visitors to the area who were driving around to avoid getting soaked. She overtook a car and caravan combination then had to slow down again when she found herself stuck behind a tractor. The road was too narrow to overtake and she had to wait until it turned off before she could put her foot down. She crested the bridge over the river and breathed a sigh of relief. Just another couple of miles and she'd be home.

The thought had barely crossed her mind when she felt the car suddenly skid when the tyres hit a patch of mud lying on the road. Turning the wheel, she tried to correct the sideways movement but to no avail. There was a horrible scrunch of metal as the car hit the side of the bridge, followed by a loud bang as the driver's airbag exploded. The noise was deafening so that it was several minutes before Emma realised that someone was knocking on the side window. The man gestured for her to unlock the door, which she did.

'Are you all right?' he demanded, bending so he could peer into the car.

'I think so.' She tentatively tried moving her arms and legs. 'Yes. Everything seems to be working OK.'

'What about your neck?' he said quickly when she went to unbuckle her seat belt. 'You can't be too careful when it comes to neck injuries. That's what they say on the television, how you should always make sure a person's neck is properly supported. Maybe you should sit there until the ambulance arrives in case you do yourself any damage.'

'Oh, but I don't need an ambulance,' she protested. 'I'm fine, really.'

'Best to make sure,' the man insisted. 'Anyhow, I've phoned them now so it would be silly not to let them check you over.'

Emma sighed. She could hardly refuse to let the paramedics treat her, seeing as they'd been summoned. She dug her phone out of her pocket and called the surgery, briefly explaining to Ruth what had happened and that she would be back as soon as possible. She had just finished when the ambulance arrived so she turned off her phone while she answered the crew's questions.

They examined her thoroughly, checking how her pupils responded to light and making sure that she hadn't been unconscious at any point before finally agreeing to let her get out of the car. The driver's door was jammed against the wall so she had to slide over to the passenger seat to get out and was surprised to find how shaky she felt when she stood up. The accident had caused quite a long tailback of traffic on both sides of the bridge, too. Emma grimaced as she turned to one of the paramedics.

'I seem to have created havoc,' she began, then stopped when she spotted a figure running towards them. Her eyes widened in shock when she realised it was Daniel.

'What are you doing here?' she began, but he didn't let her finish. Sweeping her into his arms, he stared down into her face and she was stunned to see the fear in his eyes.

'Are you all right, Emma?'

'I'm fine,' she told him shakily.

'Are you sure?' He glanced at her car and she saw the colour leach from his face when he saw the state it was in.

'Quite sure. Aren't I, guys?' She glanced at the

paramedics, who added their endorsement to her claim. Daniel took a deep breath and she felt him shudder.

'Thank heavens for that. When Ruth told me you'd been in an accident…'

He couldn't go on but she understood. He'd been as terrified about her as she'd been about him the night before. All of a sudden the doubts she'd had melted away. Daniel loved her, he really and truly did. It was the most glorious feeling to know it for certain once more.

Reaching up, she kissed him lightly on the lips. It was no more than a token but she could tell he understood what it meant when she saw his eyes blaze with joy. Emma could feel the same sense of happiness and wonderment bubbling inside her as they thanked the ambulance crew. A couple of the other drivers helped Daniel push her car off the road so that the traffic could start moving again. Once that was done, Daniel phoned the local garage and arranged for the car to be collected.

'That's it, then. Let's get you home.' He put his arm around her waist as he led her back to where he had left his car part way up the lane. Emma slid into the passenger seat, smiling as he bent and dropped a kiss on her lips.

'Mmm, what have I done to deserve that?' she teased.

'Nothing. Everything.' He kissed her again then closed the door and walked round to the driver's side. He started the engine then turned to look at her. 'I love you, Emma. I know you were hurt this morning when I told you why I had ended our relationship. I did what I thought was right, although now I can see that I shouldn't have made the decision all by myself. I just hope that one day you can find it in your heart to forgive me.'

'There's nothing to forgive. You were trying to protect me, Daniel, because you loved me.'

'Yes, I was. Maybe I went about it the wrong way but it was the only way I could think of at the time.' He took her hand and raised it to his lips. 'You meant the world to me then, Emma, just as you mean everything to me now.'

'And you mean the world to me, too, so let's not waste any more time.' She leant over and kissed him softly on the cheek. 'From now on any decisions about our future shall be made together. Agreed?'

'Agreed!'

He gave a whoop of laughter as he planted a kiss on her mouth then put the car into gear. They headed back to the surgery and it felt to Emma as though they were floating on a cloud of happiness rather than doing anything as mundane as driving. Daniel refused to let her help him take evening surgery and dispatched her straight to the house with orders to put her feet up until he got back. Emma didn't protest because she wasn't sure she was in a fit state to be seeing patients while she was functioning at this level of euphoria.

She let herself into the house and waited for Daniel to return, knowing what would happen when he did, and it was just as she had expected. They made love to each other with a joy and intensity that brought tears to both their eyes.

'I love you, my sweet Emma,' Daniel told her as he

held her against his heart. 'I want to be with you for ever, if you'll let me.'

'It's what I want too,' she told him honestly. 'Although I'm not sure about the logistics of it, with you working in London and me in Scotland.'

'Trivialities,' he assured her airily. 'We have far more important things to worry about, like when we're getting married.'

'Married?' She sat up straight and stared at him. *'Married!'*

'Uh-huh.' He pulled her back into his arms and kissed her slowly, grinning wickedly when he heard her moan. 'That's what couples do when they're in love. They get married and live happily ever after.'

'So this is a proposal, is it?' she said when she could summon enough breath to speak.

'I suppose it is.' He suddenly rolled to his feet and knelt by the side of the bed, smiling up at her as he took her hand. 'I'd better do it properly so there's no mistake. Will you, Emma Roberts, do me the honour of becoming my wife?'

'Yes,' she whispered then repeated it much louder so there would be no mistake about her answer either. 'Yes, I will!'

EPILOGUE

Three months later...

EMMA stepped in front of the mirror and studied her reflection. It was her wedding day and she wanted everything to be perfect, even though it had been a rush to get things organised in such a short space of time. Now she smiled as she took stock of the dress she had chosen.

Made from pure silk in the palest shade of cream, it fell in soft folds to the floor. The cream rosebuds that the hairdresser had pinned into her hair that morning exactly matched the colour of the fabric. More rosebuds had been hand-tied to form a posy which she would carry up the aisle. She knew she looked her best and hoped that Daniel would think so too. They had waited so long for this day to come and she wanted it to be special, a celebration of their love for each other.

A knock on the bedroom door heralded the arrival of her aunt. Both her aunt and her uncle had been thrilled when she and Daniel had announced that they were getting married. It appeared that they had known all along how she had felt about Daniel five years ago. Although he would never admit it, Emma suspected that her uncle had been doing a bit of matchmaking when he had asked Daniel to cover for him.

It had been Uncle Jim who had suggested that Daniel should think about becoming a partner in the practice, an offer which Daniel had eagerly accepted, much to Emma's delight. It had solved the problem of where they should live as once they returned from honeymoon, she would be taking up a new surgical post at the local hospital. She and Daniel would start their married life in Avondale, where they had first met and fallen in love.

'Your uncle sent me upstairs to check if you were ready,' her aunt informed her, taking a tissue out of her bag. 'You look beautiful, Emma, really beautiful.'

'Thank you.' Emma gave her aunt a hug then smiled at her. 'Shall we go? I don't want to keep Daniel waiting.'

There was quite a crowd gathered outside the local church when they drew up a short time later. Emma smiled when she spotted Alistair Grant, who was acting as one of the ushers. The source of his problems had been traced to the old chemical drums Harold Dawson had used to block access to the wind farm. Environmental services had visited Niths Farm and removed a number of other drums containing hazardous liquids. It was good to know that the community she was going to be a part of once more was no longer at risk.

The organist struck up 'The Wedding March' as they stepped inside the porch and her uncle gave her hand a reassuring squeeze. 'All set, my dear?'

'Yes.'

Emma took a deep breath as they set off down the aisle but the moment she saw Daniel waiting in front of the altar her nerves disappeared. Here was the man she loved, the man she wanted to spend her life with. From this moment on they would be together for ever.

Daniel felt his heart turn over as he watched Emma walking towards him. It was as though every hope and dream he'd ever had had crystallised into this one moment. She stopped beside him and he saw the love in her eyes when she turned to look at him and knew she could see the same emotion in his. They loved each other. They trusted each other. They were meant to be together.

Taking her hand, he made himself a promise that no matter what happened in the future nothing would spoil what they had. Maybe he had been afraid in the past but he wasn't afraid any longer. He loved Emma and she loved him. They had everything they needed to guarantee a wonderful life together.

THE SOLDIER SHE
COULD NEVER
FORGET

TINA BECKETT

To my children.
You bring me joy, every single day.

PROLOGUE

Twenty-two years earlier

"JESS. DON'T CRY."

The low words came from behind her, the slight rasp to his tone giving away his identity immediately.

Jessi stiffened, but she didn't turn around. Oh, God. He'd followed her. She hadn't realized anyone had even seen her tearful flight out of the auditorium, much less come after her. But they had. And those low gravely tones didn't belong to Larry Riley, who'd had a crush on her for ages, or her father—*thank God!*—but Clinton Marks, the last person she would have expected to care about what she thought or felt.

"I—I'm not."

One scuffed motorcycle boot appeared on the other side of the log where she was seated, the footwear in stark contrast to the flowing green graduation gowns they both wore—and probably topping the school's list of banned attire for tonight's ceremony.

The gown made her smile. Clint, in what amounted to a dress. She hoped someone had gotten a picture of that.

He sat beside her as she hurried to scrub away the evidence of her anguish. Not soon enough, though, because cool fingers touched her chin, turning her head toward him. "You're a terrible liar, Jessi May."

Somehow hearing the pet name spoken in something other than his normal mocking tones caused hot tears to wash back into her eyes and spill over, trailing down her cheeks until one of them reached his thumb. He brushed it away, his touch light.

She'd never seen him like this. Maybe the reality of the night had struck him, as well. In a few short hours, her group of friends would all be flying off to start new lives. Larry and Clint would be headed for boot camp. And her best friend would be spending the next year in Spain on a college exchange program.

They were all leaving.

All except Jessi.

She was stuck here in Richmond—with an overly strict father who'd come down hard when he'd heard Larry was gearing up for a career in the army. The papers weren't signed yet, but they would be in a matter of days. She'd done her best to hide the news, but her dad had been bound to find out sooner or later. He didn't want her involved with a military man. Kind of unreasonable in a place where those kinds of men were a dime a dozen.

Maybe she should have picked an out-of-state college, rather than choosing to commute from home. But as an only child, she hadn't quite been able to bring herself to leave her mom alone in that huge house.

"What's going on, Jess?" Clint's voice came back to her, pulling her from her pity party.

She shrugged. "My dad, he... He just..." It sounded so stupid to complain about her father to someone who flouted authority every chance he got. If only she could be like that. But she'd always been a people pleaser. The trait had gotten worse once she'd been old enough to realize her mom's "vitamins" were actually antidepressants.

Instead of the flip attitude she'd expected from Clint, though, his eyes turned this cold shade of gunmetal gray that made her shiver. His fingers tightened slightly on her chin. "Your father what, Jess? What did he do?"

Her teeth came down on her lip when she realized what he was saying. There'd been rumors about Clint's family, that his father was the reason he was the way he was.

Her dad was nothing like that.

"He didn't do anything. He's just...unreasonable. He's against me being with people like you or Larry."

His head tilted. "Me...and Larry." His mouth turned up at the corners. "I see your dad's point. Larry and I are definitely cut from the same cloth."

They weren't. Not at all. Larry was like her. He was all about good grades and toeing the line. Clint, however, lived on the edge of trouble—his skull tattoo and pierced ear making teachers shake their heads, while all the girls swooned.

Including her.

His words made her smile, though. "You're both going into the army."

"Ah, I see. Your father wouldn't like me, though, in or out of the army."

Her smile widened. "He's protective."

He made a sound low in his throat that might have been a laugh. "The thing is..." his eyes found hers again and a warm hand cupped the back of her neck "...I didn't know I was even in the running. So I'm neck and neck with Larry *straight-A* Riley."

Something hot flared low in her belly. Clint had never, ever given the slightest hint he was interested in her. And yet here he was. Beside her. The only person to notice her walk off the stage and slip out the door after getting her diploma. The only one who'd followed her.

"I—I... Did you want to be?"

"No."

The word should have cut her to the quick, except the low pained tone was somehow at odds with his denial.

"Clint…?" Her fingertips moved to his cheek, her eyes meeting his with something akin to desperation.

Another sound rumbled up from his chest, coming out as a groan this time. Then, something she'd never dreamed possible—in all of her eighteen years—happened.

Clinton Marks—bad boy extraordinaire—whispered her name. Right before his mouth came down and covered hers.

CHAPTER ONE

"CHELSEA'S NEW DOCTOR arrived today." The nurse's matter-of-fact words stopped her in her tracks.

Jessica Marie Riley blinked and turned back to the main desk of the Richmond VA hospital, where her twenty-one-year-old daughter had spent the past two months of her life—a frail shell of the robust soldier who'd been so proud of toughing it out at army boot camp.

It had always been just her and Chelsea against the world. They'd supported each other, laughed together, told each other everything.

Until she'd returned from her very first tour of duty as a former POW...and a different person.

"He did?" Jessi's stomach lurched. Her daughter's last doctor had left unexpectedly and she'd been told there was a possibility she'd be shuffled between the other military psychiatrists until a replacement could be found.

Maria, the nurse who'd admitted Chelsea and had shown a huge amount of compassion toward both of them, hesitated. She knew what a sore spot this was. "Dr. Cordoba had some family issues and resigned his commission. It really wasn't his fault."

Jessi knew from experience how devastating some family issues could be. But with the hurricane that had just gouged its way up the coast, her work schedule at Scott's

Memorial had been brutal. The shortage of ER doctors had never been more evident, and it had driven the medical staff to the brink of exhaustion. It also made her a little short on patience.

And now her daughter had lost the only doctor she'd seemed to bond with during her hospitalization.

Jess had hoped they'd finally get some answers about why Chelsea had spiraled into the depths of despair after coming home—and that she'd finally find a way to be at peace with whatever had happened in that squalid prison camp.

That tiny thread of hope had now been chopped in two. Anger flared at how easy it was for people like Dr. Cordoba to leave patients who counted on him.

Not fair, Jess. You're not walking in his shoes.

But the man wasn't walking in hers, either. He hadn't been there on that terrible day when her daughter had tried to take her own life.

She couldn't imagine how draining it was to deal with patients displaying symptoms of post-traumatic stress disorder on a daily basis, but Jessi had been handed some pretty awful cases herself. No one saw her throwing in the towel and moving on to some cushy private gig.

Maria came around the desk and touched her arm. "Her new doctor is one of the top in his field. He's dedicated his life to treating patients like your daughter—in fact, he transferred from California just to take over Dr. Cordoba's PTSD patients. At least until we can get a permanent replacement. He's already been to see Chelsea and reviewed her chart."

Top in his field. That had to be good, right? But if he was only temporary…

"What did he think?"

This time, the nurse wouldn't quite meet her eyes. "I'm

not sure. He asked me to send you to his office as soon as you arrived. He's down the hall, first door on your left."

Dr. Cordoba's old office.

The thread of anger continued to wind through her veins, despite Maria's encouraging words. This was Chelsea's third doctor. That averaged out to more than one a month. How long did this newest guy plan on sticking around?

A sudden thought came to her. "How did the hospital find this doctor so quickly?"

"This is what he does. He rotates between military hospitals, filling in…" The sound of yelling came from down the hallway, stopping Maria's explanation in its tracks. A woman headed their way, pushing a wheelchair, while the older gentleman in the seat bellowed something unintelligible, his fist shaking in the air.

"Excuse me," said the nurse, quickly moving toward the pair. She threw over her shoulder, "Chelsea's doctor is in his office. He's expecting you. Just go on in." Her attention shifted toward the agitated patient. "Mr. Ballenger, what's wrong?"

Not wanting to stand there like a gawker, Jessi stiffened her shoulders and headed in the direction Maria had indicated.

First door on the left.

All she wanted to do was skip the requisite chit-chat and go straight to Chelsea's room. But that was evidently not going to happen. Not until she met with the newest member of Chelsea's treatment team.

Feeling helpless and out of control was rapidly becoming the norm for Jessi. And she didn't like it. At all.

She stopped in front of the door and glared at the nameplate. Dr. Cordoba's credentials were still prominently displayed in the cheap gold-colored frame. The new guy really was new.

Damn, and she'd forgotten to ask the nurse his name. It didn't really matter. He'd introduce himself. So would she, and then he'd ask her how she was. That's what they always did.

Tell the truth? Or nod and say, "Fine," just like she did every other time someone asked her?

She lifted her hand and rapped on the solid wood door.

"Come in." The masculine drawl coming from within was low and gruff.

The back of her neck prickled, the sensation sweeping across her shoulders and down her arms, lifting every fine hair in its path. If she had to pick a description to pair that voice with, she'd say impatient. Or sexy. Two words you didn't want associated with an army psychiatrist. Or any psychiatrist, for that matter. And certainly not one charged with her daughter's care.

He's probably fat and bald, Jess.

Comforted by that thought, she pushed the lever down and opened the door.

He wasn't fat. Or bald.

His head was turned to the side, obscuring most of his face, but the man seated behind the gray, military-issue desk had a full head of jet-black hair, the sides short in typical army fashion, while the longer top fell casually across his forehead. Jessi spied a few strands of gray woven through the hair at his temple.

He appeared to be intently studying his computer screen. Something about his profile tugged at her, just like his voice had. She shook off the sensation, rubbing her upper arms as she continued to stand there.

He had to be pushing forty, judging from the lines beside his eyes as well as the long crease down the side of his left cheek. The result of a dimple utilized far too many times?

Something in her mind swirled back to life as if some

hazy image was trying to imprint itself on her consciousness.

"Feel free to sit," he said. "I'll be with you in a minute."

She swallowed, all thoughts of new doctors and balding men fading as worry nibbled at the pit of her stomach. Was something wrong with Chelsea? She tried to open her mouth to ask, but the words were suddenly stuck in her throat. Maybe that's why Maria wouldn't quite meet her eyes. Had Chelsea made another suicide attempt? Surely the nurse would have said something had that been the case.

Pulling one of the two chairs back a few inches, she eased into it, her gaze shuffling around the room, trying to find anything that would calm her nerves.

What it landed on was the nameplate on the doctor's desk. Not Dr. Cordoba's. Instead...

Jessi froze. She blinked rapidly to clear her vision and focused on the letters again, sliding across each one individually and hoping that an *a* would somehow morph into an *e*.

Her gaze flicked back to the portion of his face she could see. Recognition roared to life this time.

She should have realized that prickling sensation hadn't been a fluke when she'd heard his voice. But she would never have dreamed...

Images of heated kisses and stolen moments in the grass beside the creek near her high school flashed through her head.

God. Clinton Marks. A ghost from her past...a rite of passage.

That's all it had been. A moment in time. And yet here he was, sitting across from her in living color.

Worse, he was evidently her daughter's new doctor. How was that possible?

Maybe he wouldn't recognize her.

When his gray eyes finally swung her way, that hope dropped like a boulder from a cliff. A momentary burst of shock crossed his face, jaw squaring, lips tightening. Then the familiar mocking smile from school appeared, and his gaze dropped to her empty ring finger.

"I should have recognized his last name," he said. "Me and Larry. Neck and neck…"

His murmured words turned their shared past into a silly nursery rhyme. His next words shattered that illusion, however. "Still married to him?"

She swallowed. "Widowed."

Larry had died in a car accident a few months after their wedding. Right after he'd discovered from a mutual friend that she'd been seen returning to the auditorium with Clint the night of graduation. He'd asked her a question she'd refused to answer, and then he'd roared off into the night, never to come home.

"I'm sorry."

Was he? She couldn't tell by looking at him. The Clinton Marks of twenty-two years ago had worn this exact same mask during high school, not letting any kind of real emotion seep through. The earring was gone, and his tattoo was evidently hidden beneath the long sleeves of his shirt, but he still projected an attitude of blasé amusement. She'd seen that mask crack one time. And that memory now kept her glued to her chair instead of storming out and demanding that the "punk" who'd slept with her and then left without a word be removed from her daughter's case immediately and replaced with someone who actually cared.

Someone who had at least a modicum of empathy.

He did.

She'd seen it.

Experienced it.

Had felt gentle fingers tunnel through her hair, palms cupping her face and blotting her tears.

She sucked down a deep breath, realizing he was waiting for a response. "Thank you. He's gone a long time."

And so have you. She kept that to herself, however.

His gaze shifted back to something on his monitor before fastening on her face once again. "Your daughter. There's no chance that…?"

"I'm sorry?" Her sluggish brain tried to sift through his words, but right now it seemed to be misfiring.

"Chelsea. Her chart says she's twenty-one."

It clicked. What he was saying. The same question Larry had asked her before storming off: *Is the kid even mine?* Pain slashed through her all over again. "She's my husband's."

His jaw hardened further. "You didn't waste much time marrying him after I left."

She was sure it would have seemed that way to him. But Clint had been already on his way out of town. Gone long before he'd actually left. There had never been any question of him staying, and he'd used protection that night, so surely he knew Chelsea couldn't be his. But, then, condoms had been known to fail.

"You weren't coming back. You said so yourself." The fact that there was a hint of accusation in her voice didn't seem to faze him.

"No. I wasn't."

And there you had it. Clinton Marks was the same old looking-out-for-number-one boy she remembered. Only now he was packed into a man's body.

A hard, masculine body with a face capable of breaking a million hearts.

He'd broken at least one.

Only she hadn't admitted it at the time. Instead, she'd

moved on with her life the day he'd left, doing everything in her power to erase the memory of that devastating night. She'd thought she'd succeeded with Larry. And she *had* loved him, in her own way. He'd been everything Clint hadn't. Kind. Dependable. Permanent.

And willing to give up his career to be with her.

Three months later they'd married, and she'd become pregnant.

And Jessi certainly loved the child she'd made with him.

In fact, that was why she was here: Chelsea.

"It was a long time ago…" Her gaze flicked to the name-plate, and she made a quick decision about how to treat this unexpected meeting. And how to address him. "Dr. Marks, if you think that what happened between two kids—and that's all we were—will hinder your ability to help my daughter—"

"Are we really going to do this, Jessi May?" His brow cocked as the name slid effortlessly past his lips. "Pretend that night never happened? I'm interested in treating Chelsea, not in making a play for you, if that's what you're worried about."

Her face heated. "Of course I'm not."

And he was making it perfectly clear that he had no more interest in her now than he had all those years ago.

"I only asked about her parentage because I would need to remove myself from her case if it turned out she was… not Larry's."

In other words, if Chelsea were his.

What a relief it must be to him that she wasn't.

What a mess. Not quite a love triangle, but almost. There was one side missing, though. Larry had been infatuated with her. She'd been infatuated with Clint. And Clint had loved no one but himself.

Which brought her back to her current dilemma. "My daughter is sensitive. If she thinks you're treating her to work your way up some military ladder, you could damage her even more."

"I'm very good at what I do. And I'm not interested in going any further up the ladder."

The words weren't said with pride. In fact, there was an edge of strain behind them.

She believed him. The word *Colonel* in front of his name attested to decades of hard work. She knew from her father's days in the army that it took around twenty years to make that particular rank. Her dad had made it all the way up to general before his death five years ago.

In fact, her father was why she and Clint had wound up by the creek. When he'd realized Larry was headed for a military career her dad had gone off on her, using her mom's depression as ammunition for his position. The night of graduation had brought home all the changes that had been about to happen. Everyone she cared about had been on their way out of her life.

Only Larry had changed his mind at the last minute, inexplicably deciding to study at a local community college and take classes in agriculture instead.

Her glance went back to Clint, whose jaw still bore a hard edge of tension.

Me and Larry...neck and neck.

And Larry had stayed behind. With her.

The only one who knew about her dad besides her girlfriends was... "Oh, my God. You told him, didn't you? You told Larry about my father."

He didn't deny it. He didn't even blink. "How is he? Your father?"

"He's gone. He died five years ago." The pain in her chest grew. They may never have seen eye to eye about a lot of things, but she'd loved the man. And in spite of his shortcomings, he'd been a tower of strength after Larry had died and she'd been left alone, pregnant and grieving.

"I'm sorry." Clint reached across the desk to cover her hand with his. "Your mom?"

"She's okay. Worried about Chelsea. Just like I am."

He pulled back and nodded. "Let's discuss your daughter, then."

"The nurse said you've already seen her, and you've read her chart, so you know what she tried to do."

"Let's talk about that, and then we'll see her together." He pulled a yellow legal pad from a drawer of his desk and laid it in front of him. He was neat, she'd give him that, and it surprised her. Around ten pencils, all sharpened to fine points, were lined up side by side, and a single good-quality pen was at the end of the row. Nothing else adorned the stark surface of his desk, other than his nameplate and his computer monitor. So very different from the scruffy clothes and longish hair she remembered from their school days. And she'd bet those motorcycle boots were long gone, probably replaced by some kind of shiny dress shoes.

Maybe that had all been an act. Because the man she saw in front of her was every bit as disciplined as her father had been.

She shook herself, needing to gather her wits.

The only thing she should be thinking about was the here and now…and how the Clint of today could or couldn't help her daughter.

What had happened between them was in the past. It was over. And, as Clint had said, what they should be concentrating on was Chelsea.

So that's what Jessi was going to do.

If, for some reason, she judged that he couldn't help in her daughter's recovery, then she would call, write letters, parade in front of the hospital with picket signs, if necessary. And she would keep on doing it, until someone found her a doctor who could.

CHAPTER TWO

CLINT FORCED HIMSELF to stare over her shoulder rather than at the mouthwatering jiggle of her ass. The woman was no longer the stick-thin figure he'd known once upon a time. Instead, she boasted soft curves that flowed down her body like gentle ocean swells and made his hands itch to mold and explore.

Forget it, jerk. You're here for one thing only. To help Jessi's daughter and others like her.

No one had been more shocked than he'd been to realize the beautiful woman sitting across from him, worry misting her deep green eyes, was none other than the girl he'd lusted after in school.

The one he'd kissed in a rare moment of weakness, her tears triggering every protective instinct in his body.

The woman he'd handed off to the boy she'd really wanted—the one she'd married.

Unfortunately for Clint, he still didn't seem to be immune to her even after all these years.

He'd wanted to protect her.

Only he hadn't been able to back then. He couldn't now.

The only thing he could do was his job.

They reached Chelsea's room, and he shoved aside a new ache in his gut. The one that had struck when he'd realized the young woman's age was close enough to a certain deadly encounter to make him wonder whose she was.

Three months earlier and this story could have had a different ending.

No. It couldn't.

He'd done what he'd had to do back then—left—and he had no regrets.

Jessi glanced back and caught his look, her brows arching in question.

Okay, maybe he had one regret.

But it was too late to do anything about that now.

His fingers tightened on Chelsea's chart, and he started to push through the door, but Jessi stopped him. "I've been hearing things about the VA hospitals, Clint. You need to know up front that if I feel like she's not getting the treatment she needs here, I'll put her somewhere else."

His insides turned into a hard ball. He cared about his patients. All of them. No matter what the bean counters in Washington recommended or the hospital administration at whatever unit he was currently assigned to said or did, he treated his patients as if they were his comrades in arms...which they were. "It doesn't matter what you've heard. As long as I'm here, she'll get the best I have."

"But what if the hospital rules tell you to—?"

One side of his mouth went up. "Jessi May, always worried about something. Since when have you known me to play by anyone's rules?" A question they both knew the answer to, since he'd challenged almost every regulation their high school had been able to come up with.

"Would you please stop calling me that?"

His smile widened. "Is it a rule?"

"No." Her whole demeanor softened, and she actually laughed. "Because it'll just make you worse."

"I rest my case."

A nurse walked down the hallway, throwing them a curious look and reminding him of the serious issues Jessi was facing.

He took a step back. "Are you ready?"

"I think so."

Clint entered the room first, holding the door open for her.

Sitting in a chair by the window, his patient stared out across the lawn, not even acknowledging their presence. Hell, how could he not have seen the resemblance between the two women?

Chelsea had the same blond hair, the same pale, haunted features that her mother had once had. Only there was no way the young woman before him today could have survived basic training while maintaining that raw edge of vulnerability, so it was new. A result of her PTSD.

It affected people differently. Some became wounded and tortured, lashing out at themselves.

And some became impulsive and angry. Hitting out at others.

Clint wasn't sure which was worse, although as a teenager with a newly broken pinkie finger, he could have told you right off which he preferred.

Only he'd never told anyone about his finger. Or about his father.

And when he'd found Jessi crying outside the school building because of something her own father had done... he'd thought the worst. Only to have relief sweep through his system when it had been something completely different.

He drew a careful breath. "Hi, Chelsea. Do you remember me from earlier today?"

No reaction. The waif by the window continued to stare. He glanced at her chart again to remind himself of the medications Dr. Cordoba had prescribed.

He made a note to lower the dosage to see if it had any effect. He wanted to help Chelsea cope, not turn her into a zombie.

Jessi went over to her daughter and dropped to her knees, taking the young woman's hands in hers and looking up at her. "Hi, sweetheart. How are you?"

"I want to go home." The words were soft. So soft, Clint almost missed them.

Jessi hadn't, though. Her chin wobbled for a second, before she drew her spine up. "I want that, too, baby. More than anything. But you're not ready. You know you're not."

"I know." The response was just as soft. She turned to look back out the window, as if tuning out anything that didn't get her what she wanted.

Clint knew Chelsea's reaction was a defense mechanism, but having her own daughter shut her out had to shred Jessi's insides even though she was absolutely doing what was right for Chelsea.

He pulled up a chair and sat in front of the pair, forcing himself to keep his attention focused on his patient and not her mother. "I'm going to adjust some of your medications, Chelsea. Would that be okay?"

The girl sighed, but she did turn her head slightly to acknowledge she'd heard him. "Whatever you think is best."

He spent fifteen minutes watching the pair interact, making notes and comparing his observations with what he'd read of her past behavior.

She'd slashed her wrists. Jessi had found her bleeding in the bathtub and had fashioned tourniquets out of two scarves—quick thinking that had saved her daughter's life.

A couple of pints of blood later, they'd avoided permanent brain and organ damage.

Unfortunately, the infusion hadn't erased the emotional damage that had come about as a result of what her chart said was months spent in captivity.

Trauma—any trauma—had to be processed mentally and emotionally. Some people seemed to escape unscathed, letting the memory of the event roll off their backs. Others were crushed beneath it.

And others pretended they didn't give a damn.

Even when they did.

Like him?

Jessi had coaxed Chelsea over to the bed and sat next to her, arm draped around her shoulders, still talking to her softly. He got up and laid a hand on her shoulder.

"I'll give you a few minutes. Stop in and talk to me before you leave the hospital." He didn't add the word *okay* or allow his voice to change tone at the end of the phrase, because he didn't want to make it seem like a request. Not because he wasn't sure she'd honor it, but part of him wondered if she'd head back to the front desk and demand to have another doctor assigned to the case.

Clint had to somehow break the tough news to Jessi that she was stuck with him for the next couple of months or for however long Chelsea was here. There just wasn't anyone else.

So it was up to him to convince her that he could help her daughter, if she gave him a chance. Not hard, since he believed it himself. Clint had dealt with all types of soldiers in crisis, both male and female, something Dr. Cordoba had not. It was part of the reason Clint had agreed to this assignment. His rotations didn't keep him anywhere for more than six months at a time. Surely that would be long enough to treat Chelsea or at least come up with a plan for how to proceed.

If he'd known one of Dr. Cordoba's toughest cases was Jessi Spencer's daughter, though, he wouldn't have been quite so quick to agree to return to his hometown.

Being here was dangerous on a number of levels.

Jessi's not the girl you once knew.

He sensed it. She was stronger than she'd been in school. She'd had to be after being widowed at a young age and raising a daughter on her own. And according to the list-ing on Chelsea's chart, Jessi was now an ER physician. You didn't deal with trauma cases all day long without having a cast-iron stomach and a tough emotional outlook.

He'd seen a touch of that toughness in his office. Her eyes had studied him, but had given nothing away, unlike the Jessi of his past, who'd worn her heart on her sleeve.

Just as well. He was here to treat the daughter, not take up where he'd left off with the mother. Not that he'd "left off" with her. He'd had a one-night stand and had then made sure her beau had known that to win her heart he had to be willing to give up his dreams for her.

Evidently he had.

That was one thing Clint wouldn't do. For anyone.

If he could just keep that in mind for the next couple of months, he'd be home free. And if he was able to help Chelsea get the help she needed while he was at it, that was icing on the cake.

He corrected himself. No, not just the icing. It was the whole damn cake. And that was what he needed to focus on.

Anything else would be a big mistake.

"And how long will that be?" Jessi's mouth opened, then snapped back shut, before trying again. "I don't want Chel-sea's next doctor to give up on her like…"

Her voice faded away as the reality of what she'd been about to say swept through her: *Like Dr. Cordoba did. Like Chelsea's father did when he took off into the night.*

"Are you talking about Dr. Cordoba?"

She blinked. Had he read her mind? "Yes."

"He didn't give up on her." His voice softened. "His wife is very ill. He had to take a job that allows him to be home with her as much as possible. He couldn't do that and continue working long hours here. He knew his patients deserved more than that."

Oh, God. Her ire at the other doctor dissolved in a heartbeat. She'd been so caught up in her own problems that she hadn't even stopped to think that maybe he had been dealing with things that were every bit as bad as hers were. Maybe even worse. "I…" She swallowed. "I don't know what to say. I'm so sorry."

The events of the past months were suddenly too much for her, and her heart pounded, her stomach churned.

Please, no. Not now.

She'd had two panic attacks since Chelsea's hospitalization, so she recognized the signs.

Pressing a hand to her middle, she tried to force back the nausea and took a few careful breaths.

"I thought you should know." Clint leaned forward. "If you're worried about me suddenly taking off, don't be. I'll give you plenty of notice."

This time.

The words hung in the air between them, and for a horrible, soul-stealing second she thought he was hinting for her not to get her hopes up.

"I'm not expecting you to stay forever." The sensation in her chest and stomach grew, heat crawling up her neck and making her ears ring. Her vision narrowed to a pinpoint. And then it was too late to stop it. "I think I'm going…"

She lurched to her feet and somehow made it through the door and to the first stall in the restroom before her gut revolted in a violent spasm, and she threw up. She'd been running on coffee and pure adrenaline for the past several weeks, and she hadn't eaten breakfast that morning. The perfect set-up for an attack.

That had to be the reason. Not finding Clint sitting behind that desk.

Again and again, her stomach heaved, mingling with tears of frustration.

When she finally regained control over herself, she flushed the toilet with shaking hands before going to the sink, bending down to rinse her mouth and splash water over her face. She blindly reached for the paper-towel dispenser, only to have some kind of cloth pressed into her hand.

Holding the fabric tightly to her face and wishing she could blot away the past two months as easily as the moisture, she sucked down a couple more slow breaths, her heart rate finally slowing to some semblance of normality.

"Thank you." She lifted her head, already knowing who she'd find when she opened her eyes. "You shouldn't be in here."

"Why? Because it's against the rules? I thought we'd already sorted all that out." He added a smile. "Besides, I wanted to make sure you were okay."

The words swirled with bitter familiarity through her head. They were the same ones he'd said the night of their high-school graduation ceremony when she'd suddenly veered away from the rows of chairs and rushed out into the parking lot and then down to a nearby creek. Thankfully neither her dad nor mom had seen her. And an hour and a half later, when the ceremony had been over and the reception had been in full swing, she'd returned. With the lie that Clint had told her to use trembling on her tongue... that she'd been sick with nerves.

Her dad had bought it, just like Clint had said he would.

Only when she'd said it, it had no longer been a lie, because she had felt sick. Not because of nerves, but because the boy she'd always wanted—the boy she'd lost her virginity to—would soon be on his way to the airport, headed for boot camp. Leaving her behind forever.

"It's just the shock of everything."

"I know."

She shivered and wrapped her arms around herself. Clint made no effort to take off his jacket and drape it around her. It was a good thing, because she'd probably dissolve into a puddle all over again if he did.

"Have you eaten recently?"

"What?"

"I get the feeling you're running on fumes along with a heaped dose of stress. Which is probably why—" he nodded at the closed stall "—that just happened."

Leave it to him to point out the obvious. "I can eat later."

He nodded. "Yes. Or you could eat while we go over some treatment options. I skipped breakfast this morning and could use something, as well. Besides, some carbs will help settle your stomach."

Before she knew it, she found herself in the hospital cafeteria with a toasted bagel and a cup of juice sitting in front of her.

A hint of compassion in his voice as he detailed the treatments he'd like to try told her this wasn't going to be an easy fix. It was something Chelsea would be dealing with for the rest of her life. He just wanted to give her the tools she needed to do that successfully.

It was what Jessie wanted, as well. More than anything. As a mom, she wanted to be able to make things better, to take away her daughter's pain. But she couldn't. She had to trust that Clint knew what he was doing.

He certainly sounded capable.

"And what if she tries to do something to herself?" She set the bagel back down on the plate, unable to leave the subject alone.

"I'll take steps to avoid the possibility." He steepled his fingers and met her gaze with a steadiness that unnerved her. The man was intimidating, even though she knew he wasn't trying to be. Despite his reassurances, she still wasn't convinced Clint was the man for the job. Especially considering their history—which, granted, wasn't much of one. On his side, anyway.

What other option did she have, though? An institution? Bring her home and hope Chelsea didn't try to take her life again?

No. She couldn't risk there being a next time.

She'd do anything it took to help bring her daughter back from wherever she was. That included seeing Clint every day for the rest of her life and reliving what they'd done by the bank of that creek.

Decision made.

"I want you to keep me informed of every move you make."

One brow quirked. Too late she realized he could have taken her words the wrong way. But he didn't throw a quick comeback, like he might have done in days gone by. Instead, he simply said the words she needed to hear most: "Don't worry, Jessi. Even if we have to break every rule in the book, we're going to pull her through this."

And as much as the word *we* made something inside her tingle to life, it was that other statement that reached out and grabbed her. The one that said the old Clint was still crouched inside that standard issue haircut and neat-as-a-pin desk. It was there in his eyes. The glowing intensity that said, despite outward appearances, he hadn't turned into a heartless bureaucrat after years of going through proper channels.

He was a rule-breaker. He always had been. And just like his bursting into the ladies' restroom unannounced, it gave her hope, along with a sliver of fear.

She knew from experience he wasn't afraid to break anything that got in the way of what he wanted. She just had to make sure one of those "things" wasn't her heart.

CHAPTER THREE

JESSI HAD JUST finished suturing an elbow laceration and was headed in to pick up her next chart when a cry of pain came from the double bay doors of the emergency entrance.

"Ow! It hurts!"

A man holding a little girl in his arms lurched into the waiting area, his face as white as the linoleum flooring beneath his feet. The child's frilly pink party dress had a smear of dirt along one side of it, as did her arm and one side of her face. That had Jessi moving toward the pair. The other cases in the waiting room at the moment were minor illnesses and injuries.

The man's wild eyes latched on to her, taking in the stethoscope around her neck. "Are you a doctor?"

"Yes. How can I help?"

"We were at a... She fell..." The words tumbled out of his mouth, nothing making sense. Especially since the girl's pained cries were making the already stricken expression on his face even worse.

She tried to steer him in the right direction. "She fell. Is this your daughter?"

"Yes. She fell off a trampoline at a friend's house. It's her leg."

Like with many fun things about childhood—climbing trees, swimming in the lake, riding a bike—danger lurked around every corner, ready to strike.

Jessi brushed a mass of blond curls off the girl's damp face and spoke to her. "What's your name?"

"Tammy," she said between sobs.

She maintained eye contact with her little charge. "Tammy, I know your leg must hurt terribly. We're going to take you back and help fix it." She motioned to one of the nurses behind the admission's desk. Gina immediately came toward them with a clipboard.

The girl nodded, the volume of her cries going down a notch.

"Let's take her into one of the exam rooms, while Nurse Stanley gets some information."

It wasn't standard protocol—they were supposed to register all admissions unless there was a life-threatening injury—but right now Jessi wanted to take away not only the child's pain but the father's, as well.

Maybe Clint wasn't the only one who knew how to break a few rules.

But she had to. She recognized that look of utter terror and helplessness on the dad's face. She'd felt the same paralyzing fear as she'd crouched in the bathtub with her daughter, blood pouring out of Chelsea's veins. She'd sent out that same cry for help. To God. To the universe. To anyone who would listen.

And like the distraught father following her to a treatment room, she'd been forced to place her child in the hands of a trained professional and pray they could fix whatever was wrong. Because it was something beyond her own capabilities.

But what if it was also beyond the abilities of the people you entrusted them to?

Raw fear pumped back into her chest, making her lungs ache.

Stop it.

She banished Clint and Chelsea from her thoughts and

concentrated on her job. This little girl needed her, and she had to have her head in the game if she wanted to help her.

"Which leg is it?" she asked the father.

"Her right. It's her shin."

"Did she fall on the ground? Or which part of the trampoline?"

She asked question after question, gathering as much information as she could in order to narrow the steps she'd need to take to determine the exact nature of the injury.

Gina followed them into the room and was already writing furiously, even though the nurse hadn't voiced a single question. That could come later.

"Set her on the table."

As soon as cold metal touched the girl's leg, she let out an ear-piercing shriek that quickly melted back into sobs.

As a mother, it wrenched at her heart, but Jessi couldn't let any of that affect what she did next. Things would get worse for Tammy before they got better, because Jessi had to make sure she knew what she was dealing with.

"Gina, can you stay and get the rest of the information from Mr...?" She paused and glanced at the girl's father.

"Lawrence. Jack Lawrence."

"Thank you." She turned back to her nurse. "Can you do that while I call Radiology?"

Once she'd made the call, she made short work of getting the girl's vitals, talking softly to her as she went about her job. When she slid the girl's dress up a little way, she spied a dark blue contusion forming along her shin and saw a definite deformation of the tibia. The bone had separated. Whether they could maneuver the ends back in place without surgery would depend on what the X-rays showed.

Within fifteen minutes, one of the radiology techs had whisked the five-year-old down the hall on a stretcher, her father following close behind. His expression had gone from one of fear to hope. Sometimes just knowing it wasn't all up to you as a parent, that there were others willing to pitch in, made a little of the weight roll off your shoulders.

So why did she still feel buried beneath tons of rubble?

Because Chelsea's injury went beyond the physical to the very heart of who she was. And Jessi wasn't sure Clint—or anyone else—could repair it. There was no splint or cast known to man that could heal a broken spirit.

A half hour later Tammy and her father were back in the exam room, and an orthopedist had arrived to take over the case. The urge to bend down and kiss the little girl's cheek came and went. She held back a little smile. She didn't need to break *all* the rules. Some of them were there for a reason.

Hopefully, Clint knew which ones to follow and which ones to break.

He did. She sensed it.

He wouldn't go beyond certain professional boundaries. Which meant he would try to keep their past in the past. If one of them stepped over the line, he'd remove himself from Chelsea's case.

Should she talk to Chelsea about what had happened down at the creek—tell her she'd gone to school with Clint? Not necessary. He appeared to have a plan. Besides, if she heaped anything else on her daughter, she might hunker further down into whatever foxhole she'd dug for herself. She needed to give Clint enough time to do his job.

"Jessi?" Gina, the nurse from the earlier, caught her just as she was leaving her patient's room. "You have a phone call on line two."

"Okay, thanks." It must be her mom, confirming their dinner date for tonight. She'd promised to update her on Chelsea's condition, something that made her feel ill. With her father gone, Jessi and Chelsea were all her mother had left. And though her mother was no longer taking antidepressants, she'd been forgetful lately, which Jessi hoped was just from the stress of her only granddaughter's illness.

Going to the reception desk, she picked up the phone and punched the lit button. "Hello?"

Instead of the bright, happy tones of her mother, she encountered something a couple of octaves lower. "Jess?"

She gulped. "Yes?"

"Clint here."

As if she hadn't already recognized the sound of his voice. Still, her heart leaped with fear. "Is something wrong with Chelsea?"

"No. Do you have a minute? I'd like to take care of some scheduling."

"Scheduling?"

A low, incredibly sexy-sounding hum came through the phone that made something curl in her belly.

"I want us to talk every day."

"Every day?"

About Chelsea, you idiot! And what was with repeating everything he said?

"Yes. Our schedules are probably both hectic, but we can do it by phone, if necessary."

"Oh. Okay." Was he saying he didn't want to meet with her in person? That he'd rather do all of this by phone? She had no idea, but she read off her schedule for the next five days.

A grunt of affirmation came back, along with, "I'll also want to meet with you and Chelsea together."

"Why?"

"Didn't Dr. Cordoba have family sessions with you?"

She shook her head, only realizing afterwards that he couldn't see it. "No, although he mentioned wanting to try that further down the road."

"I believe in getting the family involved as soon as possible, since you'll be the one working with her once she's discharged."

Discharged. The most beautiful word Chelsea had heard in weeks. And Clint made it sound like a reality, rather than just a vague possibility. So he really was serious about doing everything he could to make sure treatment was successful.

A wave of gratitude came over her and a knot formed in her throat. "Thank you, Clint. For being willing to break the rules."

Was she talking about with Chelsea? Or about their time together all those years ago.

"You're welcome, Jess. For what it's worth, I think Chelsea is very lucky to have you."

Her next words came out before she was aware of them forming in her head. But she meant them with all her heart. "Ditto, Clint. I think Chelsea and I are the lucky ones."

"I'll call you."

With that intimate-sounding promise, he said goodbye, and the phone clicked in her ear, telling her he'd hung up. She gripped the receiver as tightly as she could, all the while praying she was doing the right thing. She was about to allow Clint back into her orbit—someone who'd once carried her to the peak of ecstasy and then tossed her into the pit of despair without a second glance. But what choice did she have, really?

She firmed her shoulders. No, there was always a choice. She may have made the wrong one when she'd been on the cusp of womanhood, but she was smarter now. Stronger. She could—and would—keep her emotions in check. If not for her own sake, then for her daughter's.

CHAPTER FOUR

THE FIRST FAMILY counseling session was gearing up to be a royal disaster.

Jessi came sliding into Clint's office thirty minutes late, out of breath, face flushed, wispy strands of hair escaping from her clip.

He swallowed back a rush of emotion. She'd looked just like this as she'd stood to her feet after they'd made love. He'd helped her brush her hair back into place, combing his fingers through the strands and wishing life could be different for him.

But it couldn't. Not then. And not now.

"Sorry. We had an emergency at the hospital, and I had to stay and help."

"No problem." He stood. "I have another patient in a half hour, so we'll need to make this a quick session."

"Poor Chelsea. I feel awful. I'm off tomorrow, though, so I'll come and spend the day with her."

When they walked into Chelsea's room, the first thing he noticed was that the lunch she'd been served an hour ago was still on a tray in front of her, untouched. At the sight of them, though, she seemed to perk up in her seat, shoveling a bite of mashed potatoes into her mouth and making a great show of chewing.

Manipulating. He'd seen signs of it earlier when he'd

tried to coax her to talk about things that didn't involve the weather.

Her throat worked for a second with the food still pouched inside one cheek. She ended up having to wash the potatoes down with several gulps of water. She sat there, breathing as hard as her mother had been when she'd arrived a few moments ago.

"Enjoying your meal?" he asked, forcing his voice to remain blasé. So much for showing Jessi how good he was at his job.

As if this was even about him.

He ground his teeth as his frustration shifted to himself.

Chelsea shrugged. Another bite went in—albeit a much smaller one this time.

Not polite to talk with my mouth full, was the inference.

Well, she'd run out of the stuff eventually. And since she was pretty thin already, he was all for anything that would get food into her system. That was one of the comments on the sheet in her file. She didn't eat much, unless someone wanted to interact with her in some way. The staff had taken to coming to her room and loitering around, straightening things and making small talk. It was a surefire way to get that fork moving from plate to mouth.

He decided to give her a little more time.

Jessi stood there, looking a little lost by her daughter's lack of greeting. He sent her a nod of reassurance and motioned her to sit in one of the two nearby chairs and joined her.

"Let's go ahead and get started, if that's okay with you, Chelsea."

Chew, chew, chew.

She moved on to her green beans without a word. Okay, if that's the way she wanted to play it, he'd go right along with it.

He turned to Jessi, sorry for what he was about to do,

but if anything could break through her daughter's wall it might be having to face some hard, unpleasant subjects. "Since Chelsea's busy, why don't you tell me what led her to being here."

Right on cue, Jessi's eyes widened. "You mean about the day I called…"

"Yes."

Her throat moved a couple of times, swallowing, probably her way of either building up the courage to talk about the suicide attempt or to refuse.

"Well, I—I called Chelsea's cell phone to let her know I was coming home early. It rang and rang before finally going over to voice mail. I was going to stop and pick up some Thai food—her favorite…" Jessi's eyes filled with tears. "I decided to go straight home instead, so we could go out to eat together. When I got there… Wh-when I got to the house, I—"

"Stop." Chelsea's voice broke through, though she was still staring down, a green bean halfway to her mouth. "Don't make her talk about it."

Whether the young woman wanted to spare her mother's feelings or her own, Clint wasn't sure. "What would you like to discuss instead, then?"

There was a long pause. Then she said, "What you hope to accomplish by keeping me here."

"It's not about us, Chelsea. It's about you."

"Where's Dr. Cordoba?" Her head finally came up, and her gaze settled on him.

"He went to work somewhere else."

"Because of me." The words came out as a whisper.

Clint shook his head. "No, of course not. He made the decision for personal reasons. It had nothing to do with you."

Jessi's chest rose and fell as she took a quick breath. "We all just want to help, honey."

"Everything I touch turns to ashes."

"No." Jessi glanced at him, then scooted closer to her daughter, reaching out to stroke her hair. "You've been through a lot in the past several months, but you're not alone."

"I am, Mom. You have no idea. You all think I'm suffering from PTSD, because of my time in that camp, don't you? Dr. Cordoba did. But I'm not."

Clint glanced at Jessi, a frown on his face. "You tried to take your life, Chelsea. Something made you think life wasn't worth living."

The girl's shoulders slumped.

"Does this have to do with your pregnancy?"

Two sets of female eyes settled on him in shock.

Hell. Jessi hadn't known?

It was right there in Chelsea's medical chart that her physical exam had revealed she'd given birth or had had a miscarriage at some point. He'd just assumed...

His patient went absolutely rigid. "I want her to leave. Now."

"But, Chelsea..." Jessi's voice contained a note of pleading.

"Now." The girl's voice rose in volume. "Now, now. *Now!*"

Jessi careened back off her chair and stumbled from the room as her daughter's wails turned to full-fledged screams of pain. She was tearing at her hair, her food flung across the room. Clint pressed the call button for the nurse and between the two of them they were able to administer a sedative, putting an end to Chelsea's hysterical shrieks. Her muscles finally went limp and her eyes closed. He stood staring down at her bed for a few moments, a feeling of unease settling over him as it had each time he'd met with Chelsea. There was something here. Something more than what was revealed in her records.

And it involved that pregnancy. She'd been calm until the moment the subject had come up.

It was time to do a little more digging. But for now he had to go out there and face Jessi. And somehow come up with something to say that wouldn't make things worse than they already were.

"I didn't know."

Clint came toward her as she leaned against the wall twenty feet away from Chelsea's door. Her stomach had roiled within her as the nurse had rushed into the room and the screams had died down to moans, before finally fading away to nothing. All she wanted to do was throw up, just like she had during a previous visit, but she somehow held it together this time.

"I'm sorry, Jess." Clint scrubbed a hand through his hair, not touching her. "I'd assumed she told you."

"She hasn't told me anything. Could it have been while she was a prisoner?"

"I'm not sure. This is the most emotion I've seen from her in the past week. We hit a nerve, though. So that's a good thing."

"I can't imagine what she went through." She leaned her head against the wall and stared at the ceiling.

Chelsea's convoy had been ambushed during a night patrol by enemy forces disguised as police officers. The group had been held for four months. Chelsea had said they'd all been separated and interrogated, but she'd had no idea one of the prisoners had died until she and the rest of those rescued had been flown home.

Jessi sighed and turned back to look at him. "The army debriefed her, but I was never told what she said, and I—I was afraid to press her too much. She seemed to be doing fine. Maybe that in itself was a warning sign."

"There was no way you could have known what she was going to do." Clint pushed a strand of hair off her cheek.

She wasn't sure she could stand seeing her daughter in this much pain week after week. And a pregnancy…

Had her daughter been raped during her captivity? The army had said there was no evidence of that, but then again Chelsea wasn't exactly a fount of information. "I think I'm doing more harm than good by going in there with you."

"Let's see how it goes for the next week, okay? Chelsea was admitted under a suicide watch. That gives you permission to make decisions regarding her health care. She could still open up."

"She doesn't even want me here, Clint. You heard her." Jessi's head still reverberated with her daughter's cries for her to get out.

"That was the shock talking. She didn't expect me to ask that particular question. At least she's getting it out, rather than bottling it all up inside."

His eyes narrowed as he looked at her face. "How long's it been since you've done something that hasn't revolved around your job or Chelsea?"

She thought for a second. "I can't remember."

"The last thing she needs is for you to break down as well, which is where you're headed if you don't take some down time."

She knew he was right. She'd felt like she'd been standing on the edge of a precipice for weeks now, with no way to back away from it.

Before she could say anything, he went on. "You said you're off tomorrow. Why don't you go out and do something fun? Something you enjoy?"

"I need to spend the day here with Chelsea."

"No. You don't. She'll understand. It might not be a bad idea to give her a day to think through what just happened."

She hesitated. "I don't even know what I'd do." Chelsea might need a day to think, but the last thing Jessi wanted to do was sit at home and let her brain wander down dark paths.

"Tell you what. I don't have anything pressing tomorrow. Why don't we do something together? It's fair season. There's probably something going on in one of the nearby counties."

"Oh, but I couldn't. Chelsea—"

"Will be fine."

Conflicting emotions swept through her. The possibility of spending the day with Clint dangled before her in a way that was far too attractive. "I'm not sure…"

"Is it because I'm her doctor?"

"Yes." He'd given her the perfect excuse, and she grabbed at it with both hands.

"That can be remedied."

Panic sizzled through her. He'd hinted once before that he might drop her daughter's case.

"No. I want you."

He paused, then shook his head and dragged his fingertips across her cheek. "Then you have to take care of yourself."

She nodded, unable to look away from his eyes as they locked on her face. Several emotions flicked through them, none of them decipherable.

"I'll try."

"How about I check the local schedules and see if I can find something for us to do? Something that doesn't involve a hospital."

Guilt rose in her throat, but at a warning glance from him she forced it back down. "Okay."

He nodded and let his hand fall back to his side. "Are you going to be okay tonight?"

Was he asking her that as a psychiatrist or as a man?

It didn't matter. The last thing she wanted was to jeopardize her working relationship with the one man who might be able to get through to her daughter. She needed to keep this impersonal. Professional. Even though his touch brought back a whole lot of emotions she hadn't felt in twenty-two years.

But she had to keep them firmly locked away. Somehow.

"I'll be fine. Just call if there's any change, okay?" She was proud of the amount of conviction she'd inserted into her voice.

"I will. I'm off at ten, but the hospital knows how to reach me if there's a problem." He took a card from his desk and wrote something on the back of it, then handed it to her. "I'll give you a yell in the morning, but until then, here's my cell phone number. Call me if you need me."

If you need me.

Terrifying words, because she already did. More than she should. But she wouldn't call. No matter how much that little voice inside her said to do just that.

CHAPTER FIVE

CLINT STEPPED ONTO the first row of metal bleachers and held his hand out for her. Grasping his fingers, and letting him maneuver through the crowd of seated spectators, they went to the very top, where a metal brace across the end provided a place for their backs to rest.

She watched the next horse in line prance into the arena, ears pricked forward in anticipation. Three fifty-five-gallon drums had been laid out to form a familiar triangle.

Barrel racing.

The speed event looked deceptively easy, but if a horse knocked over a barrel as it went around it, the rider received a five-second penalty, enough to cost a winning ribbon.

"I used to do this, you know. Run barrels."

"I know you did."

Her head swiveled to look at the man sitting next to her, completely missing the horse's take-off.

"You did?"

He smiled. "I came to the fair on occasion. Watched a few of the 4-H events."

The thought of Clint sitting on one of these very bleachers, watching her compete, was unnerving. How would she have missed him with the way he'd dressed back then? He hadn't exactly looked the part of an emerging cowboy.

Exactly. She would have noticed him.

Which meant he'd never actually seen her race. She settled back into place.

"I didn't realize you were interested in 4-H."

His gaze went back to the arena. "I wasn't."

Something about the way he'd said that...

"Do you still have your trophy?" He was still looking straight ahead, thankfully, but her gasp sounded like a gunshot to her ears, despite the noise going on around her.

The metal brace behind her groaned as more people leaned against it. Jessi eased some of her weight off it.

"How did you know I...?" She'd only won one trophy in all her years of entering the event.

"I happened to be in the vicinity that day."

How did one *happen* to be in the vicinity of the fair? It spanned a large area. And the horse arena wasn't exactly next to the carnival rides or food.

"You saw me run?"

"I saw a lot of people compete."

Okay, that explained it. "So you came out to all the horse events?"

"Not all of them. I had a few friends who did different things."

Like run barrels? She didn't think so. Neither did she remember him hanging out with any of her 4-H friends. And the only year she'd won the event had been as a high school senior.

The next horse—a splashy brown and white paint—came in, and she fixed her attention on it, although her mind was going at a million miles an hour. The rider directed the horse in a tight circle near the starting area and then let him go. The animal's neck stretched forward as he raced toward the first barrel, tail streaming out behind him.

"Here!" the rider called as they reached the drum, using her voice along with her hands and legs to guide the horse around the turn. She did the same for the second and third barrels and then the pair raced back in a straight line until they crossed where the automatic timer was set up. Nineteen point two three seconds.

The announcer repeated the time, adding that it put the horse and rider into second place.

Clint leaned closer, his scent washing over her at almost exactly the same time as his arm brushed hers. The dual assault made her mind blank out for a second. So much so that she almost missed his question. "I always wondered. Why do some of them start with the left barrel rather than the one on the right?"

Play it cool, Jessi.

"B-because horses have a dominant side, kind of like being right- or left-handed."

"Interesting. So your horse was right-handed?"

She swallowed. So he *had* seen her. She'd hoped maybe he'd heard that she'd won from a friend, rather than having been there in the flesh. What did it matter? So he'd seen her race. No big deal.

But it was. And she had no idea why.

"Yes, she was."

Neither of the next two horses beat the time of the leader. Despite her wariness at coming out today, and her horror at realizing he'd watched her the day of her win, she could feel the muscles in her body relaxing. He'd been right to suggest she take a day off.

A *real* day off.

"Do you think Chelsea—?"

"The hospital will call me if they need me. We're both off duty today."

She frowned. "She's my daughter, Clint. I can't help but worry about her."

"I'm not asking you to put her from your mind. I'm asking you to enjoy your day. It's what she would want."

She sighed. "She did seem happy when I told her where I was going." Jessi had insisted on stopping to see Chelsea before they'd left, although she hadn't told her that she and Clint were going together.

"Exactly." He bumped her with his shoulder again. "And she's probably going to ask what you did. So let's make it good."

Jessi's eyes widened. How was she supposed to respond to that?

She was still trying to figure it out when she heard a weird screech of metal, then Clint's arm was suddenly behind her, crushing her tightly against him.

"Hold on!"

She thought at first it was because a new horse had started the course, but then she sensed something falling, followed by screams.

When she glanced back, she saw that the metal support had broken free—probably from the weight of everyone leaning against it—and was dangling from the far side of the bleachers. And on the ground...

Oh, Lord. Fifteen feet below them were five people who'd evidently tumbled backward off the top seat when the structure had given way. Others were now on their feet in a panic, trying to rush down the stands to get to the ground. One person tripped and landed on another spectator a few rows down.

"Stay here," Clint muttered.

Like hell. "I'm coming with you. I'm a doctor, too, remember?"

Someone in the judges' booth called over the loudspeakers, asking for everyone to remain calm. And also asking for medical assistance.

Clint cautiously made his way down, trying to make sure he didn't trample on anyone, and again holding her hand as he took one step at a time.

By the time they reached the bottom they could hear a siren that cut off just as it reached the wide dirt aisle that separated the main arena from campers and horse trailers. The crowd opened a path to let it through.

One of the victims was now on her feet and waving away offers for help. Another person had disappeared, evidently also unhurt. But the remaining three were still on the ground, although one was sitting up, holding his leg.

"I'm a doctor," Clint said to him. "Can you hold on for a minute while we check the others?"

"Go," the man said, his thin, wiry frame and rugged clothing suggesting he was a farmer or someone who worked with livestock.

Jessi motioned that she'd take the far patient, a woman who was on her side, moaning, while Clint took the last remaining patient, a child, who was writhing on the ground and crying. They pushed through layers of people who wanted to help.

"I'm a doctor, let me through," she said to a man who was kneeling next to the woman. The man backed up to make room in the tight circle.

The EMT vehicle stopped and two medical workers jumped from the back just as Jessi crouched near her patient. The woman was conscious but obviously in a lot of pain.

"Where does it hurt?"

"Brandi," she gasped, ignoring the question and trying to roll onto her back, only to stop with a moan. "My daughter. Where's Brandi?"

Jessi glanced to the side, but couldn't see Clint through the bodies of onlookers, but his patient had looked to be a little girl.

"How old is your daughter?"

"She…she's five. Pink shorts." Talking was an obvious struggle for her.

That had to be Clint's patient.

"Someone's helping her right now. Where does it hurt?"

"M-My ribs. It hurts to breathe."

Jessi did a quick rundown of the woman's vitals. Everything seemed good, except for a marked tenderness on her right side. "Did you hit your head at all?"

"No. Just landed flat on my side. I couldn't get up."

One of the emergency services workers knelt beside her. "What have you got?"

Jessi glanced at the man, who looked to be almost as young as Chelsea. "Possible rib fractures." She read off the woman's vitals. "How's the little girl next to us?"

"Fractured wrist, but she looks good to go."

Jessi's patient broke down in tears. "Is that her? My daughter?"

It was amazing someone hadn't been more seriously injured or even killed in that fall. But luckily the bleachers had been built on dirt rather than a harder surface like concrete or asphalt.

She turned to the EMT. "Can you ask Dr. Marks if his patient's name is Brandi? It's her daughter, if so."

"Sure. I'll be right back."

Asking everyone to move back as he did so, she finally had a clear line of sight to Clint. He gave her a reassuring wink that made her smile.

God, how familiar that was. And it still made a jolt of electricity go through her system.

The girl was indeed Brandi, and within minutes everyone had been bundled up into two ambulances, which were creeping back between the throngs of horses and people, and soon disappeared. The sirens were off this time, probably trying not to spook the horses and risk more accidents.

Clint grasped her elbow and eased her over to the side. "They're taping off the bleachers."

Her adrenaline was just beginning to dissipate from her

system. "I felt the piece of metal give a little bit earlier, but it's been here for ages. I had no idea it could come loose."

"Just an accident."

"Thank God it wasn't worse. How about the person who fell, trying to get down?"

"Evidently they were all okay, since we didn't have any other patients."

With the excitement dying down, people were moving over to the rail next to the arena as the remaining barrel racers moved back into position.

"Do you want something to eat?"

She glanced up at him. "You can eat, after all that?"

He tweaked her chin. "They're all fine, Jess. Let's enjoy the rest of the day."

Their patients may have been fine, but Jessi wasn't so sure about herself. The memory of his hand grasping hers as he'd hauled her up the steps wound around her senses. She missed his touch. Wanted to reach over and...

The cell phone on Clint's hip buzzed. The hospital? Her whole body stiffened as dread rose up to fill her being.

Clint's system went on high alert as he put the phone to his ear.

"Marks here."

"Clinton? Clinton Marks?"

Frowning, he tried to place the feminine voice on the other end of the line. While the light Southern drawl was familiar, it definitely wasn't anyone from the hospital, because they would have called him "Doctor." If this was some telemarketer, they were about to get an earful for scaring Jessi.

And she was scared. He could read it in her stiff posture and the hands clenched at her sides.

He decided to go ultra-formal. "This is Dr. Marks."

"Well, *Dr.* Marks—" there was an air of amusement

to the voice now "—this is Abigail Spencer, Jessi's mom. Chelsea's grandmother. You remember me, don't you?"

Hell. That's why she sounded familiar.

He mouthed "Your mom" to relieve Jessi's fears, wondering why she was calling him instead of Jessi.

Jessi evidently had the same idea as he did, because she frowned and checked her phone. Maybe it was dead or something.

Clint and Jessi's dads had both been stationed at the same base, so he'd seen her parents quite a bit during his school years. His memories of Mrs. Spencer were of a kind woman with blond curls very like her daughter's and a quiet smile. So very different from his own mother's tense and fearful posture that had cropped up anytime she'd heard that front door open. Or how she would place her body in front of her son's until she had gauged what mood her husband had brought home with him. He rubbed a thumb across his pinky. His mother hadn't always been able to protect him, though.

Which was why the Spencer household had seemed so strange and alien to him. He'd never been able to shake the feeling that Jessi's mom had seen right through to the hurting kid hidden beneath a rebellious leather jacket and spiked hair. He brought his attention back to Jessi's mom as the silence over the phone grew awkward. He cleared his throat. "Of course I remember you. How are you?"

"Anxious to see my granddaughter. But Jessi told me that's not a good idea right now. I want to ask why. It's been over two months."

He didn't understand what that had to do with him, unless Jessi had used him as an excuse to deflect her visits. But whatever it was, that was between the two of them as far as he was concerned.

"I'm sorry, Mrs. Spencer. I really think you should talk to your daughter about that, because I can't discuss Chelsea's treatment. Jessi would have to give written authorization to—"

A poke to his arm made him look at the woman beside him. She shook her head.

Mrs. Spencer's voice came back down the line. "I can do better than that. Why don't you come over for dinner tonight? Jessi will be here, and we can hash all this out between the three of us." There was a pause. When her voice came back it was on the shaky side. "I'm her grandmother. Don't you think I'm entitled to know what's going on?"

"Again, that's not up to me." He felt like an utter jackass for saying those words to a woman who'd been nothing but nice to him during his time in Richmond, but Jess was staring holes right through him. "Jessi has medical power of attorney at the moment."

"She's trying to protect me, but I don't need protecting." An audible breath came through the receiver. "Won't you please come to dinner?"

There was no way he was going to walk into a situation like that without Jessi being fully aware of what was coming, and he wasn't willing to admit her daughter was standing right next to him. Not without Jess's approval. "Tell you what. Call your daughter and talk to her. If she's in agreement with me coming over tonight, I'll be glad to." How was that for admitting he had no other plans for a Friday evening?

Another poke to the arm, harder this time. "What are you doing?" she whispered.

He gave her a helpless shrug.

Unlike Jessi, he'd never married, instead throwing his whole life into helping others who were dealing with traumatic events stemming from their military service. It had been the least he could do for his dad, who, like Chelsea, had felt all alone.

"Okay, I'll do that." A quick laugh made a warning

system go off in his head. "Do you still like corned-beef brisket?"

She remembered that? He'd eaten over at their house exactly once, which was when he'd discovered how over-protective her dad was—the polar opposite of his. And he hadn't liked Clint. At all. Clint had never been invited back to the house again.

"I love brisket." Not that he thought there was a snow-ball's chance in hell that Jessi would agree to him coming over and talking about Chelsea's condition. If she'd wanted her mom to know how treatment was going, surely she would have told her by now.

"See you around seven, then."

Not quite sure how to answer that, he settled for a non-committal reply. "Thank you for the invitation, Mrs. Spen-cer."

The phone clicked off.

He met Jessi's accusing eyes. "Why did you let her in-vite you to dinner?"

As if he'd had any choice in the matter. One eyebrow went up. "I think the more important question is how did she get my number and why is she calling me, instead of you?"

"I don't know what you—"

Her phone started playing some samba beat that made him smile. Jessi groaned. "Oh, Lord. How am I going to get you out of this?"

"Don't worry about trying. I can come, if it's okay with you." Why he'd said that he had no idea.

"Hi, Mom. No, I'm...out at the fair." She licked her lips, while Clint handed money to the man in the funnel cake booth. "I know, I'm sorry. It was a spur-of-the-minute thing. A friend invited me."

She listened again, her face turning pink. "No, it's not a *guy* friend."

Pretend feathers all over his body began to ruffle and quiver in outrage as he accepted two plates from the vender. Uh…he could show her he was a guy, if she needed proof. Scratch that. She'd already seen the proof.

"Don't sound so disappointed, Mother." She rolled her eyes and glanced back at him. "You did what? How did you get his number?"

Her lips tightened, and she plopped down on a nearby bench, shutting her eyes for a second. "That's right. I forgot I left his card on the refrigerator. What were you doing at my house, anyway?"

Clint shifted beside her, uneasy about listening in on the conversation.

"Mom, you are going to spoil Cooper rotten. You know he has a weigh-in coming up."

Cooper? He set one of the plates on her lap and kept the other for himself. Did Jessi have another boyfriend? Visions of some muscle-bound hunk lounging in her bed came to mind.

No, she would have said something to him.

And exactly when had he given her the chance? He'd asked about Larry, but not about any other man who might be waiting in the wings.

"What? Clint *already* agreed to come? Wow, he sounds a little desperate, doesn't he?"

She stuck her tongue out at him, just as he took a bite of his fried cake, making him relax in his seat. "Okay, I'm about done here, so I'll start heading back that way. Love you."

He hadn't exactly agreed to go, and he was glad Jessi had heard for herself his side of the conversation. His smile widened. It would seem Mrs. Spencer could play loose and easy with rules, too.

She got off the phone and picked her cake up with a napkin he held out to her.

"Desperate, am I?" He didn't try to hide the wry tone to his voice.

"What could I do? If I said you couldn't come to dinner, she'd make up her own conclusions. And I couldn't exactly admit that you were sitting right next to me, eating funnel cake, could I?"

That part was his fault. He'd been the one to pretend they weren't together.

"So who's Cooper?" He dropped the question as if it were no big deal. Which it wasn't.

"A communal beagle," she said, as she swallowed. "Mmm...that's good stuff."

Also good was the dot of powdered sugar on her lower lip. One he was just able to refrain from licking off.

"A communal...beagle?"

Her tongue sailed across her lip, whisking away the sugar. "Okay, I guess that does sound weird. He adopted me about a year ago...came waddling up to the door and scratched on it. No one ever claimed him, so Mom and I have been caring for him between the two of us. He's on a diet. Supposedly." Stretching her legs out in front of her, she went on, "When I have to work late, Mom takes him to her house. You'll probably meet him tonight. Since you're evidently coming to dinner."

She munched down on another piece of cake, moaning in enjoyment. "That is if you still have room for food after this."

"You haven't asked me if I had plans for the evening."

Her eyes widened. "Oh, God. I'm sorry. Do you?"

"No. But I don't want to make things any harder for you than they already are." The tortured look when she'd discovered her daughter's pregnancy came back to haunt him. "I know this isn't easy, Jess."

"No, it's not." She paused, setting her food back on her plate. "Can you let me set the tone of the conversation?

Mom will just worry herself sick if she knew the extent of what Chelsea is facing. And she hasn't seemed herself recently either. She was on antidepressants for several years, so it has me worried."

He frowned, surprised by the information. But people sometimes hid their problems well. "Does she know about the suicide attempt?"

"Yes. But she wasn't there when it happened. She only knew…afterwards."

He touched her hand. "You sure you want me to come?"

"I'm not sure of anything right now. But Mom is right. Chelsea is her granddaughter. One she hasn't seen in over two months. It's time to start letting her know what's going on. I—I just want to feed her the information in bits she can process. She's been through a lot in the past five years."

Since her husband's death.

"I understand." He withdrew his hand and sat up straighter. "I'll let you answer specific questions, and I can fill in any of the medical gaps. How does that sound?"

"Perfect. Thanks so much, Clint."

Well, at least she hadn't thrown his card away. Then again, she hadn't kept it in her wallet either. "If you're done, I'll take you back to the house. I'm pretty sure you don't want us arriving in the same car."

She handed him her plate and waited until he'd thrown them both in a nearby trash receptacle to answer.

"Probably not a good idea." She smiled and stood to her feet. As they made their way back to the parking area, Clint had one thought. He hoped tonight went a whole lot better than his day had.

Jessi's plans for a relaxing evening at home looked like they were shot to hell. Between helping her mom set the table and dragging her makeup bag from her purse to touch up the dark circles under her eyes, she was getting more and more antsy. It was one thing to spend a few relaxing hours at the fair. It was another thing entirely to eat a meal with him while her mother grilled them about Chelsea's condition, which of course she would.

She'd just put the last swipe of mascara on her lashes when the doorbell rang and Cooper started up with the baying his breed was famous for. She froze, the makeup wand still in her right hand. Sucking down a breath, she quickly shoved it back in the tube, blinked at herself in the bathroom mirror and headed to get the door.

By the time she got halfway down the stairs she saw her mother had beaten her to it, apron wrapped around her waist. The door opened, and Cooper bumbled forward to greet the newcomer.

As Clint bent to pet the dog, Jessi couldn't help but stare. He'd evidently showered as well, because his hair was still damp. Dressed in a red polo shirt that hugged his shoulders and snug black jeans that hugged other—more dangerous—parts, he looked better than any funnel cake she'd ever had. He straightened and went over to kiss her mother's cheek, while Cooper continued to snuffle and groan at his ankles.

His eyes came up. Met hers across the room.

A sting of awareness rippled through her as his gaze slid over her white peasant shirt and dark-wash jeans before coming back up to her face. One side of his mouth pulled up into something that might have been a smile. Then again, it could have just as easily been classified as a modified grimace. Either way, the action caused that crease in his cheek to deepen and her heart rate to shoot through the roof.

Sexy man. Sexy smile. Stupid girl.

Hurrying the rest of the way down the stairs, she grabbed Cooper's collar and tugged him back into the house, while greeting Clint with as much nonchalance as she could muster under the circumstances. "Glad you could make it."

Not that there'd been much choice on either of their parts. Her mom had made sure of that. And right now the woman was the perfect hostess, ushering Clint in and offering him a drink, which he declined. That surprised her. He'd been such a rebel in high school that everyone had assumed that he'd played it loose and easy with alcohol, although she'd never actually seen him touch the stuff.

Her mom glanced at her in question, but Jessi shook her head. She needed all her wits about her if this evening was going to go according to plan. If she could help it, they were going to avoid talking about Chelsea as much as possible, and when her mom pressed for information, she would be honest but gloss over some of the more depressing aspects of her granddaughter's present situation. Like the fact that she either didn't want to talk about what had precipitated her suicide attempt, or she had simply blocked out that portion of her life. Who knew which it was? And it wasn't like Clint had had much time to get to the bottom of things. He'd been her doctor for, what…a little under a week?

"You look lovely," Clint said to her once her mom had gone to the kitchen to put the finishing touches on their meal. Cooper, obviously hoping for a few dropped morsels, puttered along behind her.

"Thank you." She bit her lip. "I'm really, really sorry you got caught in the middle of this."

"It's fine. I haven't had a homemade meal in…" He paused. "Well, it's been a while."

A while since someone had cooked for him? Jessi found that hard to believe. A man like Clint wouldn't have any trouble finding dates. He was even better looking now than he'd been in high school, although she never would have believed that possible. Gangly and rebellious as a teenager, he had filled out, not only physically—which was impressive enough—but he now had a maturity about him that had been lacking all those years ago. Oh, he'd made all the girls, including her, nervous wrecks back then. But as a man—well, she'd be hard pressed to say he wasn't breathtaking in a totally masculine way. From the self-assured smile to the confidence he exuded, he gave her more than a glimmer of hope that this was a man who could help her daughter.

"Have a seat," she told him. "Mom will be back any minute, and I'd like to set some quick ground rules. Like I said earlier, I haven't told her much about Chelsea's behavior—she knows about the suicide attempt, but not much about her time at the hospital. I wanted to keep it simple until I felt like there was some ho—"

Her voice cracked as an unexpected wave of emotion splashed over her, blocking the one word she wanted to believe in.

"Until you felt like there was some hope?" He finished the sentence for her. "There's always hope, Jess. I think we'll start seeing a little more progress in the coming weeks."

He shifted to face her. "Exactly what do you want me to say to your mom? I'm not comfortable with lying."

And yet he'd been the one to suggest she lie to her father about what happened after she'd run out of the gym during graduation all those years ago. To protect himself from her dad's wrath? Or to protect her?

Maybe it had been a little of both.

"I don't expect you to lie. You said there's always hope. If you could just keep that as a running theme when you talk about Chelsea, it would help Mom feel better."

"She's going to ask to see her, you know. Is there a reason you don't want her to?"

"I'm worried about her, like I told you earlier. I want to…be there when she sees Chelsea."

And I want you to have time to work your magic first. She didn't say the words, but she wanted them to be true. She trusted him. Why that was she couldn't say. She hadn't seen them interact that much. But he'd said he'd do his very best for Chelsea and she believed him. She just hoped it was enough.

Five minutes later, they were called into dinner. Cooper settled under the table with his head propped on Clint's right foot, despite all her efforts to deter him.

"He's fine," Clint said. "As long as he doesn't expect me to share any of that delicious-looking brisket."

They all laughed, and Jessi gave a quick sigh of relief. She'd half expected her mom to grill Clint on Chelsea's prognosis from the moment they sat down, but it was mostly small talk as Jessi munched lettuce leaves with nerves that were as crackly as the salad. The feared topic didn't hit until they were halfway through her mom's famed brisket, which, despite being as succulent as ever, was getting tougher and tougher for her to force down.

"Jessi tells me that she thinks Chelsea is dealing with PTSD. Is that what you're seeing, as well?"

Clint dabbed his mouth with his napkin and nodded. "We see quite a number of veterans who come back with issues related to what they've seen and done."

"Does that mean you have some ideas on how to proceed?"

Jessi's eyes jerked to his and found him watching her. She put her fork on the table as she waited for him to answer.

"We're keeping our options open at the moment. I'm still working through the notes from her previous doctor."

"That's right. I forgot you'd just moved home. What

perfect timing. Or were you just so homesick that you couldn't bear to stay away any longer?"

Jessi sucked down too much of the water she'd been sipping and choked for a second, but Clint didn't miss a beat. "Doctors are transferred to other locations on a regular basis, just like any other member of the armed forces." He gave a rueful twist of the mouth. "We both know about that, don't we?"

Way to go, Clint. Find something you have in common and use it to evade the real question.

Kind of like he'd done when she'd asked him why he had to leave the day after graduation. "I've already signed the papers, and that's when they told me to show up" had been his answer. She'd bought it at the time. But now? She had a feeling he'd just wanted to avoid her making any demands on him after their shared time together.

Which stung even more now than it had when he'd said the words.

Jessi's mom smiled back. "I'm sure you've done your share of moving, just like we did when Jessi was little." She paused then said, "I'm really glad you're back, though, and that you'll be the one treating Chelsea."

Clint's face registered surprise. "Why is that?"

Cutting into another section of her meat, her mom glanced up with a hint of sadness mixed with what looked like relief. "Because you, more than anyone, know what it's like to live with the effects of PTSD."

CHAPTER SIX

THE ROOM WAS silent for five long seconds.

Clint knew, because he counted every damn tick of the clock. He hadn't told Jessi or anyone else about his dad and the problems he'd had. Could his mom have mentioned it to Abigail or someone else from their past?

Worse, did Jessi know?

Even as the questions ducked through his cerebral cortex, looking for a believable response, he thought he saw pity flit through Jessi's eyes, although right now her mouth was hanging open in shock.

But, eventually, he had to say something. The ache in his pinky finger sprang to life, reminding him of all the reasons he'd decided to join the military and leave Jessi far behind. He clenched his fist to rid himself of the sensation and made a decision.

He was going to tell the truth. Air his dirty laundry— at least about his father. After all these years.

"Yes. I do know."

Jessi's fork clattered to her plate, and her mouth snapped shut. "Mom, I don't think that's an appropriate thing to blurt out at the dinner table."

Wounded green eyes, so like her daughter's, widened. "Oh, I'm sorry. I didn't realize. I just assumed that everyone knew—"

"It's okay," Clint said, his thumb scrubbing across the crooked joint, a habit he used as a daily reminder of why his job was so crucial. Because PTSD didn't affect just the individual soldier...it affected everyone around them, as well. "I didn't talk about my problems much. And for a long time I didn't realize that something could be done."

Jessi finally spoke up. "*You* had PTSD?"

"No. My dad did. It was back when I was in high school."

Differing emotions flickered through her eyes. Sadness. Shock. Then finally the one he'd hoped never to see: guilt.

"Clint, I—" Her tongue flicked across her lips. "You never told any of us."

"Would *you* have?"

He knew she'd catch the inference. That her father—a tough army boot-camp instructor—had been vehement in his opposition to her being involved with anyone in the military. After Mrs. Spencer's words, he now wondered if it was because Jessi's dad and the entire base had witnessed the hell his mom had gone through because of his dad. Because of the way he'd used the bottle to blot out the demons related to his war deployment. It hadn't worked. He'd just created a living hell for everyone around him. Clint wouldn't want any daughter of his to go through what his mom had on a daily basis.

Whatever Mr. Spencer's reasons, it had ended up saving Clint's hide down at that creek. It—and his enlistment papers—had given him the perfect out for leaving Richmond. He'd jumped at the excuse, although he now realized that's all it had been. An excuse. He'd been afraid *of* his dad and *for* his dad. Had run away from the possibility that he might turn out to be just like him. But most of all, he hadn't wanted anyone to know the shame he'd felt.

The irony was, they had known, according to Abigail.

"No," Jessi said. "I wouldn't have shared my secrets with just anyone."

The hint of accusation in her voice was unmistakable. Because she had shared *her* secret with someone: him. But he hadn't returned the favor by telling her his. Maybe because he hadn't wanted to add any more to her plate. Maybe because the only thing he'd wanted at the time had been to erase the pain in her eyes.

Instead, he'd ended up making love to her and adding to his long list of sins. Which included leaving her the very next day. He'd thought it was to protect her.

Not that it had done any good. Jessi's own daughter was now struggling with trauma related to her military service, so he hadn't ended up protecting her from anything. Just his own ugly past and uncertain future.

Little had she known back then that he had harbored a secret crush on her. Maybe it had been part of the whole badass, wanting-to-redeem-himself syndrome. The same reason he'd enlisted. A need to redeem himself and maybe even his father—or at least to make peace with what had happened.

Clint's job, though, had turned into a passion he just couldn't shake. In some small measure he *had* redeemed himself. Each time he was able to help an emotionally wounded soldier have a shot at a normal life, he was somehow giving his father the help he'd never received when he'd been alive. And in doing that—Clint flexed his damaged finger again—he helped protect their sons and daughters.

Abigail broke into his thoughts. "I really am sorry. I just assumed that Jessi knew, since you went to school together."

They'd done more than just that. Which was something he could not—would not—think about right now. Not with her mom sitting there, looking more than a little mortified.

"It's fine…"

"Don't worry…"

He and Jessi spoke at exactly the same time, which caused everyone to laugh and broke the tension instantly. Even Cooper gave a quick *woof* of approval.

And although he'd been the one to say, "Don't worry," he was worried. More than a little. Because every time he caught Jessi watching him, his gut slid sideways.

"I have some peach ice cream for dessert," Abigail said, "if anyone wants some."

He glanced down at his watch. Almost nine. He could safely take off and claim to have survived the evening. "Thank you, but I probably should be heading home. I have an early morning tomorrow."

He pushed his chair back, dislodging Cooper from his foot in the process. The dog's nails clicked on the hardwood floor as he slid from beneath the table and pressed his cheek against Clint's calf. Reaching down, he scratched behind the animal's ears.

"Are you sure?" Abigail asked.

"Yes, unless there's something I can do to help clean up."

She smiled. "Not a thing." A quick frown puckered her brow. "I almost forgot. When can I see Chelsea? I don't want to set her treatment back, but if I can just spend a minute or two with her to assure myself that she's really—"

"Of course." He glanced at Jessi for confirmation. "How about if we make it for the next time Jessi and I meet with her? Friday at three?"

Jessi nodded her approval. "It's okay with me. I want to talk to you a little bit about her condition first, though, okay, Mama? I don't want you to be shocked by what she might say…or not say."

"I wasn't born yesterday. I know it's bad. I just want to see her."

"I'll pick you up on my way home from work, then. We can go together." She kissed her mother on the cheek, something that made Clint's chest tighten. Despite Mr. Spencer's heavy-handed ways, this had been a house of love. It was obvious the two women were close. And he was glad. Glad that her teenage angst hadn't left any lasting scars.

His arthritic pinky creaked out a warning shot when he curled his hand around the chair to push it back in.

"Thanks again for dinner, Mrs. Spencer."

"You're very welcome, and I'm glad you came. I already feel better."

As he started for the door, he was surprised to find Jessi right behind him. "I'll walk you to your car."

He opened the door, forgetting about Cooper. The dog bounded out before he could stop him.

"It's okay," Jessi said. "He does it to everyone. He won't go far."

The walk down the driveway was filled with the scent of magnolia blossoms, a smell he remembered well. Unbeknownst to Jessi, he'd sat in front of her house for hours the night of graduation, listening for any sounds of fighting, or worse. It had been hard back then to remember that not every father struck out with his fists.

But there'd been nothing that night. Just the muggy heat and that rich floral scent—something he connected to Jessi every time he smelled it. Even now, memories of the soft carpet of moss he'd felt beneath his hands as he'd supported his weight swirled around him. Of her face, soft and flushed, tilting back as he'd trailed his mouth down her neck.

Damn. He never should have come here.

He quickened his steps, only to have her hand touch his arm as they reached his car. He turned to face her, keys in hand, ready to get the hell out of there. The faster he left, the sooner he could regain his sanity.

Which right now was nowhere to be found. Because all he wanted to do was kiss her. Right in front of her house. To relive a little of the magic he'd experienced all those years ago.

"Why didn't you tell me…back then?" she asked.

He might have known this was why she'd wanted to come with him. "I thought I'd explained that. It was my problem, there was no reason to involve anyone else."

"God, Clint. I bawled my eyes out about my dad's stupid rules without even knowing what you—"

"I didn't tell you because I didn't want anyone to know. Besides, it doesn't matter anymore. It's all in the past."

"And your dad is gone."

His jaw clenched. His father's liver cancer, brought on by years of alcohol abuse, didn't mitigate the fact that Clint wished he'd known sooner how to help him. "So is yours."

"Yes. I'm just glad he's not suffering. The strokes came faster at the end…"

"I'm sorry." He put his arm around her, meaning to give her a quick squeeze and release her. Instead, somehow she wound up against his chest, palms splayed against his shirt, staring up at him with those huge eyes.

The same eyes that did something to his insides every damn time she looked at him. It had happened in high school. And it was still happening now. He leaned back against the car door, still holding on to her.

She bit her lip for a second. "For what it's worth, I'm glad you were the one—back then. And I'm glad it's you now."

Whoa. If that wasn't a kick in the gut, he didn't know what was. She was glad he'd been the one who'd taken her virginity and not Larry? He'd beaten himself up about that for years afterwards.

And what did she mean, she was happy it was him now? She had to be talking about Chelsea.

"I had no idea who she was, Jess, until you stepped into that room. I swear."

"I didn't know it was you either. Until I saw the nameplate on your desk."

Her fingers came up and touched the line of his jaw, and she smiled. "I never believed that rebel freedom air you put on back in school."

He cocked a brow. "Oh, no? And why was that?"

"Because you looked so lost at times. I just never understood what caused it back then."

Before he had time to tense up, she continued. "Mama is right, you know."

"How's that?"

"You are the absolute best person to be treating Chelsea." She closed her eyes for a second before looking up at him again. "I'm so glad you're here, Clint. So glad you came home."

The squeezing sensation in his chest grew. The tightrope he was toeing his way across was thinner than he'd realized...harder to balance on than he'd expected.

"Promise me you won't drop the case," she added.

That's exactly what he *should* do. Especially now. Bow out and ask someone else to step in. Transfer the hell out of that hospital and go back to California.

A thought came to him. Was this why Jessi was in his arms, staring all doe-eyed at him? "I can't make you that promise. I have to do what I think is in the best interests of your daughter."

"I know. Just promise me that tomorrow, when you walk into that office, you'll still be the one treating her."

He was suddenly aware of her fingers. They were still on his skin, only now they'd moved slightly backward, putting his senses on high alert—along with certain parts of his body. "I'll be there for her."

"Good. Because I think I'm about to do something very, very stupid."

He didn't need to ask what it was. Because he was on the verge of doing something just as stupid.

But it didn't stop him from tugging her closer, neither did it stop his lips from closing over hers in a sudden crazy burst of need.

And once their mouths fused together, he was transported to the past. Twenty-two years, to be exact. He'd been unable to get enough of her. Her taste. The faint scent of her shampoo or body wash, or magnolias—whatever the hell it had been that had filled his senses, intoxicating him more than the booze he'd been offered earlier ever could have.

A faint sound came from her throat. He was fairly certain it wasn't a gasp of protest, since her arms had wound around his neck and her body had slid up his as she'd gone up on tiptoe. He buried his fingers in the hair at her nape, the slight dampness probably due to the Virginia humidity, but it brought back memories of perspiration and bodies that moved together in perfect harmony. Of…

The sound of Cooper's plaintive howl split the air a short distance away, followed by the sound of the front door opening. Abigail's voice called out the dog's name.

Cursing everything under the sun, he let Jessi pull free from his lips, even though the last thing he wanted to do was let her go. He wanted to drag her into the car and drive right to the creek to see if that night had been everything he'd remembered it being.

Abigail's voice called the dog's name again. The bushes shielded them from view, so Clint didn't look. Besides, his gaze was glued to Jessi's pale features.

Even when Cooper decided to lumber over to them, instead of going to the house, he didn't break eye contact.

"Sorry. I'm sorry." The gutted apology as she backed up one step, then two, made his lungs burn. The back of her hand went to her mouth, and she pressed hard. Her feet separated them by another pace, then she reached down to capture Cooper's collar. "Please, don't dump her. This was my fault. Not hers."

As she led the dog back to the front door, Clint gave his head a silent shake. There was no one else. He couldn't leave. Not yet.

Chelsea couldn't afford to lose two doctors in the space of two weeks.

Which meant Clint couldn't afford to start something he would never be able to finish. He'd made love to Jessi once and had barely been able to find the strength to walk away. If it happened twice, there was no hope for him.

So, from now on, he would tread carefully. And keep his distance from Jessi and her mom as much as possible.

CHAPTER SEVEN

CHELSEA WAS TALKING.

Not a lot, but Clint had noticed a subtle shift in her de-meanor over the past several days as they met for their sessions. She was more interested and less withdrawn. He wasn't sure what had caused the change, but he was all for it.

Besides, it kept him from having to deal with the dev-astating consequences of that kiss he and Jessi had shared beside his car. And the suspicious thoughts that had crept into his mind in the meantime.

Had she tried to manipulate him into staying?

No. Jessi wasn't like that. When he'd left all those years ago, she'd never said a word to try to make him change his mind. Yes, she'd made him promise that he'd remain on her daughter's case—right before she'd locked her lips to his, but it wasn't as if she was the only one who'd been thinking along those lines. He'd been just as guilty. And she'd been very careful to maintain her distance ever since. Their consultations were now over the phone—despite their earlier agreement to meet with Chelsea together—and her voice during those calls was brisk and businesslike.

Just like the doctor she was.

And she was smart. She knew exactly the right ques-tions to ask regarding her daughter's state of mind. According to the nurses, her visits to Chelsea occurred during his off hours. He had no doubt she'd somehow found out his schedule and was purposely coming when he wasn't around.

As grateful as he should be for the breathing space, he found himself irritated at the way he missed her presence.

What else could he do, though? He'd always prided himself on his self-control, because it was something his dad had never had much of. And yet Clint lost it every time he was around Jessi.

Every. Damn. Time.

It had been true twenty-two years ago, and it was still true today. He just couldn't resist her. The good girl that he'd had a secret crush on in high school had turned him into an impulsive, reckless creature. One he feared, because he recognized the beast all too well. He'd looked into impulsive, reckless eyes so like his own during his teenage years.

That raw, angry kid had morphed into a cool, rational man somewhere along the way, and in doing so had found himself. Had found an antidote that worked. But it only functioned if he didn't let anyone get too close.

Today would be the test. Jessi was due here with her mom in a little over an hour. He'd warned himself. Scolded himself. Immersed himself in work. All to no avail.

His heart was already pounding in anticipation of seeing her—trying to justify being with her one more time.

Just one kiss. He could stop anytime he wanted.

Sound familiar, Clint?

Substitute *drink* for the word *kiss* and you had his dad in all his lying glory.

Not good.

His assistant pushed open the door. "Dr. Marks? Miles Branson is here for his appointment. Are you ready for him?"

"Yes, send him in. Thanks, Maria."

As hectic as his morning had been, with two new patients and a flurry of consultations, he shouldn't have had time to think about Jessi at all. But she'd found her way into every nook and cranny of his brain and surged to the forefront whenever he had a free moment.

Like now.

Miles came in and, after shaking Clint's hand, lowered himself into one of the chairs across from him. Another PTSD patient, this particular man had made great strides in his treatment over the past couple of weeks. It could be because of that new baby girl he had waiting at home for him.

"How're Maggie and the baby?" he asked.

"Both beautiful." The smile the man gave him was genuine, and the furrows between his brows seemed less pronounced than they'd been when Clint had arrived. He scrolled through his phone for a second and then handed it over.

Miles's wife and a baby swaddled in a pink blanket lay on a hospital bed. She looked exhausted but happy, while it was obvious their daughter was trying out her new set of lungs, if the open mouth and red, angry-looking face were anything to go by.

"Beautiful. You've got a great pair of girls there." Clint pushed the phone across his desk.

"I'm a lucky man." He smiled again, glancing down at his wife and daughter. "You know, for the first time in a long time I actually believe that."

"I know you do. Are you ready to try for a reduction of your medication?"

"Can I do away with it altogether?"

Clint paused for a second. While his superiors were very conscious of time and money, his only concern was for his patients. He'd been known to ruffle a few feathers along the way, but had still somehow made it up the chain of command. While paroxetine wasn't addictive, like the benzodiazepine family of medications, he still felt it was safer to reduce the dosage gradually while maintaining a regular therapy schedule as they progressed.

In the two years since Miles had first been seen by other doctors, the man had gotten engaged and then married to a wonderful woman who knew exactly what he was battling. And, thank heavens, this man hadn't shown the agitation and anger issues that Clint's dad had.

"Let's knock it down from sixty milligrams a day to twenty and go from there." He grabbed his prescription pad and wrote out a new dosage recommendation. "We'll maintain our sessions, and in a couple of weeks, if all goes well, we'll reduce them even more. How does that sound?"

Miles sat back in his chair, his posture relaxed and open. "It sounds like living. Thanks, Doc."

For the next forty-five minutes they went through the new father's moods and actions, detailing where he'd struggled, while Clint made notes he would transcribe later. Together they made a plan on how to deal with the next several weeks, when having a new baby at home would put more stress on both him and the family.

When they finally parted, he opened the office door to let Miles out and his glance immediately connected with Jessi and her mom, who'd arrived fifteen minutes early for their session with Chelsea. He nodded at the pair, walking Miles over to his assistant's desk and giving a few last-minute instructions on scheduling.

Taking a deep breath, he finally turned and made his way over to the pair in his waiting area. Jessi, dressed in a casual white-flowered dress that stretched snugly across her top and waist, stood to her feet. Flat, strappy sandals showed off pink toenails and dainty feet. He swallowed when he realized he'd been staring. All his misgivings from earlier came roaring back. He shoved them aside.

"Sorry to keep you waiting," he muttered, his voice a little gruffer than he'd expected. But seeing Jessi up close and personal created this choking sensation that closed off the upper part of his throat.

Her mom was the one to break the stare-fest. "We were a little early, at my insistence. I'm anxious to see my granddaughter."

"I'm sure you are."

Abigail was in a pair of jeans with a white button-down shirt. At almost sixty, she was still a beautiful woman, with high cheekbones and eyes very like her daughter's. And her granddaughter's, for that matter.

"Do you want to meet in my office or head down to Chelsea's room? Jessi gave a little shrug, no longer attempting to look directly at him. Maybe she felt as uncomfortable as he was about this meeting. "Wherever you feel is best."

Her mom spoke up again. "I haven't seen Chelsea's room. Do you think she would mind if we met her there? I'm curious about where she's been staying." She blinked a couple of times. "Not that I'm saying there's anything wrong with the hospital. It looks modern and well cared for."

Not what she'd expected. She didn't say the words, but he could imagine her thoughts.

The VA's reputation had taken a beating in the press over the last year. And not without reason, but the corruption was slowly being weeded out, and Clint hoped the end result would be a system of hospitals the country's servicemen and women could be proud of.

Clint had done his best to make sure his patients received the best treatment possible. And he knew there were a lot of other dedicated doctors who also cared deeply about their patients. The waiting lists were staggering, and, yes, it would probably be much easier to find work in the civilian sector for better pay and a lighter workload. But that wasn't why he did what he did.

"You're fine," he assured Abigail. He turned to his assistant. "Could you call down to Chelsea's room and let her know we're on our way?"

"Of course, Doctor." She picked up her phone and dialed as Clint nodded toward the hallway to their right. "Jessi, you know the way."

She stood and slung the strap of her purse over her arm, making sure her mother was following her. She glanced back at him. "Any last-minute instructions?"

"No. Chelsea's been more open, as I told you over the phone. I think that's an encouraging sign." Not that they'd made definitive steps in her treatment. The new class of antidepressants he'd prescribed was kicking in, though, so he had hopes that as the fog of despair continued to lift, she would start looking to the future, instead of crouching in the past. They had yet to talk about the specifics surrounding her months in captivity. She'd reiterated that she hadn't been tortured or assaulted, but as to what exactly had happened during that time, there was still a large swath of information that was missing. Clint had even tried going through channels and seeing if her superior officers knew anything more. But they were what Clint would label as "careful" with their words. It hadn't been anything in particular that was or wasn't said. It had just been the way the information had been delivered. And every story had been told in an identical fashion.

For Clint, that fact alone raised a huge red flag.

"Nana!" he heard the greeting even before he reached the room. And the happiness in that one word was apparent. As was the sight of the two women embracing, while Jessi stood back to allow the reunion to happen.

"How's she really doing?" she asked him in a low voice

as Abigail sat on the edge of the bed, her arm around her granddaughter.

"Just like I said. She's talking more."

"Any idea yet on the why?"

The why of the suicide attempt.

"We haven't made it that far, yet."

The exchange ended when Abigail waved her daughter over. "Doesn't she look wonderful?"

She didn't, and they all knew it. Still pale and frighteningly thin, Chelsea did not have the appearance of a soldier who'd been through the worst that boot camp had to offer... who had survived a stint as a POW. She looked like a fragile piece of china that might shatter at the slightest tap.

While they talked, Clint grabbed two chairs from an empty room that adjoined Chelsea's and added them to the two that were already against the pale gray walls—Clint had learned how important equalizing the setting was, which was why his office had three identical chairs. One for him and two for those who met him there. His rank was above that of many of his patients, but that didn't mean he had to act the part.

"Dr. Marks?" Jessi's voice interrupted his thoughts.

Although it rankled at some level, he knew it was better for them to address each other in a formal manner in public, although he'd told Chelsea—in vague terms—that he and Jessi had known each other in the past. It was easier to be as truthful as possible, while holding back information that could be deemed harmful to her treatment.

"Sorry," he murmured. He turned to Chelsea. "Do you feel up to sitting with us?"

"Yes." She swung her legs over the side of the bed, waving off her mom, who'd immediately moved to help her. "It's okay. I can do it."

She was in a set of flannel pajamas that Jessi had evidently brought in during one of her other visits. Ideally, he would have liked her to be dressed in normal clothes for their meetings. And in recent days she'd made more of an effort.

So why was today different?

Was she trying to appear fragile, warning away any talk that crept toward painful subjects?

It was too late now to ask her to change, and he didn't want to do anything that would upset Jessi's mom in the process. Besides, he had another client in an hour and a half and he wanted to make sure that Chelsea wouldn't be cut off in the middle of anything important.

They sat in a circle. Chelsea and Abigail glanced at him expectantly, while Jessi's gaze was centered on the folded hands she held in her lap.

"Chelsea, it's been a while since your grandmother has seen you, am I correct?"

The young woman's hand snaked out and grabbed Abigail's. "I'm glad she's here."

"So am I."

He wasn't going to push hard this session, he just wanted to reintroduce the family and make sure everyone knew that their old ways of interacting might not work in this new and different world. Chelsea had gone to war as one person and had come back another. They all had yet to see where exactly that left her mom and grandmother, although the reunion had gone much more smoothly than he would have expected.

Even as he thought it, Abigail pressed her fingertips to her eyes and wiped away moisture that had gathered beneath them. "Oh, no, Nana. Don't cry." Chelsea wrapped her arms around the older woman. "Mom, there's a box of tissues in my top drawer. Would you mind getting me one?"

Jessi jumped up and headed toward the small end table beside the bed. She drew out the top drawer, found the

box and withdrew it. Then she stopped. Chelsea was facing away from her mother and couldn't see her, but Clint
could. A strange look crossed her face as she peered at
something inside that drawer. She started to reach for it
then withdrew her hand.

Chelsea, as if realizing something was wrong, swiveled around in her chair. "Can't you find…? Oh, no, Mom.
Please don't."

But it was already too late, because Jessi had reached
back into the drawer and withdrawn what looked like a
wad of tissues. Glancing at Chelsea and seeing the horror
in her eyes, he realized that's not what that was. Not at all.

Even as he looked, Jess smoothed down the bottom edge
of the thin paper and came forward a couple of steps, only
to stop halfway. It was a doll of some sort.

No. Not a doll. A baby. Painstakingly crafted from the
tissues in the box in her drawer.

"Chelsea, honey." Jessi's voice dropped away for a
second before coming back again. "What is this?"

CHAPTER EIGHT

JESSI SLUMPED IN a chair in Clint's office. "I don't understand. What could it mean?"

Her daughter had refused to talk about the strange item, withdrawing back into her shell until Clint called a halt to the session and let Chelsea crawl back into her bed. She'd silently held out her hand for the doll and laid it carefully back inside the drawer.

The act made Jessi shiver.

She'd sent her mom home with a promise to stop by later, and Clint had ordered the nurse to call him immediately if there was any change.

"I don't know what it means. Maybe she miscarried while she was overseas. Maybe it's something she made as a coping mechanism. There could be any number of explanations, but until she tells us we won't know for sure."

"Will you ask her again tomorrow?"

"I'll see how she is. We may have to work our way toward it slowly." He dragged his fingers through his hair and leaned back in his chair. "It could just be a dead end."

"Who makes a doll out of a box of tissues? It just doesn't seem…normal."

When he stared at her, she closed her eyes. "Sorry. That didn't come out right. It's just that everything seemed to explode out of nowhere two months ago."

"I know. It just takes time."

"What if she never gets better? What if she's like this for the rest of her life?"

He reached across and covered her hand with his. "Thoughts like that aren't going to help anyone."

"Did you struggle with those kinds of thoughts during high school? About your dad? Did *he* ever get better?"

When he went to withdraw his hand with a frown, she grabbed at his fingers, holding him in place.

"Oh, God, Clint, I'm so sorry," she whispered. "I'm just worried about Chelsea."

"I know." He laced his fingers through hers. "I gave her a sedative, so she should sleep through the night. We'll start fresh in the morning."

"I want to be there when she wakes up."

He studied her for a minute or two, before shaking his head with what looked like regret. "I don't think that's a good idea, Jess. When you and your mom left, she was agitated and withdrawn. I don't want those memories to be the ones that resurface when she opens her eyes. Give her a day."

"A day?" She couldn't believe he was asking her to stay away from the hospital for an entire day. "I'm not the only one worried. Mom is, as well."

"I'll call you as soon as I see her. Are you working tomorrow?" He let go of her hand and reached for one of his pencils, jiggling it between his fingers as if he needed something to keep him busy. Or maybe it was a hint that he needed to get back to work.

"I'm on the afternoon shift, starting at three. I'd better get out of your hair." She stood to her feet, then thought of something. "What if you get a call in the middle of the night?"

"If something serious happens, I'll be in touch."

"Promise?"

"Promise." He must have read her dubious smile, because one side of his mouth curved into that familiar half smile. "Would you like me to pinkie-swear, as well?"

Despite her worry, she found her own lips twitching. "Would you, if I asked you to?"

"Yes."

Something icy hot nipped the air between them. She held her breath and then released it in a long stream. "Or you could come and spend the night at the house. Just in case."

Why on earth had she asked that? It was too late to take back the offer, although she could clarify it. "On the couch, of course."

His eyes softened, but he shook his head. "I have to work for a couple more hours. Besides, I don't think my staying with you would be a good idea, Jess. Things never quite remain that simple between us. And I meant what I said about taking myself off the case if I think my objectivity has been compromised."

Oh, Lord, that's right. He'd intimated that he'd hand Chelsea over to someone else if things got too personal between them. "I wasn't asking you to sleep with me. Not this time."

She'd gone that route once before, asking him to make love to her by the creek, desperately needing a few minutes out from beneath her father's thumb.

"I don't remember complaining the last time you did."

No. But then again she hadn't seen him volunteering to hang around the next day—although it had probably been too late for him to back out of boot camp by that time. And who was to say he would stick around in Richmond now? Some servicemen loved the adventure of a new place every couple of years. Not Jessi. Once she'd gotten to high school, her father had finally seemed willing to settle down and stay until she graduated. Then she'd married Larry, who hadn't known she'd had a dalliance with his friend. Not until that last day of his life.

She blocked out the thought and concentrated on the here and now as Clint got up and opened the door to his office.

She walked through it and then hesitated on the other side. "So you'll call me tomorrow."

"As soon as I have some news. Yes."

They said their goodbyes, and already his manner was more aloof. Businesslike.

Once she got to the front door of the hospital she lifted her chin and made a decision. If Clint could keep his personal life separate from what happened at the hospital, then she could, too. For everyone's sakes, she was going to have to learn to take her cues from Clint, adopting that same professional demeanor whenever she was here.

No matter how hard it was starting to be.

The suicide had come out of nowhere, and while it hadn't been one of Clint's patients it brought home the thin line he was walking with Chelsea and Jessi. The entire hospital was on edge because of it.

It wasn't easy for any doctor to lose a patient, no matter what anyone said. True impartiality was hard to come by at the best of times…and with Jessi it seemed to border on the impossible.

He'd felt the anguish radiating from every pore of her body when she'd lifted that macabre paper figure out of her daughter's drawer. And it had taken a lot of self-restraint to remain in his seat, observing Chelsea's reactions, and not rush over to make sure the woman who wasn't his patient was okay.

While he and Jessi hadn't been involved emotionally in the past—a thought he stubbornly clung to, no matter what his gut said—there could be nothing at all between them now.

Not just because of his patient. Not just because of his and Jessi's past. But because of his job and his own personal baggage.

Once they found a replacement for him, he was headed back to San Diego. It was either that or request that his transfer to Richmond be made permanent, something he couldn't see happening. He was the one they called on for temporary assignments. It's what he wanted. Moving around a lot kept his mind on the job at hand, rather than highlighting his lack of a personal life. And the unlikelihood that he'd ever have much of one.

Not that he hadn't tried. He'd been in serious relationships. Twice. But both times the woman had left, saying she felt he was withholding himself emotionally.

He had been. Somehow he could never quite let his guard all the way down. His every move was calculated. Controlled. And that's the way he liked it.

He was very aware that wasn't what most women looked for in a man. He was just not husband material.

Because of his dad?

Hell, the second Jessi had mentioned his father in his office he'd tried to yank his hand away, very aware that his crooked finger was right there for her to see. And ask about. The last thing he wanted to talk about was his past. Jessi's father might have been a pain-in-the-ass drill sergeant—but at least he'd loved her enough to care about who she saw. What she did.

His cell phone beeped. When he glanced at the caller ID, he winced. Jessi. The very person presently haunting his every thought. And it was already midmorning. He was supposed to have called her to let her know how Chelsea was.

He pressed the answer button and bit out an apology.

"Sorry, Jess. We've been swamped and I hadn't had a chance to call you yet."

She brushed aside his apology with a cleared throat. "Was she okay when she woke up?"

Despite the worry in her tone, her voice flowed over him, soothing away some of the worst parts of his morning. A few muscles in his jaw relaxed.

"I haven't had an in-depth conversation with her. Just a few minutes of small talk as she ate breakfast. We're due to have a therapy session at two."

"But she's okay."

He realized what she was looking for, and all the day's heartache came roaring back. "She doesn't seem to be obsessing over what happened yesterday. I'll call you when I've talked to her again."

"Hmm." She didn't say anything more.

"I know I promised. I'm sorry." He gritted his teeth.

"No, it's just that I have to be at work at three, and I'll probably be just as swamped with patients as you seem to be, since it's a holiday."

Ah, yes. Father's Day. Something he tried to forget every year. He glanced down at his left hand, where the crook in his finger reminded him of a whole childhood of fear and unhappiness. That wasn't the only reason he wasn't crazy about this particular day. At this point in his life, he didn't see himself ever carrying the title of father, even if he found someone and married her. He was close to forty, and had never really given kids much of a thought.

Maybe he should ask Jessi if the day held any special significance for Chelsea, though…good or bad. He should be prepared for any eventuality.

"Will Father's Day add to Chelsea's stress levels?"

There was silence over the line for a long minute. "No. Larry died before she was born. She only knows him through pictures." There was something sad about the way she said it.

He forced the next words out even as his insides tightened. "You didn't have much time together."

"No, we didn't. The worst thing is he might still be alive if someone hadn't…" The words ended on a strangled note.

Something burned in his gut. "If someone hadn't what, Jess?

"It doesn't matter. What does is that I have a wonderful daughter from our union. That's what made the hard times after his death bearable."

The image of Jessi mourning her husband was enough to make that burning sensation tickle the back of his throat. She'd had a daughter with the man. And as much as he told himself he didn't care, the cold reality was that part of him did—the same part that had leaped when he'd first realized who Jessi was and had wondered if Chelsea might be his.

But she wasn't. And if he was going to do his job, he had to remember that and keep on remembering it.

"About my session with her. How about if I send you a text, rather than trying to call? That way you can check in when you've got a free moment."

"That would be fantastic. Thank you, Clint. But please do call if something changes. I'll set my ringer to vibrate just for your number. If it does, I'll know it's important, and I'll find a way to answer, or I'll call you right back."

The tension in his gut eased and something warm and dangerous took its place. She was going to be listening for his call and his call only.

Okay, idiot. It's in case of an emergency. It's not like she's putting your number on speed dial or anything.

"So you have the number here, if you have any questions or need something, right? I remember you said my card was on your refrigerator." He glanced at the business card on his desk, since he hadn't quite memorized his Richmond number yet. "Or do you need me to read it off to you again?"

"Nope. I've already programmed it into my phone. In fact, I have you on speed dial," she said. "Just in case."

CHAPTER NINE

FATHER'S DAY SHOULD be outlawed.

Or at least the giving of gifts involving any type of motor should be banned. So far that afternoon, Jessi had treated a leg that been kissed by a chain saw, a back injury from an ATV accident and a lawn mower that had collided with a lamppost before bouncing back and knocking its new owner unconscious. Not to mention assorted other minor injuries. And she still had two hours to go until the end of her shift. The one thing she hadn't seen had been the screen on her cell phone lighting up or feeling its vibration coming from the pocket of her scrubs.

All was silent with Clint and her daughter.

Sighing, she grabbed the next chart and headed for the curtained exam room. Patient name: William Tuppele. Complaint: the words *fishing hook* and *earlobe* ran through her head before she blinked and forced her eyes to read back over that part.

Okay. So it wasn't just things with motors that should be banned from this particular holiday.

When she entered the room, a man dressed in hip waders with a camo T-shirt tucked into them sat on the exam table. And, yep, he was sporting a shiny new piece of jewelry.

She looked closer and gulped. Had something behind his ear just moved?

Stepping farther in the room, she glanced again at his chart. "Mr. Tuppele." She omitted the words *How are you?* because it was pretty obvious this was the last place the man wanted to be. Instead, she aimed for cheeky. "Catch anything interesting today?"

Instead of smiling, the man scowled. "Great, I get a nurse who thinks she's a comedienne."

She bristled, but held out her hand anyway. "I'm Dr. Riley. How long have you been like this?"

"About an hour." His gaze skipped away from hers, his words slurring the slightest bit. "My son caught me with his hook. It was his first fishing trip."

"Hmm." She kept the sound as noncommittal as possible, but from the way his face had turned scarlet and—she tried not to fan herself openly—the alcohol fumes that bathed every word the man spoke, she would almost bet there was no "son" involved in this particular party. Rather, she suspected a male-bonding episode that had gone terribly wrong.

Hip waders and booze. Not a good combination. They were lucky no one had drowned. "Did someone drive you to the hospital?"

She certainly didn't want to let a drunk loose on the roads.

"One of my buddies. He's down in the waiting room."

Jessi could only hope the *buddy* had been less generous when it came to doling out those cans of beer to himself. She made a mental note to have someone check on his friend's sobriety level.

She sat on her stool just as the worm—and, yes, it was indeed a piece of live bait—gave a couple of frantic wiggles. Lord, she did not want to touch that thing, much less have to handle it. But the best way to remove a fishing hook was to cut off the end opposite the barb and push the shank on through, rather than risk more damage by pulling it back out the way it had gone in. That barb acted like a one-way door. They went in, but they didn't want to come out.

The worm moved again.

"Hell," said the man. "Can you please get this damned thing off me? It stinks."

And it's creeping me out.

Mr. Tuppele didn't say the words, but she could well imagine him thinking them, because the same thoughts were circling around in her head, too. Maybe this was the worm's way of exacting revenge on anglers everywhere.

And maybe she could call one of the male nurses.

Ha! And give her patient a reason for his earlier sexist remark. Hardly. "When was your last tetanus shot?"

"Haven't been to a doctor in twenty years. Wouldn't be here now if one of my...er, my son hadn't been so squeamish about taking it out himself. "Is my ear going to be permanently pierced? I don't cotton to men with earrings and such."

She smiled despite herself, tempted to match his it-was-my-son fib and tell him that, yes, he would be permanently disfigured and might as well go out and buy a couple of nice dangly pieces of jewelry. But she restrained herself. "No. I knew a man who had his ear pierced in high school but had to stop wearing an earring when he went into the military. It's all healed up now."

At least she assumed that's when Clint had stopped wearing the single hoop in his ear, because there was no sign of it now. And how was it that she had even noticed that? Or remembered what he'd worn back then?

She'd kind of liked his earring, back in the day.

"Good. Don't need anyone getting any strange ideas about me."

Too late for that, Mr. Tuppele. She already had a few ideas about him. And they went much deeper than men sporting earrings. "Let me set up. I'm going to call in a nurse to give you a shot to numb your ear."

"I don't need it numbed. I just need that damned thing out."

"Are you sure?" The rest of the staff was going to thank her patient for sparing them the need to get close to that wriggler.

"Just do it."

"Okay." Trying not to shudder, she got her equipment together, praying the worm died before she had to deal with it. As disgusting as she found it, she felt a twinge of pity for the creature. It hadn't been its choice to be cast into a river for the first hungry fish to gulp.

Gloves in place, she squirted some alcohol on the wound in back of his ear, waiting for the string of cuss words to die down before continuing. She grabbed her locking forceps and clamped the instrument right behind the worm. If the barb had gone all the way through his ear, she could have just cut it off and backed the hook out, worm and all. But while there was a tiny bit of metal showing in the front of the lobe, the barb was still embedded in the man's flesh. It was going to hurt, pushing it the rest of the way through. She got a pair of wire cutters and took a deep breath, then moved in and cut the eye, leaving as much shank as possible behind that worm.

"Okay, I'm going to have to push the barb through the front, are you sure you're okay?"

"Fine."

Holding the front of the man's earlobe with her gloved fingers, she used the forceps to push hard, until the barb popped through.

The man yelled out a few more choice words, but he'd

held remarkably steady. Having a hook shoved through your ear was evidently a surefire way to sober up. Fast.

"All right, the worst part is over. I just need to pull the hook the rest of the way out." Holding a tray beneath his ear so she wouldn't have to touch the worm, she removed the forceps and used them to grasp the barb in front. Then she pulled steadily, until the worm plonked onto the instrument tray and the hook was the rest of the way through his ear.

Praying the creature didn't find his way off the counter and onto the floor, she set the tray down and used a piece of antiseptic soaked gauze to sponge away the blood and dirt from the front and the back of the man's ear and then took a piece of dry gauze and applied pressure to stop the bleeding. "Can you hold this here? We'll need to get you a tetanus shot as well as some antibiotics, just in case."

Mr. Tuppele did as she asked and squeezed his earlobe between the two sides of gauze. But when she carried the worm over to the garbage can, the man stopped her with a yelled "Hey!"

She turned toward him, still holding the tray. "Yes?"

"That thing dead?"

She glanced down. It wasn't moving any more, thank God. "I think so."

"Touch it to make sure."

Horror filled her to the core. She hated fishing. Hated bugs. Broken bones, bullet wounds, she could whiz through with ease, but anything that wiggled or crawled or stared with cold-blooded eyes she was just not into. "I'll let you do the honors." She held out the tray and let the man jab the worm with a finger while she cringed. Thankfully it remained limp, even after two more pokes.

"Damn. I was hoping to use that one again."

Again? Hooking himself once hadn't been enough?

She gave a mental eye roll. "Sorry about that. It was probably the alcohol."

"There ain't that much in my blood."

And... Okay.

Dumping the worm and the cleaning gauze into the trash bin, she turned back to face him. "I'll have the nurse come in with the shot and your prescription. Make sure you see your doctor if that ear puffs up or doesn't seem to be healing after a couple of days. Or if you develop a fever."

She took the gauze from him and checked his ear, before pressing tiny round bandages over the front and back of the puncture wound. "You can take those off in a couple of hours."

The man managed to mumble out a "Thank you."

Her phone buzzed, making her jump.

Clint. It had to be.

Patting the man on the back and telling him to take care, she went out and gave instructions to the nurse and asked her to send someone out to check on his buddy. By that time her phone had stopped ringing. "Anyone else waiting for me?"

The nurse grinned. "Not at the moment. But the new barbecue grills are probably being fired up even as we speak."

"Heaven help us all."

Hopefully, that wave of patients would come through after she was off duty. She forced out a laugh, even though she was dying to grab her phone and call Clint back. He knew she was on duty. Knew she'd get back to him as soon as she could.

The nurse got the injection ready and carried it into the room, leaving Jessi alone in the hallway. She took out her phone and glanced at the readout, even though she knew who it was.

C. Marks.

Hitting the redial button, she leaned a shoulder against the wall, an ache settling in her back at all the bending she'd done today.

"Marks here."

"Clint? It's Jessi. What's up?"

"Just calling to see how much longer you were on duty."

Jessi glanced at her watch. "I have another half hour, why?"

"I thought we might get together and talk about Chelsea."

"Is something wrong?"

"No, she's fine. No major developments, but no setbacks either. I just haven't eaten, and I assume you haven't either. Would you like to go somewhere? Or I could come to the hospital and eat with you in the cafeteria."

She grimaced, glancing at the room she'd just come from. "No. The food here isn't the best, and I'm not really hungry. I could do with a shake, though, while you get something else."

She was still puzzling over his sudden change of heart.

"A shake sounds fine. How about we get it to go?"

Okay, she hadn't thought this far ahead. "And go where?"

"We could go to the park on the east side."

The park? She glanced out at the streetlights that were already visible in the darkening sky. "Sounds like a plan."

"Good. I'll meet you at the front entrance of the hospital, okay?"

"I'll be there."

Maybe somehow in that period of time she could shake off all thoughts of sitting inside Clint's car in a dark park, sipping on a milk shake. Or the fleeting images of what they could do once they finished their drinks and had said all they needed to say.

A warning came up from the depths of her soul, reminding her of days gone by and how badly he'd broken her heart. But only because she'd let him.

You can't head down that road again, Jess.

No, she couldn't.

Well, if her heart could make that decree, then she could somehow abide by it.

So she would have to make one thing very clear to herself before he came to pick her up. She would not kiss Clinton Marks again. Not in the dark. Not in a park.

The impromptu rhyme made her smile.

And if *he* kissed her instead?

As much as she might wish otherwise, if that ever happened, then all bets were off.

Because she might just have to kiss him back.

CHAPTER TEN

"YOU USED TO have an earring in high school."

A swallow of his milk shake went down the wrong way, and Clint gave a couple of rough coughs before turning in his seat to stare at her. In the dim light of the parking lot at a nearby burger joint, he could just make out her questioning gaze. He'd decided against going to the park, worried about being *too* alone with her.

This was more public, although he wasn't exactly sure what he was worried about. Surely they could both handle this situation like adults. Running into each other from time to time was part of adult behavior.

And going to the fair and having dinner with her and her mother?

All part of being back in his hometown. It meant nothing. At least, he'd better make sure it didn't.

And what about her asking about his earring?

Jessi must have changed clothes before leaving the hospital, because she wasn't wearing a lab jacket or rubber-soled shoes but a pair of slim, dark jeans, lime-green T-shirt and a pair of shoes that had a wedged heel. Not what he would consider doctor gear at all. In fact, she looked much more like the teenager he'd known in high school than a mom with a grown daughter.

He felt like an old fuddy-duddy in comparison, still

in his shirt and tie. He could have sworn the kid at the drive-through window had eyed Jessi with interest. Clint had thrown the teen a glare in return, which had felt like something Jessi's actual father might have done.

When had he turned into such a square?

Maybe when he'd seen the emotional wounds of those returning from battle. And how they reminded him of his own.

"I did have an earring. I took it out the night before I reported for boot camp."

The night of their graduation. The night he'd made love to Jessi. It had marked the end of an era for him, a journey from childhood to becoming a man. Removing the earring that night had been something the old Clint wouldn't have done. He'd have reported to boot camp and waited until someone ordered him to take it out. But he hadn't. After watching Jessi's house for a while that night, he'd gone home—avoiding the after parties and festivities that had gone along with graduation—and stared at himself in the bathroom mirror. God, he'd wanted to stay in Richmond that night. For the first time he'd thought of doing something other than running away. And it had been all because of Jessi.

Instead, he'd unhooked the small gold hoop and pulled it from his ear. As if that one act would give him the courage to walk away when everything inside him had been yelling at him to stay and fight for her, shoving aside his fears about what might happen if he did. What kind of life he might drag her into, if he stayed.

But, even if he'd decided to risk it all for her, Jessi was already spoken for, at least according to Larry and all their friends.

The image in the mirror that night had told him which of them had had a better shot of giving Jess a good life. The choice had been obvious—at least to him. He had just been a screwup from a dysfunctional family, his finger a constant reminder of what that brought.

He hadn't wanted that for her.

So he'd let her go. An act his teenage self had decided was the mature thing to do. He still had that old hoop in a box somewhere.

Jessi unexpectedly reached up, her fingers cool from holding her frozen drink as they touched his chin. Using gentle pressure, she turned his head to the right, leaning over to look. Her breath washed across his skin, the scent of vanilla catching hold of his senses and making him want to sneak a taste of her mouth.

"Is there still a hole where your earring used to be?"

What was with all the questions? And why had he ever thought sitting in a car—or anywhere else—with her was a good idea?

Just being an adult. Proving he could control his impulses.

He swallowed. "I haven't really looked in a while. Why?"

"We had a guy come into the ER tonight who'd hooked himself while fishing and I had to push the barb all the way through his ear. He was worried his family would think he'd pierced it." She gave a soft laugh. "He wanted to know how long it would take to heal. I told him he should be more worried about the risk of tetanus than a tiny hole."

Her nose wrinkled. "The worst thing was there was still a live worm attached to the end of that hook."

"Well, that had to be an interesting scenario."

"I almost couldn't do it." She let go of him and leaned back in her seat. "Did you ever have to do something and wonder if you'd be able to get through it?" She made a sound in her throat. "Never mind. Of course you have."

He could think of two at the moment. One was leaving her behind twenty-two years ago. And the other was not touching her now, when everything inside him was strain-ing to do just that. "I think everyone eventually gets a case like that. Or at least wonders if the patient would be better off with another doctor."

Jessi suddenly bent to get her milk shake. In the process the lid came off, dumping the cup, and half of its contents, right onto her lap.

He moved to grab it just as her cry of dismay went up. "Oh, no. Clint, I'm so sorry. Your car."

"I'm more worried about you turning into a block of ice." He sent her a half grin as he tried to scoop some of the shake back into the cup. It only ended up sloshing more onto her shirt and jeans.

"Don't move." He got out of the car, cup in hand, and strode into the restaurant to throw it away, exiting a few seconds later with a fresh empty cup and a handful of napkins.

Together they corralled most of the spillage between the paper cup and a spare lid, and then sopped up the re-mainder with the pile of napkins.

"I always was the clumsiest girl in high school."

"Don't do that."

"What?"

"You used to cut yourself down for things, even when they weren't your fault."

He could always remember some self-deprecating com-ment or other she would throw out there in school, making everyone laugh and passing it off as a big joke. But there had always been a ring of conviction to the jibes that had made him wonder if she didn't actually believe all the "I'm such a klutzo" and "Wow, am I ever a nerd" statements.

She glanced up at him, her hand full of napkins. "Everyone did that. Even you."

Yes, he had. And he knew for a fact that he'd believed

most of what he'd said. Maybe that's why it bothered him so much when she did it.

"Let's get you home."

"I'll pay for whatever it costs to clean your seats."

He shook his head. "They're leather. I'll just wipe them down with a damp rag. They'll be fine. You, however, might need to be hosed off." He said it with a grin to show he was joking.

"Thanks for being so understanding," she said, as he gathered up the rest of the trash and got out of the car once more to throw it all away.

Understanding? Hell, he was barely holding it together. He put the car in Drive and followed her directions to her house. "Come on in while I change. We can talk about Chelsea over coffee, if that's okay?"

"Sounds good."

No, it didn't. It sounded idiotic. Impulsive. And he should leave. Now. But something drove him to open his car door and follow her up the steps to her house.

It's just coffee. She hasn't propositioned you. You're her daughter's doctor, for God's sake.

He was the one who'd called to arrange this meeting in the first place.

Which meant he should have asked her to come to his office, not a fast-food joint.

But surely Jessi had patients who were acquaintances or the children of acquaintances during her years of working in the ER. And it would make sense that she might meet them in the hospital cafeteria or a coffee joint to catch up later. It was kind of hard to work in a town where you grew up—no matter how large—and never expect to run into anyone you knew.

Only Jessi was more than an acquaintance.

And what they'd had was more than a quick hello and goodbye.

That was years ago. They'd spent a little over an hour down by a creek, hopped up on hormones and the thrill of graduating from high school. And she'd been distraught by her father's unbending rules.

It was in the past. All of it.

And that kiss beside his car at her mother's house a week ago?

Fueled by memories of that shared past. It wouldn't happen again. Not if he could help it.

She unlocked the door, glancing behind her as if to make sure he was still coming. "I'll get you that rag if you want to wipe the seat down while I change. I'll leave the front door open."

"Sounds good." And if he were smart, he'd leave the rag just outside the door afterwards and take off in his car before she could come back out of her bedroom.

And that would be just as unprofessional as kissing her had been.

At least that was his mental excuse, because after wiping up the few drops of milk shake from his seat he found himself back inside her house, calling up the stairs to her and asking her what she wanted him to do with the rag.

"Just put it in the sink and have a seat in the living room. I'll be down in a few minutes."

Instead of doing as she asked, he rinsed out the rag and hung it over a towel bar he found in her utility room. Then he spotted the coffee machine on one of the counters and a huge glass jar filled with those single-serving coffee filters that seemed to be all the rage nowadays. He had one of the machines at home himself. The least he could do was make the coffee while he waited. He'd just found the mugs when Jessi came traipsing back into the kitchen, this time dressed in a white floral sundress similar to the one she'd worn during dinner at her mom's, her feet bare, hair damp as if she'd showered.

He tensed, before forcing himself to relax again.

Of course she'd had to rinse off. She'd had a sticky drink spilled in her lap. It meant nothing.

"Sorry, Clint. I didn't intend you to get the coffee ready, too."

"No problem. I just thought I'd save you a step." He realized something. "Where's Cooper?"

"At Mom's. He's a communal pet, remember? I get him tomorrow."

"Ah, right."

She reached in a cabinet. "What do you take in your coffee?"

"Just sugar."

She set a crystal bowl down and then went over to the refrigerator and pulled out a container of milk. "Help yourself."

"Thanks."

They worked in silence until the coffee was done and they'd moved into Jessi's living room, which was furnished with a huge sectional and a center ottoman. Pictures lined the fireplace mantel and as he took a sip of his coffee he wandered over to them. There were several snapshots of Chelsea doing various activities and one of a more formal military pose. She was soft and natural in every photo except the last one, since official portraits were supposed to be done sans smile. But even in that one there was a spark of humor lighting her eyes that the woman back at the VA hospital lacked.

There was one picture of Jessi and Larry in their wedding attire. Both of them looked so young. Larry would be forever ageless, never having had a chance to really grow up and become a man.

He might still be alive if someone hadn't...

Her earlier words came back to mind. If he *were* still

alive, Clint would probably not be standing here in her living room right now.

He probably shouldn't be, regardless.

And the sight of the two of them smiling up at each other sent something kicking at his innards. A slight jabbing sensation that could have been jealousy but that made no sense. He'd been the one who'd left. What had he expected Jessi to do? Dump Larry and wait for him to come back for her?

He hadn't. He'd never set foot in Virginia again until now. And if he'd known who Chelsea was before he'd agreed to come, he doubted very seriously he would be standing here now.

"Clint?"

Her voice reminded him that he was still staring at the picture. "Sorry. Just seeing how Chelsea was before she deployed." He turned and sat on the shorter leg of the sofa perpendicular to her. "She smiled a lot."

"Yes. She was happy. Always. Which is why it's so hard to see her like this and not know how to help her."

"I'm sure it is." He took another sip of his coffee, wishing he hadn't added quite so much sugar.

"Did she talk at all today?" Jessi tucked her legs up under her, smoothing her hemline to cover her bare knees.

"She shared a little about what her days in captivity had been like. What she did to pass the time."

"You said on the phone there weren't any breakthroughs. You don't consider that one?"

That was a tricky question to answer. Because while it was technically more than Chelsea had told him in the past, she'd spoken without emotion, as if she were using the information itself as one more blockade against questions that might venture too close to painful subjects. Like that macabre tissue paper baby she kept in her nightstand.

"It does help to know a little about what went on. But

she's not talking about her captors or about her rescue. Just about what she did. Reciting her ABCs and having conversations inside her head."

Jessi slumped. "It's been almost two and a half months."

He didn't mention that sometimes the effects of PTSD lasted a lifetime. His dad, instead of getting better, had slowly sunk into a pit filled with alcohol, drawing away from those he'd known and loved. And when he or his mom had tried to force the issue... Yeah, that was something he didn't want to talk to Jessi about.

"I know it seems like forever. But she was held for four months. It takes time. Sometimes lots of it."

She stared down at her cup for several long seconds before glancing up with eyes that held a wealth of pain. "It sounds so terrible for me to say this out loud, but I'm afraid to have her home again. Afraid the next time she tries something I won't get there in time to stop her."

Clint set his coffee cup down on a tray that was perched on an ottoman between the two seating areas. He went over to sit beside her, setting her coffee aside as he draped his arm around her shoulder and drew her close. "Jess, you're dealing with some aftereffects yourself. Maybe you should talk to someone."

She lifted her head. "I'm talking to you."

"I mean someone objective." The second the words came out of his mouth he wished he could haul them back and swallow them whole. He tried to clarify his meaning. "It would be a conflict of interest for me to treat you both."

He realized that explanation wasn't any better when she tried to pull away from him. He squeezed slightly, keeping her where she was. "I'm not explaining myself very well." Hell, some psychiatrist he was. He couldn't even have a coherent conversation with this woman.

"No, it's okay." She relaxed, and her arm snaked around his waist with a sigh. "I'm being overly sensitive."

No, she wasn't. And Clint was drawing closer and closer to a line he'd sworn he wasn't going to cross with her. But with her head against his chest and her hand curled around his side, her scent surrounded him. *She* surrounded him.

Her fingers went to his left hand and her head lifted slightly, staring at something. Then she touched his damaged finger. She bent a little closer. "What happened?"

Damn. He tried to laugh it off. "An old war wound."

"You never mentioned going to war."

He hadn't. That particular war had been fought here on American soil. Not even his father had known what he'd done to his son with that hard, angry squeeze.

"I was making a joke. A bad one." He shrugged. "It's not important."

Her head went back to his chest, but her finger continued to stroke his crooked pinkie, the sensation strangely intimate and disturbing on a level that was primal.

He needed to get up and move before either of them did something they would regret.

Then she lifted his hand to her mouth and kissed his finger, the delicate touch ramming through his chest and driving the air from his lungs.

Her tongue trailed across the skin, and his hand tightened slightly on her shoulder. He wasn't sure whether or not it was in warning. And if it was, was he warning her not to stop? Or not to continue? His body responded to the former, rejecting the latter. Because he did want her to continue. To keep on kissing him with those featherlight brushes. And not just there. Everywhere.

"Jess," he murmured. "I think I should move back to the other seat."

She stopped, still holding his hand. "Does that mean you're going to?" Her whispered words were as much a caress as her touch had been.

Heat swirled through him.

"Not if you keep talking to me in that tone of voice."

She let go of his hand and moved hers a little bit higher, smoothing over his biceps until her palm rested on his shoulder. And when she looked up at him, he was lost.

Decision made.

He was going to kiss her. Just like she'd kissed him. Softly. Gently. And with just enough contact to drive her wild.

CHAPTER ELEVEN

IT WAS AS if the past twenty-two years had rewound themselves.

The second his lips touched hers, Jessi was back by the creek, her only worries her father's strict rules and getting to school on time. And it felt so good. So carefree.

If only she'd known how free she'd been back then.

But she could experience it again. With the same man. Just for a little while.

She'd always thought Clint had been invincible all those years ago. But her mom's comment about his father and discovering that crooked little finger showed her he wasn't. He was just as human as she was. Back then…and maybe even now.

Jessi threaded her fingers through his hair, hearing Clint's low groan as he moved to deepen the kiss, shifting her until she lay half across his lap, one of his hands beneath her shoulders, his other splayed flat on her stomach. It was that hand that made her go all liquid inside. It wasn't doing anything special but it was between two very sensitive areas of her body, both of which were doing their damnedest to coax his fingers to slide their way.

A gentle touch of his tongue was enough to get her full attention.

Yes!

Surely he wouldn't stop this time. It had been ages since she'd been with someone. So long that the slightest movement of his body had her eagerly lapping up the sensations like a person deprived of food and water, and desperate for any sign of relief.

She was ready for that kind of relief. For him.

Clint.

And here he was, in her house. And there was absolutely no one around. Not her mom. Not Chelsea.

Just the two of them.

So she pressed closer to him, deepening their kiss, his soft lips making her feel dizzy with need.

And finally…finally, the hand at her waist woke up, his thumb drawing little circles on her belly that had her moaning with anticipation, arching up into it with a mental plea that he evidently heard. Because with a single movement it slid up and over her right breast, that circling thumb finding her nipple without hesitation. Her sundress had a built-in bra, but it was thin, just a shelf of netting with a piece of elastic beneath it, so his touch was heady and intimate, arcing straight down to her toes and then back up again.

When his fingers moved away, she whimpered in protest. His mouth slid from hers, depriving her of another point of contact.

"Clint…"

His hand moved to the back of her head, supporting it as the scrape of his chin along her cheek put him at her ear. "I don't want to stop."

The moment of truth. She sensed he was giving her time to compose herself, to give her a chance to put an end to things even while telling her he didn't want to.

She made a dangerous decision.

"Then don't."

His fingers tightened on the back of her head. Then

his other hand went to the thin strap on her sundress and tugged it down her arm, leaving one shoulder bare.

There was a slight hesitation, then that wicked thumb went to work, brushing the joint where her shoulder met her arm. "Is this what you want?"

"More." The word came out as a shaky whisper. She hardly dared to believe she was goading him to continue. But this was exactly what she needed. To have someone just sweep aside her normal code of conduct and make her...*feel* again.

"How about this?" His fingertips moved higher, trailing from beneath her jaw down the side of her neck and along her collarbone. Light ticklish touches that made her ache and squirm.

She wanted him everywhere at once, kissing her mouth, cupping her breast, filling her with his heat where it counted the most. So she took his hand and placed it on her breast, where she wanted it.

"You read my mind, Jess." The words came out in a half growl that made her shiver.

He ducked beneath the edge of her sundress and found her bare skin. He paused then curved his palm over her, the light friction on her nipple sending a low sound up her throat.

"Hell, woman. You need to warn a man before you go braless."

Encouraged by the rough words, she bit her way up his jaw and then smiled against his mouth. "My dress has a bra. You just missed it."

"Could have fooled me." His thumb and forefinger captured the tight bead and gave a gentle squeeze that made her squirm again. "But in that case..."

He removed his hand and urged her off the couch and onto her feet, while he sat, legs splayed.

"Wh-what are you doing?"

"I want to see you—all of you—but at the rate I'm going, I'm not going to make it that far." A quick flash of teeth accompanied the words.

She smiled back at him, his meaning giving her a shot of courage and daring her to tease him back. "I think I can help with that. What would you like to see first?" Balling the skirt portion of her dress, she slid the hem part way up her thighs, keeping her attention focused on his face.

A muscle worked in his jaw, and he placed his hands flat on his thighs. "Let's start from the top. And work our way down. Just like we did in school."

The reminder of how his hands had trailed from her face to her breasts and finally down to that last forbidden place made hot need spurt through her. And the way his knuckles turned white as his long fingers dug into his thighs told her that need wasn't one-sided.

"Okay, let's do that." She let go of her skirt and trailed the back of her right hand down her neck, like he'd done moments earlier, only she didn't stop at her collarbone. Instead, she dragged her fingers along the edge of her bodice—one strap still draped over her arm. The second strap flipped down.

"Next?" she asked, waiting for direction.

"Peel it down. Slowly." The low words weren't abrupt and bossy, rather they coaxed her to do his bidding. Dared her to cross a threshold to a room she'd never entered before. Her times with Larry had been good, but they'd been to the point. Vanilla sex that had been a sharing of hearts and minds, even if it hadn't been superimaginative. Then again, they'd had such a short amount of time together, there hadn't been a chance to venture much further than that.

And that wasn't something she was going to think about.

Not when Clint was right here, holding the door open and asking her to step through it.

This was what she wanted—what she expected from Clint. Wild and raw and real…echoes of the rebellious boy he'd once been. The one who had whispered to a matching defiance within her, drawing it out and fulfilling her in ways she never would have imagined.

So she crossed her arms and took a strap in each hand and pulled with slow, steady pressure that made the fabric of her dress roll back on itself, revealing the upper swell of her breasts. She kept going until she got to the most crucial part, then hesitated.

"Jess." The whispered word shifted her eyes back to his. But he wasn't looking at her face. He was staring at the half-exposed portion of her body, the heat in his expression taking away the last of her inhibitions. She tugged, and he swallowed.

"You have no idea how much I want to drag you down here and finish this."

"Then do it." She let her arms go to her sides, making no attempt to hide herself from him.

He reached behind him and retrieved his wallet from his pants. Her mouth watered, thinking he was going to pull a condom out and do exactly what she'd suggested. And a packet did appear, but he made no move to haul her down onto the couch.

"Here or in your bedroom?"

"It doesn't matter." It was the truth. She wanted him. Badly, and she didn't care where it happened, as long as it happened. And soon.

He smiled again and set the condom on his thigh, making her tighten inside. Because six inches north of that packet was a bulge that left no question as to whether or not he wanted her.

"Does that dress have a zipper?"

It took a second for the question to register, and when she glanced up at him she saw that he knew exactly where she'd been looking. That he'd meant for her to measure the distance between possibility and reality. Because nothing was for sure until he slipped that protection over himself and thrust into her.

"Yes."

"Can you reach it?"

She nodded, her now shaking fingers going to the side of her dress, finding the pull tab then sliding it down to her hips, her other hand holding the rest of the garment in place.

"Let it go," he murmured, his meaning clear.

Releasing her grip, the fabric slid to the floor, leaving her standing in front of him clad only in her panties.

She expected him to tell her to remove those as well, but instead his fingers went to the button of his slacks and undid it.

"Once those come off, honey, it's all over." His bald words made the breath stall in her chest. As did the fact that he was sliding his own zipper down and ripping the condom open.

She wanted to do that. "Wait."

Wary eyes moved to her face. Oh! He thought she was stopping him.

Hurrying to correct him, she said, "Let me."

He took the condom from the packet. "Next time."

Next time!

Her lips parted as he drew the waistband to his briefs down and exposed himself. And unlike her, Clint had no inhibitions. None. Not the last time they'd been together. Not this time. His eyes burned into hers as he sat there. He toyed with the open condom.

The nub at the apex of her thighs tightened, making her squeeze her legs together, aching for some kind of relief.

She licked her lips. "Put it on."

"First your panties."

Hurrying to do as he asked, she hooked her thumbs into the elastic and started to bend over to slide them down, only to have him interrupt her. "Watch me as you do it."

Shifting her focus back to his face, she finished, stepping out of her underwear and standing back upright.

"Beautiful," he murmured. "Even more now than then."

He finally rolled the condom down his length, and took himself in hand. "Now come here, honey."

She moved between his still splayed legs and shuddered when the fingers of his free hand slid in a smooth move up her thigh and found the heart of her. Just the process of removing her clothing while he'd watched had made her body moist and ready.

"Hell. Just like I remember."

By the time he'd finally touched her by the creek, she'd been shaking with desire. One flick of his finger had sent her over the edge. She'd been so embarrassed, only to have him shush her and tell her how much he liked it. When he'd finally entered her, she had already been riding the crest of that same wave, shattering right along with him.

The Clint of today slid one finger inside her, wringing a moan from her. He stayed there, just like that, not moving. She shuddered, needing him so badly she couldn't speak.

"Spread your legs for me."

Somehow, she shuffled her legs farther apart.

"Perfect." He sat up straight, the pressure of his finger inside her holding her right where she was, putting his face dangerously close. Too late, she realized that was what he'd been aiming for all along. "How much will it take this time, Jess?"

Another reference to their first time together.

He added a second finger and pushed deep, using the pair to edge her hips closer. Suddenly off balance, she was forced to clutch his shoulders. "How much, Jess?" he repeated.

Then, as she watched, he moved his mouth until it was pressed against her…and let his tongue slide right across her.

It was as if he'd lit a fuse inside her. Her nails dug into his shoulders and every muscle in her body stiffened as what he was doing blotted out everything except the sensation of his tongue moving backward along her in a slow, drawn-out motion. The fuse ran out of line in a millisecond, and she detonated, crying out as his fingers finally moved, pumping inside her while she convulsed around them.

Then she was in his lap, his hands gripping her butt as he thrust hard into her, filling her beyond belief. She wrapped her hands around his neck, her mouth going to his ear as she rode him furiously, whimpering as her climax continued to crash all around her. He gave a muttered oath and then jerked his hips forward, holding her tight against his body as he strained upward for long seconds, the pressure inside her causing a new wave of convulsions.

When his muscles finally went limp, his arms encircled her back, thumb gliding along her spine.

She drew a deep, careful breath, registered Clint's heavy breathing and smiled, the problems of the day melting as his scent mixed with her own and filled her head. She nuzzled his cheek and then went back to his ear.

"I guess I'm not the only one who went up pretty fast."

His fingers tightened around her, although his voice was light. "Is that a complaint?"

"No. It was sexy, watching you lose control."

He drew her mouth back to his and kissed her long and deep. "Is that so? In that case, maybe we should find out which one of us holds out longer…the second time around."

CHAPTER TWELVE

"It's just been a long time, and I was upset."

Not the first words a man wanted to hear when he woke up after a night of passionate lovemaking. But there they were, and Clint was at an obvious disadvantage, since he was lying on her couch, an afghan draped over his privates, while Jessi hovered above him, already dressed, looking both worried and...

Hungry.

It was there in her eyes as they slid over his body and then darted back to his face, as if she was doing her damnedest not to look at him.

They'd never even made it back to her bedroom last night, instead using the long L-shaped couch to its full advantage.

Well, if she thought he was going to make it easy for her...

He slid up and propped himself up one of the throw pillows as he eyed her right back.

"Well, that's a hell of a good morning."

She took a step closer. "Sorry. I just don't want you to think..."

"That last night meant something other than great sex?"

Her eyes widened. "That's not what I was going to say."

"So it did mean something," he said, not sure which he preferred.

"No." She held out a hand to stop him from saying anything else. All that did, though, was give him a way to reach out grab her wrist.

She half laughed, half screamed. "Clint, stop. I'm trying to be serious."

"Oh, honey, so am I."

She let him drag her to the sofa and haul her down on top of him, where a certain area of his body was already displaying its delight at this turn of events.

"Wait. Let me finish my thought."

Leaving his fingers threaded in her hair, he looked at her, knowing his next words were not what he wanted to say at all. Hell, he didn't want her to say *anything* except what she wanted him to do to her. But he forced the words out. "Okay, so talk."

She drew an audible breath. "I just didn't want you to think last night had anything to do with Chelsea."

Her eyes trailed away from him, but the words themselves hit him in the chest like a bucket of ice water, sluicing away any hint of desire and leaving a cold trail of suspicion in its wake.

A sour taste rose up in his throat.

"I hadn't thought that at all, Jess." He rolled until she was wedged between him and the back of the couch as he stared at her. "Until just this very second. Did last night have something to do with her?"

"No! Yes. There are just things that you don't know. About how her father...about how Larry died. Not even Chelsea knows. But if someone from our past sees you, I'm afraid she could find out."

"I think you'd better tell me, then."

Jessi's eyes filled with tears. "A few months after we got married he told one of his friends I was pregnant. Well, the friend had seen us—you and me—leave graduation together and come back within minutes of each other. It got him thinking. He suggested Larry ask me whose child I was carrying." There was a pause before she continued. "We had a huge fight, and he accused me of sleeping with you. When I wouldn't deny it, he said Chelsea probably wasn't even his."

She shifted against the couch, and he eased back to give her some breathing space.

Clint could barely open his mouth. "His death?"

"He stormed off...so very angry. He went to a bar, and then a few hours later his car hit an embankment. He died instantly."

Hell. He felt like the biggest ass in history.

He leaned his forehead against hers, guilt causing his muscles to cramp. One more thing destroyed by his lack of control all those years ago. "Dammit. I'm sorry, Jessi. I had no idea."

So many mistakes: if he hadn't impulsively raced after her that night. If he hadn't stayed there with her and done the unthinkable... If he hadn't left her to deal with it all afterwards.

The small box of baggage from the past morphed into a shiny new trunk of regret.

They remained like that for a minute or two until Jessi gave a little sniff.

He scooted back some more, giving her a chance to compose herself, trying to ignore the quick swipe of palms across damp cheeks. The last thing he wanted to do was hurt her.

Then...or now. But it would seem he'd done both.

And he knew what he had to do to keep from hurting her further.

He sat up and slid off the sofa, conscious of her eyes following his movements as he gathered his clothing and headed for the bathroom just down her hallway. After he'd flushed and washed his hands, he dressed quickly, avoiding his image in the mirror as much as he possibly could, because whenever his eyes met those in the reflection, angry accusations stared right back at him.

How had he let this happen again?

When he was around her, his common sense went out the window, and he let his emotions rule.

Just like his father. He didn't hit, but his actions caused just as much damage. Dammit, they'd culminated in a young man's death. Someone Jessi had loved.

He had to take himself off Chelsea's case. It was no longer about remaining objective but about doing what had served him—and everyone around him—well for the last twenty-two years: staying away from emotionally charged situations.

If he'd known the details about Larry's death, he would have taken himself off Chelsea's case that very first day. This time, though, he wasn't going to let Jessi carry any of the blame for what just had happened between them. Nope, he was going to stuff it into his own bag of blame. One that seemed to swell larger every time he laid eyes on her. When he returned to the living room, Jessi was still there, seated on the sofa, only this time she had a phone to her ear.

"Of course, honey," Jessi said to whoever was on the line. "I'll check with Dr. Marks and see how soon we can arrange it." Her glance met his and she mouthed, "Chelsea."

Jessi's daughter was calling her? Right now?

He sat beside her, suddenly very aware of all inappropriate things they'd done in this house last night.

The second she clicked off the phone, she finally looked at him. Really looked at him. "Chelsea wants to talk about something." She licked her lips as if afraid of saying the next words. "She wants us both to be there."

* * *

Please, don't quit yet.

The words chanted through her skull as Clint dropped her off at Scott's Memorial to pick up her car and then waited for her to follow him back to the VA hospital.

They hadn't said much once she'd got off the phone, and the interior of his car had been filled with awkward silence and a sense of dread that had blocked her stomach and clogged her throat.

How could she have been so stupid to think last night wouldn't have any serious repercussions? Her only excuse was that it had felt so good to be in his arms. So right.

Only it wasn't right.

The timing had always been lousy when it came to her and Clint. If he'd stayed all those years ago, she never would have married Larry. But she never would have had Chelsea either.

And just like last time Clint wouldn't be there for the long haul. As soon as they'd found a replacement for him, he'd be gone.

He would waltz out of her life once again.

It's just not meant to be. It never was.

The words trailed through her head as if dragged on a banner behind a plane for all the world to see.

Her subconscious rejected them, though, cutting the line and watching as the lettering fell to the ground in a swirl of white canvas and belching smoke.

Before she had a chance to come to any conclusions, Clint pulled to a stop in one of the few parking spaces that had another spot beside it. She slid her car next to his and took a couple of deep breaths before she got out and went to where he stood, waiting. "You won't say anything, will you?"

Clint looked at her as if she had two heads. "About

what? Larry? Or about us having a second one-night stand?"

A flash of intense hurt zinged through her chest, making her gasp for air.

As if realizing what he'd done, he hooked his index finger around hers. "Sorry, Jess." He gave a squeeze before letting her go. "I seem to spend a lot of time issuing apologies nowadays."

She tipped her chin back. "Let's just see what she wants." The words came out sharper than she'd meant them to, but maybe that was a good thing. She could put her armor back in place and pretend last night had meant nothing. "We can discuss everything else later. If we could avoid arriving at her room at the same time, that would make me feel more comfortable."

"So you want me to hide out in my office for a few minutes before joining you."

Saying it like that made Jessi realize how cheesy and paranoid the idea sounded. "You're right. Let's just go together."

Once they got to Chelsea's room, they found her seated on the bed, that eerie tissue-paper baby on top of the nightstand. Jessi tensed. That had to be what she wanted to talk about.

She leaned down and kissed her cheek. "Hi, sweetheart."

Chelsea grabbed her around the shoulders, wordlessly hugging her tight for a minute or two. Then she whispered, "I'm sorry for putting you through what I have for the past couple of months. I love you, Mom. Always remember that."

A chill went over her at the solemn words. She stood up and glanced at Clint. "All that matters is that you start feeling better."

"I think I will as soon as I get something off my chest."

Once they were all seated, Clint started things off with some light conversation, never even hinting that he'd been with Jessi in anything other than a professional capacity. Instead, he asked about Jessi's day at work yesterday, subtly guiding her to tell the fishhook-in-the-ear story. Chelsea actually laughed right on cue.

"You hate worms," her daughter said.

"I do. I still remember you bringing in a jar of dirt for me on Mother's Day. Little did I know that that you and Grandpa had spent hours digging up earthworms to put in it."

Chelsea grinned again. "You screamed when one of them dug through the dirt and slithered along the inside of the jar. Grandpa laughed and laughed."

Jessi smiled at the memory of Chelsea and her dad's conspiratorial glances at each other as they'd handed her their "gift."

"You always were the fearless one."

"Not always." Chelsea's smile faded. "I need to tell you something. Something about when I was held in Afghanistan."

"Okay." She glanced at Clint, but he simply nodded at her.

Setting the doll in her lap, Chelsea took a deep breath. "You were right about my pregnancy. I was expecting when I was captured. I hadn't told anyone because it meant a ticket straight home—and I didn't want that. The whole thing was so stupid. It was an accident. I kept meaning to do something—say something—but I put things off... and put things off." Her eyes came up. "And then we were ambushed."

Jessi's heart contracted. "Did they...did they do something to you, honey?"

"No." Chelsea glanced up at the ceiling her eyes filling with tears and spilling over. "I mean, they didn't hurt me physically. They isolated me and made me change into a long, loose tunic. Then they wrote a script and forced me to read it in front of a camera."

Jessi had never heard about any message, but she didn't say anything, just let Chelsea continue talking.

"As one month turned into two, the isolation started to get to me, and I began talking to the baby. Every day. I went from just wanting her to go away to needing her for my own survival."

Her?

Oh, God, had they made Chelsea deliver the baby and then stolen it from her? Was that what the doll was all about?

When Chelsea's words stopped, Clint voiced the question that Jessi couldn't bring herself to ask.

"What happened to the baby?" The line of his jaw was tight, as if he too was struggling with his emotions right now.

"She died."

"Oh, Chelsea…" Her mind went blank as she tried to find the words to say. But there was nothing.

"She died, and I couldn't do anything to save her."

"Your captors didn't help?"

She shook her head. "I didn't want them to know I was pregnant, because I wasn't sure how they'd react to an unmarried woman carrying a child. So I hid my condition. It wasn't hard under the robes. I was in my cell most of the time, and I figured once I delivered, they'd let me keep her, or maybe even let us go."

Clint spoke up. "How far along were you when you were captured?"

"Around three months." She turned to glance at him. "I lost track of time after a while, but I think she was born around four months into my captivity."

Too small. Without the help of modern medicine the baby wouldn't have had much chance to survive.

Chelsea continued. "She came in the middle of the night. She was so tiny. And absolutely perfect." Her fingers caressed the doll. "She never even cried. I held her for a long, long time, praying for her to take a breath." Her voice broke for a second, but then she continued. "After a while, I knew she was dead, and I was afraid if anyone found out, I'd be killed, too—and I didn't want anyone other than me touching her. So I tore off a piece of my robe and wrapped her in it, then I scratched a hole in the dirt floor of my cell with my fingernails and buried her. I was rescued less than a week later."

A couple more tears trickled free, and Jessi reached over and held her hand, her own vision blurry.

"I'm so, so sorry, Chelsea." Her daughter had dealt with all of this by herself. There'd been no one there to help her...no one to comfort her. Her own heart felt ready to shatter in two.

A box of tissues appeared on the tiny table in front of them. Chelsea took several of them and wiped her eyes and then blew her nose before turning to look at her.

"Once she was gone, I realized just how alone I was. I couldn't even mark my baby's grave. And if I died there, I would be just like her. Dumped in a shallow grave somewhere. No one would even know I existed. After I got home, I started thinking maybe that would be for the best. That the baby should have survived. Not me. That I should be the one forgotten, instead of her."

Clint leaned forward. "You wouldn't have been forgotten, Chelsea. People would have grieved deeply, just like you grieved for your baby. You have a mother who loves you. A grandmother. Comrades in your unit. And you're right where you should be. You're here. Alive. Everything you did while in that cell had to be done. It gave you a chance to survive. Gave you a chance to make sure your baby would never be forgotten.

"If you had died, her memory would have died with you." He paused, keeping his gaze focused on her. "And yet look at what's happened. Your mom now knows about her. I know about her. You'll probably talk to more people about her as you live your life. She won't be forgotten. Your very survival makes that a certainty."

Chelsea seemed to consider his words for a minute, and then nodded as if coming to a decision. "I'd like her to have a grave here in the States. A marker with her name on it."

"Of course we'll do that." Jessi wondered if the ache in her heart would ever stop. She'd been about to be a grandmother of a baby girl who might have survived, given access to modern medical facilities. But those were things she could never say to Chelsea—*would* never say to her. They would decide together whether to tell Chelsea's paternal grandparents. Larry's parents were still alive, and Jessi and Chelsea kept in touch with them regularly. As for her mother…

They could think through all that later. The important thing was that Chelsea was talking. Working through things she hadn't told another soul.

She had to ask. "Does the father know?"

"No. I never told him, and there seems to be no point now." She licked her lips. "And he could get in serious trouble if the truth were made known."

"Why?"

"He's an officer, and I'm not. We weren't supposed to get involved with each other to begin with."

Jessi shot Clint a glance that was probably just as guilt-filled as she feared. But he wasn't looking at her. At all.

"Did you love him?"

"No. And he didn't love me. It just happened. Neither of

us meant for it to, and we've never gotten together again. It was just the one time."

God. Chelsea could have been describing exactly what had happened years ago, only with different players. And Chelsea was right about one thing. Larry had found out and the consequences had been disastrous. And so very permanent.

Her stomach clenched and clenched.

And unlike Chelsea, she hadn't learned from that mistake all those years ago. She'd gone right back and done it again.

Jessi hadn't been able to resist Clint.

She never had. He'd been just as taboo as that officer Chelsea had spoken of.

Chelsea glanced at Clint. "You told me during our first meeting that you were here to help me get through this. So I'm ready to try. I promise to work really hard."

Clint stiffened visibly in his seat.

Chelsea, totally unaware of the strained dynamics in the room, kept on talking. "Did you go through boot camp, Dr. Marks?"

"I did." Nothing in his voice betrayed his feelings, but Jessi knew. She knew exactly the struggle going on inside him right now.

"Then you know a soldier agrees never to leave a wounded comrade behind."

He gave a quick nod.

"I may not be missing a limb or have any visible external injuries except these…" she held out her wrists, showing the scars "…but I am wounded. So please, please don't leave me behind."

CHAPTER THIRTEEN

THEY WERE MAKING PROGRESS.

It came in fits and starts, but the past week had seen Chelsea come further than she had since she'd been at the hospital.

And Clint was still on her case, even though in his heart of hearts he knew he shouldn't be. But Chelsea's words had reached to the heart of who he was as a soldier, and he knew that he would have wished more than anything that someone had been there for his father. But they hadn't. He'd dealt with his demons alone. That's not what he wanted for Chelsea.

Besides, since that session, Jessi had been careful to keep her distance, speaking to him only when he asked her something during joint sessions or when he saw her in the halls at the VA hospital. It was like she was walking on eggshells around him.

Well, so was he, around her. And the edges of those shells were beginning to feel damn uncomfortable beneath his feet.

But as long as he could maintain things for another few weeks, they should be fine. Chelsea had gotten her wish not to be abandoned "like her baby." And she was gradually starting to believe that none of what had happened had been her fault. She'd soon be discharged and start doing her sessions on a weekly outpatient basis—which meant he'd be seeing even less of Jessi.

And that made his chest tighten in ways he'd never thought possible. In fact, he hadn't felt this way since...

Since the day he'd left her twenty-two years ago.

Just like he'd leave her again once his transfer papers went through.

And, yes, he was prepared to put in for one, even though a little voice inside of him whispered that when this was all over—when Chelsea was no longer his patient—he could ask Jessi out on a real date and woo her the way he'd once dreamed about.

Except nothing had changed. Not really.

He was still not the right man for her. He was still too cautious—too afraid to let himself be with any one woman.

Besides, Jessi had already experienced the worst parts of coming from a military family, having a daughter who'd served and come back with serious issues. Did she really need to be involved with a man who dealt with wounded soldiers day after day? Wouldn't it just remind her of all she'd gone through with Chelsea?

Never had he felt the weight of responsibility more than he did right now.

"Dr. Marks?" One of the nurses popped her head into the room. "Peter Summers just called. He's asking for a refill of his methadone prescription."

Another complicated case.

He sighed. Peter's maintenance dosage of the drug was dependent on his showing up for his sessions, the last two of which he'd missed. A longtime addict, methadone was meant to replace cravings. The treatment regimen was highly regulated and required sticking to a precise schedule. That meant outpatient sessions and progress reports. Clint would have followed those guidelines even without the corresponding laws, just because it was the right thing to do.

Hell, it didn't seem like he'd been too worried about doing the right thing when he'd been rolling around on Jessi's couch.

And thoughts like that would get him nowhere.

"Would you mind calling him and setting up a new appointment? Tell him he can't have a refill without coming in."

Consequences. Larry's tragic death came to mind. The consequences of his fling with Jessi.

Well, someone else besides him might as well learn the meaning of the word.

"Will do." The nurse jotted something down onto the paper in her hand. "Oh, and I didn't know if you knew, but there's someone waiting to see you. At least, I think she is. She's come down the hallway and almost knocked on your door twice before going back to the waiting room and just sitting there."

He glanced at his planner. He wasn't scheduled to see anyone for another couple of hours. "Any idea who it is?"

"It's Chelsea Riley's mother."

His throat tightened. Jessi was here to see him? Had almost knocked on his door twice?

"Is she still here?"

The nurse nodded. "She's in the main waiting area."

He pushed his chair back and climbed to his feet. "Has she been to see Chelsea yet?"

"No, that was the strange thing. She came straight here without asking anyone anything." She shrugged. "I thought you might like to know."

"Thank you." He shoved his arms into his sports jacket. "If I'm not in my office when you get hold of Peter Summers, could you leave me note with his next session date? Or let me know what he said?"

"Sure thing."

With that, the nurse popped back out of the room, leaving him to struggle with whether to go down to the waiting area and talk to Jessi or to pretend he knew nothing about it and either wait for her to come to him or to leave, whichever she decided.

Consequences, Clint. You have to do more than talk the talk—you have to be willing to walk the walk. Even if it means walking away.

Despite his inner lecture, he wandered down the hallway—like the idiot he was—and found her in the waiting area, just like Maria had said.

Jessi's head was down, her hands clasped loosely between her jeans-clad knees. She could have been praying. Hell, maybe that's what he should be doing right now. Because just seeing her was like a fist to the stomach. A hard one. Hard enough to leave him breathless and off balance.

And all those emotions he'd worked so hard to suppress boiled up to the surface.

The waiting room was full, only five or six seats empty in the whole place and neither of them next to where Jessi was perched. He moved in, catching the eye of an older man, who, although gaunt, still sat at stiff attention. Clint nodded to him, receiving the same in return. He finally got to where Jessi was seated.

"Jess?"

She glanced up, the worry in her green eyes immediately apparent. She popped to her feet. "I was just coming to see you."

"I know. One of the nurses told me."

Her teeth came down on her lower lip. "I figured it must look weird. I just couldn't get up the nerve to…" She glanced around, bringing back the fact that the room was full and now more than one or two sets of eyes were following their exchange with interest.

"I'll take you back to the office," he said. "And I'll run down to the cafeteria and get us some coffee." He wasn't sure how smart it was to be alone with her. But as long as he kept the door unlocked, they'd be fine. At least, Clint hoped so.

He went to the cafeteria and ordered their coffees. She liked hers with milk, something he shouldn't remember, but did. He dumped a packet of sugar into his own brew and headed back to his office.

When he pushed through the door, he noted she still wore the same haunted expression she'd had earlier. Setting her coffee on the desk in front of her, he went around to the other side and slid into his office chair. "What's going on, Jess?"

"It's Mom. I—I felt like I had to tell her about…about Chelsea's baby, since she and my mom are close." She blinked, maybe seeing something in his face that made her explain further. "I'd already talked to Chelsea about it. She knew I was going to tell her."

"And how did your mom react?"

Her clenched fingers pressed against her chin. "That's just it. She's in the hospital. And I don't know what to tell Chelsea. I know she's going to ask as soon as I go in there."

Shock spurted through his system. "What happened?"

"I think I told you, she hasn't been quite herself lately. Anyway, when she heard the story, she seemed to be handling it okay, then she suddenly started feeling a weird pressure in her chest." Jessi blew out a breath. "It turns out one of her arteries is 90 percent blocked. She needs bypass surgery. She'd been having symptoms for about a month, but didn't want to worry me."

He immediately went to reach for her hand then stopped when Jessi slid hers off the top of the desk and into her lap.

Keeping her distance. Asking for his professional opinion.

Of course that's what it was. She'd already told him what she needed to. She wanted to know whether or not she should tell her daughter about what had happened. She hadn't come to him for comfort or anything else.

Just medical advice about her daughter…his patient.

Right now, though, the last thing he wanted to do was think this thing through. What he wanted was to get out of his chair, walk around the desk and grab her to his chest, holding her while she poured out her heart.

Impulse control.

With his recent track record, holding her was exactly what he shouldn't do.

He took a sip of his coffee and let the heat wash down his throat and pool in his stomach, adding to the acid already there. "I think you should tell her the truth about your mom's condition. Maybe not the events preceding the attack but that her doctor found a blockage in an artery and has decided it needs to be addressed as quickly as possible."

"So you don't think I should tell her about Mom knowing what happened with the baby?"

"Not unless she asks you point-blank. The truth might eventually come out, but I don't think you need to hurry into any kind of explanation right now. That can wait until after the surgery. When your mom—and Chelsea—are better."

The truth might eventually come out.

Great advice, Marks, considering your and Jessi's current situation. And what had happened to her late husband once that truth had indeed come out.

None of that mattered at the moment. "When is the procedure scheduled?"

"They want to do it as soon as possible. This afternoon, in fact."

He sat back in his seat. "Maybe it's good that this happened when it did. At least you were with your mom at the time and knew what to do."

"Did I, Clint? What was I thinking, just blurting something like that out?"

"You said she'd been having symptoms for a while. Besides, I'm sure you didn't 'blurt it out.' You were doing what you thought was best for your mom and for Chelsea."

Like he was doing, by continuing to treat Jessi's daughter? Actually, yes. Nothing had happened to suggest that this couldn't all work out for the best as far as Chelsea was concerned.

"I just never dreamed it might lead to—"

"I know." He paused. "Do you want me to be there when they do the procedure?"

"Don't you have patients?"

Not a direct refusal. More like a hesitation…trying to feel him out, maybe?

"I have one more to see in about an hour and a half. What time is her surgery scheduled for?"

"Five." Her hands came back onto the table and wrapped around her mug.

"I'll be done in plenty of time to get to the hospital." He waited until her eyes came up and met his. "Unless you don't want me there."

There, if she wanted reassurance, he would give it to her. And he had a feeling she could use a friend right now, even if they could never be anything more than that.

"I'd actually like you to be there, if it's not too much trouble."

"Of course it's not."

This time her fingers crept across the desk and touched the top of his hand. He turned his over so it was palm up and curled his fingers around hers.

"Thank you so much, Clint. I know it's hard after everything that went on between us."

"Not hard at all."

They sat there in silence for a few long seconds, hands still gripping each other's. Only now he'd laced his fingers through hers, his thumb stroking over her skin.

A few minutes later she left—with his promise to be at the hospital before her mom's procedure.

And somehow in that period of time he was going to give himself a stern pep talk about what he should and shouldn't do as he sat with her in the waiting room.

And all he could do was hope that—for once—his heart decided to cooperate.

CHAPTER FOURTEEN

JESSI PACED THE waiting room of the hospital an hour into her mom's surgery, her chaotic thoughts charging from one subject to another. Her daughter had been so upset by the news that she hadn't asked if Jessi had told her about the baby.

Or asked any deeper questions about why Jessi had told Clint before she'd told her.

That was good, because the last thing she needed to do was heap one more tricky situation onto the pile.

And tricky was the best way she could think of to characterize her and Clint's relationship.

There was no way she could be falling for Clint all over again. They hadn't seen each other in over twenty years. But as they'd worked together, treating patients at the fair, there'd been a feeling of rightness. A rightness that had continued when they'd made love at her house a week later.

Except feelings didn't always mean anything, at least where she was concerned, because she'd always had a thing for Clint. Even back in high school.

It didn't make a difference then, Jessi, and it's not going to make a difference now. He's going to leave. Just you wait and see.

All those confused feelings had to do with Clint being her first. After all, you never really forgot your first love, right? And she *had* loved Chelsea's father. Very much. If it hadn't been for their argument, Larry would still be alive. Would she even be giving Clint a second glance if he were?

Something else she didn't want to think about because it just made her feel that much worse.

The man in question was seated in one of the cushioned chairs in the hospital waiting room, elbows on his knees, watching her pace. She went over to him. "How do you think it's going?"

One corner of his mouth turned up. "You mean since the last time you asked me? All of five minutes ago?" He patted the chair next to him. "Why don't you sit down? Wearing a hole in the linoleum isn't going to help anyone right now."

She blew out a breath, worry squeezing into every available brain cell and wiping away any other thoughts. Plopping down in the chair, she leaned back and closed her eyes. "What if Mom or Chelsea finds out what we've done?"

"Where did that come from?" His arm went around her shoulders and eased her closer.

"I just don't want to make anything worse for either of them."

"No one's going to find out."

"Larry did." She was immediately sorry she'd said it when his body stiffened.

"Sorry, Clint. I'm just worried."

"I know." He sighed. "You need to stop pacing."

Her eyes opened, and she cranked her head to the right to look at him. "I already did."

"Not there." He nodded at the floor, then his fingers went to her temple and rubbed in slow circles. "I mean up here. You're driving yourself crazy. Nobody's going to find out, unless one of us tells them. And I don't see that happening."

"Thank you," she murmured. "You've been a lot cooler about all of this than I have any right to expect."

He chuckled. "Cool, huh? I don't know if I would call it that, exactly."

She wasn't sure what he meant by that, and she was too nervous to try to figure it out right now. All she knew was that she was glad he was there with her.

Jessi leaned into Clint a little bit more, allowing herself to absorb a little of the confident energy he exuded. That energy was something that had drawn her to him as a high school student, and it wasn't any less potent now.

"How long are they going to be?"

"Jess, it takes time. The doctors felt pretty sure going in that everything was going to run according to plan."

"Yes, but anything could happen." Even as she said it, she allowed her eyelids to slide together, letting his clean scent wash through her, canceling out the sharp bite of disinfectant and illness that came with being at a hospital. She was used to those smells, for the most part, but right now, when she was worried about her mother, they were reminders that sometimes things went wrong, and people died.

"It could, but it probably won't. I think she's going to be just fine."

His words were so inviting, offering up a reality that was in stark contrast to the gloomy paths her own thoughts were circling.

"I hope you're right."

This time when her eyelids slid closed, she allowed them to stay like that, lulled by his easy assurances.

Maybe because that's what she wanted to believe.

Either way, she found herself emptying her mind of anything that didn't revolve around the man beside her. And of how right, and good, and…restful it felt to be with him right now.

Dangerous to let him know that, though.

A hand squeezing hers brought her back. She blinked, the harsh glare of the overhead lights flooding her system.

Heavens, she'd fallen asleep. While her mom was undergoing bypass surgery.

"Jess, the doctor is heading this way."

She jerked her head off his shoulder so fast she thought it was going to bounce to the floor and roll down the hall. Dragging her attention to the present, she glanced past the wide door of the waiting room to see that her mom's doctor was indeed striding toward them, no longer wearing his scrubs.

Standing, she waited for him to reach her, vaguely aware that Clint had climbed to his feet beside her, his fingers at the small of her back as if knowing she still needed that connection.

Even before the doctor reached them, he flashed a thumbs-up sign and a smile. "Everything went really well, better than we could have hoped for, actually," he said. "The harvested vein went in without a hitch and her heart is going strong. She should feel better than she's felt in quite a while. Her other arteries still look pretty good. With a change in diet and exercise, hopefully they'll stay that way for a long time to come."

Relief rushed through her system. "So she's going to be okay?"

The doctor nodded. "Absolutely. Barring anything unforeseen, we'll release her in the next few days. She'll need someone home with her for about a week after that. We checked her insurance, and it'll cover a home nurse."

"Thank you so much. When can I see her?"

He smiled. "She's in Recovery at the moment. You know the routine. Once she's moved into a room, we'll let you see her." For the first time his glance slid smoothly to Clint. "But just you right now."

The touch at her back moved away.

Chelsea hurried to make the introductions, but left out why Clint was there, waiting with her.

The surgeon held out a hand. "Dr. Marks, good to meet you. I served as an army doc before moving over to private practice. I appreciate all you do for our military."

She tensed, wondering if Clint would question why he'd moved when there was so much need—much like she'd done when she'd heard about Dr. Cordoba resigning his commission. All Clint said, though, was, "I'm happy to do it. The country needs both civilian and military doctors. I'm glad you were there for Jessi's mom."

If Dr. Leonard thought it was strange that Clint was there with her or that he'd called her by her first name, he gave no hint of it. He simply nodded and let them know he'd send a nurse out to get Jessi when her mother was settled in. Then he turned around and headed back the way he'd come.

She glanced up at Clint. "Thanks for waiting with me. If you need to get back to the hospital, I understand."

"I already told you, I'm done for the day. I'll stay and make sure everything is okay."

"Thanks again." She bit the side of her lip. "Sorry for falling asleep on you. I can't believe I did that."

His fingers touched her back again. "You've been carrying a lot of weight around on those strong shoulders, Dr. Riley. Maybe it's time you let someone else help with the load from time to time."

Was he offering his services in that regard? And if he was, did she dare let him?

Maybe she already had just by accepting his offer to be here during the surgery.

"I'm sorry you've gotten dragged into my family's problems. Both in high school and now."

He turned her and laid his hands on her shoulders—

ignoring everyone else in the room. "No one 'dragged' me." He squeezed softly before letting her go. "Either then or now. I'm here because I want to be."

And later, after Chelsea was better. Would he still be there?

Something she didn't dare even think about at the moment. Because who knew when that would be. It could be years before Chelsea was well enough to function without the help of someone like Clint. Although she imagined the emphasis would be on counseling later, if there came a time that she didn't need medication to help her cope.

And Jessi knew how things worked in the military. Clint would be transferred out of here, either sooner or later, whereas she had settled her life in Richmond for the long haul. Her mom and daughter were here—not to mention Cooper—and she couldn't imagine leaving them.

Not even for Clint?

She stepped back a pace, not willing to face that question quite yet. Besides, there was nothing between them other than what boiled down to a couple of one-night stands.

One-night stands.

Why did that explanation make her throat ache in a way it hadn't all those years ago?

Hadn't it? Her subconscious whispered the question into her ear, but Jessi raised a hand and swished it away, making Clint frown.

"You okay?" he asked.

"Yes. Just relieved." She took another step back. "Seriously, you don't have to sit here with me. I'm sure you've got other things to do."

His frown grew deeper. "If you're worried about Chelsea or your mom finding out, don't. I won't tell them I was here unless you want me to."

"No!" She cleared her throat and lowered her voice

when she realized a couple of pairs of eyes in the waiting room had shifted their way. "I don't want to have to explain why."

Because she wasn't even sure of the answer, and she was afraid to look too closely at the possibilities. She might just discover something she was better off not knowing.

She'd already had her heart broken. Not once. But twice. Once by Clint and once by her husband's accusations. She didn't want to risk another crack in an already fragile organ.

Clint's voice was also low when he responded. "I already said I wouldn't say anything. So don't worry about it."

But he sounded a little less confident than he had a few minutes ago, when he'd assured her that her mother would be just fine.

"Thanks."

They both sat down, but this time without talking, and Clint didn't put his arm back around her. She tried to tell herself she was glad. But deep inside it made her feel lonely, yearning for something she was never going to have.

And what was that exactly?

A relationship with Clint?

Those four words caused a shudder to ripple through her. Her arms went around her waist, even though the waiting room wasn't chilly.

God, she hoped that's not what she was looking for. Because that wasn't on the cards for her or for Clint. Going down that road would be a recipe for disaster.

She would do better on that front, starting now. Despite her earlier thoughts, she needed to start relying on Clint less than she currently was.

The problem was, Jessi honestly didn't know how she was going to back away when the time came.

Because that crack in her heart was just waiting for an excuse to widen. And she had a feeling it was already far too late to stop that from happening. The crowbar was there in hand, poised and ready.

Or maybe it wasn't her hand that wielded that power at all.

What if, in the end, Clint was the one to decide if her heart came apart in jagged pieces or remained intact?

When the nurse finally came down to tell her her mom was awake and ready to see her, Jessi was relieved to be able to walk away from her spinning, panicked thoughts... and to put her attention firmly where it should have been all along: on her mom and Chelsea...and off Clint.

CHAPTER FIFTEEN

THE SUN WAS peeking out from between heavy storm clouds. Both figuratively and literally. At least as far as Chelsea was concerned. A good omen.

Jessi's mom was home and recovering after her bypass surgery. Clint had seen Jessi in passing, but she had her hands full at the moment with her job, her mom and her daughter.

Which brought him back to the item on his desk.

Transfer papers.

Or rather a request to terminate his temporary assignment in Richmond and head back to Cali, where, from what he'd read on the internet that morning, all was sunny and bright. Not a cloud in sight.

And, hell, he could use a little more light right now to clear his head.

To sign or not to sign, that was the question.

No, it wasn't. He'd eventually put in that request. It was only a matter of time. And willpower.

Willpower he'd been sorely lacking in the past several weeks. To stay would be a mistake. Something he'd convinced himself of time and time again.

His presence here in Richmond brought back memories of not-so-happy times for all of them.

How many times had Jessi mentioned Larry's name?

Hell, he hadn't even known the man had died when he'd arrived here, much less the reason for it. And Jessi had been carrying that around for all these years.

And being here with her was a definite reminder of his own bitter childhood. People from his past knew more than he'd realized—judging from Mrs. Spencer's comments at dinner. They'd evidently talked amongst themselves about his father's problems.

And Clint's explosive reactions when he was around Jessi? Also reminders of what a lack of control could cause—had caused. He might have enjoyed it at the time, but there were consequences for everything in this life.

He'd have to leave some time or other. Why not now? Chelsea was scheduled to be released from the hospital next week. She'd continue her sessions as an outpatient… a victory he should be cheering, instead of acting like he was about to be shot off to the moon, never to be heard from again.

Maybe he'd request deployment instead. That should take him far enough away. Or he could just let the army decide where he was needed, rather than ask to return to San Diego.

Chelsea popped her head in, as if she'd heard his thoughts. "Have you heard anything about my grandmother yet?"

He slid the transfer papers beneath a file folder, not willing to let her see it. No need to cause a panic. It would take time for the orders to go through, anyway.

"No, just that she's been released." He smiled at her. "And you really should learn to knock, young lady. I could have been with a patient."

He motioned at the chair across from his desk.

Her lips twisted. "You're right. Sorry."

"No problem." He tapped the eraser end of his pencil on the smooth gray surface of the desk, the hidden papers glaring at him from their hiding place. "As I was saying, your grandmother seems to be doing pretty well, according to your mom. She just has to take it easy for a few weeks."

Just like he did. He'd seen firsthand the problems that jumping into something with both feet could bring.

"Hmm…"

"And what does that sound mean?" He forced a light smile, although it felt like the corners of his mouth were weighted down with chunks of concrete.

Chelsea's own light attitude vanished. "I was hoping to do something, but I guess it can wait until Nana's feeling better."

"Anything I can help with?"

"I'm not sure. Maybe. I was telling Paul that I'd like to hold a memorial service for my…for the baby. He said he'd like to come. So did some of the others in our group."

Paul Ivers, a young man who'd moved over to sit by Chelsea during one of their group sessions. When had this particular conversation taken place?

"I don't see why that couldn't happen at some point."

"I'd want you there as well, if that's okay. You've helped me so much."

"I haven't done anything, Chelsea. You've come this far under your own power. I've just been here to listen and facilitate."

"Maybe you don't think you've done much, but I do. And you said you knew each other before. I asked Mom about that, and she said you, she and my dad were all in school together. My dad's not here anymore, so it would mean a lot if someone who knew him came."

Me and Larry, neck and neck.

He'd been a stand-in for the man back then. The last thing he wanted was to be one now.

Was that what he'd been when he'd made love to Jessi

back at her house? A stand-in for a man who was dead and gone? A man whose death he'd helped cause?

"Please, Dr. Marks?" Chelsea's voice came back again.

Clint sat there, conflicted. He believed in keeping his word whenever possible, something his father had never seen fit to do.

In fact, a lot of the strict rules governing his life had come about because of his dad's poor judgment. Maybe that wasn't such a bad thing. Those rules had served him well, until he'd come back to Richmond. "I can't promise anything, Chelsea, but if I'm still here, I'd love to come."

Her eyes widened then darkened with fear. "You're thinking of leaving?"

He hurried to put her mind at ease. "I simply meant if you hold the service five years from now, there are no guarantees I won't have been transferred somewhere else by then."

His buzzer went off before he had time to think.

When he answered, his assistant said, "Mrs. Riley is here."

His already tense muscles tightened further. Hearing Jessi referred to as Mrs. anything stuck in his craw.

Jessi Marks. Now, that had a nice ring to it.

No, it didn't.

Hell. This day was turning out to be anything but the good omen he'd hoped for fifteen minutes earlier. It was morphing into a damned nightmare.

"Oh, good," said Chelsea. "We can ask her what she thinks."

Perfect. He had a feeling Jessi was going to love this almost as much as he did.

He responded to his assistant, rather than to his patient. "Send her in."

Jessi scooted through the door, her face turning pink when she spied her daughter sitting in one of the chairs.

Then her eyes crinkled in the corners. "Hi, sweetheart. I was just headed down to see you."

"Were you?" Chelsea's lips slid into a smile. "Guess you decided to stop by and see my doctor first."

Pink turned to bright red that swept up high cheekbones like twin beacons of guilt.

Chelsea waved away her mother's discomfiture and stood up to catch her hand. "Anyway, I'm glad you did, because we have something to tell you."

"We do?"

"You do?"

He and Jessi both spoke at once, then their eyes met. Hers faintly accusing as she met him stare for stare. She was the first to look away, though.

Chelsea blinked as she glanced from one to the other. "I don't actually mean 'we' because I kind of sprang this on Dr. Marks."

That was one way of putting it.

She glanced at him again. "Is it okay if I tell her?"

"That's completely up to you." He had to force the words out as invisible walls began to close in around him. So much for his quick, silent escape. What a damn mess. No matter which way he spun, seeking the nearest exit, he only dug himself in deeper and deeper.

Pulling her mom over to the chairs, they both sat down, then Chelsea told Jessi what she'd told him, in almost exactly the same way. As if she'd been rehearsing the words over and over until she'd got them perfect.

His insides coiled tighter.

Once her voice died away there was silence in the room, except for Clint's phone, which gave a faint pinging sound as it received a message of some type.

Jessi licked her lips, her gaze flicking to Clint for a mere second before going to rest on her daughter. "I think that's a lovely idea."

"I asked Dr. Marks about letting the group come…and I invited him, as well. He said he'd be there, if he was still in Richmond."

"'Still in Richmond'?"

The words curled around a note of hurt, the sound splashing over him in a bitter wave.

This wasn't how he'd wanted her to hear the news.

Chelsea's hand covered her mother's. "No, I mean he said that if I had the service five years from now, he might have been transferred somewhere else by then."

Jessi's body relaxed slightly.

Did she care that he might move away?

Of course not. She had to know as well as he did how utterly foolish it would be for them to go any further than they already had. And she'd withdrawn a little over the past week, changing their working relationship into one of professionals who were collaborating on a patient they had in common. Only to Jessi she was no patient. She was her daughter—someone she loved with all her heart and soul. He saw the truth of it each time the women looked at each other and in the way Chelsea touched her mom, as if needing the reassurance of her presence.

To be loved like that would be…

Impossible. For him, anyway.

And he needed to pull himself together before someone realized how jumbled his emotions had become.

"Of course I'll be there." The words came out before he had time to fully vet them. So he added, "If I can."

"When do you want to do this?" Jessi's voice became stronger, as if she saw this as a way for her daughter to close this chapter in her life and move on to the next one. One that Clint hoped with all his being would be full of laughter and happiness. This family deserved nothing less, they'd been through so much over the years.

He did not need to add more junk to the pile. They both

had enough to deal with right now. He decided to change the subject. "How's your mom?"

"Good. The home nurse is with her this morning. She's getting stronger every day. In fact, she said today that finding out…er…finding out about her blockage might have been one of the most positive, life-affirming experiences she'd ever gone through. She feels tons better and is raring to get out of bed and go back to work on her garden and play with Cooper." Jessi shook her head and squeezed Chelsea's hand. "I think I know where you got your stubbornness from."

"Mine?"

Laughing, Jessi said, "Okay, mine, too."

That was one thing Clint could attest to. This was one strong trio of women, despite the momentary flashes of pain that manifested themselves in physical reactions: Abigail's heart blockage. Chelsea's suicide attempt. Jessi's reaching out to an old flame during a crisis?

Yes. That was exactly it.

It should have made him feel better—set his mind at ease about leaving in the months ahead. Instead, a cold draft slid through his body and circled, looking for a place to land. He cleared his throat to chase it away. It didn't work. It lay over him in a gray haze that clung to everything in sight, just like the morning dew. What it touched, it marked.

And that mark was…

Love.

He reeled back in his seat for a second, trying to process and conceal all at the same time.

He loved her? Heaven help him.

How could he have let this happen? Any of it? All of it?

He had screwed up badly. Had let his emotions get the best of him, just like he always had when he was around this woman.

The transfer papers seemed to pulse at him from beneath the binder with new urgency. The sooner he did this the better.

And his promise to Chelsea?

"What do you think Nana would want me to do?" Even as his own thoughts were in shambles, Chelsea's were on the brink of closing old wounds and letting them heal.

"I think Nana would want you to be happy, honey."

"Can we have the service next week, then? I don't know how long the members of the group will keep coming to sessions. We can have a private memorial for just our family later, if Nana feels up to it."

"We can have it anytime you want."

And in that moment he knew he had to see this through. He had to be there for Jessi, just as she had to be there for Chelsea. Abigail wasn't up to taking on that role yet. And Larry was no longer there.

And he wanted to. Wasn't that what love was about? Sacrificing your own comfort and well-being for someone else's?

Like he'd done once upon a time?

He peered into the past with new eyes. Eyes that saw the truth.

He'd loved her even then. Even as he'd been preparing to hand her over to another man. One whose father didn't drink himself into a rage and let his fists do the talking.

A normal, mundane life.

Something Clint hadn't been able to give her. Because back then he'd had anger issues, too. Toward his father, who'd dished it out. Toward his mom, who'd sat there and taken it. Toward the world in general, for turning a blind eye toward what had been going on in homes like his.

The military had helped him conquer most of his anger, but only because it had instilled discipline in its place, and had channeled his negative energy into positive areas.

But his life still wasn't peaceful. It was filled with patients like Chelsea, who scrabbled and clawed to find some kind of normalcy.

Jessi had been through enough. She'd deserved better than him back then, and she still did today.

She deserved a professor or architect or poet. A man who brought beauty into her life. Not memories of days gone by.

I'm going to have to give her up all over again.

And he was going to have a few more scars to show for it.

He realized both pairs of female eyes were on his face, both wearing identical expressions of confusion. One of them had said something.

"I'm sorry?"

Chelsea bit her lip. "I asked if next Sunday would work for you? Or do you have other plans?"

"No. No plans." Once he'd said it, he realized he could have come up with an excuse. Like what? A date? That would go over really well with Jessi. Besides, he'd meant what he'd thought earlier. He wanted to be there for her... and for Chelsea. Like the family he'd never had?

Maybe. Maybe it was okay to pretend just for a few hours—to soak up something he'd never be able to have in real life.

Like a wife and daughter?

Yes.

Even if they both belonged to a man who could no longer be there for them.

So he would act as a stand-in once again. For an hour. Maybe two. And he could pray that somehow it was enough to get him through the rest of his life.

CHAPTER SIXTEEN

SHE WANTED TO hold Clint's hand, but she couldn't.

Not in a cemetery, while mourning a tiny life that had been snuffed out before its time. Standing next to him would have to be enough.

Only it was so hard. Hard to remain there without touching him.

Curling her fingers into her palms, she forced them to stay by her sides as a chaplain she'd never met talked about life and death…commemorating a granddaughter she'd also never met.

A hand touched hers. Not Clint's, but Chelsea's. Her daughter's fingers were icy cold, her expression grim, eyes moist with grief as the minister continued to speak.

"In the same way this marker serves as a reminder that a tiny life was placed into Your loving arms, we, like Marie Elizabeth Riley, need to place our trust and hope in You, the Author and Finisher of our faith, that we will one day see her as she was meant to be. Whole and full of life…"

The sudden rush of tears to eyes that had been dry took Jessi by surprise, overriding whatever else the chaplain was saying. She fumbled in her purse, letting go of Chelsea's hand for a second as she searched for a tissue.

Clint, still, solemn and heartbreakingly handsome in a dark blue suit, pressed a handkerchief into her trembling hands. She glanced up at him to find him watching her, something dark and inscrutable in his gray eyes. Was he irritated at her for blubbering? But this baby would have been her first grandchild…would have probably survived if Chelsea had had access to health care.

And that was another thing that had driven her daughter crazy with guilt. All those what-ifs. *If* she had just spoken up…*if* she'd admitted she was pregnant, instead of fearing a reprimand or, worse, of being sent home in flurry of paperwork and inner shame…*if* she'd told her captors the truth. The baby's father had never been notified. Chelsea saw no reason to cause trouble for a man with whom she'd had a one-night stand.

Jessi knew what that was like. She'd had two of them. Both with the same man.

The chaplain asked everyone to bow their heads, so Jessi closed her eyes. And felt a hand to her right clasp hers once again. Chelsea.

And then, out of nowhere, warm fingers enveloped her other hand, lacing between hers.

Clint.

Oh, God. The tears flowed all over again. She'd wanted to hold his hand, and he'd not only read her mind, he'd found a way to accomplish the impossible.

A flicker of hope came to life in her chest.

Maybe it wasn't impossible. He had certainly made love to her like she'd meant something to him.

Then again, he'd done the same thing all those years ago. Maybe it was different now. They were both older. Wiser. They'd both lived through things many people never had to experience.

She tightened her grip around both hands, allowing herself to feel connected to him in a way that had nothing to do with sex. Or need. But was something deeper. More profound.

No.

Not happening.

And yet he'd made the impossible possible.

As the prayer went on, Clint gave her hand a quick squeeze, then released it.

When she peeked between her lashes, she saw that she wasn't the only one who had a male hand linked with hers. The young man next to Chelsea stood so close their shoulders and arms touched. And his index finger was twined around her daughter's.

She swallowed. Maybe, just maybe, she could let herself believe. Just like the chaplain said.

The seed took root and spread throughout her being, twisting around her heart and lungs until she wasn't sure where they started and the belief ended. Maybe that was the way it was meant to be.

She could talk to Clint. Somehow find out if he felt the same way. Surely he did. Otherwise why would he have held her hand?

Because she'd been crying? Maybe. That was why it was important to talk to him. And she would. Just as soon as the service was over, and she'd made sure her daughter was okay. Her mom was at home. They still hadn't told Chelsea about the circumstances behind the heart episode, and they'd both agreed to keep that quiet. Her mom also felt it was best for her to stay at home for this particular event. Neither of them wanted anything to mar the service. And although Jessi trusted Clint not to say anything, one of them could inadvertently let something slip without realizing it.

The prayer ended, and Chelsea took the white rose in her hand and gently kissed the bloom, then placed it across the bronze marker that had been set in the lush grass beside Larry's grave. Grass that hadn't needed to be turned up, since there was no body to bury this time. The back of

Jessi's throat burned. Larry would have loved his daughter. And his granddaughter, if he'd been able to see past his own hurt and pride. Two lives, needlessly lost.

But at least there was now a place where Chelsea could come and remember—along with a concrete bench that had been placed at the foot of the graves, a gift from her mother. She hoped they could come here each year and remember.

The service ended with a flautist from their church playing "Amazing Grace," the light, bright sound of the instrument giving the hymn a sense of hope and peace. It's what Chelsea had wanted, and as her daughter moved to stand beside the same young man as before, a quick glance was shared between the two of them. Jessi looked at him a little more closely. Surely it was a good thing that her daughter was beginning to look past the pain in her heart and see a future that was brimming with possibilities.

Like Jessi herself was?

When she gave Clint a sideways look, she saw that his attention was also on the pair. She could have sworn a flash of envy crossed his expression before disappearing. His gaze met hers, and he nodded to show her he had noticed, then he leaned close, his breath brushing across her ear as he murmured, "Try not to worry. Paul's a good man."

Words hung on the tip of her tongue, then spilled past her lips. "So are you, Clinton Marks."

His intake of breath was probably not audible to anyone except him, but even so he froze for several seconds at her comment, while his brain played it over and over in that same breathy little whisper.

She thought he was a good man?

Emotion swelled in his throat, and he forced himself to stand up straight before he did something rash right in front of her late husband's grave. Like crush her in his arms and kiss her like there was no tomorrow. Tell her that he loved her and would always be there for her.

As the last notes of the song died away, people began to filter out of the cemetery. Chelsea leaned over to Jessi and said, "I'll see you later on at Nana's?"

"I probably won't be there for a few hours, okay? There's something I need to do first," said Jess.

"Okay." The two women embraced for several long seconds then broke apart. Paul walked her daughter over to her car and held the door open, leaning over to tell her something before closing it.

"What do you have to do?" Clint asked.

If he was smart, he'd say his goodbyes right now before he got caught up in some kind of sentimental voyage that would end with him dragging her back to his place.

"I thought we might go back to my house for a little while."

He waited for her to tack a valid reason on to the end of that phrase. But she didn't. Instead, she simply waited for him to respond to the request. One that had come right on the heels of her other shocking comment.

He should end it right now. Cut her short before she could say anything else with a brusque, "Not a good idea and you know it."

Right. He could no more bring himself to say something like that than the moon could grow an oxygen-rich atmosphere. Or maybe it could, because right now he was having trouble catching his breath and his head felt like it was ready shut down.

He glanced back at the markers, Larry's name biting deep into his senses and grinding them into something he no longer recognized. Needing to get away before it took another chunk from him, he said, "Sounds good. Are you ready?"

"Do you want to follow me back?"

Honey, I'd follow you anywhere, if I could.

Maybe things weren't as dire as he'd painted them. Would it be so bad if he and Jessi somehow tried to make a go of things?

That paper on his desk came to mind. He could just tear it up and dump it in his waste can, and no one would be the wiser.

The thought grew as they walked to the parking lot together. With no one else around, Clint took her hand again, gripping it with an almost desperate sense of reverence. This woman did it for him. She met him right at his point of deepest need. And she had no idea.

And if she wanted to go back to her place and discuss Chelsea's case, he was going to be crushed with disappointment. Because he wanted her. In the past. Right now in the present. And in the days that stretched far into the future.

Whether or not any of that was possible was another matter. But maybe he shouldn't worry about leaping right to the end of this particular book. Maybe he should turn one page at a time and savor each moment as it came.

Because who knew how long anything in this life was going to last? Wasn't today a reminder of that?

He saw her to her car and smiled when he did the exact same thing young Paul had done. Opened her door for her and then leaned across it. Only instead of saying something, he kissed her. Right on the mouth. Right in the middle of a public parking lot.

And he didn't give a rip who saw him.

One page at a time. And he was loving the current chapter because, instead of a quick peck and retreat, Jessi's lips clung to his for several long seconds. When he finally forced himself to pull back, she gave him a brilliant smile. "I think we're on the same page."

A roll of shock swished through him. Coincidence.

It had to be. Unless Jessi had suddenly become a mind-reader.

Then again, he found it pretty damned hard to hide his feelings from this particular woman. They bubbled up and out before he could contain them. That's what had gotten him into trouble when they'd been in high school and again a couple of weeks ago. It was impossible to be near her and not want to touch her. Hold her. Make love to her.

He didn't respond to her words, just said, "I'll meet you at your house." Because if he was wrong, if she wasn't feeling the same deep-seated need that he was, he'd end up eating his words and feeling like a fool.

The fifteen-minute drive seemed to take forever, but finally she pulled into the driveway of her house. They got out of their cars and stared at each other for a minute before coming together.

Then he was reaching for her and dragging her into his arms, kissing her with a fervor he had no business feeling. But she kissed him back just as hard, her hands winding around his neck, going up on tiptoe so she could get closer.

Her tongue found his, leaving no doubt in his mind where her thoughts were headed. And that was fine by him, because his had been there for hours…weeks.

"Keys." His muttered words were met with a jingle, then he swept her up in his arms and strode to the front door. "Unlock it."

It gave him a thrill to note that her hands shook as she twisted around to do as he asked, because he knew his were trembling just as hard, along with every other part of his body. Half in anticipation of what was to come and half in fear that somehow it was all going to fall apart before they got inside…before he got the chance to strip her clothes from her body—in her bedroom this time—and drive her to the point of no return.

Because he was already there. There was no turning

back from the emotions that were throbbing to life within him. He couldn't bring himself to say them, so he would show her instead. With his mouth. With his hands.

With his heart.

And hope that somehow she'd be able to decipher their meaning.

He kicked the door closed, trying not to trip when Cooper suddenly appeared, barking wildly and winding around him. He let Jessi down long enough for her to let the dog out into the backyard before hauling her back up into his arms. This time he lifted her higher so that his mouth could slant back over hers, his fingers digging into the soft flesh of her thighs, her waist. Right on cue, her arms went back around his neck and she held on tight.

Clung as if she were drowning.

Well, so was he.

"Bedroom," he muttered against her mouth. Could he not get anything out other than one- and two-word sentences?

Evidently not.

And if she was going to stop this parade, she had the perfect opportunity to drag her lips from his and tell him to put her down, that they were going to sit on that long sofa and talk.

She didn't. "Down the hallway, first door on the right."

Then she was kissing him again, her eyes flickering shut even as his had to remain open to avoid tripping over furniture or running into a wall as he made his way down the hallway and arrived at her bedroom. He paused in the doorway and eyed the space, noting the frilly pillows on the bed and the hinged frame that held two pictures on the nightstand. One of Jessi with another man. And one of her holding that man's baby.

Larry.

His chest tightened, and he pulled back slightly, rethinking this idea.

"What's wrong?" Her breathless reply washed over him.

He nodded at the nightstand, and she glanced in that direction and then tensed before looking back up at him. She shook her head. "It's okay, Clint. He's been gone a very long time."

She didn't say that she didn't love him, or that Larry wouldn't mind if he could see them.

Just that the man had been gone a long time.

He stood there, undecided. Could he lie in that bed and thrust inside her, while her dead husband watched them?

"Take me over there," she murmured.

He didn't want to. Wanted to suggest they go back to the familiar sofa in the living room. But his feet had ideas of their own. He carried her over to the small table and watched as she tipped the frame over onto its front so that the pictures were no longer visible.

"Better?" she asked, one corner of her mouth curling.

It was. A little, anyway. "Yes."

"Okay, now put me on the bed—" her fingers sifted through the hair at the back of his neck, sending a shiver over him "—and take off all my clothes."

"Your wish—" he wiped Larry from his mind and dropped her from where he stood, then smiled at the squeal she gave as she bounced on the mattress and lay there staring up at him "—is my command."

She licked her lips. "Then come down here and start commanding me."

CHAPTER SEVENTEEN

BEFORE HE COULD do as she asked, Jessi sat up and scooted to the edge of the bed, allowing her legs to hit the floor. Then she grabbed him behind the knees and dragged him forward a step or two, parting her legs until he stood between them.

"I thought I was doing the commanding," he said.

"Changed my mind," she said with a laugh, removing his keys and wallet from his pockets and putting them on the bed. "Because you'll end up having all the fun, like last time."

His brows went up. "I don't remember hearing any complaints."

"That's because there weren't any." Reaching for his belt buckle, she slid the loop out in one smooth move that made his mouth water. "And I don't think you'll be hearing any complaints now. At least, not from me."

With the buckle undone, she moved to the button of his dress slacks.

Hell, she wasn't going to hear any complaints from him either. Although his ideas for maneuvering her to the point of no return were not going according to plan.

Or maybe she'd had the very same thoughts about him.

His flesh twitched.

And he was already too far gone to back out now.

Down went his zipper. "Wait."

She stopped and met his eyes. "Am I doing something wrong?"

No, she was doing everything exactly right. And that was the problem. He really *was* too far gone. His body was pumping with anticipation. Too much too soon and he was going to have trouble not letting go in a rush. It was why he hadn't let her touch him last time.

"No, honey." His hand tangled in her hair, resisting the urge to drag her forward and show her exactly what he meant. "I just don't want you to do anything you don't want to do."

One perfectly arched brow went up an inch, and she licked her lips. "And if I want to?"

Even as she said it, she peeled apart the edges of his slacks and pushed them down his hips, until they sat at midthigh.

No trying to hide what she did to him at this point, because it was right there in front of her. Her hands moved around to the backs of his thighs, sliding over his butt and grabbing the elastic waistband of his briefs. "Are you ready?"

Oh, he was ready all right. But he wasn't so sure he was ready for what she wanted.

Dammit, who was he kidding? He was a man. He wanted it. Wanted every last thing she could think of doing to him.

And he wanted it now.

"Do it."

That was all it took. She dragged his underwear down in one quick tug, her nails scraping over his butt in a sensual move that set all his nerve endings on high alert.

He bobbed free, inches from her face. Her thumbs brushed along the outsides of his legs as her hands curled around the backs of his thighs, holding him in place. Then she leaned forward without hesitation, her mouth engulfing him in a hot, wet rush that made him grunt with ecstasy.

She remained like that for several seconds, completely still, her eyes closed, nostrils flaring as if the sensation was heavenly.

Hell, lady, you should be standing in my shoes.

He struggled like a wild man to contain the warning tingle, using every bit of ammunition in his bag of tricks to keep from erupting right then and there. Tangling his hand in her hair, he dragged her backward until he popped free. "Damn, woman. You're going to get more than you bargained for if you keep that up."

She laughed. "Haven't I told you? I love bargains. Especially when I get more bang for my…buck."

The pointed hesitation before she said that last word made his flesh tighten in anticipation. A silent promise to give her exactly what she wanted: a hard, fast bang that was, oh, so good.

Just like last time.

But this time he wanted to draw out his pleasure. And hers.

So, keeping his fingers buried in her hair, he drew her forward again, watching as she slowly opened her mouth.

Yes!

He edged closer, dying to feel her on him, then pulled away at the last second. He repeated the parry and feint several times with a slow undulation of hips that was a blending of obscene torture—emphasis on the torture. At least for him.

She clenched the backs of his thighs, trying to tug him closer, while he remained just out of reach. "Clint. Please…"

"What do you want, Jess?"

"Right now? I want you."

That was all it took. He pushed her backwards on the

bed, knocking the frame off the end table in the process, and shoved her full skirt up around her hips. Black satin panties met his hungry eyes. He jerked them down and then kicked his way out of the rest of his clothes, cursing when one foot got hung up in the waistband of his briefs. Once free, he tossed a condom packet onto the bed and lay down, hauling her on top of him, until she was straddling him, her skirt pooling around her hips.

"You wanted to be in control, Jess? You've got it."

Her eyes trailed from the straining flesh outlined beneath the fabric of her skirt up his bare chest, until her eyes met his. "In that case, do you want me clothed? Or unclothed?"

Unclothed. His mind screamed the word, mouth going dry. He had to force himself to say, "Your game. Your rules."

She gave him a slow smile. "Mmm. I like the idea of making my own rules." Taking her skirt in hand, she pulled the black silk up his erection in a long, slow move that made him rethink his assessment. Then she let it slip back down the way it had come.

Okay, clothed was pretty hot, too. Especially when she continued to hold his gaze, and he knew she could spot every muscle twitch in his cheek, discern every time he had to hold himself in check. Like now, when myriad sensations began to gather in his chest. In his gut...

"Jess..." It was meant to be a warning, but her name came out as a low hum of air.

One of her hands crawled beneath her skirt and found him. And the tactile awareness of being able to feel what she was doing but not see it made the act seem secretive and forbidden. An exotic ritual that defied time and space.

She slid forward and shifted her hips up and over his ready flesh. He braced himself, but she didn't come down on him in a rush, as he'd expected. Instead, she brushed him across her skin, back and forth, her eyes closing, lips parting. He swallowed hard when he realized what she was doing—using him on her body, giving herself pleasure, rocking her hips in time with her hand.

Holy hell. This was as hot as her mouth had been.

Worse.

Because then she'd only been pleasuring him. Now she was bringing both of them to new heights of throbbing awareness. Every cell in his body wanted to thrust home and end the torment. He could just slide up and inside her in one fast move, and she would probably let him... probably welcome him. But the shifting expressions on her face were too entrancing to do anything but lie there and take whatever she wanted to dish out.

"God, Jess. You're killing me here."

"What do you want?" She turned his earlier words around and pushed them back at him.

Only he knew exactly what he wanted. "I want you to make yourself come."

Her fingers tightened, and her movements became quicker, bolder, her breasts straining beneath her shirt as she brushed herself against him—or brushed him against herself—he didn't know which it was and didn't care. He was dying to cup her, to scrape his thumb across those hard nipples now visible even through her blouse and bra, but he wanted this round to be all hers.

All around him, he felt her slick heat. Lust spiraled through him, growing stronger with each stroke, even as her movements became more purposeful. Reaching sideways, Clint found his wallet and the condom just inside it. He wrapped his fingers around the plastic wrapper, gripping it tight, hoping he'd still have the sanity to use it when the time came.

Jessi's breathing quickened, her teeth coming down on her lip as her body continued to feign the motions of sex.

Good sex. The kind of sex that didn't come along every day, with every woman.

No, there was only one woman he'd ever shared this kind of connection with.

Her body stiffened suddenly, pressing hard against him. Then she went off with a cry, her body pulsing against the tight need of his erection. Tearing into the packet, he reached beneath her skirt and sheathed himself in a rush before plunging into her and losing himself in the continued contractions of her orgasm.

Using her hips, he pulled her down onto himself as hard as he could, already too far gone to try to last any longer. Instead, he pressed upwards in greedy thrusting motions as he allowed himself to plummet mindlessly over the cliff of his own release, falling, falling, until there was nowhere else to go.

Nothing registered for several seconds—or it might have been minutes. Hours, even.

When he could finally breathe again, finally think, he gathered her to his chest, his fingers sliding up through the damp strands of her hair and holding her close.

"Remind me not to put you in charge ever again."

"So you *are* complaining." She snuggled closer.

"Never."

He kissed her brow, her taste salty with perspiration, and allowed his eyelids to finally swing shut...no longer afraid he was going to miss something crucial.

With one last sigh, he propped his chin on her head and allowed his body to relax completely.

Something tickled the side of her arm.

There it was again. It wasn't Cooper, because he was in the living room, and the bedroom door was shut.

Her mind reached out to grasp something, only to have

it shift away uneasily. The sensation returned. A light rhythmic stroke trailing up toward her shoulder now.

Her eyes opened to find someone standing beside the bed, watching her.

Clint.

"Hello, sleepyhead. I fed Cooper and let him out. Hope that was okay."

"Mmm…"

Since his voice sounded as rough as hers felt, she wasn't the only one who had fallen asleep after the second time they'd made love.

In her bed. In her house. And the second time he'd undressed her slowly. Carefully. Kissing his way down her body in a way that had made her heart melt, even while her senses had been kicking into high gear.

Like now. Only it was her heart that was soaring, rather than her libido. Because Clint was still here. He hadn't hightailed it out of here like she'd half expected. The hope she'd grasped earlier continued to grow, picking up speed as she finally acknowledged the possibilities that this might just work out between them.

"Hey, yourself. What time is it?" She rolled onto her back to look at him fully.

"About five in the afternoon." A hand reached up to scrub the stubble on his jaw. "Do you have to work?"

Work? At a time like this?

"Have you been walking around the house like that?" The man had fed Cooper and let him out…stark naked?

He smiled. "Why? Does it bother you?"

"Define bother."

He laughed. "So, about work…"

"No. No work, but I need to check on Chelsea and my mom, like I told them I would."

"I thought you might. Otherwise I would have let you sleep. As it was, if Cooper hadn't scratched at the door, I was going to wake you in a completely different way." He found one of her hands and linked his fingers through hers.

She closed her eyes, happiness flowing over her. "Wow. You're up for a third round?"

"Believe me, I'm up for all kinds of things. Round or otherwise." A quick glance down showed he was already up and ready.

"Mmm." She let out a sigh as a thought came to her. Talk. That's what she'd meant to do at some point, only she'd gotten sidetracked. She dipped a toe into the water. "Do you think Chelsea and Paul are going to start seeing each other?"

"I think it's a possibility. Why? Is that a problem?"

"Do you think it's a good idea?"

"Don't know. They've both been through some tough times. They'll either be able to support each other, or they'll drag each other down."

A shiver went over her. "I hope I never have to live through anything like the past couple of months ever again. How do you deal with patients who are in such pain on a daily basis? I think it would eat at my heart." She hesitated before continuing. "And after what happened with your dad…"

Lifting his hand to kiss it, his crooked little finger caught her attention. She changed her aim and kissed that knuckle instead.

He stiffened at her act. "My dad is the reason I'm in this line of work."

Pulling away, he reached down and picked something up off the floor. She frowned, and then saw it was the picture frame he'd knocked off. Flipping it over, he went to put it on the nightstand then stopped, his jaw tightening as he stared at it.

"Clint?"

He shook his head, throat moving for a second. Jessi swiveled her eyes to look at the frame.

The glass on Larry's side had broken, a series of jagged, cobweb-looking cracks distorting his features and obscuring half of his face.

When she glanced back at Clint he looked...stricken. That was the only word she could think to describe it.

She reached out a hand. "Hey, it's okay. It's only a cheap frame. I can get another one."

He set it on the table but wouldn't quite meet her eyes. Something was wrong. Very wrong.

"Jessi, I need to tell you something."

A wave of foreboding licked at her toes, then her ankles. Soon it was waist deep and rising.

She reached out to touch him, but the second she did, he backed away and found his trousers, sliding into them and fastening them before he looked at her again.

"I was going to wait and tell you later, but this seems as good a time as any." A muscle worked in his jaw. "They've found a permanent replacement for Dr. Cordoba. He arrives in two weeks."

She wasn't sure what this had to do with them. "Chelsea will continue her sessions with him, then."

"Yes." He scooped his dress shirt from the floor and pushed his arms through the sleeves.

Why was he getting dressed? This was good news. They wouldn't have to hide their relationship anymore.

Right?

"So that means we'll be able to see each other without—"

"No." His lean fingers moved quickly to button up his shirt. "We won't. I'm putting in my transfer papers. You knew this was only a temporary assignment. Just until they found another doctor. I'm going back to San Diego."

What? Her mind screamed that word over and over and over until it was hoarse with grief and confusion.

He'd made love to her last night as if he couldn't get enough. As if she really meant something to him. And now he was leaving?

Shades of the past came back to haunt her. Hadn't he already done this once before? Screwed her and then taken off without a backward glance?

The ominous wave was still rising, faster than ever, splashing up her neck and cresting over her head until she couldn't breathe. Horror washed through her at all she'd done with him last night, at how truly and freely she'd given herself to him.

In. Love.

And he'd felt nothing. *Nothing.*

As the silence drew out, he finally broke it by saying, "I should have told you before…" He motioned at the bed.

He hadn't been willing to change his life for her twenty-odd years ago so why had she thought he would now?

Sitting up and not bothering to cover her nakedness, she glared at him, welcoming the anger—because it kept away the tears. "Yes, you should have. But, then, you wouldn't have had one last trip down memory lane, would you? Treating patients isn't the only thing you're good at, Dr. Marks. You're also an expert at using people, and then ditching them when you've had what you wanted."

She climbed to her feet and stood there. Refusing to be vulnerable. Refusing to care what he did.

Only she knew deep inside it was a lie. The cracks in the picture frame now mirrored the ones in her heart, splitting wide open and spilling everything inside her into the dust that had become her life.

"Jess, that's not the way this—"

"No!" If he said one more word she was either going to burst into tears or slap him across the face with all her might. "Just go. Have Chelsea's new doctor call us when he arrives."

He grabbed the rest of his clothes and shoved his bare feet into his dress shoes. "I'm sorry, Jess."

Tossing her head, she bit out a quick reply. "Don't be. It was a blast from the past. We had our own mini high school reunion right here in my bedroom, but now it's time to pack up and get back to our own lives, in our own cities."

She didn't ask him exactly when he was leaving. She didn't want to know.

Clint's throat moved as he looked at her for another minute. Then he said, "Goodbye, Jessi."

With that, he turned around and walked out of the bedroom, his receding footsteps on the hardwood floor marking his location and searing the message into her brain. There was no slowing of his pace, no hesitation as the front door opened and then closed.

Clint was leaving. And this time he wasn't coming back.

CHAPTER EIGHTEEN

A WEEK WAS all it took to change his life forever.

He'd filed expedited transfer papers, asking them to put him wherever they needed him, preferably deployed overseas. He wound up at the VA hospital in New Mexico instead.

It might as well have been the other side of the world.

He sat at a desk that looked exactly like his previous one and wondered how he'd gotten here. Aimless. Rootless. And, thus far, patientless. They were letting him get settled in.

Right. Like that's what he needed. More time to think about what had happened that night in Jessi's bedroom.

He'd been all set to tell her how he felt, and then he'd picked up that frame and seen the damage he'd caused.

To her marriage. To her life.

At that moment he'd felt as shattered as that glass.

Being with Jessi again had wreaked havoc with his insides, turning him back into that impulsive screwup he'd been in high school.

He couldn't risk messing up her life a second time. Neither could he ask her to pick up and move away the next time he got his transfer papers. Jessi's life was in Richmond. With Chelsea and her mom—and those two graves.

Clint's place was with his patients. The one thing he knew he was good at.

She'd be okay without him. Seeing Chelsea get better would give her hope for a new beginning. He'd soon be relegated to the past again—where he belonged.

His phone rang. He glanced at the readout and his mouth went dry, his blood pressure spiking.

A Richmond area code.

Only it wasn't Jessi's number. He didn't recognize it. Damn it!

When would the hope finally die? It was over. He'd ended it himself—and she hadn't been sorry to see him go. She'd not said one word to discourage him. Instead, she'd practically shoved him out the door.

Checking the door to his office to make sure it was closed, he pressed the speakerphone button and stared at the open case file in front of him. So much for trying to get up to speed.

"Hello?"

"Dr. Marks?"

He recognized the voice immediately. "Chelsea? Is everything okay?"

"I don't know. I mean, everything's fine with me. It's Mom."

His heart plummeted. "Is she all right?"

"No." There was a pause, and then her voice came through. Stronger. With just a hint of accusation. "I saw you holding hands at the memorial service. How could you just…leave like that?"

"I was transferred. You know how it works."

A curse word split the air, and Clint picked the phone up and put it to his ear, even though he knew his assistant wouldn't be able to hear their conversation through the thick walls.

Chelsea's voice came back through. "You're right. I do

know how it works. And there's no way you'd be able to get the okay for a transfer that fast unless you asked for it to be expedited. Or unless you'd been sitting on it this whole time."

"What does it matter? The Richmond hospital was a temporary assignment."

"Did I say something? Do something?"

"No." He hurried to set her mind at ease. "This had nothing to do with you, Chelsea. I'm proud of how hard you've worked on your recovery. You've faced the past head-on and now you're ready to move into the future."

A laugh came over the phone, but it was without humor. "That's what you always told us during group, wasn't it? That we had to face the past and see it for what it was without running or hiding from the truth. But in the end that's not what you did, is it?"

Hell, how had a tiny slip of a girl managed to read him so well? He had run. He'd taken one look at that broken glass, and instead of facing his fears, instead of talking to Jessi about everything that had happened, he'd turned tail and run.

Because he was afraid to face the future. Afraid his past would somehow catch up to him and splash its ugliness on to Jessi.

In reality, he'd been looking for an excuse to flee ever since he'd seen her sitting in his office that first day.

Why? Because he loved her, and just like back in high school he'd hightailed it out of town rather than having the courage to tell her how he felt and let her decide what to do with that information.

"What happened between me and your mother isn't any of your business."

"Sure it is. She's. My. Mother." She took an audible breath. "When I was in trouble, you never hesitated to bleed every detail of my therapy to her, because…she had a right to know the truth. She's listed as my next of kin. Well, guess what, Doctor, that works both ways. I'm her next of kin. I have a right to know. Did you even care about her at all?"

He swallowed. "Yes."

"Well, she cares for you, too. She's been smiling and saying all the right things, but she's not okay. She looks awful."

"I'm sorry."

"Not good enough. You might outrank me, but I'm going to tell you straight up what I think."

He smiled despite himself. "There's no question you and your mom are related."

"Yeah? Well, here it is. You're no better than a common deserter."

Shock rolled through him. "Excuse me?"

"You heard me. When the battle inside your head got tough, you turned around and walked away, instead of acting like a soldier and facing it, the way you told us to do. She's not the enemy, Dr. Marks. I don't know what it is you're fighting, but I suggest you figure it out and come back and face it. Otherwise you'll regret it for the rest of your life."

She looks awful.

He'd rushed off so sure that he was doing the right thing and saving the woman he loved a whole lot of pain.

What if he'd ended up *causing* her pain instead?

Hell. He was an idiot. "Reprimand noted and accepted."

"Good. You said you cared about her. Do you love her?"

He smiled, making a decision he should have made twenty-two years ago. "I think your mom deserves to hear that from the source, don't you?"

"Then get back here and tell her. Because I'm pretty sure she loves you, too."

* * *

Jessi pulled her sticky scrubs away from her midsection, fanning the fabric against herself as she headed into the parking lot. It was an hour past the end of her shift, and she was only now able to leave the hospital.

A gang war had seen her dealing with multiple gun-shot wounds. Two had died en route to the hospital and another three had needed surgery. One of them had a broken finger in addition to other more serious wounds, but that small injury had been the one that had made her finally break down and admit the truth. That she missed Clint. Terribly.

She had a feeling Chelsea knew something was wrong, and her mom—almost completely recovered from her surgery a month ago—had also cast some worried looks her way. She had no idea why. She'd been acting cheerful, even if that's all it was. An act.

Straightening her back, she quickened her pace. This was ridiculous. How long was she going to keep moon-ing over something that was never going to happen? She needed to pull herself together and forget about...

Keys in hand, she paused halfway across the parking lot. Someone in uniform stood near where she'd parked her car, the tall military bearing painfully familiar. How many times had she seen that stance?

Her dad. Her daughter. In a military town, it was im-possible not to recognize the proud upright posture. Only this went beyond that. This was...

Clint.

Oh, God. Something inside her urged her to turn around and dash back to the safety of the hospital.

No. She was not going to let what that man did or didn't do dictate her actions and emotions any longer. So she walked toward him, trying not to look directly at him as she did so, afraid he'd see the misery in her eyes.

When she reached her car she saw that she was right, he was standing right next to it. She'd have to pass in front of him to get to the driver's door.

"I thought you'd left," she said, her voice sounding as chipper as ever.

"I did." He didn't move. Didn't crack a smile at her tone. "I came back."

Her heart took a swan dive. What? Had he decided he hadn't tortured her enough?

She swallowed. "Why?"

"Because I'm done running. When you told me about Larry and his death, it was like a hole opened up and swallowed me whole. If I hadn't followed you that day…if I'd let him chase you outside instead, you'd still be one big happy family."

He drew in an audible breath. "And then I broke that frame, Larry's frame, and it was as if the universe was sending me a message. That I'd screwed up your life once before, and I could very well do it again if I stayed."

Her own breath caught in her lungs before whooshing back out. "Why didn't you say something?"

"I thought I was doing you a favor."

"Well, you didn't. I—" He cut her off with a finger pressed across her lips.

"Let me finish, while I still have the nerve. I came back to tell you I love you. I have since high school when I found you crying beside the creek." He paused. "I gave you up once, thinking it was for your own good, but I'm not going to do it again. Unless you tell me to go."

She pushed his hand away.

"Twice." The correction came out before she could stop it. "You gave me up twice. Why should I believe you this time?"

"Because it's the truth, Jess. I swear it." He took a step forward.

She tried to force herself to move back, but she couldn't. She just stood there, staring up at him. Maybe the summer heat had gone to her head and he was a mirage. After all, he didn't look hot at all.

Okay, so he looked superhot in that uniform, but not in the way she'd meant it.

"So what changed your mind this time?"

She had to know he hadn't just come back on a whim. That he was here for the long haul this time.

"That's a complicated question. I've never been truly terrified of anything—not even my father. But you scare me, Jess. The fear that I might not be good enough for you because of my past. Larry's death just seemed to echo that fear. It took a wise young woman to set me straight."

She frowned, until something clicked. "Chelsea."

He nodded. "Yes. She challenged me to come back and face my fears. So here I am. This is my battleground, and I'm not going to retreat. Not this time. Unless you tell me to."

He was handing her the power. Just like the last time they made love. Only this time it wasn't a game, and she had to be very sure of her heart. Trust that he wasn't going to leave, this time. That he wasn't going to take off like Larry and do something crazy, instead of sitting down and talking out their problems.

Did she trust him?

Yes. If he had the guts to face his fears, then she owed it to herself—and him—to do the same.

"Well, I guess we're at an impasse, then," she said in as serious a voice as she could manage, when all she wanted to do was throw herself into his arms and kiss him until neither of them could breathe. "Because I'm not going to tell you to leave. And you're evidently not going to leave on your own."

His eyes clouded for a second, but he stood firm. "No, I'm not."

"Then you'll just have to stay." She thought of something. "Wait. What about your transfer?"

"It hasn't been officially approved, it was still in the works, but they let me move early. My current contract is almost up, so I can resign my commission—go into private practice—if that tilts the odds in my favor. We wouldn't have to move. Ever. We could stay right here in Richmond."

This time she did throw herself at him, wrapping her arms around his neck. "Those odds were already tilted once I saw you standing here. I love you, too, Clint, no matter what you decide to do. You do so much good for people like Chelsea. And if the paperwork on your transfer goes through before you can cancel it, I'm coming with you."

He grabbed her up and held her tight—so tight that she felt the air rush from her lungs. She didn't care.

She loved this man. More than she ever had.

Leaning down, he caught her mouth in a kiss that held a wealth of love and longing. "There's only one thing I want to do right now."

She laughed. "Really? Can it wait until I've had something to eat?"

"It could, but…" He withdrew and reached inside the jacket of his uniform, pulling out a small jeweler's box.

Her hands went over her mouth, afraid the sun and heat were still playing tricks on her. "Clint?"

He snapped the box open to reveal a ring. Small and twinkling and perfect. "It was my grandmother's. Mom gave it to me before I went into the service. She said I might need it one day. She was right." He smiled. "I'd get down on one knee, but I'm afraid I'd be seared permanently to the pavement if I did. Damn, I'm screwing this all up. I should have waited to ask you to marry me until dinner, when we could have champagne, or until I had the ring resized—"

"No. This is the perfect place. The perfect ring. And you're the perfect man for me." Tears gathered in her eyes. "And I accept your proposal, Colonel Clinton Marks."

He kissed her again. Then Jessi unhooked the chain from her necklace and let him slide the slender ring onto it, where it dangled in the hollow of her collarbone. Fingering it while heat waves danced over the black tar surface of the parking lot, she blinked. "Where's your car?"

"Someone offered me a lift."

She could guess who that might be. "Chelsea again?"

"Yes."

"So you've been standing in the parking lot for over an hour?"

"Not quite. I had a little help tracking your movements."

Ahh…so that's why Chelsea's text—asking her to let her know the second she got off work—had been waiting for her when she'd switched her phone back on.

She clicked the button to unlock her car. "I guess we should put her out of her misery, then."

"Already done. I told her if you weren't home in an hour to assume we were out celebrating somewhere."

"Oh? You were that sure of yourself, were you?"

He grinned. "You have no idea what I've been through over the past month. I wasn't sure of anything, least of all myself."

"So what kind of celebration were you thinking of?"

He slid into the passenger seat and waited for her to join him. "I was thinking of something small and private."

"Interesting." Her pulse rate sped up, despite her earlier words about eating something. "So whose turn is it to be in charge this time?"

He eased his fingers deep into her hair and turned her

face toward him. "How about if from now on we make sure it's an equal partnership?"

"Yes," she breathed as he leaned down to kiss her again, allowing her senses to begin that familiar climb. "That's the perfect solution."

EPILOGUE

"Do you, Jessica Marie Riley, take Clinton Shane Marks to be your lawfully wedded husband?"

Clint faced Jessi as she said the words that would legally bind her to him. Only they were already bound by cords much stronger than anything the minister could say.

Jessi had convinced him that the broken frame didn't represent what he'd done to her life all those years ago. Instead, it symbolized a breaking free from the mistakes of the past in order to face a future that was clean and new. They were getting a second chance, and Clint didn't intend to waste one second of it.

After they'd repeated the rest of the vows, he gripped her hands and let the emotion of doing so pour over him in a flood. And it was okay. No more shoving them behind a wall and hoping they'd stay there. He wasn't his father. He knew how to control those unhealthy feelings, while giving himself over to the ones that made two people into one.

"You may kiss the bride."

"Gladly." He wrapped his arms around Jessi's waist and reeled her in. "Love you," he whispered against her lips.

"Love you, too," she mouthed back.

Only then did he allow himself to really kiss her, putting his heart and soul into the joining of their lips.

"Whooo…" The sound came from the seats behind them, growing in volume the longer the kiss went on.

Clint smiled and leaned back, allowing his hands to slide down her arms until he was clasping her fingers once again. His grandmother's small diamond glittered up at him, a promise of the future. A promise further evidenced by the ultrasound in a drawer in his office desk. Jessi was expecting. A surprise to both of them. And for someone who'd thought he'd never be a father, it was another emotional first. A good one, though.

Jessi squeezed his hands and then turned to motion Chelsea and her new fiancé up to the front.

Paul had proposed just a week ago, and Chelsea had accepted, so there would be more wedding bells in the future. And probably more births along this crazy path they were all on. Her daughter hugged her long and hard, while Paul shook Clint's hand and wished him well.

Then Clint wrapped his arm around his new bride, while the minister introduced them as Mr. Clint and Mrs. Jessica Marks.

Smiles and cheers from some army buddies and their families and friends came from all around them.

This was where he belonged. He'd faced his deepest fears and they hadn't destroyed him. They'd given him hope.

Hope for a future filled with happiness as well as trials, but, most important, love.

"Shall we?"

Jessi grasped his hand and ran down the aisle, half dragging him along with her.

"What's the rush, Mrs. Marks," he asked.

They reached the door and pushed through it. "I've been waiting all morning for the chance to smash a piece of wedding cake all over your face."

"That's more exciting to you than us getting married?"

"No." She threw him a happy grin. "It's what comes after that has me all worked up."

"Dare I ask what that is?"

"You could, but you might not want me to explain in a public venue."

He laughed, his heart lighter than the frothy layers of his bride's cream-colored dress that fluttered around her knees.

"Then lead on, woman. We've got a cake to cut."

* * * * *

MILLS & BOON
MEDICAL
Pulse-Racing Passion

Set your pulse racing with dedicated, delectable doctors in the high-pressure world of medicine, where emotions run high and passion, comfort and love are the best medicine.

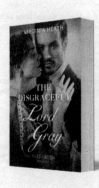  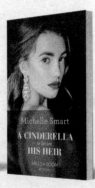

MILLS & BOON

THE HEART OF ROMANCE

A ROMANCE FOR EVERY READER

MODERN

Prepare to be swept off your feet by sophisticated, sexy and seductive heroes, in some of the world's most glamourous and romantic locations, where power and passion collide.

HISTORICAL

Escape with historical heroes from time gone by. Whether your passion is for wicked Regency Rakes, muscled Vikings or rugged Highlanders, awaken the romance of the past.

MEDICAL

Set your pulse racing with dedicated, delectable doctors in the high-pressure world of medicine, where emotions run high and passion, comfort and love are the best medicine.

True Love

Celebrate true love with tender stories of heartfelt romance, from the rush of falling in love to the joy a new baby can bring, and a focus on the emotional heart of a relationship.

Desire

Indulge in secrets and scandal, intense drama and plenty of sizzling hot action with powerful and passionate heroes who have it all: wealth, status, good looks…everything but the right woman.

HEROES

Experience all the excitement of a gripping thriller, with an intense romance at its heart. Resourceful, true-to-life women and strong, fearless men face danger and desire - a killer combination!

To see which titles are coming soon, please visit

millsandboon.co.uk/nextmonth